PRESUMED
GUILTY

Praise for the work of Mark McGinn

McGinn's private investigator novel, *Deceit*, is dark, gritty and intense and his style is taut and atmospheric. Deceit delivers action, suspense and an insider's look into politics, law and life 'Down Under'. It's most highly recommended. *Jack Magnus, Readers' Favorite*

Though a resident of Sydney, Clay Tempero, (*Deceit*) introduced in McGinn's *Trust No One* (2013), would be right at home anywhere as a PI who doggedly pursues a case while wrestling with his own demons or rocky past. McGinn knows his way around the legal system and genre conventions. He also has a facility for the odd turn of phrase: cocaine usage is described as 'vacuuming with straws'. *Kirkus Review 2014*

Trust No one is an intriguing mystery set against the backdrop of Sydney. Sharp and witty dialogue, and memorable characters. *Rocking great reads, 2015*

A suspenseful, alarming, spine chilling horror, thriller short story (book). Very well written. Never a dull moment from start/finish. Make another great scary movie or TV series. Very easy for me to give the short story (book) 5 stars. *Tony Parsons MSW (Washburn)*

Best Served Cold is Mark McGinn's first novel. His familiarity with the legal system is evident throughout the novel, and the basic formula of the legal thriller (throw an innocent person into jail, get them caught up in a conspiracy, and then get them out) is used well by McGinn, as he puts his own spin on these plotline developments. *Booksellers NZ*

Best Served Cold has a great plot and cast of characters. A tightly written story that gripped me all the way to a terrific ending. *Paul Thompson, journalist and editor, Fairfax Media*

Mark McGinn

Merlot
Publishing

Acknowledgements

First thanks to my wife, Ena, for her love and patience toward an unbidden cave dweller in the house, and to Anna Rogers, who continues to provide great support and incisive editorial skills for my projects.

Published by Merlot Publishing

10 Priorsford Court, Christchurch New Zealand

A division of www.mcginncrime.com

2016

ISBN 978-1-5136-1860-9

Part One
PRE-TRIAL MOTIONS

1

A TRIO OF BALD bulbs illuminated Lottie's reflection in the bathroom mirror. She tilted her head forward trying to catch clues of emerging grey in the flaming red. She needed Ben's eyes. At forty-four, it could be worse than a bit of grey. No kids meant the worst effects of gravity had been deferred in the short term.

She thought about another story that had gone south. Ben would feign sympathy but, as editor of *The People*, he'd be secretly pleased.

She had hopes that this weekend in their getaway in Akaroa would be better than the last. Then he was focused on his own problems. He moaned about his deputy, about the Montague Company, about his bloody car audio, about the need to take Viagra. She'd petted him, fed his ego and made excuses for him the whole time.

He didn't see the real problem. What normal married couple couldn't talk about their work and careers? You'd think after three years they'd have found a way. God knows, she'd tried. The stone wall between them was as impenetrable now as it was when she started editing *Uncover*. How the hell do you counter the 'integrity to our own companies' theme? What did that even mean?

She heard him come in downstairs. Good. His arrival signalled that she wouldn't have to cook for him too late in the evening, when she might be tempted to eat again. Minutes ago, she'd finished her own meal of burger and fries. She'd bought him fish. She'd never been able to eat fish but she could cope with cooking it – just.

On the Monday, when she'd last returned to Auckland, they'd stared at each other in silence before she'd left, then she'd pecked him on the cheek and expressed hope that their next weekend would be better. He'd said, 'Might be better if you spent less time with the neighbourhood watch next door. That woman has her binoculars trained on us, even in the dark.'

Doris Knowles probably was a bit of a busy-body. But she was lonely and harmless.

Another noise.

In response to his arrival she called, 'I'm up here. About to have a shower. Wanna scrub my back?'

No answer.

She waited. Something stopped her from moving, from turning the shower on. Was he trying to scare her again? He liked surprising her – sneaking up to make her jump. He could be a schoolboy pain in the arse when he did that.

She listened for his movement. A dog barked in the distance. Probably the mutt three houses away, the one that people in the burger bar complained about. Cars passed on the street below. Someone tooted a horn, a farewell or a greeting.

'I've already heard you, so forget about it. I know you're here.'

Nothing.

'C'mon, Ben.' Her tone an indication she was tired of this game.

She listened more intently. The dog had stopped. No cars passed.

The floorboard at the landing of the stairs creaked.

At that moment, she realised that although she'd closed the door downstairs, she hadn't locked it.

Her call was less sure now. 'Ben?'

Nothing.

She stared at the door handle vulnerable in her nakedness. All her clothes were in their bedroom, next door.

She felt paralysed.

The handle moved down – slowly.

As the door opened towards her, her heart pounded. Anger now. This shit wasn't on. It was unnecessary. She'd have a piece of him. She lunged forward, yelling, 'Cut it out.'

Short of breath, Lottie wrenched the door open. She gasped and reeled.

In her final seconds of life, the last thing she saw was the weapon.

2

'**ON THE CHARGE OF** rape, do you find the defendant guilty or not guilty?'

Defence counsel Sasha Stace noticed a slight tremor in the court official's hand as the verdict question was asked. Her client, Labour MP Roy Andrews, was probably the calmest person in court, despite the possibility of a guilty verdict and jail sentence.

With determination, Sasha focused not on the jury, but on the bland file cover in front of her. She avoided eye contact with the twelve strangers. Mac, her stepfather and lifelong mentor, advised her long ago about finding the eye of jurors. There were times when you must, there were times when it was advisable and there were times when you never did. Now was a 'never' moment. Although it would make no difference to their verdict, she wouldn't betray her anxiety.

'Not guilty,' the foreman said, formal and cold, his eyes locked on the official.

'On the charge of unlawful sexual intercourse with a minor, do you find the defendant guilty or not guilty?'

'Not guilty.'

A chorus of 'Yes' and spontaneous clapping crawled to a stop.

In the Christchurch High Court Sasha knew she should feel victorious, taste the sweet flavour of victory. Instead, there was bile in her mouth. She knew what the young girl would be feeling. She'd exploited the inconsistencies in her evidence, little things like the order of events, how she'd been confused about what came first, who she'd told and when. Sasha believed the girl had told the truth but she did her job. Now, thanks to her, the girl had been branded a liar.

The courtroom quiet returned. 'And is that the verdict of you all?' the woman asked.

The jurors all nodded, decisive.

Through the stale air, a shriek. 'What's wrong with you people? How can you do this to my daughter?'

Sasha saw prosecutor Tom Carson turn to look. The judge and officials also looked. Sasha did not turn to look, to see a mother's distress, to show her shame. Neither did the jury. Their attention was on the judge. Their eyes could not be further away from the mother. The court attendant demanded silence. He quelled the shrieking but not the sobbing. Sasha dropped her chin while Justice Bowen thanked the jury, then addressed Andrews, flanked by men in the khaki green of prison escort garb. 'Mr Andrews,' he said, hiding what Sasha knew would be his disgust, 'you are discharged and free to go.'

Andrews did a fist pump for his supporters as he left the dock. He'd told Sasha he would. He couldn't bring himself to consider the possibility of the verdict going against him. He'd congratulated her on 'wiping the floor with the little bitch'. He and Sasha stood in the holding cells when he'd said that and, despite their warmth, Sasha felt a chill run through her. Andrews enjoyed the contest, saw it as a high stakes intellectual game in which every possible ploy had to be used to secure his acquittal.

When Sasha was raped, she wasn't physically hurt. The late Justice Peter Niven didn't smother his penis with avocado-infused olive oil as Andrews did. Niven slipped her a date rape drug. He took her, not just without consent, but without her knowledge. She was bruised, but not hurt in the way Alice was hurt.

But it still hurt. In the night's dark, in the constant determination not to be a victim, in the men who looked like Niven, walked and talked like Niven, it still hurt. When it happened to Sasha, she was forty. Alice was fourteen. A teenage girl held a criminal to account, despite the risk, the possibility of disbelief. Others to come would show that courage, but now, Sasha's only thought was that she got rapists acquitted.

Everyone stood as the judge exited. Carson, wiry and looking beat, offered a bony hand in the usual polite gesture of congratulation counsel use. 'Well done.'

Fluorescent light caught sweat on his face, the unhealthy colour of a barked tree. He added, 'Should've had you batting for us. My fault.' He forced a smile as he walked past, disappointment in himself palpable.

Sasha nodded and mumbled a heartless thank you, then tied the pink ribbon around the Andrews file on which she recorded, 'Final criminal trial!!' She sat for a moment as the court emptied. The attendant ambled over. His gait was the benchmark for slow-moving justice but his height lent a presence that bolstered his commands for silence. Below wispy grey hair, deep lines ran a horseshoe from both sides of his cheeks to thin lips. Perhaps his daily working environment had taken its own toll. He whispered, 'You okay, Ms Stace?'

With no other sitting scheduled, he needed to lock up the legal bear pit in which she'd spent the last three days. She gave him the smile: the one where she showed no teeth but also, according to others, where the skin around her eyes didn't crinkle. 'All good, Maurice,' she said. He didn't need to know the truth.

In the courts law library, she pulled a journal from a shelf, taking nothing in. Thoughts of Mac and his reaction to her giving up criminal cases distracted her. Her phone vibrated. Andrews texted to say she was expected at the post-verdict party. He'd hired a floor at a central city hotel, a venue that once hosted the Beatles. When she left the library, she was met by a misery sky, a low pall in sync with her mood.

On the way to meet Mac, her cell phone rang. Relief. It was not her happy client insistent that she share his joy. Loren Steel said she was calling on behalf of the Law Society's local Standards Committee.

Sasha wondered why, even though she knew she'd done nothing wrong, her heart skipped a beat when someone in authority stopped her. Such needless guilt.

'Sasha, do you have any relationship with Quentin Fisk?'

'I've only opposed him in court. Nothing more than that. Why do you ask?'

'Very good. The committee, pursuant to Section 144, would like you to investigate on its behalf, an allegation of misconduct against Mr Fisk.'

Steel continued her formal tone and explained the allegation. They agreed terms and conditions, including Sasha's fee. When the call ended, Sasha thought of Mac again. Some good news to balance what he'd see as the bad.

3

THE COFFEE HOUSE HAD a dark knotted wood floor and cream-painted windows. Hard surfaces swirled voices around Sasha and Mac. She'd suggested the venue without thinking how Mac, eighty next year, would cope with his slight deafness if the place was busy.

Mac said, 'Did you know this was the last place in Christchurch I brought Natalie to?'

She nodded. The café was also significant for other reasons. It had been a backdrop of history between her and Mac since he'd begun bringing her here as a little girl. But it was also the place where they confronted her troubles, personal and professional, a place where Mac had offered so much support, something she now needed again.

Before she could respond, Mac changed the subject. 'I hear Ben Tyler can bury his wife now. Charlotte, isn't it?'

'Yes. Dreadful business. Nearly three weeks. Seems the police are no closer to finding the killer.'

'Have you visited him?' he asked.

She looked down. 'I phoned him. Passed on my condolences.'

He waited, an embarrassing silence that illuminated her failure to be more personal. For more than a dozen years she and Ben had been in a relationship. They had fled Christchurch after a nightmare case she'd prosecuted, and virtually dragged Mac and her mother Natalie to Sydney with them. But her relationship with Ben ended after she caught him in bed with Lottie.

'I know I should've seen him but I just haven't been able to bring myself to do it.'

Mac sounded bewildered. 'But you parted amicably in the end?'

'I know. But with each passing day, it just got harder and harder until it was impossible.'

'I see,' he said, disappointment in his voice. 'Still, you'll go to the funeral?'

Sasha kicked air under the table. Ben Tyler and his murdered wife were not on her agenda. She said, 'I can't.'

'Sasha.' He sounded mortified.

She looked up and saw deep lines in his forehead. 'Diplock and I have a fixture in the High Court. It's been adjourned three times and the last time was final.'

'I see.'

Another pause, long seconds. 'Sad all round,' he said and proffered a hand across the table. 'I understand. Good that you made contact. It wouldn't have been easy.'

She took his hand in both of hers, a silent thank you for the reprieve.

Mac smiled. 'Bubbles for your victory this morning, then?'

Sasha let his hand go. 'A celebration, maybe. But not the victory. Definitely not that. No justice done there.'

'But I popped in,' Mac said. 'Heard you cross-examining the girl. She was all over the place.'

A cacophony intruded. Looking around, Sasha recognised two lawyers in a group of five women. Their tone and lascivious expressions suggested men and their foibles were the subject of discussion.

'Because I took her all over the place, Mac. Tied her in knots, got her mind spinning on an axis of confusion. Like every good lawyer does, right?'

Mac heard her sarcasm and gave a familiar look, one that said, 'Here we go again', mixed with good old-fashioned disappointment. After a lifetime of love and emotional support, at its height when she was a pregnant seventeen-year-old, she still childishly hated to disappoint him. She'd always wondered whether he'd truly supported Natalie's requirement to adopt the baby out, or simply maintained a united front with her mother.

'I know, Mac. You've heard it all before, right?'

A woman, early thirties, dressed in the house uniform of black shorts and top and black apron, approached with laminated menus and a cheery voice. 'Anything to drink, to be going on with?'

Mac shot Sasha a glance. 'Looks like a couple of house reds might be in order.'

Sasha fixated on initials lightly carved into the top of the table.

'Two house reds, in less than two,' the waitress said, confident of her time promise.

Sasha glanced at her watch. She'd counted things for as long as she could remember. It didn't matter whether it was time, cars, whatever. Her favourite was the beat of her own drum but for now, she would monitor the waitress.

'Mac, did it never get to you?'

'What, exactly?'

'The gamesmanship, the deceit, the whole damn thing.'

He looked pensive. 'I've wondered about that old chestnut, that it was better for ten guilty men to go free than have one innocent man condemned. And remember, I had one innocent man condemned and hanged.'

'At least you were fighting to save his life. What's nobler in advocacy than that? Dad and I both sent innocent men to their deaths, albeit in different circumstances.'

'Well,' Mac sighed, 'we've been all over that, have we not?' His face said 'endlessly' but he was kind enough not to use the word. That was his way.

'I know. But Alice was a frightened, confused little girl, Mac. A little girl who was raped and whose ordeal made it extremely difficult to recall the details and their sequence under pressure. In the name of so-called justice, I helped Andrews violate her again.'

The waitress returned. One minute fifty seconds. She eyed Mac as he pulled his wallet. 'No, you're good,' she said. 'Pay on the way out.'

Mac thanked her. When she left, he said, 'You weren't the only able advocate in court. Tom Carson knows when he presents the prosecution case that...'

'I'll be picking her to bits,' Sasha interrupted. 'She was a carcass after my cross-examination and in my closing address I felt like a vulture picking over the remains.'

Mac sighed again. 'We don't need the courtroom melodrama now. We both know you were doing the thing you took an oath to do, without fear or favour.'

The silence between them was not uncomfortable. Her mother used silence as a weapon, a punishment cruel and unusual. Many times,

Sasha had wondered what Mac saw in Natalie.

They sipped wine. 'Passable,' Mac said. Over the rim of the glass, he added, 'Might it not be the case that you have, with considerable justification, overempathised with the complainant?'

First to know about Niven, Mac engineered the judge's removal from the bench. His courage spared her the need to be courageous but he hadn't quite grasped her situation. Sasha had done several sex crime cases since then. 'You crafty old bugger,' she said with a half-smile aimed at appeasement. 'Are you a counsellor now?'

He looked at an empty third chair between them and pointed in her direction. 'Your Honour, would you please instruct the witness to answer the question.'

Her cell phone rang. She didn't recognise the number and terminated the intrusion.

Mac said, 'So?'

'It's more than Niven, Mac. I struggled to find my normal enthusiasm when I spoke to the bright-eyed hopefuls at the law café earlier this afternoon. I preached the values of being human, not losing what's important, getting beyond being good at advocacy.'

He gave her a look of approval.

She added, 'I used to believe questions about guilt or innocence were self-indulgent, the duty to the court, and then to the client, was the essential focus of all good lawyers. Many of my colleagues still hold to that. I admire their tenacity.'

Mac looked solemn. 'You can still practise criminal law Sash, just turn down sex cases. That would be understandable.'

As usual, Mac knew where she was going. She'd been his protégé for such a long time. He could see change afoot – for himself as well as for her.

'I won't make any fanfare about it,' she said. 'I'll just become too busy to accept new criminal briefs.'

'Been a big part of your practice, Sash. Better a live donkey than a dead lion, not so? The criminal justice system needs people like you. It needs people capable of reflection more than it needs automatons. The thing you're going through is what humanises the system.'

She didn't want this debate. She couldn't win it. The soul of legal probity from whom she'd learned so much implored her, through Bambi eyes, to reconsider. He wanted her to return to the fork in the road, the alternative route where she'd always advocated for the 'system'. She wanted to tell him the change in her practice would allow more time for her to care for him. But she dared not. He'd not only reject the need, he'd be disappointed that she'd even thought that necessary.

'I'm so over criminal law, Mac. Is there a better sign of that than feeling sick when a verdict goes my way? It's not just sex cases. It's living in a world where one shower a day isn't enough.' She shook her head. 'I can't do it any more. I want to move on. I need to move on.'

'You don't think you can help get justice any more. Is that what you're saying?' The disappointment in his tone, across his face, was unmistakable. 'You'll just leave that to others, those more willing to sail close to the wind with their tactics than you are?'

She gave the small shrug of a confounded child. 'I've been approached by the Law Society to assist with disciplinary conduct cases. There's one on the way. They're sort of criminal, aren't they? Criminal lite?'

Mac stroked his chin between thumb and forefinger. 'You won't be popular.'

'Popular? I might be a bottle blonde but I'm not brainless Barbie. Not yet.' She forced a smile. 'You're not going to tell me you practised criminal law to be popular.'

'I practised criminal law for exactly the same reasons you do. Like you, I questioned what I was doing. Many times. But I always came back to the same principle. The right to a defence keeps a police state at bay. The cornerstone of a decent society.'

The cell phone rang again, this time a relief. 'Same number,' she said. 'Wellington. Do you mind?'

Mac gestured agreement.

'Sasha Stace.'

'Ivor Grange.'

The café was noisy. Sasha squinted in concentration and inserted a finger in her other ear. 'Sorry, who is this?'

'Ivor Grange, parliamentary secretary for the attorney general.'

'How can I help you?'

'Two things. The AG wants to thank you for your efforts on behalf of our man, Andrews.'

'Just doing what the party paid me to do, Mr Grange.'

'Quite. And call me Ivor, please. Andrews and the party have reached what is referred to as an understanding. Tonight's news will be full of his gratitude and support from the party in what has been a difficult and traumatic time for him. In return, he'll resign from Cabinet with immediate effect, avoiding any unnecessary personal focus that might detract from our party's performance in the House.'

She sat more upright. 'Or adverse perceptions of the party and who it supports.'

'Quite.'

Mac tilted his head.

'Which brings me to the second reason for my call. The AG would like to meet you. He'll be in Christchurch the day after tomorrow if you have an hour to spare.' He sounded hopeful.

'I think, Ivor, our work is done, is it not?'

'As far as that man is concerned, yes, it is. In time, he will leave a vacancy within the party.'

Looking at Mac, Sasha wondered where the hell the conversation was going. Was Grange sounding her out to replace Andrews? 'I've always adopted an apolitical stance on these things, Ivor.'

'A factor that makes you very suitable, Sasha.'

The echo on the line was not helped by more raucous laughter behind her. She pushed her finger deeper into her spare ear, and crushed the other with her phone. 'Suitable for what, may I ask?'

For reasons unknown to her, Mac was grinning. Then the cogs turned over.

She asked, 'Is this what's referred to as an approach?'

'The AG thought it appropriate you were warmed up to the idea before you both meet. There'll be an appropriate process, of course – always is.'

'Of course.'

'Are you willing and able to meet? One would think your office would be discreet.'

4

CARSON'S FAILURE IN THE Andrews case was good news for Quentin Fisk, or QF, as he liked to be known at work. In his high-backed leather chair, at a desk big enough for three, he smiled at the press coverage of Andrews' resignation as MP for Christchurch Central.

He swivelled to look at the mountains and imagined himself in the Beehive, manoeuvring the current idiotic attorney general out of his job. What would Mother have said if he, Quentin Fisk, influenced New Zealand's judicial appointments?

He'd all but given up aspirations to the High Court bench, and didn't want a lower court appointment. Although, he remembered, Mother had always exhorted, 'Never say never.' A sensible approach to life, avoidance of being backed into corners. He'd had enough of those: up against bike shed walls, into stinking lavatory cubicles – as many possible tight jams as gangs of schoolboy bullies could conceive.

A grey jumbo jet was a distant moving contrast in the duck-egg sky, all powerful, defying gravity. How much easier life would've been, would now be, with another few centimetres of height. His win-loss ratio in trials would be all the better without the need for built-up heels. He rubbed a finger under his nose and heard the sawing sound of whiskers he once grew to a broom-like black moustache. 'Ill-informed people,' his PA once said, 'might think the moustache reminded them of an insurance salesman, or a pimp.'

The PA's arse was her redeeming feature in an otherwise average body, with average looks and average clothes. But that arse! Low and large enough to park a bike in. He turned back to the local newspaper, *The People*, and sneered at the lawyer whose photograph was placed next to the Andrews piece. Sasha Stace QC. Tall, photogenic Sasha Stace, a Queen's Counsel, a leader of their bar. Lucky in her genes, she had far more gravitas than she deserved. Carson handed her the prominent victory yesterday. Sadly, she was destined for bigger things. Nothing he could do about that.

He turned the page and it cracked like a whip. On the bottom of page two, his own headline – 'Court dismisses prosecutor's plea'. He'd read that piece of fiction. Averill, with tea and sympathy, warned him about it. He cut the article out for the ledger, the book that was a reminder of slights and insults against him, Mother's most important recommendation. He glued the cutting into a red-covered, A5 exercise book, normally locked in his desk drawer.

The story covered his loss in the Employment Court and ran to three columns on half a page. The paper highlighted the negative decision against him: that he'd acted in a high-handed, unfair and unreasonable way in giving the employee a dismissal letter immediately following her explanations for lateness. The judge said a fair employer would have taken time to consider those explanations which he considered to be reasonable. No coverage of the fact the stupid woman had received repeated warnings.

Worse was the happy tone of the paper's editorial. It celebrated his further drop in the political polls for his candidacy to represent Labour in Spreydon, despite the fact his rival did not even live in the electorate.

Fisk thumped the article with his fist, pressing down the glue. This was not the first time Ben Tyler's paper had undermined him. It was time Tyler paid. He cheered himself by flicking through the pages of records he'd kept over the last ten years – big red ticks, the signal that retribution was complete. Justice. He had no idea when he'd be able to tick off *The People* but the day would come.

A light door knock. Fisk heard it click open before he'd had the chance to call, 'Come.' He scrambled to lock the ledger away. Averill poked her plump cheeks through the gap.

Oozing irritation, Fisk said, 'Have I not asked everyone to wait till I call?'

'Sorry, QF. Zoe's here and she's in a bit of a hurry. Will you see her?'

He beckoned his PA in. 'Shut the door, Averill, and do the chair swap.' He put on his suit coat and admired two joined moons amplified by the woman's tight red skirt. He wondered how much of her chest had been caught by the hidden camera opposite his desk. He would check the tape tonight, as he did every night when he spent time away from his office. She looked smarter today, more alluring in her black fishnets. He swallowed hard and felt his temple pulse. Soon.

Averill complied. It was an open secret that staff disciplinary meetings with QF were conducted 'on the potty', a lower chair than normal. Tom Carson had attempted several times to get him to drop the practice. When Averill withdrew, Fisk raised the level of his own chair.

He heard the knock and counted silently to five. 'Come.'

Zoe Underwood strode in and placed her shapely figure in front of his desk.

Not looking up from a notepad he said, 'Sit.'

Zoe complied, clicking a ballpoint pen while she waited.

Fisk's eyebrows knitted together. 'That's annoying, Zoe.'

'I'm kind of busy, QF. What's up?'

He leaned back in his chair, put his hands together and tapped the tips of his forefingers. 'Busy?' he said, pretending surprise. 'We like busy. We pay you to be busy. Billable busy. That's what we like around here.' He offered a canine smile.

'Something cryptic in that?' she asked.

'Not at all. I assigned you billable work in the Fisheries prosecution.' He noticed her lipstick was darker than normal, the colour of blood under fluorescent lights. And she'd given only a poker face reaction to his comment. He added, 'I've learned you palmed it. Did Top Cat okay that?' Fisk knew he hadn't.

'Mr Carson wasn't involved. I made a judgment call. Trisha's load was light and she's in need of court experience. It wasn't the first case she did on her own and she had a good OC.'

Fisk felt heat behind his eyes. He stopped tapping his forefingers and drew a deep breath. 'The ability of the officer in charge is irrelevant. Those are judgment calls I get to make. I'm the managing partner here. If you recall, I hired you and Trisha. You might've been here a year or so longer than her...'

Unruffled in tone or appearance, Zoe interrupted, 'Two, actually.'

Cool, calm and collected – that's what Top Cat liked about her. Fisk had pushed for a less dominating personality, a shorter woman, less attractive. He'd reluctantly agreed that Zoe's shoulder-length hair, the colour of buffed copper, azure eyes and wide smile made her a head-turner. A discreet show of pert breasts before jurors wouldn't harm a prosecution case. In fact, shirt buttons open, Zoe could argue for or against a motion and pretty much remain mute.

But the lech Carson got his way.

Underwood's chin came up, haughty. She knew she was attractive, knew she was smart and, despite her youth, was trying to undermine him in front of the rest of the firm.

He wouldn't have that. He wanted to slap his palm on the desk, make her jump. He wanted to say, 'I don't fucking care if it's ten years, I make those calls, not you.'

Despite what people did, how they made him feel, he seldom said those things. Declaring his hand compromised his ability to execute the justice ledger.

5

'SAW THE NEWS ABOUT Andrews.' Ted gave a gap-toothed smile as Fisk stepped out of his red Subaru. 'When do you put your hat in the ring?'

Fisk held a thumb up. 'Any day now.'

'A formality, you reckon?'

'Oh, yes. I've got backing in the right places. Once I'm over that line it's only a matter of time.'

The two men had been neighbours for more than two years. They'd exchanged vegetables over the fence, both happy to discuss Fisk's brilliance in court. They'd had several discussions about trial tactics and Ted visited him in court, offering praise for his advocacy and even the odd suggestion. Praise he didn't mind. The suggestions he could do without.

Ted, in his early seventies, looked pained. 'The wife and I feel sorry for that wee girl, though.'

'You needn't, mate.'

'How do you mean?'

'It was an Oscar-winning performance,' Fisk said. 'Right down to the inconsistencies in her evidence.'

'Never.'

Fisk nodded. 'She's been well rewarded. You can sleep easy.'

Ted looked confused, as well he might. He didn't know how or why Andrews was indebted. And he wouldn't understand the out-of-court machinations and balancing acts that achieved both a friend's acquittal and resignation.

Fisk pointed to the tomatoes that had climbed above his side of the fence. 'Fancy a swap? Couple of kilos of Russian Reds for some of the corn you've got growing down the back?'

Ted looked behind him, drew on his rollie and blew a thin streak of smoke from the side of his mouth. 'The corn's a way off yet.'

'I trust you,' Fisk said. 'You'll be good for it. Graham loves corn on the cob.'

A little look of anxiety as Ted beckoned him closer. 'A small matter I need to mention, Quentin.'

Fisk smelt tobacco and beer on the man's breath. He was going to ask for free legal advice again. Why was it people matey with lawyers thought specialised knowledge didn't have to be paid for? Perhaps Ted thought sucking up to him was sufficient payback. Well, it wasn't. He encountered this everywhere. It was why he didn't cultivate friendships outside the bar.

'Yes.' He made his response sound more tired than interested.

Ted looked a bit embarrassed. He should.

'You know our bedroom – the wife and me – it's this side of the house?' He pointed at the ocean blue stucco wall a few metres back from the brown palings between them.

'It might surprise you to know I haven't been aware of that.' The dog smile. 'I don't make a point of peering in my neighbour's windows to see what secrets lie within.'

'No, no. I wasn't suggesting that, Quentin. God, no. A senior prosecutor isn't going to do that, is he? No, this is about playing your overture, the Beethoven thing.'

'It's Tchaikovsky. The *1812*. What about it?'

'The missus reckons it's a bit loud. Says the cannons make the glass in our windows shake. I know she's imagining it but she's wondering if you could wind it back a bit.'

'You're firing her cannons, then?'

Ted looked embarrassed. 'You know how it is.'

'No. Friends with benefits, people you can require to leave – that's more my thing.'

Ted revealed fingernails with half the garden under them as he raked back a dry nest of thatch above red-lined eyes. Face hopeful, he said, 'I can report to the war office the communiqué has been dispatched, right?' He looked proud of his little analogy.

Fisk nodded. 'You can, Ted. I'll take the submission under advisement. How's that?'

Inside, Fisk poured himself a gin and tonic, with ice and a slice, and called, 'Daddy's home. Come on, Graham, out you come.' In the living room, he held his free hand out in front of him as if in a dark room, feeling for an unseeable wall.

Graham gave him a hard-eyed stare and didn't move.

Fisk cajoled with no positive result. 'In your own time, then. I'll get dinner ready.' He mused over the chat with Ted and smiled. A step closer to the goal now. He'd boasted about the levels of service he'd bring to his role as an electorate MP. Ted had been impressed. But in truth, a Cabinet minister was what mattered. It wasn't about doing the work, it was having the power that made the difference.

In the temperature-controlled room, Fisk opened windows behind lace curtains and turned off the radio that served as Graham's company during the day. On the opposite side from his neighbour, his back section Spreydon townhouse faced the local school's bike sheds. He'd like to be in Fendalton or, better still, on the hilly slopes of Cashmere or Sumner. Mother told him Spreydon wasn't a suburb for up and coming lawyers. He'd countered her snobbishness with his need to be close to the good Labour people of Spreydon, Sydenham and Hoon Hay. That's who he'd be representing. He didn't mention it was a temporary bolt hole until he cracked a system that would return his investments on the horses.

Fisk read a reminder about the service date for his car. He'd had a turbo acceleration installed in his Subaru. Foot hard on the accelerator, his head now jerked back into the rest so fast that, according to his mechanic, he was in danger of getting whiplash.

'Whiplash is for sissies,' he'd replied.

Graham had the run of the house between the kitchen–dining area and the adjoining living room but Fisk ensured the other doors and windows were secure as he came and went. He didn't want Graham to escape or come to any harm. He prepared Graham's meal of raw apple and cabbage and inspected the bottom of the cage for the day's droppings. Parrots didn't show an illness until it was well advanced. The vet had told him to closely monitor the bird's excrement for signs of change. As usual, Graham was well.

Fisk removed his suit coat and put his head through a crudely made poncho covering his upper body. 'TV time,' he announced.

Graham didn't move but mimicked the call. He was happy when he did that.

Drink in hand again, Fisk turned on the six o'clock news. Now Graham moved. Fisk knew he would. It was a daily ritual. Sitting on his shoulder Graham squawked, 'Daddy home.'

'Good boy, Graham. Giz a kiss.' He held his arm up and the bird bobbed and clawed its way sideways until it reached his hand. Fisk felt the cool claws on his skin, made a smooching noise, produced spittle and the parrot stretched its beak towards his mouth and nibbled Fisk's lips.

Fisk said, 'Heard people talking about love today.'

Graham cocked his head, showed a cold eye.

'Isn't that a load of crap, Graham? Love. Who needs it? Crap, eh?'

Graham returned to the shoulder platform and squawked, 'Rap'.

Fisk smiled, stroked the bird's soft back feathers. 'That's right, crap.'

Graham, like all lorikeets, needed a lot of attention and affection. Fisk got it back. TV time was their spiritual union although the bird often misbehaved when Mother was on screen.

Fisk held up his G and T and said, 'Not too much.' Graham dipped his curved beak, took a drink, sat upright and shivered. He moved a short distance away from the deposit he'd left on the poncho. 'Good boy,' Fisk said. He looked at the framed photo of his twin sister on the television, a nuclear-powered smile for a ten-year-old. It was thirty years ago, to the day, their birthday, that she was raped and strangled.

6

'IT SOUNDS SERIOUS,' SAID Kate Quigg, Sasha's PA. She looked concerned. 'What will lawyers think of you going after one of their own?'

Sasha said, 'The Standards Committee doesn't embark on investigations lightly.'

'But lawyers investigating lawyers – how is that even fair?' Kate said. 'Why don't you have an independent outfit do it, like the cops?'

She wasn't the first person to ask this. 'Sometimes, legal ethics are complicated,' Sasha said. 'Lawyers experienced in the challenges provided by clients are the best people to wade through complaints. Anyway, disciplinary hearings often involve a person who's not a lawyer as part of the tribunal.'

Sasha moved to her desk overlooking leafy Cranmer Square and poured water for the two of them. 'In this particular case,' she said, 'Mr Fisk had been instructed by a client to object to a rezoning of land near the client's home. It's alleged Fisk failed to declare he was a trustee of the organisation that owned the land and wanted it rezoned.'

Kate pulled a face. 'Sounds a bit dodgy, even to me.'

Without thinking, Sasha produced her censorious finger. 'You shouldn't say, "Even to me." That's putting yourself down.'

Kate's smile was impish and she gave a little shrug.

When she returned from Sydney, Sasha had looked up her former PA, but the matronly gatekeeper had retired to a life of bowls, golf and Probus lunches. She did, however, volunteer that her neighbour knew of a young woman, Katherine Quigg, who'd grown up on the wrong side of the tracks, been in a bit of strife as a teenager. But in a work trial, Kate had proved to be obsessive about detail without that impacting on her energy and productivity.

Sasha said, 'I'm investigating two allegations of professional misconduct. It's said that Fisk had a conflict of interest between his client and his trust. Knowing that, he then failed to raise that conflict and advise his client to seek independent advice.'

Kate brushed a lock of brown hair from one eye. 'Who owned the land?'

'An animal welfare group. I'd have to look up the name.'

'Oh. That's sad. Trying to do good for poor animals that can't speak for themselves and now you're after him.'

'Sometimes people do stupid things. He might be innocent. We'll have to wait and see.'

She didn't look convinced. Sasha added, 'Conflicts like this are avoidable, Kate. You don't accept money from a client you can't represent properly. The same goes for withholding information you know is important to the client's interests.'

Kate still looked as if Sasha was the bad guy. 'Well, did he get anything for himself? she asked, tone challenging.

'I don't know. But if he's done what's been alleged against him, it would still be dishonest.'

'I guess.' Her concession was reluctant.

'All lawyers have a duty to protect the public from the unprofessional behaviour of any of us.' Sasha's tone had become strident and she dropped her voice. 'If we can't stop it through education, we have to be seen to take tough action when it happens.'

Kate asked, 'What happened about the land?'

Sasha looked out to the square below, feeling discomfort in her back when she moved. She stretched. Soreness visited her whenever she was involved in difficult cases, which was now most of the time. She silently cursed Andrews.

'Long story short, the Selwyn Council didn't rezone the land. But that didn't happen in time for Fisk's client. He was desperate to prevent any subdivision and bought the trust land for $700,000. More than a quarter of a million above its valuation and well above what the trust paid for it.'

Wide-eyed, Kate said, 'Wow. I guess it sounds like the client has a reason to be pissed.'

The bell above Kate's workstation tinkled. She said, 'That'll be the attorney general and Mr Grange.'

Sasha fastened the top button on her jacket and smiled. 'Do you think I should see them?'

'No. They didn't make the appointment through me.'

'Fair enough. Send them away.'

7

IN THE FLESH, MARTIN Ellis was diminutive to the point of being weedy, much more so than he appeared on television. His eyes were a darker grey than his pin-striped suit. Italian if Sasha's guess was correct.

'Mr Attorney,' she said, offering her hand.

His was damp and limp, a fish well past its best. 'Martin, please.' He flashed a practiced, for the camera, smile. 'Allow me to introduce Mr Go-to Man.'

Grange's handshake was noticeably different. He said it was nice to put a face to her name. His striking feature was the thick, grey airport runway on top of his head, not a single strand out of place. Despite claiming to be a non-drinker, he had a florid complexion.

Sasha remembered his previous invitation to informality. 'Good to meet you too, Ivor.'

Kate took coffee orders. When she left and the three of them were seated opposite a glass-topped table, Ellis waved a hand around the room. 'Pretty much what I expected for a leader of the bar,' he said. 'But a set of All England law reports – impressive. Pretty rare, I'd have thought.'

'Know every case,' Sasha said, grinning.

Ellis lifted his eyebrows at Grange. 'Also impressive.'

'I'm joking, of course. They were my late father's. Can't bring myself to do anything but retain them. They go where I go.'

Kate returned, set down the coffees and Ellis nodded his appreciation. 'Your own personal barista too. Not many go that far.'

At the door, Kate faced Sasha and, away from the men's line of sight, she made a wrist gesture by her groin. Sasha bit down on her lip, hard, then pretended to turn her cell phone off. It gave her precious seconds to compose herself. Kate was the living exemplar of a lack of deference.

Recovered, she said, 'Life's too short for drinking boiling water with brown powder in it, Martin.'

Grange tapped his fingers on the manila folder across his knees.

Ellis said, 'Indeed. Ivor tells me you understand this meeting is an informal approach.'

Sasha nodded and gave no clue about her excitement – a new opportunity for fulfillment in the law.

Ellis continued, 'With these sorts of appointments, you'll understand the importance of clear criteria and transparency. Both critical.'

'Of course,' she said, 'who would disagree?'

Ellis said, 'I'm told by those in the know that you tick all the right boxes.'

'Surely not?' Sasha said, faking surprise.

Ellis glanced at Grange as if seeking reassurance. 'Legal ability and experience are givens, of course, but also certain qualities of character.'

'Ah, that lets me off the hook.'

Ellis was almost comically earnest in response to her nervous levity. 'Also givens are honesty and integrity, but what we like about you, Sasha, is you have good judgment and common sense. We also think you're apolitical and willing to accept public scrutiny.'

She wondered how he'd formed those views but decided to drop the humour. It had fallen embarrassingly flat. 'Thank you. I take it, "we" is a reference to your Cabinet colleagues?'

'And the bench,' Ellis said emphatically, 'your potential colleagues.'

'Public scrutiny isn't always straightforward,' Sasha replied. 'The judiciary faces increasing criticism for displeasing the government in interpreting the statutes, or when sentencing offenders.'

Grange said, 'We travel a middle road, paying no great heed to the Sensible Sentencing Trust or the prison reform soapbox.'

Ellis glanced at Grange, to check if he'd finished. 'We know about the Niven matter,' he said.

'Are you referring to the late Justice Peter Niven?'

Ellis said, 'Of course.' He leaned forward and dropped his voice. 'We believe you conducted yourself with the utmost dignity in what can only have been the most appalling of circumstances.'

'Kind of you to say. I don't know what you know, but I've never discussed that man with anyone other than close personal friends.'

Grange joined in. 'The only reason we raise the subject is we know you were in Queensland at the time he died. In point of fact, within close geographical proximity.'

Sasha wondered how they knew even that much. She forced a smile. 'And you're looking for a personal assurance I had nothing to do with his fall. Is that it?'

Ellis stuck two fingers inside his white collar, moved them to his Adam's apple. 'No, no. Good heavens. We don't believe that for a second – we wouldn't be here otherwise. We understand from the Queensland police they didn't interview Mr Tyler, who we believe was your partner at the time.'

'They didn't speak to me and therefore couldn't have spoken to anyone else.' She folded her arms. 'Few people know that man raped me on the evening I attended his swearing in party. Eventually I confided in Mr McClintock, who was instrumental in Niven's removal from the bench, as I'm sure you know. If I recall, I didn't even tell Ben Tyler until the day before we left Noosa. Since my honesty and integrity are, as you say, givens, it wasn't possible for anyone I knew to be involved in Niven's death.'

But it was possible. She'd told Ben in the morning and Niven was found the following morning. The authorities believed he died late the previous afternoon.

'May we ask,' Grange said, 'whether you have any ongoing relationship with Mr Tyler?'

Although she was well over their break-up Sasha was miffed Grange wanted to go over this rocky ground. If it wasn't for the fact she was keen to become a High Court judge, this would be the point to politely ask them both to leave.

She finished her coffee and was about to answer when Ellis said, almost apologetically, 'Sasha, these questions are necessary only because of Niven. It was a serious misjudgment appointing him to the bench. His conduct showed we need to be extra careful. It isn't just the potential judge, but also their relationships and associations that need looking into.'

Relationships. She felt her heartbeat knocking and rubbed a hand over a tiny wrinkle in her black skirt. She realised they needed to know if there was dirt on Ben, a skeleton rattling to be released from an insecure cupboard. 'How much old information are you wanting?'

Grange replied, 'Just anything potentially embarrassing to the government. At the moment, the public service is an incontinent lot. We're trying to act on that as we speak.'

'Ben Tyler and I parted company in Sydney – it was a relationship that had run its course. He returned to Christchurch before I did, to take up his position at *The People*. I returned, following my mother's death a year later. Mac, who's my stepfather, wanted to come back. I thought the day would come when I might need to look after him. Frankly, that may be a barrier to furthering your approach – my commitment to Mac.'

'On the contrary,' Ellis said. 'We need the judiciary at all levels of our system to be in touch with community challenges and responsibilities.'

After a pause, Grange said, 'Pretty much to a man – and woman,' he added hastily, 'our judges are in stable relationships. As far as we know, you have no significant other in your life apart from Mac. Is that correct?'

He'd asked the question with a concerned tone: the implication that living life on one's own might be a disqualifier. She wanted to quibble, use the Human Rights Act and illegal grounds of discrimination. But she knew, in this instance, that wasn't at all persuasive. She said, 'You mean apparently stable relationships.'

Both men looked at their polished shoes, and Grange drew a fingertip across the folder he'd nursed throughout the meeting.

'I'm sorry,' Sasha said, 'but my instinct is to avoid those types of assertions or judgments without evidence. I'd hope that's why I'm suitable for this role.' She considered offering to put up a profile on nzdating.com but thought better of it.

'Touché,' Ellis said. He glanced at Grange. 'Look Sasha, we'd like your hat in the ring.

The parliamentary secretary opened his folder. 'This is an expression of interest form we'd like you to complete,' he said, his tone formal and cool. 'As you know, Marshall Hall will consult the various legal luminaries required and he'll ask you to confirm what we've just discussed – that no historical matters will cause difficulties after your appointment.' Grange handed her the form.

Sasha grinned. 'I look forward to hearing from the solicitor general. When he was here in Christchurch as the senior prosecutor, a dozen years ago, if I recall, he had me join the independent prosecutors' panel. I've never forgiven him.'

The two men chortled. 'A judge with a grudge,' Ellis said. 'Now that might be a barrier to appointment.'

They stood, Ellis serious again. 'Due process, of course, but once that's done,' he said, nodding at the form, 'it might be appropriate to get your secretary to arrange a fitting for the ceremonial wig and gown.'

Sasha restrained herself from rubbing her hands with glee. Grange got to her door first and as Sasha was about to open it, Ellis, behind her, said, 'By the way, Sasha. I heard you were investigating Quentin Fisk on behalf of the local standards committee.'

'That's right. Professional misconduct.'

Ellis nodded, looked grave. 'As you'd expect, he's done the appropriate thing and kept Marshall informed.'

Why had he introduced Fisk into their farewell? She kept a neutral expression. 'Yes, that would be appropriate.'

Seconds of silence passed while Ellis and Sasha locked eyes. Neither of them blinked. He tilted his head slightly. 'I'm confident you'll do a good job, Sasha.'

'Thank you.' She hoped her exaggerated nod showed she had finished discussing Quentin Fisk.

Ellis missed or ignored the signal. In a tone of regret, he said, 'Quentin tried to help a client and it's rebounded dreadfully. I'm sure you know how these things work. I hope it's not too indelicate to say, Sasha, that he drew the nutter straw with that man, Yuile.' He looked at Grange.

'Definitely. Been terrible,' Grange said. 'The man plagues our office with calls. I've had to warn him about police intervention if he does not cease and desist. He's a vexatious crusader, Sasha.'

'I'm seeing Mr Yuile next Tuesday. I'll be happy to reinforce the necessity for proper behaviour.'

'Sound idea,' Ellis said. 'In view of what we were talking about before, we wouldn't want you so caught up in these tawdry proceedings that you became collateral damage. Quentin's been a fine servant to the law.' He gave a nod, similar to Sasha's own, then offered his hand. 'We'll be in touch, Sasha.'

8

OUTSIDE ON CRANMER SQUARE, cars rushing their way, Ellis buttoned his suitcoat. 'What do you think? Pass muster?'

Grange mirrored his boss's move with his jacket. 'Potential there, I'd have thought. Might not be quite as malleable as one would prefer.' A moment of silence. 'You think she got the message about Fisk's proceedings?'

Ellis shook his head. 'I noticed what you noticed. There's a bit of an edge to our Sasha Stace, propriety that's more than skin deep. Almost too proper. We need to keep an eye on her. We don't want anything rebounding. Not with our plans. Can't afford that. Let's get her used to the idea of being a High Court judge, have her covet the role a bit more before we apply more pressure. You might even have to come up with another plan to help Fisk. I suggest we watch her closely. Quentin will just have to be patient.'

Grange said, 'He's not known for that.'

'If he wants to be in Cabinet, he'll bloody well have to be. Let him know we've had a word.'

9

ULTAN O'ROURKE, DEPUTY EDITOR of *The People*, slid his thin frame into the front passenger seat of Ben Tyler's car. 'How are you bearin' up, mate?' he asked in his broad Ulster accent.

'Feeling like shit. I just need to get today over with.'

'Understandable, of course.'

At 10.50 a.m. Tyler pulled into the traffic on Fendalton Road. There was a pig squeal of rubber on asphalt behind him, followed by the prolonged sound of a car horn. In the rear-vision mirror, Tyler saw an angry male face, fist clenched above the steering wheel. Tyler responded, 'I'm going to my wife's funeral, you prick.'

'Benjamin. We don't want the good Lord takin' both of us as well. Why don't I drive?'

'It wasn't your good Lord that took Lottie, Ultan.'

Tyler had inherited his deputy, a rare appointment of an Australian-based journalist into a New Zealand editorial role. He came with impeccable credentials: arts and political science honours degrees from Oxford, an MBA at the Darden School of Business in Virginia, and a heritage of breaking big stories about bigger government issues.

After several minutes of silence, O'Rourke asked, 'Did I tell you my white overalls have been stolen?'

'Your tatty car painting outfit?'

'Aye.'

'Well overdue for replacement, I'd say. Listen, you have any more thoughts about what we were talking about last night?'

'About Charlotte's killer?' The Irishman stroked his ginger goatee. 'I've been thinkin' the sheer brutality suggests it was more personal than business.'

'Or made to look like that when it was still business.'

'Seriously, Ben?'

'Who knows for certain? The competition between us for advertising dollars was fierce. Uncover could allocate a resource for at least three months or more. Got to be story related. I reckon something that needs to be kept hidden from the public.'

'Well, that's personal in my book, but I take your point. Anyway, I thought you and Charlotte didn't talk about business. An Iron Curtain of communication between you.'

Tyler glanced at O'Rourke. 'That was at her insistence. I kept telling her we didn't work in the same space but she insisted on this thing she called, "integrity to our own companies".'

'What's that supposed to mean?'

'She was worried about me being able to do things with her commercial info, deals she had on the go.'

O'Rourke said, 'Your mate Orson Plummer won't be happy about our commercial operations. He certainly wouldn't want those in the public domain. Known to be a prudent man with money is Mr Plummer.'

'Jesus. Plummer's no mate of mine. Not after Lottie skinned him financially. But he's got no interest in Montague Media.'

'He's coming on to the Montague board.'

'Never!'

'Aye. Only a matter of time before Plummer knows you've got your feet under the editor's desk. I'm thinkin' a low profile might be the go for you in the next little while.'

'How do you know this and I don't?'

O'Rourke smiled. 'Connections, mate.'

Tyler and Lottie had left Sydney as soon as the money came through – no goodbyes and no forwarding address. After the bitter acrimony between Lottie and her former husband, breathing anything like the same air was impossible.

Ben thrust his head back against the seat when they came to a red light. 'What could he do?'

'Well,' O'Rourke drew the word out. 'Not fire you outright. With a sufficient grudge, he could convince other shareholders to require a management restructure. Perhaps leavin' only one New Zealand group editor, turnin' all current editors at New Zealand Montague papers into deputies.'

'That'd be a bloody act of war.'

'I don't see those Aussies bein' too fussed about a loss of editorial control over here, do you? They've always seen New Zealand as an outpost of sheep shaggers. Profitable sheep shaggers, mind.'

After three years, would Plummer have enough bitterness from a poisonous divorce to make everyone else suffer? Tyler was still thinking about the possibility of an Aussie takeover when he realised O'Rourke had moved on.

'Hello. Earth to Benjamin!'

'I'm listening,' Ben said, irritated at being caught daydreaming. 'You mentioned political shenanigans, or the church. You bloody Micks know about the latter. How many paedo priests have been defrocked now?'

'We don't defrock,' O'Rourke replied, feigning offence. 'We rotate. Off to greener pastures, more appreciative parishes.'

After a short silence, Tyler said, 'I overheard her on the phone. About two weeks before she was killed. She whispered the words "corrupt culture". I reckon I wasn't supposed to hear.'

O'Rourke narrowed his eyes. 'You hear anythin' else?'

'My hunch is it's political.'

'As I said, with…'

'Nah. It was her demeanour – she looked anxious. A story about a pollie getting caught with his dick in a new orifice isn't worrying. I reckon it was bigger than that. I'd recognise the signs. Whatever it was, it had her on edge.'

'I don't know mate. Murder? Lottie made friends more than she made enemies.'

'Well, I'm certain it wasn't random and I don't think it was a local, a burglary gone wrong. Neither of us lives in Akaroa. She was followed and whoever followed her was either happy to kill me as well, or knew I wouldn't be there.'

'You tell the coppers all this?'

'I had three hours with them. They weren't interested. Their sole focus was on me and my movements. They're suspicious I'm still alive after being attacked. They asked about my phone calls, what I did between when I discovered her and when I called them, et-fucking-cetera.'

'Only natural, I guess, especially if you're right and it's not a local involved. Who's runnin' the inquiry?'

'DS Rod Black,' Tyler said, incredulous.

'Christ almighty. You've got history there, mate.'

'Tell me about it.'

The car radio broke in. 'We've just had breaking news in relation to the murder of journalist and editor Charlotte Kay, allegedly killed by an unknown intruder just over three weeks ago. Police have advised this station's crime reporter that an arrest of the alleged killer is imminent. Repeat, breaking news just to hand....'

Ben exhaled loudly and shook his head.

Ultan slapped him on the shoulder. 'Thank the Lord, mate. You must be relieved.'

Tyler swallowed, unable to speak.

10

THE CAFÉ'S RADIO BLARED when the owner adjusted the volume. Sasha tuned in when a familiar voice, a radio newsreader with the tone of a graveside priest, referred to the attorney general. '…and Minister of State Services, Martin Ellis, has ordered a joint police and auditor general inquiry into government department leaks, said to have occurred over the last six months. At this morning's Beehive press conference, Mr Ellis said there had been an interception of another attempted leak of confidential trade negotiations. It is understood these negotiations were between the governments of New Zealand and China.

'In other political news, Trevor Wright, leader of One New Zealand, announced today his party would contest every seat in the next general election. He pledged, if elected, to ensure an end to the gravy train of fat-cat lawyers making a pile of cash from the Waitangi Tribunal. He said ONZ will make legal fees part of treaty settlements rather than additional costs to the growing taxpayer largesse.'

'Good luck with that,' the owner said to the white-haired customer paying for his food and pot of tea.

Sasha waited in line with Paul Diplock QC, a lawyer with more seniority at the bar. Despite that, or perhaps because of it, Diplock had been a good friend to Sasha for many years. Although she'd never flirted or encouraged him, her instinct was that he fancied her. His wife died unexpectedly about the time Sasha became a Queen's Counsel twelve years ago.

In the Amuri coffee shop, dressed in sober courtroom clothing, they waited to pay for their lunch selection. It was the adjournment of a family at war over a deceased father's estate. Each of them had a plate of sandwiches, a sausage roll and an over-brewed coffee, but Sasha was concerned that she'd return to court with every thread and pore infused with the fumes from the café's deep fat fryer.

The customer in front said, 'He's got a good point, though. Bloody treaty settlements are increasing the national debt and the lawyers are all on legal aid to sue the government – that's you and me, mate, in case you haven't noticed.'

The owner glanced at Sasha, looked sheepish, then jabbed numbers into his electronic till. 'Crocodile tears,'he said. 'Wright doesn't give a bugger about taxes. He says what he likes to wind people up. He knows he'll never get the chance to implement his policies.' He handed over change.

'You think the government's doing the right thing then, shelling out millions of taxpayer dollars?' Without waiting for an answer, the customer continued, ''Cause we know the big money ain't trickling down to those who need it – just to lawyers with their snouts in the public trough.' He accepted his change and moved off, disgruntled.

'Sorry about that.' The owner totted up the cost of Sasha's food and drink.

'No need,' Paul said behind her. 'He's not alone in his thinking. I don't think we lawyers have crowned ourselves in glory. But given the historical lack of trust between the government and Maori, I don't see there's a better alternative.'

Seated, Paul looked around for eavesdroppers. 'So. The High Court bench, Sasha.' He sounded surprised.

'Other than Mac, there aren't many people I can talk to about this. And he'd push me in his own inimitable way, just as he did before I took silk.'

Diplock looked impassive. His piercing blue eyes, above a long Roman nose, appraised her over half-rimmed specs. 'Bit rich coming from you, Sasha. When I was considering the bench, you did your best to talk me out of it.'

Out on Durham Street, a lawyer, anger in his face, chopped the palm of one hand with the other. His client cowered, no place to hide. As he watched the professional bullying, Diplock said, 'If I recall, you trotted out loneliness, isolation and giving up the thing that led us to becoming senior lawyers in the first place.' He looked back at her.

Sasha smiled. 'Money? Should've had more treaty claims work'.

'Giving people a voice. That's what you said, did you not?'

His recall was perfect. They were the things Mac told her when he'd turned down the opportunity. 'Can't deny that.'

'Well, what's changed?' he asked.

'The approach coincided with my resolution to drop criminal trials. And I'm getting older. There're people younger than us on the bench.'

'And look at the bloody appeal rates. When I was asked, I felt I was getting older and I'd have felt a lot older if I'd finished my legal career as a judge. When you're a judge you don't get to go back to your office and complain about grumpy judges like we've always done. You don't get to gossip about who should've recused themselves from which cases, who's had a brain fart when half the relevant evidence is overlooked, about the sour-faced personal assistants they have, etcetera, etcetera.'

'Quite right. As judges, our focus will be on members of the bar, an echo of the same conversations with a bit more informed vitriol.'

Diplock gave her a look of disbelief and pity.

She said, 'You may be right. But then, there'll be no more up at the crack of dawn or surviving on three hours of sleep a night. That's appealing, yes? I'll have staff, including research counsel to do the leg work, and a good pension to retire on. Name on the honours list – just for doing my job.'

'That's not you, Sasha. And besides, those things aren't real reasons, proper reasons.'

'I know, I know. What is real, though, is I'll have more inner peace than I've had in a long while. Besides, the bench gives you a view of the whole picture, not just the bits we do our best to persuade the jury about. We get to curb the excesses of bureaucrats, determine where the truth lies instead of crafting slanted versions of it. Someone we both know once said, "Bugger the law, let's have a bit of justice."'

Diplock laughed, a snorting sound, just short of mocking. 'Well, if you feel that way, maybe it *is* time you left the bar.'

For a few seconds they stared at each other in silence. Diplock looked no less tired than Sasha felt, legal battle scars etched deeper every year.

'If it's what you want, you must do it, Sasha.' He sighed and dropped his shoulders. 'Could be endless days of deciding this stuff.' He waved a hand in the direction of the court from which they'd just come. 'Deciding which of the intractable and dogmatic hyenas has the best feed of the carcass. Or, if you're lucky, sending a hapless bugger off to life imprisonment for the lack of a moment's reflection and adequate self-control.'

It was then, that the change in her relationship with Paul Diplock hit her. She hadn't thought about this before. He knew before she did. There would be an adjustment, one that neither of them wanted. 'I don't want the change to come between us, Paul.'

He forced a smile. 'And the first time you find against me?'

'Come on, you know it won't be personal. Start now. Build a bribe account to minimise the risk.'

'You'll be way too expensive. How far has the process gone?'

'The paperwork's done. I've been fitted for the red dressing gown.'

11

BEN TYLER SAT IN the front row of mourners on a manicured oval lawn bordered by red and white roses. Today, his paper had criticised the lack of progress in the murder investigation in the past three weeks, an editorial already out of date.

Grayson Kaye lifted a framed photo of his sister Lottie, flaming hair falling over her shoulders, eyes that chased the viewer like the Mona Lisa. He put his lips to the glass, then replaced the picture on her polished rimu casket. His manicured fingertips lingered before he turned and faced a hundred other mourners who'd gathered on his stately lawn in Cashmere's Hackthorne Road.

'It's hard to believe,' Kaye said, face heavy with grief, 'that dear Lottie has been gone a whole three weeks. Harder to believe that she was taken in such a brutal way.' Kaye looked at Rod Black standing in the wings, dark suit, navy shirt, sober tie in a tidy knot. The cop fiddled with his ear, the top of it missing courtesy of a bullet.

Tyler had covered the injury to Black. A woman, half Black's age, chest falling out of her top, had caught his eye outside a south city supermarket. Turning to gawk had saved the detective's life. There was no love lost between the two men. As a result of Black's miss-management of a murder case, Tyler's stepfather had been forced into an ignominious retirement. The Teflon cop had escaped unscathed but ever since, Tyler had put Black's performance under the microscope.

Tyler looked around the mourners: his ex, Sasha Stace, wasn't there. He'd guessed wrong.

Kaye said, 'So gratifying to hear, only minutes ago, that the police have identified her killer. It's a blessing Mum and Dad haven't had to cope with this.'

Black gave an almost imperceptible nod at the grieving brother.

Kaye took a deep breath of the light nor'west wind, a determined act to rally himself. 'But we're not here to dwell on the tragedy of Lottie's death. We can't change what's happened.' He glanced at his notes.

'Lottie and I grew up in this city. More recently, she and her husband Ben holidayed in Akaroa together, on as many weekends as they could manage while she worked in Auckland.'

Tyler dried wet eyes behind dark glasses. Ultan O'Rourke sat on one side of him, his night editor on the other, a smattering of other staff in close proximity.

Kaye continued, 'It's why we're here today and not in Auckland. I'd like to acknowledge work colleagues and friends who've travelled from Sydney and throughout New Zealand. Thank you for coming.'

Kaye summarised Lottie's education and spoke of happy times together, bussing into the city to watch movies, swims at the local school pool followed by ice cream and lollies on the walk home, a walk today's children would consider unreasonable. The activity and spending money allowed their mother to get on with gardening and their father to socialise with mates at the working men's club. Tyler could tell from the murmuring around him that Grayson and Lottie's experiences weren't uncommon. It wasn't a lot different in his own family.

'Despite the fact she was three years younger than me, she was the first to try alcohol. I remember, she was twelve when our father blamed me for the apparent loss of a favourite Irish whiskey in a green jar on the mantelpiece. I argued it was evaporation. Not even I believed Lottie would've been responsible. It was years before she 'fessed up to being the secret tippler.'

The audience chuckled. Kaye told of his sister's pride in her journalism degree and in landing jobs on Sydney community papers, followed by the *Daily Telegraph* and the *Sydney Morning Herald*.

He produced a weak smile. 'In pursuit of her ambition to be the best in her business, Lottie was fearless. She won awards for uncovering corruption in business and in politics. It didn't make her many friends. Even in her own world of journalism, she attracted more envy than admiration.' Voice faltering, Kaye said, 'But she stuck to her beliefs. Her strength of character always came through.' He sipped water and wiped an eye with the back of his hand. 'Once she made up her mind about what she wanted, she was unstoppable. Enough stubborn determination to burn.' A backhand dab of the other eye. 'But that wasn't all there was to Lottie. She was also a loving woman, someone who would show compassion towards others, particularly the lonely and the isolated. Her life's been cut short. She was only forty-four, but if we can take anything from this awful tragedy, it's that she loved what she did. And she lived life to the full.'

Kaye laid his hand briefly on the casket, then moved towards Tyler, who stood. The two men embraced, long and tight.

The service over, Tyler accepted hugs, condolences and handshakes in his workgroup huddle. He heard Grayson Kaye nearby. Loud, Kaye said, 'No, no. That's not right. I don't believe that.' Rod Black and his sidekick, fleshy-faced Detective Barry Hart, stood next to him and looked in Tyler's direction. Kaye looked tortured as he followed the direction of Hart's sausage finger.

The two cops walked towards Tyler. To O'Rourke, he muttered, 'More bloody questioning.'

'Christ almighty,' the Irishman said. 'Now they have the killer, you'd think they could at least let you bury your wife in peace.'

Hart put his hand on Tyler's shoulder. 'Ben Tyler, I'm placing you under arrest for the murder of Charlotte Kaye. You do not have to say anything. If you do say anything, what you say may be recorded and given as evidence in court. Do you understand?'

Tyler stepped back a pace and shook his head. His voice was paralysed. His look to supporters pleaded for help. They were just as dumbfounded. Indignation kicked in. 'What the hell are you doing? Are you mad? I did not kill my wife. What is this?'

Tyler was led down the sloping section to Hackthorne Road. He saw a uniformed constable in an unmarked car. Beyond that, a Subaru. The man who grinned behind the wheel was Quentin Fisk.

12

TYLER HAD A SLEEPLESS night. The bunk-bed in the basement police cell and the confidence the cops had in their case kept him awake. They'd only interviewed him once. He didn't count that night in the Akaroa hospital, when Black took away his blood-stained clothes. He'd tried to answer questions about timing of events. Black was preoccupied with mobile phones – his and Lottie's, where he was when he got his injury, what happened to the crowbar in his office, his inheritance and whether he owned a white boiler suit. But in the end his written statement said it all.

In the creeping light of a new day, Tyler reflected on his years reporting police and court rounds. Further interviews of a suspect invariably helped the police. After sufficient sweat time, suspects contradicted themselves, advanced new lies with which to condemn themselves at trial. The more they talked, the easier the prosecution case got. But in his case, Black hadn't even attempted that strategy. Not a good sign.

Now, he sat caged inside a police truck, wearing yesterday's funeral clothes. They smelled of the cells' unique inhospitable odours – surfaces embalmed with fluids forced and excreted from the fearful, the intoxicated, the deranged, the guilty and the innocent. The company of three other prisoners was no relief, despite attempts at humour.

One man had failed to honour bail conditions and had been arrested. Another was up for robbery and another for burglary and rape. Tyler resisted joining the banter about their captors, dumb-fuck pigs who didn't know their arses from their elbows. They blew hard about their smart briefs outsmarting witnesses and conning judges with a sob story. They didn't believe their own bullshit. Head in his hands, he concluded Black and Fisk must have more than a drive to get even. The stakes were too high for games. But, what?

In court, Tyler forced himself to walk upright and look confident in the short distance from the cells to the dock. The court clerk, a skeletal woman with acne visible from metres away, told him what everyone knew – that he was charged with murder. Between now and his trial, the prosecution would continue to build a heavy case against him. Yet Black must already have enough to obtain his committal for trial. How good that case was, he would find out when police opposed his bail application.

The prosecuting sergeant, a sandy-haired man cling-wrapped in a stretched police uniform, sought a remand for one week. Surprisingly, the police didn't oppose Delia Lang's bail application. Tyler first took this lawyer's advice a few months ago when he'd dismissed a difficult employee. Lang impressed him with her forthright approach, to say nothing of her good looks.

He was required to surrender his passport, to meet reporting conditions and not to associate with people in Akaroa without supervision. He was not considered a flight risk or likely to interfere with witnesses and his lack of criminal history also counted in his favour. The police stance had to be a tactic to avoid outlining the strength of their case, something they'd have to do if they opposed bail. Perhaps it was also a tactic to help Fisk weaken any argument he was behind a prosecution with an ulterior motive.

Formalities completed, Tyler and Delia Lang who was Montague's corporate counsel, walked away from the criminal section of the court. Outside, a media posse waited under the chestnut tree closest to the building. When Tyler appeared, they thrust themselves and their audio equipment in his direction, squawking like chicks in the nest when mother returned.

'What comment do you have, Mr Tyler?'

'Who do you believe killed Lottie, Ben?'

Delia, strawberry blonde, prominent cheekbones, tall and striking in her black suit, pushed past them. She insisted they had no comment. Tyler paused, his shoulders hunched, his face drained of colour. The part of him that was prudent said he should take his counsel's lead. The part of him wanting to front-foot Fisk and Black said he should fire a shot. That part won. In a flat voice he said, 'I did not attack my wife, I did not kill my wife. I want people to know that. I've told the police that and I want everyone else to know it.'

As he spotted his car waiting in Armagh Street, he heard a woman journalist ask why he'd been arrested, why the police hadn't accepted his denials. More upright now, an edge to his tone, Tyler said, 'Imagine for one second what it's like to lose your wife and then be wrongly accused of her murder? Try that, just for a second.' He paused, then continued. 'It won't have escaped your attention my paper has been critical of both Quentin Fisk and the police on different occasions. It's also no secret Mr Fisk harbours certain political ambitions following the retirement of Roy Andrews. I'm sure he doesn't want me to be reminding voters about his pedigree.'

A reporter known for conspiracy theories asked, 'Are you saying this is a malicious prosecution?'

Delia glared at Tyler. 'We're making no further comment at this time. Thank you.'

In the black leather seats of O'Rourke's car, Delia said, 'This will be a bloody show trial, Ben. You need a heavy weight trial lawyer. Murder isn't corporate counsel territory. You know that, don't you?'

Tyler scratched the stubble on his face and neck, the sound of sandpaper on wood. 'I don't want an out of town hotshot wheeled in. Gives the wrong impression, the whiff of desperation.'

'We won't need to do that. We've got a silk down here who does our defamation cases. She's hauled a few editorial arses out of the fire, I can tell you.'

13

'NO,' SASHA SAID, ARMS folded.

Delia Lang looked surprised. 'No?'

Sasha's jaw tightened, her shoulders ached, but she knew she'd given the right answer. 'No.'

Instead of taking her routine Saturday morning walk around Hagley Park, she was in her office, at the urgent request of Montague's corporate counsel. She'd read Tyler's statement to the police. Pete Wells, local general manager of *The People*, sat next to Delia and looked more shocked than his in-house lawyer. He'd developed a sudden tic in his right eye at Sasha's rejection of their plea to defend Tyler.

For twenty minutes they'd outlined what they knew of the case against their editor. Sasha shared their belief in his innocence. Not for a second did she believe Ben would've murdered his wife. That wasn't just because they'd lived together for all those years. He was not capable of such a horrendous act.

It disturbed her that Rod Black was the officer in charge of the case. That was his role when she'd led a prosecution, the one where she'd unwittingly sent a man to his death. After that, she couldn't get out of Christchurch fast enough. She was comfortable saying no because she knew good criminal lawyers who'd provide a great defence.

Sasha said, 'This isn't about Ben. The combative nature of high-powered criminal trials has worn me down, Delia. I've seen colleagues burn out, become quite distressed, suicidal even. The stakes in cases like this are enormous, matched only by the pressure on counsel.' She forced a smile. 'Do you know Mac, my stepfather and mentor?'

Delia shook her head.

'Well, he's getting on in years. Giving up criminal law means more time for me to look after him.'

Delia looked defeated. 'Ben wants you, Sasha,' she said, pleading. 'He says you're the only one he trusts to leave no stone unturned.'

'And we do pay you a large retainer,' Wells said.

Delia turned on him. 'Jeez, Wellsy, this isn't about the bloody money.'

Wells looked down, but it was true. Montague did pay well. Sasha could argue the money was for civil litigation but Delia saved her from the quibbling response.

She faced Wells again. 'Give us a few minutes, will you, Pete.'

He looked reluctant to leave, affronted that a woman probably twenty years his junior had assumed control of a critical meeting. She picked it. 'Bit of lawyer stuff to catch up on, okay?'

As Wells left the office his movement gave life to the fragrance of the pink lilies Sasha had placed on her bookcase. They lightened the room and softened her workplace but they didn't soften her stance with Delia. She'd turned down what they thought was a reasonable request. She'd rationalised her absence from the funeral, despite her late mother's voice in her ear, you've got to do what's right. If she couldn't contemplate attending Ben's wife's funeral, how could she defend him from allegations he killed her?

When Wells had gone Sasha changed the subject. 'We seem to be bumping into each other a bit more these days. How's it going with Montague?'

Delia's smile was effortful with no impact around her eyes. She cleared her throat. 'Sasha, I've found out … I'm not sure how else to say this except come to the point.'

Sasha felt her stomach tighten and her shoulders stiffen as she sat upright in her chair.

In the pause, Delia looked away for a second, brushed strands of hair off her cheek, then looked back. 'I'm your daughter, Sasha. The biological daughter you adopted out.'

Sasha's mouth opened, an involuntary action.

'I know,' Delia said. 'Bit of a bombshell. I've been carrying it around for several months and I just can't do it any more.'

Sasha's heart had a sudden and urgent need to vacate her chest. She said, 'Bit of a bombshell? Talk about understatement.'

Delia said, 'I know. I'm sorry. But you know, Sasha, I'm not sorry I found you.'

Sasha got into cross-examination pose, arms folded across her chest. She'd given no thought to whether this day would ever arrive. Surely there was a careful process to prevent this kind of shock? She worked at keeping her voice steady. 'How did you find me?'

'My ex was a social worker. When my folks died about ten years ago, I hounded him to help me with the Adult Adoption Information Act. I knew roughly what it involved, but he had expertise in the process. Long story short, he found you'd never sought to restrict identifying information. I hadn't either.' A pause. 'Neither had you made any enquiries.'

It sounded like a nice piece of self-justification.

'No,' Sasha said softly. 'Keeping my identity open wasn't a conscious decision. Still, I expect I would've been contacted by the department responsible if your enquiries were legitimate.' Her tone was harsher than she intended.

Delia's cheeks coloured. 'The enquiries never went through the right channels.'

'That would put you at significant risk.'

'Well,' she said, doubtful, 'only if I could be tied to an illegal process. My ex, Alex, was the one exposed.'

'Where is he now?'

'No idea. Last I knew he was heading to Europe. I dumped him.'

'After you got what you wanted?'

She grimaced slightly. 'Sort of. He was needy.' Hope in her voice, Delia asked, 'Did you want to give me away to focus on your career?'

'I see how it might seem like that. At seventeen, I didn't know what I wanted. Delia, I...'

Leaning forward Delia interrupted. 'Look, I don't just want to work with you, Sasha. I'd like to get close to you. And I need to work with you on Ben's case. The firm was delighted when I said I'd secured you.'

'You said what?'

'I know, I know. I'm sorry.'

This was more than a little presumptuous. Despite words of apology, she didn't look particularly contrite. The question now was whether she stuck to her guns or began to forge a relationship with her daughter. She hoped the outcomes wouldn't be mutually exclusive.

'Well, I'm sorry, Delia, you'll just have to tell them I'm not taking the case. Not wanting to be involved is not personal to you or Ben. It's about me taking control of what I want, my future career, my life.'

Delia apologised again, close to tears. 'I tend to do that, I'm afraid. Bottle things up and then blurt them out.'

It was a point of difference between them. The height, the physical appearance, the interest in the law, perhaps even bottling things up – they were like Sasha – but not blurting things out.

'Okay, I accept that. You wouldn't want to keep that information to yourself without ever knowing if I also wanted to know. I get that. I just need a bit more time to get my head around this, Delia.'

She nodded emphatically. 'I get it. I really do.'

'When I say I don't want to try another murder case, I need you to understand that's not down to the way you've delivered the news about us. Okay?'

An unhappy nod now. Then she said, 'Look Sasha, is it unreasonable to ask that you at least see Ben? He knows we're meeting today.'

'Does he know what you've just told me?'

She looked horrified. 'Of course not.'

With Mac's disappointment in her head, meeting Ben didn't sound too unreasonable. Maybe she could promote Diplock to him as defence counsel.

'Perhaps. I've got your card. I'll give you a call tomorrow and let you know.'

14

BETWEEN THE HOURS OF 2 and 4 a.m., unable to sleep, Sasha tested the effectiveness of her soundproofed garage. It took a work out over her drum kit before her mind began to settle. She concluded that yesterday's second meeting, as mother and daughter, was better than the first.

It was still early days, but Sasha recognised in Delia a familiar style of conversation. She reminded herself that the good in her was not entirely down to carrying her genes or those of an unknown father. The environment in which she had flourished will have added so much to who she was.

In a car accident a decade ago, both Delia's adoptive parents were killed. Since then, a younger brother had committed suicide. Sasha, with no real counselling skills, felt compelled to respect Delia's unwillingness to talk about these terrible events. Maybe the sad history might help her build what Delia wanted.

She had a thousand questions for her. She'd once told her investigator friend, Clay Tempero, he had sixteen years of his daughter's life to catch up on. Now, she had thirty-three to explore. What were her parents really like? Yesterday, they did the surface stuff: name, rank and serial number, her brother's death, although she was definitely more uncomfortable talking about him than anyone or anything else. What did she enjoy doing? Reading? What were her favourite foods, pet hates? But it struck Sasha, even in her mad swirl of emotion, how much more she wanted to know, despite the bomb Delia detonated. Sasha knew of people in the same situation who'd made a different choice, been too frightened to seek out an unknown parent or child, avoided a connection that might shatter dreams and serenity.

Daring to dream explained why she was now looking at the four-storey building occupied by *The People*. She was going to see Ben, mostly for Delia, and to relieve pangs of conscience. Mac's dissonant tone about avoiding Ben still jarred but his happiness did jump more than a notch when she told him she'd agreed to be considered for the High Court bench.

The building in front of her looked distinctly gloomy. Was it the morning sun behind the building, or her attitude to the impending meeting inside? The sharp perpendicular lines and tombstone windows spoke of the Black Death architecture of England's fourteenth century, copied 600 years later when this building was designed. Yet the city wouldn't willingly be without it or the cathedral, lording over The Square, fifty-three strides away. Along with other things, these buildings were part of being home, but home wasn't always comfortable.

Over the drum kit she had wrestled with what to say. Her one personal experience of Lottie was as unpleasant as it was unforgettable. The image of her in Ben's bed returned. Her red hair fanned on a fat pillow, his body hidden by a sheet, his face undoubtedly between her naked thighs. That was six years ago and she'd thought that life since had been better for them both. Until now.

Through the smokescreen doors on the second floor, she turned left. A man with a grumpy tone was telling a reporter their productivity wasn't up to scratch, a cutting remark about needing to produce more than mucus. Sasha paused at the desk of Ben's PA, a woman she hadn't seen since she was last in Christchurch. Jane had broken in a handful of editors who'd come and gone. Her smooth face lit up behind rimless glasses. 'My goodness, Sasha Stace.' She brought diamond-clad fingers to her cheeks. 'How long is it?'

'Too long, Jane. How have you been?' she asked.

Jane gestured around her. 'You know, same old, same old. Faces come and go but the work, at least for me, is pretty much the same. What about you? I'm sorry, I didn't even think to seek you out at the funeral.'

Sasha's heart skipped a beat. 'Same here – I'm sorry. Quite a turnout, wasn't it?'

A male journo hobbled out of an office next to Ben's. Tall, brown hair everywhere like loose electricity, angular face. He covered big stories and had a bit of a rep for being curmudgeonly. When he saw Sasha looking in his direction, he smiled. Hell, what was his name?

'Lovely to see you, Sasha. Been too long.' He patted her arm and limped on.

Jane chuckled. 'His first act of kindness in a week. You always turned the lights on in this place, Sasha.'

'Way too kind, Jane.'

Her mouth turned down. 'You and Ben,' she said, nostalgia in her tone. 'You went away together but...' Her jaw tightened. 'I want you to know you've always been a friend of *The People*, Sasha. And we'll always be a friend to you.'

'Thank you, Jane.' The heat in Sasha's skin shot up and she scratched her neck before tilting her head towards Ben's open door. 'Are Delia and Pete with him?'

Jane put a finger in the air, moved it up, her signal for the general manager's office. She whispered and touched Sasha's hand. 'Private tête-à-tête. He fancies her. Poor man's deluded if he thinks he's got a snowball's chance in hell.' Jane chuckled in silence – small eruptions of padded shoulders. 'Nothing changes, Sasha. Go on in.'

At Ben's open door, Sasha heard him on the phone. She paused at the shelf outside his office, current and past copies of *The People* on display. The government's apology to Te Arawa iwi over treaty grievances was still in the news. So was the debate about whether land should be handed over because it had special significance. The Christian Heritage Party was disbanding, police had said they were closer to an arrest involving the deaths of Maori twins no more than babies. There was more news of measures about the government's anti-leaks sweep, including an attempt to dig dirt on Martin Ellis.

Sasha overheard Ben say, 'No progress.' He sounded exasperated. 'And there won't be any bloody progress now I've been charged. They're not interested in considering anyone else. I'm presumed guilty. A domestic gone wrong, pure and simple. Makes the trouble with my shitty car audio pale into insignificance, I can tell you.'

A pause.

'I'm going to take leave. Ultan will take over. We'll make acting appointments for others. My tragedy is their luck.'

Another pause, longer.

'Yeah, he expects to pick up the seat. I've briefed the team, though. We play this down the middle. Editorials will be well grounded in facts, no speculation about what he might or might not do. I don't want any jury judging me thinking I'm trying to get revenge on him behind the scenes. We'll keep all copy balanced, stick to the facts. Just do the job we're good at. It won't be easy for some. They'll want to maximise the defence perspective in the copy.'

'Cheers, mate. Appreciate the support.'

Sasha knuckled the open door and walked in. The cynical part of her felt the call was staged for her benefit, all the right things said. He'd know she was waiting. Cynicism wasn't the sole province of journalists.

Ben looked the epitome of the busy executive. His office, denied morning sun, was cool, but he'd rolled the sleeves of his white shirt to the elbows. His black tie was loosened below an unbuttoned collar, and ever diminishing brown hair, once a full bird's nest, was now simply mussed. Perhaps he still drew a hand through it as he always did when contemplating difficult things ahead.

He moved easily from behind his desk, arms out, initiating a hug. Sasha tucked her left arm behind her back and extended her right hand. Extra lines hung below his eyes, the skin underneath them like a bruised peach. 'You look great,' he said. 'But then you always looked great. Coffee?'

'Please.'

At the door, he caught Jane's attention, then pointed at the large oak table, with matching chairs upholstered in old, stretched and buttoned leather.

'Big office,' Sasha said, looking around. His handwriting was on the whiteboard at the end of the office. Names and designations appeared as possibilities for the latest staffing decisions forced by his departure.

'Big job. Look, I appreciated your call, Sasha. Very much.'

She thought she should tell him that she regretted not coming to see him earlier. Instead she said, 'I'm sorry we're meeting in these circumstances.' She was torn between using Lottie's name and referring to her as his wife. For a long time, she'd been able to box her up in a dark attic, a piece of history she couldn't throw away but didn't want to see again. She added, 'No one should lose their life in that brutal way.'

'Thank you.'

Both of them avoided mentioning the funeral.

Wells knocked and led Delia into the room. They both greeted her as if she was a long-lost friend. Jane followed with a near brimming coffee plunger, best china cups and saucers, digestive biscuits neatly overlapped next to chocolate thins organised to look like brown-uniformed sentries at rest. Ben depressed the plunger, taking care to avoid a Ruapehu-like eruption. It was painful to watch and the silence hung heavily. He was flanked by Wells and Delia. Delia's smile was warm, her good teeth just visible. Sasha made a point of looking at her watch.

At last Ben spoke. 'I just want to say how much I appreciate you coming, Sasha. I know you were reluctant and I get that.'

Sasha gave a tiny nod, resisted the ubiquitous, 'That's okay'.

'I need you, Sasha.' Ben glanced sideways at Delia and added, 'We all need you. I know that's not what you want to hear and no one's more deserving of a break from crime and murder trials than you. Perhaps I, more than most, understand that.' His tone was apologetic. 'I don't deserve your help, I know. But we both know how much crap I'm in here.'

Sasha said, 'If I were in your situation, I'd want Paul Diplock QC. In my view, there's no better court brawler than Paul. He's who I'd go to.'

Ben frowned while he thought. 'I don't doubt his ability, Sasha, especially if you recommend him. But you're the only person I have real confidence in for a trial like this, especially with Fisk involved.' He paused, perhaps assessing the impact of his reply.

Sasha didn't cooperate with clues.

'I said earlier, I'm presumed guilty. It's you I need to defend me on this awful charge.'

Sasha drank coffee while the others mounted their pleas in Ben's support. It was like a job interview in reverse. The three of them submitted all possible grounds for their appeal to her: the longstanding and successful relationship with Montague both in New Zealand and Australia, the mutually beneficial loyalty, the company's high regard for her, unfettered access to any and all corporate assets she might need. They even suggested Sasha wouldn't be reversing her retirement from criminal law, just delaying it.

It was hard, partly because she admired their advocacy. It was a model of what she'd recommended to the final year students she mentored at the law faculty. Empathy first and foremost in persuasion, making the unpalatable more palatable. She filled her lungs with air and, with a forced calm, exhaled. The effort did little to bolster her resolve and she had another go at promoting Diplock. It was futile. Collectively, they insisted no disrespect to her colleague, but they expressed greater confidence in her.

Their pleas took twenty-two minutes. When she stood, others followed, respectful but unsure. 'I'll sleep on it, let you know in the morning.'

Jane was away from her workstation. Sasha lingered outside where she'd waited earlier. Congratulatory comments and back-slapping would decide it. She would walk away and stay away.

'Jesus Christ, Pete,' Ben said. 'I need to take up prayer.'

15

THE PICTURES SHOWED BLACK and Fisk standing at the foot of the wheelchair ramp leading into Akaroa hospital. Black looked uneasy as Fisk strutted towards a small scrum of media personnel on the lawn in front of the building.

Sasha was curious why Fisk had attended the homicide scene rather than Tom Carson. Perhaps the privilege of seniority allowed Carson to delegate late-evening callouts. Still, it was unusual for the attending prosecutor to talk to the media instead of a senior detective. That Quentin Fisk was doing so, was not a good sign.

She had recorded a political debate about government treaty payouts to iwi and the recording had captured the 'breaking news' of a homicide at Akaroa. Sasha recognised a local TV3 reporter who had a camera unsteady on her shoulder. A journo held a microphone with a Radio Live logo; another she recognised was from Radio New Zealand. A tall brunette, hair past her shoulders, face away from the camera and wearing a cap, looked like she was writing in a notebook. She would check with Ben but, by process of elimination, she was probably from his paper. Sasha wondered how the reporter felt later when she discovered her boss was a suspect. She stabbed the volume up button on the remote.

The fat man from Radio Live wiped his brow. The sound was poor and voices were muffled. 'Mr Fisk, can you confirm the deceased is award-winning investigative reporter and editor, Charlotte Kaye?'

Fisk flinched at the intense television light but dropped his arm shield almost as soon as he raised it. His expression was solemn, his voice grave. 'I cannot confirm the identity of the deceased or anyone else thought to be involved at this time. The deceased's next of kin are yet to be advised.'

'But it's true, isn't it,' asked the TV3 reporter, overexcited, 'that this is nothing short of a brutal murder. Are people in this town safe?'

The brunette with the notebook filled Fisk's pause but the

microphone struggled to pick up her voice. It sounded like she'd asked about leads or suspects.

'All I can confirm,' Fisk said, 'is that between seven-thirty and nine this evening, a person was killed and another is believed to be injured, although I have no information as to the seriousness of those injuries. I'm confident the police will soon find and arrest the perpetrator. My role as a senior prosecutor is to give advice concerning matters of evidence at the scene should that be necessary. Thank you. I can't add any more at this time.'

Now, as Sasha walked with the one-way traffic on Durham Street, towards Armagh, her thoughts were on Fisk and Black teaming up. They would be a handful for Delia, even with a more experienced leader. Her plea and Ben's appeal came to mind. She felt her jaw tighten. She didn't want this case. Taking on Fisk and Black together would require more than a twice daily shower.

And yet…

The one possible advantage anyone had of ensuring Fisk behaved himself belonged to her through the current disciplinary case.

No. She wasn't responsible for his courtroom conduct. That was the trial judge's role. She would have to turn it down.

Sasha enjoyed the heat radiating from the red bricks of Environment Court building and distracted herself from Fisk by counting unregistered cars. There was always something to count, always would be. On a Holden wagon, she was not the first to notice the out of date registration card. Pink graffiti soiled the windshield. An arrow pointed to an expired rego with words, 'I wish my driver wasn't Maori.' She checked for observers, then scratched at the word 'Maori' with a thumb nail, until it was gone.

At the corner of the building, Sasha buttoned a cream tailored jacket that offered nothing against the scything cold wind that funnelled up Armagh Street. At the Beer Café, she waited in a booth opposite the long side of the bar, facing the Avon River. On the far side of the bridge from where Mac would emerge, the green willows came close to touching the bank.

Her Mills Reef chardonnay was delivered by a man with a long brown ponytail and the shady outline of a growing moustache. He placed the wine on the table, and appeared to smile with sympathy. Sasha could see his mind at work – a fifty-year-old woman coming to a bar on her own. The gold in his teeth reminded her of Clay Tempero. She had once asked if there was anyone special in his life. He had said he was 'between women'. Would that be his status again?

Was she ever special, or just one side of a relationship sandwich? She'd made the running then, but had been on the rebound from Ben.

She didn't blame Clay for not coming to Christchurch. How could she? She'd never invited him. He had a shot at establishing a relationship with his daughter and had reconciled with his father. It would've been selfish to ask to put her needs first. Besides, they'd been casual, never lived together. In contrast, she and Ben hadn't lived together yet he followed her to Sydney.

No, that shouldn't be the test. Living together wasn't a sign of commitment. Look at the increasing number of couples who commuted. It was how Ben and Lottie ended up.

After a while Ben stopped asking Sasha for them to live together and called her a commitment phobe. Tilly, her Sydney barista friend, helped her to see his point of view. No father to remember, a hard-working but emotionally distant mother, subconscious feelings of abandonment. Perhaps his allegation was true.

The TV monitor in the bar showed more protests about land and property ownership. If it wasn't fear that rich immigrants would buy up land, it was fear that more government owned land would be handed over to Maori tribes. It was said Maori would do what they liked with it, including charging other New Zealanders for access. As with many debates on social and economic issues, more heat than light was generated. Despite different New Zealand cultures, the anti-immigrant camp was united.

Mac came into view, framed by smudged glass in the small iron-casing window. His worried face triggered a thought about his doctor's appointment and it struck her that the bridge he crossed was where her father had fallen, clutching his chest. John Stace had successfully prosecuted a capital murder trial in which Mac was junior defence counsel. The two men had been good friends before her father died. She only ever knew him through Mac and Natalie.

She knew Mac wouldn't be around forever, that one day his wise counsel would be lost to her. She'd tried to thrust thoughts of his death aside but they keep returning, a maudlin probe at the edge of more rational thought.

As he stood at the bar, the paunch over Mac's belt filled his pin-striped waistcoat. He saw her, grinned and mimed the offer of a drink. A wave of emotion hit her, a flush of body heat, the impulse to cry. Christ, what's wrong with me? She bit her bottom lip. Get a grip, he's not gone yet.

When he sat at her table Sasha asked, 'How did it go?'

'How did what go?'

'You know, at the doctor's.'

He gave a dismissive wave. 'Doc reckoned I need to enlist younger pallbearers.'

Fisk and Black walked into the café and headed to the bar. Fisk, who came up to Black's shoulder, looked for a seat. Beer in hand, he saw Sasha and motioned with his head for Black to follow. He was smirking. By now, he'd have been served with notice of the disciplinary investigation.

'Have I heard correctly?' he asked.

His brown eyes bulged. He had an alert, semi-intelligent look about him, like a German shepherd. On second thoughts, smaller, terrier-like.

'Are you talking to me?' Sasha made her tone as unwelcoming as possible.

He pointed a stubby finger at Mac. 'I don't know your date here so it's reasonable to conclude I'm talking to you.'

'I have nothing to say to you, Mr Fisk.'

'I heard you were defending your old boyfriend.'

Sasha glanced at Black. Head down, he looked embarrassed before he excused himself for a bathroom visit.

'You heard wrong,' Sasha said.

Fisk stared at Mac. 'Are you not going to introduce us, Sasha?'

'We're having a private meeting. You're intruding.'

Undeterred, Fisk sat by Mac, offered his hand. 'Quentin Fisk.' He gave a well-practised, trust me smile, like a salesman in search of confidence. 'I'm from the prosecution service.'

'Really,' Mac said, a little inflection of scorn. It was how Sasha had heard him respond to so many witnesses, and it never failed to draw smiles from jurors.

Fisk flushed, dropped his hand and then turned to Sasha. 'You with that holier than thou attitude and only taking winnable cases. I thought it unlikely you'd get involved. You'd have understood why Lottie would divorce Tyler if he hadn't murdered her for her money first.'

He looked like a little boy bursting with a secret. The smirk reappeared. 'But I can't say too much, since you won't be involved.' He ran a finger across closed lips, then gave a toddler's wave before turning to find Black standing at the bar.

Sasha stared in their direction and Mac said, 'Obnoxious little toad.'

'That doesn't begin to cover it.' She updated Mac in confidence about the disciplinary matter. 'If for no other reason, he shouldn't be running this case against Ben. A half-decent lawyer would've kept their head down.'

Mac said, 'I've heard Carson is quite unwell.'

'Even so, Fisk could and should brief this out, Mac. He's got that, "I'm going to get you now" look all over him. He can't possibly be objective about Tyler with the various editorials that've been written about him.'

'Can't say I have a lot of sympathy for your former partner.'

'You know he wouldn't have killed his wife, Mac.'

'Like you, I thought I knew him, once.'

She reached over and grabbed his hand. 'I'm well over all that. You don't need to be anti Ben on my account.'

Mac pensive, looked out at the river, then back at her. 'But you've declined to act for him,' he said. 'You've got bigger fish to catch – a new career to look forward to.'

Fisk, who occasionally glanced Sasha's way, was enjoying the moment. It was clear he and Black were a team, a dangerous team, one with a record for closing in on suspects prematurely and the other with a win at all costs approach.

'Representing Ben and becoming a judge aren't mutually exclusive, Mac.'

He sounded alarmed. 'What do you mean? You don't need to get involved, Sasha. Not with the High Court bench so close. Anyway, a couple of weeks ago you were telling me how over criminal law you were.'

He was right. She'd said all that and more, not only to Mac but to Delia, Wells, Kate and Paul Diplock. She'd considered all the reasons not to help him. But what about her belief in his innocence, encountering a vengeful prosecutor with dodgy motives. What about the dream team of Fisk and Black, the smarminess, the virtual goading? What about Delia needing help? Then there was Natalie in her ear – You must do the right thing. And although she'd never admit it publicly, beating Fisk meant a chance to get even with Black after he'd refused to listen to her all those years ago. His stance had cost a man his life, put Ben's life in jeopardy, even her own. Did holding a grudge put her in the same class as Fisk? Maybe. But to walk away would be wrong. As much as it was inconvenient, she couldn't. Not now.

'I am over it. That's still true, Mac.' She could see his puzzlement. She jerked her head in Fisk's and Black's direction. 'I just think with that lot, there's more at stake than my disenchantment. Announcements about my retirement from criminal law are a little premature.'

She wanted to tell him about Delia but she'd let Fisk get too far under her skin. She silently cursed the man and clenched her fists under the table. Later.

Sasha breathed deeply. 'Now, this doctor of yours,' she said. 'The truth, the whole truth and nothing but the truth.'

16

FIFTY-FIVE-YEAR-OLD Edwin Yuile, a horse-faced deputy principal at Selwyn Primary, didn't seem shocked by the treatment meted out to him by Quentin Fisk. It was as if he expected the lawyer to do the dirty on him. In his brown suit, he sat back on Sasha's sofa and sipped cold water.

'Mr Yuile, how did…'

Yuile held up a hand, fingers spread, as though stopping an errant pupil.

Sasha frowned, conscious this was Natalie's controlling gesture. She'd always resented it.

In the squeaky voice of a child's soft toy, he said, 'It's Edwin, please. And may I call you Sasha?'

She nodded. 'How did you come to be involved with Mr Fisk?'

Yuile moved his tongue back and forth inside his top lip, a gum cleaning operation, while he considered his response.

'I seem to recall,' he said, scratching the top of his dank brown mane, 'that he door-stopped me one summer's night. I was mildly annoyed as I'd been delayed by a stroppy parent at the school and risked missing the beginning of the six o'clock television news, Channel One, of course.'

'He approached you?'

'I've said that.'

'With what purpose?'

'I was going on to say he had a woman with him, same height as I recall. I only mention the height because…'

'I'm sorry to interrupt, Edwin, but I'm a bit pushed for time and I know Mr Fisk is short – shortish in stature. His purpose?'

'Of course. He asked me whether I was aware of developments occurring in the vacant half-acre section next to my property.'

'And were you? Aware, I mean.'

'No, not at all. I was, without putting too fine a point on it, rather peeved to hear what he had to say about the building plans.' Yuile removed a small, black, hard-covered notebook from his jacket. A green ribbon slithered from within.

Yuile said, 'I made notes, straight after he left.' An equine smile – lots of pink, tongue-cleaned gum. 'Time spent in thoroughness is never wasted, Sasha.' Like a police officer in court, he asked, 'May I refer to notes?'

Sasha wanted to say, what purpose would they have if you didn't, you pompous prat. Would a High Court judge have those thoughts? She fetched a yellow-lined notepad, thinking one sheet would suffice. Kate would copy the relevant pages of his notebook when he'd finished.

Yuile found the place he'd marked. 'He said the woman with him was his secretary, Averill somebody. He didn't introduce us properly.' He looked up. 'Not just corrupt, is our Mr Fisk. I think we can add rudeness to his list of attributes.'

Sasha gestured for Yuile to continue.

'After he'd told me about the development plans he asked me what I thought. Naturally I was horrified. I've made a lifestyle decision to live semi-rurally. I have a few goats on my property. They're excellent for keeping the wide open spaces in order. Don't get me wrong. I'm sympathetic to the animal welfare movement. Who wouldn't be?'

He was not convincing. The words were right but nothing else about the man indicated he'd be sympathetic to anything but his own causes. 'What happened next?' she asked.

'He said there was a consents procedure.' Finger back in place. 'I, of course, knew this. I teach social and community studies.' He smiled, thankfully without gums.

Sasha's concentration wandered. She overheard Kate explaining to a potential client the rules of engaging a barrister, her role as a lawyer. Barristers cannot take instructions directly from clients but instead, from other lawyers called solicitors. Then her mind went to Ellis and Grange. May we ask whether you have any ongoing relationship with Mr Tyler? She skipped to Mac and his concern for her. One more trial, albeit difficult, wouldn't break her psychologically.

'He said I could object and he'd be prepared to assist. Naturally, I agreed and asked him what was necessary.'

'When did he tell you about the purpose of the development?'

Yuile looked back at his notebook and it crossed her mind Ellis and Grange would want to know she'd decided to defend Ben Tyler.

'That came next. He said it was for building a small farm, some wildlife reserve – a form of animal rehab place – like Willowbank. I'm familiar with that place. We've had school trips there. Nice idea but difficult to see how a wildlife reserve would be replicated out in Selwyn. I suppose it's possible, but imagine the heavy machinery and excavation involved.' He looked incredulous. 'Plausible maybe, but utterly intolerable.'

'I think you told the Law Society that although you hadn't met Fisk before, his firm once represented you in the purchase of your Selwyn property.'

The hand reappeared. 'A minor correction. I wrote to the Law Society, but in essence, that's correct. What I forgot to record was he also told me he was from the prosecution service. It gave him an air of gravitas, turned him from being just another lawyer into one more trustworthy. No offence, of course.'

'On that matter, have you been in touch with the attorney general's office to complain about Mr Fisk?'

He looked surprised. 'No. Should I have done?'

'No.'

She recalled Grange's words. It's been terrible. The man plagues our office with calls. I've had to warn him about police intervention if he does not cease and desist. He's a vexatious crusader, Sasha. 'What about the attorney general's staff? Has anyone contacted you about your concerns, suggested that you stop ringing them or there might be consequences?'

Surprise turned to shock. 'Absolutely not. Has this been suggested? Perhaps Fisk has impersonated me, attempted to discredit me before we even got started?'

'I don't know, Edwin. But I accept your assurance. Let's get back to Mr Fisk's visit.'

Yuile exhaled loudly. 'Well, he said the advertising period in which to object was almost over. I said I hadn't seen the advertisement. He asked if I'd had a letter from the council. I said I had, but I assumed it was a local council property rates invoice. They always send these out well in advance and I'd put it aside. I have the payments automatically scheduled.' He looked bewildered. 'He was annoyed – at me.'

Sasha knew that Fisk, realising the consent would've been granted without his intervention, was annoyed at himself. 'And then?'

Yuile looked back at his notes. 'We were at my kitchen table and he pulled out a notice of objection, which he asked me to sign. It was typed up as a document produced by Fisk, Carson & Co.'

'The firm was specifically named?'

'Yes. When you folded the document lengthwise in half, it had a backing sheet to it. The words "Notice of Objection" were halfway down the page and the firm's name was typed at the bottom, like a footer. To me, it added a sense of formality and demonstrated legitimacy.'

Sasha made that note, the little detail added to authenticity. 'Did he say what he'd do with this notice of objection once you'd signed it?'

Yuile frowned when he couldn't find what he was looking for. 'I haven't got that written down. I remember he said he had to present it or file it with the other lawyer.'

'Serve it?'

'Yes, that's it,' Yuile said, gums on display. 'Like a legal game of tennis, I suppose.'

Fully engaged now, she asked, 'And the other lawyer, did he say who that was?'

'I asked him, but he was vague.' Yuile looked at his notebook. 'A lawyer, a pansy pushover, he said, he'd forgotten the name – a firm in the city.'

'Did you see Mr Fisk again after he came to your property?'

'No. Although I have notes of several telephone calls.'

Sasha got him to go through notes of four calls. They were all assurances Yuile's objection was in hand – his need to lodge a formal statement for the Environment Court, a planning hearing to follow.

'And did he send you a copy of the objection notice?'

'That was part of the "We'll keep you informed promise".'

'Did he ever ring you?'

'No, I made all the running, but I didn't mind. I don't like the thought of lawyers turning on the meter when they decide their revenue needs increasing.'

'At any stage from the first moment he contacted you, until you bought the adjoining land, did he ever tell you he was either working for, or connected in any way with, the animal welfare trust.'

'Definitely not. He told me, based on my objection, and evidently I was the only objector, the trust was preparing for a full-scale defended hearing. He said it would cost me seven or eight thousand dollars and even if we won, he said it was inevitable the trust would appeal, leading to further costs. I felt like he was frightening me off. I couldn't understand why. With my fees, he would have benefited from that, wouldn't he?'

Realising this complaint would go the distance, Sasha said, 'I'm sorry to ask you this. I assume, since you're in a teaching role, you have no criminal convictions?'

Yuile reddened, lowered his chin.

'I only ask because it's better I know now, than have any issues of credibility arise later that might catch us by surprise.'

Sasha waited him out, a tactic Natalie taught her. It almost always paid off when interviewing witnesses.

When he replied his voice was less grating, 'There was … when I was eighteen, almost thirty years ago. I assume the new clean slate law means it can't be raised.'

'That depends on the offense and the circumstances in which that information is sought. If you were cross-examined at a disciplinary hearing, it might be relevant. You'd better tell me what it was.'

He whispered, 'It was an indecency charge.'

'Not a child?' she asked, horrified.

'Good God, no.' He moved his hand over his mouth and mumbled.

'I'm sorry,' Sasha said. 'Did you say, on a boat or goat?'

He looked away as he said, 'Goat', then gabbled the rest. 'My eighteenth birthday. I was under the influence and blindfolded at the time. My lawyer said it was best to plead guilty and put it behind me. It was the last case called in the Balclutha court, a benefit of an alphabetical call. The *Otago Daily Times* reporter had left. My father ran the local rag so it was never going in that.'

17

'**TWICE IN TWO DAYS**,' Mac said, smiling. 'This place will have to give us a discount.'

Sasha and Mac were among the mid-morning coffee crowd, less raucous than the drinks after work mob. Their black coffees arrived with little aluminum jugs of hot water. Mac also ordered a piece of caramel chocolate slice. As always, he offered some to Sasha and, as always, she declined. It occurred to her that her choice reflected who did most of the talking. She wondered whether she should eat more when she was with him. Their best times together were always when she did most of the listening.

'I'm assuming your facial expression means you want to talk about my health warning signs,' Mac said with a hint of guilt. 'After last night, I'm surprised you haven't got a new diet to present.'

Sasha pointed at the slice. 'Have I said anything? Chided you about your sweet tooth?'

'Wouldn't make any difference if you did. I think you know that.'

She sipped the coffee. 'Before we got on to your health last night, there was a piece of the story about Tyler's trial I didn't tell you.'

He finished chewing and said, 'Well, you know my thoughts about that. I haven't changed my mind.'

'No and I don't expect you to, Mac. I don't really disagree with you. A focus on the bench is a priority. But I've thought more about it. If I'd known Ben was the target for an arrest and Quentin Fisk and Rod Black were leading the prosecution, I'd never have said anything about retirement. If you recall, you tried to talk me out of that.'

'It was more your disillusionment I was discussing. Thoughts of retirement grew out of that. Yes?' He took another bite.

'True. Frankly, little has changed in that domain and I'll be clear what I expect of him. Fortunately, there's no reason why representing him and becoming a judge are mutually exclusive. They both sipped. 'Anyway, the second chair is Delia Lang, Montague's corporate counsel.

Have you met her?'

'No. I did happen to see her in court when I had lunch with Bowen J. the other week.'

'Anyway, she asked me a few times to mentor her – a while back.'

'Well, she'll get that now, won't she?' He took another bite of his slice.

'I've got news about her, Mac. Big news.' She realised that in the moment of revelation, she was now almost in the same situation as Delia. 'That baby girl I had thirty-three years ago. It's her, Mac. Delia Lang.'

Mac inhaled his food and coughed violently, causing Sasha to stand and look for help. Mac waved in the negative and while he regained composure, Sasha fetched water.

After several swallows, Mac croaked, 'How did this come to light?'

She told tell him the whole story.

Another cough, his voice strained, 'She's manipulated you, Sasha. Is she even genuine?'

Sasha hadn't considered the possibility. Her heart lurched. 'Well, there's the physical resemblance. Our ages are a perfect match. No imposter would risk getting that wrong. But I didn't ask for DNA proof, if that's what you mean.'

He still looked sceptical.

'Mac, I refused to represent Ben even after she told me. But she asked if it was unreasonable to at least see him. After you and I talked the other day, I felt bad about the way I managed the funeral.'

'I wonder about the timing. She left telling you this news until after you refused to represent him.'

'And I continued to refuse after she told me.'

This wasn't going at all like Sasha hoped. She felt her shoulders drop, her excitement at the prospect of sharing the news now in the ether. She hadn't anticipated Mac's reaction.

He looked her in the eye. 'Do you believe that she wants more than a professional relationship – something personal?'

'I've had a second conversation with her, about her life, pretty superficial stuff, to be honest.' She told him the details. 'So yes, I think she does and, what's more, I'm open to that.'

With Mac's circumspection, she added nothing about the increasing yearning that was pulling her towards Delia, an unbidden and even greater desire than being on the bench.

18

MAC HAD SOFTENED A little by the end of their coffee together. He expressed interest in meeting Delia but Sasha sensed she would need to push to make it happen.

Clay was her focus now. It had been thirty-two minutes since his flight had landed. She freshened her lipstick and fired a spray of Chanel No. 5 at each side of her neck.

Being in his arms couldn't come soon enough. His uncertainty that first time – after a day poring over security DVDs, then the meal he'd cooked for them. That night in Rushcutters Bay was as clear in her mind as if it were last night. Uneasy at making the running again, she felt like a woman less than half her age: flushed, stomach churning. And she'd told him it was his professional services she needed. She looked around to see if others were staring at her.

He was the seventy-seventh passenger to come through the door but counting hadn't calmed her nerves. On his trolley, a soft bag with a red tie around the handle. He carried a matching smaller bag over his shoulder. In black jeans and blue shirt, he was looking fit. In fact, in response to his disgustingly healthy appearance, she held her tummy in.

He was close. 'Christ, you're not getting any shorter, Sash.'

A curious opening but they hugged and he kissed her on the lips in a non-lingering way.

'Nice to see you too,' she said. 'Were you stripped searched by multiple people?'

'Your lot make our luggage handlers look like sprint champions and that, I promise you, is no mean feat.'

Sasha thought he was keen to change the subject when he said, 'So! Urgency coupled with media mystery.'

'Off to see the client now,' she said. 'Charged with murdering his wife. I need your nose on the case. Some dodgy players are involved.'

Glancing sideways, she caught the gold glint in his grin. He said, 'You're learning.'

'I remember the lesson. You said trusting people was a significant performance failure of mine.'

She buzzed the window down and inserted the card that released them from the car park. 'How are Felan and the Reprobates?'

'You make them sound like they're in a band,' he said. 'I've just tried calling Felan now. This trip deprives him of an opportunity to book up a large lunch with me on his expense account.'

'Sorry about that. I'm sure he'll find a suitable substitute.'

'That's what worries me – the vulnerability of unsuspecting women half his age.'

'Nothing changed there, then. What about the team?'

'Also much the same. We still think we have the ability of twenty-somethings, still imagine we're bowling at one-thirty clicks.' His tone became more serious. 'But I have to say, you're not popular with the Reprobates. I had to persuade them a couple of weeks' break from cricket is more likely to help my dodgy hamstring than harm it.'

'I'm sure they'll get over it. It'd be too bad if they win without you, though.'

'Not sure how to take that,' he said.

As they headed down Memorial Avenue, Clay asked what was hidden behind the 10-metre hedge.

'My golf course,' she said with enthusiasm. 'Russley.'

'I thought you charged like a wounded bull but you've obviously progressed to the full Pamplona event.'

Another glance, unsure if he was serious. 'I don't own the bloody course. It's where I play.'

At the red light, Clay said, 'But you're a sit-down kind of girl for recreation. You still drumming?'

'Not as much as I'd like. I don't run or mountain climb but I walk, you know that. And I'll have you know, I play the odd good shot for a novice. The pro says my swing isn't too bad. Reckons I should invest in longer shafts, though.'

'Naturally,' he said.

Moving at the green light, Sasha sensed his stare. 'What's that supposed to mean?'

'It means you're a natural at most things you turn a hand to.'

She thought of putting her left hand where his jeans bulged, to massage gently and feel the creeping resistance in the seam, the hydraulic anticipation. But Natalie appeared in her head and she settled for hoping for another opportunity.

'Speaking of turning things, I have a confession about last night's web of mystery.'

'Yes?'

'The client. It's Ben Tyler.'

She counted off three seconds before he almost shouted, 'Tyler! You're defending Tyler? He married that woman who...'

'Indeed,' she interrupted. She was not surprised by his disbelief. 'Would you have flown over if I'd told you?'

'I'd have tried to talk you out of defending him. Who's he supposed to have murdered?'

'That woman, as you put it – his wife.'

'No!'

The lights were red again. She turned to face him. 'He says he didn't do it.'

'He would. The dock is the most popular place to declare one's innocence. Well, only marginally more popular than prison. I read prison musters were...'

'A form of communion for the innocent. You've used that one on me already, but in Ben's case, I believe him.'

Clay exhaled through his teeth, a sigh of frustration. 'You want to believe him.'

'No, that's not right. I do believe him.'

They pulled away at the green. A hoon, approaching fast from behind, veered right at the last minute and overtook Sasha. The roar of his throaty Triumph died quickly. 'Tosser,' Sasha said.

'Methinks the lady doth protest too much.'

'Not you. That idiot,' she said, pointing.

'An oversupply of testosterone. Makes men do strange things – men like Tyler, perhaps. I start with the premise if the cops make an arrest for murder, they're confident they'll prove it, even if it's just a case of circumstantial evidence.'

'Let's reserve judgment,' she said. 'Suffice to say, the prosecution dream team of Black and Fisk is enough to make any defence counsel wake with night terrors.'

'But why you? Is it even ethical, given your personal history with the bloke?'

'More ethical than impersonating a police officer with dodgy search warrants and no less ethical than having sex with the boss's wife in his firm's cleaning cupboard.'

Several times, she'd wondered what had precipitated the change from the boy next door to a dogged determination to be unorthodox? It'd been a point of friction in their past – her need to work within the law to assemble evidence, his need to push the boundaries in the pursuit of justice.

Sasha saw him wince, then scratch his head. 'Burnt my moral pulpit a while ago, didn't I?'

'It's not an unreasonable question.' Sasha's tone was more conciliatory. 'Technically, my client is Montague and my instructing solicitor is Montague's corporate counsel.'

'A bullshit version of the truth,' he said.

'I didn't want the bloody case. I'd said no but that had nothing to do with Ben.' Sasha told him why she was ditching crime from her work.

'You're saying the turnaround is down to believing Tyler and concern about this prosecution dream team?'

'Pretty much. Black and his sidekick are enough of a worry. However, he's teaming up with a prosecutor who's dodgy.

'Sounds like you have sensible reasons not to be involved.'

This hadn't gone well. Sasha decided to pick another time to tell him about Delia.

19

IN BEN'S OFFICE, INTRODUCTIONS complete, Sasha confirmed she'd take the case. The relief in the room was palpable so she reminded the assembly of what was ahead of them. Delia would be her 'junior', in compliance with a bar convention that silks have second chairs in court. Clay would provide the day-to-day legwork and assistance as required.

'There are two conditions,' Sasha said. Delia tilted her head and Pete Wells drew back as if to avoid a punch. Ben was unmoved. 'You all know my reluctance to take this case and the reasons why.' She eyeballed Wells. 'I'm taking it partly in recognition of the relationship I have with Montague.'

Wells studied his shoes, guilt-ridden over his weekend remark about how well the company paid her.

'I'm also taking it because of concerns about the prosecutor, his ambitions and the Law Society complaint you've recently published about him. I'm investigating that for the society so hope to be a positive influence on his conduct during the trial.'

Three heads nodded.

'The first condition is related to my intended change of direction. I'm tired of deceit, lies and cover-ups and their impact on me and others dear to me. I'm over it, big time. And I'm particularly over my own team behaving like that.' She looked at Ben. 'Therefore Ben, if during my defence of you, I learn you've lied to me, or attempted to mislead me, I'm out.'

Delia said, 'Hang on a minute, Sasha, that's…'

She gave Natalie's stop sign before she realised. 'Not negotiable,' she said. 'The consequences of any attempted deception will be yours to manage, not mine. Given what I've said, I hope you'll respect the reasons for the conditions and comply.'

Wells and Delia were both about to speak again when Ben said, 'Agreed. Second condition?'

'You stay out of the media, Ben – no photographs, no statements, no public appearances. If you have any planned, cancel them. You're nothing more than a grieving husband, keen to clear his name, but you'll only do that through me.' She lifted her head a few degrees. 'Understood and agreed?'

'Understood and agreed,' they said, a choir in harmony.

Clay cleared his throat, which prompted Sasha to say, 'And another matter – a third condition to my continuing involvement, if you will. Nothing less than full cooperation with Clay.'

'Agreed.'

'Are we all on the same page?' she asked.

Delia nodded. Wells looked at Ben. They also nodded.

Outside, as he and Sasha walked to her car, Clay said, 'Haven't seen you quite like that before. To think you're on their side, too.'

'You think I'm tough on my own team?'

'If I was Tyler, I'd be frightened to make the slightest slip.'

'No bad thing. But if you or he thinks I'm hard work, wait till you see Quentin Fisk in action.'

20

IN THE OFFICE EARLY, Sasha caught up with invoicing and reading various journals and notices alerting practitioners to law changes. With a plan to drive to the murder scene in Akaroa, she wore blue jeans, a pink shirt and a silver necklace that Clay had given her in Sydney. She was tempted to have the roof of the Audi sports open, but was dissuaded by the cool wind. This flexibility in her routine and attire didn't come easily to judges – she decided to enjoy it while she could. Ordinarily, she'd have her second chair with her but Delia had a case in court.

No respecter of the 100 kilometre an hour limit, Sasha flew over the grey straights of road. Lake Ellesmere looked brown and unwelcoming on her right, the odd lonely tree bowed to traffic in permanent submission to the Canterbury nor'wester. Her thoughts turned to Mac. She'd put to him that his talk of getting younger pallbearers was bluster. He'd conceded, under cross-examination, that he had 'a problem with the old ticker'. He'd said he didn't want to worry her. She'd chided him she wasn't a little girl any more, but in her arguments and protests, she'd proved the opposite.

As she passed the sheep-dotted embankments to her left and the man and dog outpost of Little River, her anticipation began – the first glimpse of the harbour. First, there was the ear-popping climb and the heady wind around the bends. After that, the ultimate crest beyond the Hilltop Tavern and sun that glinted off a serene blue sea, encircled by the rugged hills of Banks Peninsula.

Out of the car, Sasha stretched her legs and back and gorged on the view, a city girl's private homage and the only time she ever thought about being Piscean.

Back on the road, she steered around groups of risk-taking, lycra-clad fanatics on two wheels. At one point a pair of them forced her well over the center line but she restrained the urge to share her colourful invective beyond the car's interior. Around Duvauchelle, then the Takamatua hill, she buried her foot and remembered being the seventeen-year-old passenger next to her then boyfriend in his old Chrysler. They were coming the other way, downhill at 140 kilometres an hour on the steep gradient. All she could think about was the looming compulsory stop. Logically, it was in their favour, designed to help the inexperienced with no judgment for the speed of oncoming four-wheeled missiles. As they hurtled downhill, the sonorous wind howling its death call past the windows, she could think only of a village idiot playing vehicle roulette, driving through that stop sign while they plunged into deathly disaster. It was both exhilarating and terrifying. She didn't know it then, but a different terror lay in wait. She'd gifted her virginity to that boy and between them they managed the unthinkable.

But was it unthinkable Delia would turn up? Sasha was enjoying the idea of seeing more of her, a future relationship. But she'd resolved not to rush into it. Perhaps she might be more like an older sister, seventeen years older. Yes. She'd like that. A lot.

Not much bad happened in Akaroa. Its courthouse was turned into part of the town's museum back in the eighties, long after it had been decommissioned. The 500 or so permanent residents were a service-focused lot, providing visitors with food, accommodation and idyllic scenery. Depending on your point of view, the town came alive in summer and hibernated in winter. It was proud of its old French influence and narrow, French-named streets with no need for anti-crime cameras.

The murder scene was situated between the two ends of town: the old hotels and guest houses at one, the modern bars and restaurants at the other. For now, she'd park close to the Bully Hayes café in Beach Road. Neither city, nor classic rural town, this place celebrated its own unique funkiness – the residents and the tourists, the old and the new, the French and the Maori, the hills and the harbour.

Despite the heart-warming journey, she felt uneasy as she sat beneath the café's black umbrella. She had the sense of being watched. She was used to being observed. Her cases attracted big galleries, although she didn't know why, and she got stared at in shops, in bars, by the lecherous and the curious. What was happening now felt covert. She had a good look around. People were milling, fetching and carrying. Others, like her, were waiting. It was just before the mid-morning coffee rush, if a rush was to be had in Akaroa.

Imagination in overdrive, she focused on the large weeping palm at the end of a row of five Norfolk pines. One had been butchered to the shape of an umbrella. The palm took her back to a ten-day jaunt in Thailand where she and Ben rode elephants. He'd urged his mount to move faster than hers, some competition in his mind.

She'd made a photo album of that trip for the two of them but since they'd parted, she hadn't looked at it or anything else from their years together. Yet she knew where it was at home. She subscribed to the gone but not forgotten philosophy, and did so without guilt. Mac's mantra had always been 'Guilt is a wasted emotion unless you use it on the other side's witnesses'.

She had some now, though. She'd turned down Ben's request for them to travel together. The police still had the car he was driving that night and although a ride would've met his practical needs, it felt too chummy for her. All she wanted today, was to be professional.

With no table staff in sight, she stood to go inside.

'Penny for them,' the voice said behind her.

Caught by surprise, she flinched. It wasn't the first time Ben had snuck up on her when she'd been deep in thought. Despite an unconvincing smile, he looked relaxed, almost inappropriately so, given the morning's agenda.

'A penny? Just a little less than a legal aid lawyer. You saying I'm cheap, or my thoughts are worthless?'

He kept the smile but his eyes were serious as he stared, trying to read her mood.

'You know me,' he said.

'I thought I did.'

He looked away.

Damn. So much for professionalism. 'Come on,' she said, 'let's get coffees to take away.'

21

WITH THE AROMA OF coffee and food behind them, the smell of sea salt cooking on the warm beach stones was pungent. The house, an old two-storey cottage, was pristine white, with a blue trim. Sparkling in the morning sun, it looked a most unlikely place for a grisly murder.

Ben rolled the sleeves of his cream shirt up to his elbows and led her to the back of the property. 'Lottie's rental was under the carport,' he said, pointing.

The police booklet of photos confirmed this. In fact, little had changed from the night of the murder. There were still three strands of retractable washing line hooked onto a metal pole. The grass around its base and under the hedge fencing had survived the scything reaches of a mower. Beyond the front of the carport the property's boundary, a retaining wall, stained timber planks arranged like a xylophone, at its edge.

'I put my car up behind hers,' he said. 'Well, it wasn't mine. It was a loan from Sounds for Cars. I'd bought a new audio system and the bloody thing hadn't been working properly for weeks after they'd installed it.'

He stopped and stared, seeming to replay his next moves. Sasha didn't want to interrupt his thought process. She hoped this return to the scene would stimulate new memories that would help them.

He said, 'I got my overnight and computer bags from the trunk and headed over here to the back door.'

There was a dry outlet pipe set into the wall, the colour and size of a Cuban cigar. The old wooden door had been lovingly restored, the knob handle and lock set at a low height. It took a long rod key, the type that sat comfortably on a warden's hip.

Sasha asked, 'Was it open?'

He ran a hand through his hair. 'No, but it was unlocked.'

Through the back door hallway, a curtained nook was to the left. The police photo of this had been taken from the opposite direction.

'I got to about this point,' he said, pensive.

It occurred to Sasha he was doing a good job of containing his emotions.

'Well, I think I did, I don't know for sure. It was about here I came to. I don't know what happened. It wasn't until I got to my feet that I felt the pain in my head.'

Sasha pulled the curtain. The wooden hoops slid effortlessly along the rail but not in silence. 'The assailant could've hidden here,' she said, 'but you'd have heard the curtain open.'

'Not if it was already open. It would've been dark when I came in.'

At the stairs Ben looked up to the landing. On the wall above, a framed print, bush in the foreground, the harbour and the peninsula hills beyond. His walk was slow and wary. He hunched as if expecting another blow from the hidden intruder. From behind, Sasha heard his panting, a noisy struggle for breath, as if he'd completed a hard run for the first time in a while. At the landing they walked over old blood stains, now brown, and headed to the top.

'Just a minute,' she said, unsure why she was whispering. 'Do you remember seeing blood here on the night?'

'I just thought she'd cut herself. Wouldn't have been the first time. She was a bit careless with knives.'

They moved to the bathroom door. It was shut and Ben stopped.

Sasha asked, 'Was it open or closed on the night?'

'Ajar.' He was still gasping.

'Open it.' She tried to sound encouraging.

His face pleaded for relief but she gave a small nod to continue. He opened the door, then swivelled his head. 'I can't do this.'

'Tell me what you saw.'

His voice disintegrated as he sobbed the words, 'Blood. There was blood everywhere.'

Sasha stepped forward, started to touch his shoulder, then dropped her arm as he moved through the door and fell to his knees. He crawled to the bowl and retched. For a moment Sasha closed her eyes while he vomited coffee into the bowl no longer speckled with Lottie Kaye's blood.

Upright again, he lurched like a drunk, rinsed his mouth at the basin, then passed her without speaking, a flash of anger in his eyes. His look said this was cruel, unnecessary and even, she thought, vindictive. That she'd finally taken revenge for that night when she discovered their infidelity.

22

UNSETTLED BY BEN'S REACTION, Sasha tilted her head back against the door frame. She needed to push on, let him have space to recover. She checked off the bathroom scene against what was in the police photos. How different now from the carnage that night. Towards the end of the booklet, death scene photos and morgue shots made their sickening appearance. Unlike criminal bar colleagues who were desensitised to death, she'd never got used to seeing past the body, the last horrible seconds, imagining the life once led, the bereaved left behind. She'd chided herself for melodramatic self-indulgence. It didn't help deal to or with the prosecution's tactic of presenting the macabre.

Pictures showed Lottie Kaye's naked and battered body. The side of her head visible to the lens had been caved in and her facial features were close to mashed beetroot. Two teeth sat in a pond of dark blood. Pictures of her forearms revealed what appeared to be defensive wounds, the skin around them dark with bruises. The tops of her hands were bloodied. Under stark light a diamond ring gleamed on a mangled finger.

There was blood on the toilet cistern, the seat below and the wall above. Another more viscous substance, probably brain matter, was also on the wall. There was a shot of the ceiling, a grille underneath. A close-up showed it was enveloped in dust and fur and it too looked to be blood spattered. The top of the round white rubbish bin, half a metre or so from the Lottie's head, was spotted with blood, as was the foot-controlled pad.

The glass shield of the shower on the other side of the bathroom was spattered, as was the lower part of the bath's exterior. It looked like a heavy blunt instrument had been used in a forehand–backhand movement, collisions with both sides of her head.

A trio of naked bulbs above a mirror illuminated a curved line of blood spots, tails forming as they hit the glass. Lottie's nose was bent at an impossible angle and her red hair was blood soaked. Sasha knew, from the savagery of the killing, that Lottie had not encountered a routine burglar. There was purpose and brutal determination at this scene, way beyond bad luck and opportunism.

Downstairs, Ben sat sideways on the sofa facing the front door. Sasha tiptoed across the floor and sat next to him, apologising to his back. He clutched a fat striped cushion to his stomach as if it was his most precious possession. He turned and faced her with the expression of a hurt puppy, astonished to be kicked.

She said, voice soft, 'Sometimes it helps when witnesses physically return to the scene. Their memory can be enhanced, a trigger effect.'

'Who would want to remember what I've seen?'

His face was pale, his eyes wet. She apologised again. 'Can we talk more about what happened when you found her?'

He pulled the cushion to him, a tighter hug, and closed his eyes. 'It was obvious she was dead. What had been done – it was unsurvivable. I didn't even check for a pulse. I knelt to pull her to me, to say goodbye. She was warm, her blood was still warm.'

'Did your knees touch the floor?'

He looked surprised. 'How would I know? Is that important?'

'Can I get you to demonstrate? I was going to do that in the bathroom but we don't have to go there. We can do it here.'

He looked unsure. But it was important, critical. She withheld her reasons, not wanting to influence the demonstration. She placed her jacket over the back of a chair at the dining table. 'I'll lie here, on the floor as if ... you know.'

Sasha adopted the position of Lottie's body but Ben looked as though he wanted to be elsewhere. Turning her head away from him, she said, 'Now, show me what you did.'

She heard him walk back to the stairway. She called out, 'What are you doing?'

'I've remembered this.' He returned, carrying a bath towel. 'There was one on the rail. I grabbed it and placed it over her lengthwise, like this.' He crouched beside her.

'To avoid getting her blood on you?'

'No. She was naked. It was a dignity thing.'

'Oh, right,' Sasha said, disappointed.

'Problem?'

'The prosecution argues you didn't get any blood spatter on your front because you were wearing protective clothing.'

'This is what I did,' he said, and Sasha felt his arm slide under her shoulder. 'I pulled her to me with one arm, cradling her head to my chest. Like this.'

His chest was hot, his shirt damp, and Sasha could smell his deodorant, working overtime. She thanked him. As they separated, she observed his knees weren't on the floor. It explained why there was no blood on them when Lottie's body was cloaked in blood and the floor covered.

When Sasha shared her observation, Ben said, 'The towel would have been between my legs and her stomach.' He stood and offered a hand. The gesture brought back memories of karate they used to do together. He was good at putting her on the floor. Before things turned sour, they'd practised routines in her living room overlooking Rushcutters Bay, each of them barefoot in white dressing gowns. When Sasha wanted sex with him, she'd do the moves with nothing on under her gown. He'd always know and his distraction from the bout was obvious. He'd manoeuvre her falls so she'd end up on the cream sofa, a softer than normal landing. And he'd put his hand down as he did now, and she'd pull him on top of her.

Looking confused, he asked, 'What?'

'I was just thinking.'

'About?'

She gripped his hand and pulled herself upright. 'How, if all that wasn't horrific enough, you now face the nightmare of a trial.' She glanced at the kitchen. 'If there's coffee, I'll make you one. I think you'll be able to keep it down now.'

'A triple gin would be good but coffee'll do. Plunger's in the pantry.'

Coffee poured, they returned upstairs to a little balcony overlooking an aquamarine sea. Sasha's bare heels rested on terracotta tiles that provided mountainous obstacles for a few resident ants. The steam from their coffee mugs was just visible in the warming day. Sasha thought she could see the silver sheen of small Hector's dolphins as they breached the surface, but it would be rare if they came this far down the harbor.

They sipped in silence until their mugs were nearly empty. Sasha decided to break the silence. 'In the bathroom, Ben. You were able to pull yourself away from her and…'

'Lottie. Not her, Lottie.'

'Of course. Lottie.' Their eyes locked in more silence.

'I'm trying to treat this like I would any case, Ben. Our history is…'

'Long,' he interrupted. The beginnings of a sad smile tugged at his mouth. 'And for the most part, warm and loving, yes?'

'It's not useful for either of us to spend any energy on the past. For one last time, I need to be at the top of my game, not just for you, but for me. And I want rid of the sour taste lingering after that Andrews trial. That's important to me, Ben, but what's at stake for you is much greater.'

'I know that. But we can't do this without discussing Lottie, the history between her and me.'

'Come on,' Sasha said, 'let's walk to the lighthouse.'

23

BEN HAD FIRST MET Lottie within a year of relocating to Sydney from Christchurch. She'd started tutoring a journalism course, so had got him along to give students a dose of reality. He'd talked about the practical, unglamorous side of the job – the challenges of editing, leading a team of cynical and independent-minded people, increasing circulation in a competitive market and so on.

'Things progressed between you,' Sasha said.

'Not for a while. We started seeing each other when you were doing that nursing home murders case. Orson Plummer, her husband, introduced us at a media awards do. She slipped her card into my dinner jacket pocket.'

'You had a dinner jacket? You didn't have one when we went to cocktails at Government House in Sydney.'

Ben smiled. 'I remember that – and the idiot who fancied you.'

'Which idiot?'

'The fat prick, the one the cop wasted.'

They walked on a few metres in silence, side by side. Sasha pointed at the white hexagonal lighthouse as it came into view. 'People paid one dollar for that, did you know?'

'I should know that.'

'These things were decommissioned in the seventies. When it stood in its original position, at the heads, the idea was to push it into the sea.'

Ben's smile was wry. 'Christ, the heritage nut bars would be apoplectic.'

'Almost. Interested folk formed a preservation society and approached the then Marine Department, who thought their plan to relocate it was bonkers.'

'How do you know this stuff?'

'Mac. You remember he was close to my dad?'

'I do.'

'Before Dad took up the law, he'd been in the navy. He was keen on lighthouses. I was about twenty when the building was moved here. Mac told me Dad would've been interested had he been alive.' She looked Ben in the eye. 'He'd have been one of those nut bars you mentioned.'

Ben winced. 'Sorry. Editorial licence.'

Sasha led them up to the broad base and past the giant red door to lean on the railing fence. The tide was still out and the smell of salty kelp and detritus was heady. Pieces of driftwood were the shape and size of everything between blanched pencils and discarded prosthetics.

'What happened with you and Lottie after we parted company? I'm imagining things got easier.'

'Yes and no. No, because Plummer fired up the closer Lottie got to freeing herself of him. It was bitter to the end – beyond the end. And easier, yes, because I could dedicate time to support her. O'Rourke tells me Plummer is coming onto the Montague board. If he doesn't already know I'm editor of *The People* it won't be long before he finds out.'

'You think Plummer could be involved in this?'

'Not on his own. He'd need help getting in and out of the country without passing through immigration. I can't see him planning to murder his ex-wife and leaving an easy trail to be discovered.'

Sasha opened her shoulder bag and pulled out Ben's written statement to the police. 'We need to talk more about this, particularly after you found her.'

He read the record of his account. 'Not much more I can add.' He looked sad. 'After finding Lottie, it's a blur, a complete blur. To be honest, I remember hardly anything and that's bloody frustrating. I must have been in shock.'

Out on the harbour, several yachts were anchored, one with a dinghy in tow – matching paintwork, a nautical mother and child. Kids' voices rose from the stony beach below, a series of what sound like suggestions followed by whines.

Looking at the statement, Sasha said, 'You came in the back door, were hit over the head, came to, discovered Lottie dead in the bathroom and called the police?'

'Correct.'

'You arrived before the killer could get away.'

He gave a downturned smile. 'Not the first time my timing's been out.'

'We don't have the neighbour's signed statement yet, but I've been told she says she came into the house, called out and got no response, went upstairs, saw Lottie dead, then came down and found you on the floor by the nook.'

He looked confused. 'I don't get that.'

'No chance you passed out again after calling the police?'

He shrugged but Sasha could tell he was annoyed that he couldn't be more definite.

'What about the smashed glass in the front door? Do you know anything about that?' she asked.

'Didn't see that until I was put in the doctor's car. As I said, I arrived through the back door and left by the front.'

'The police didn't find a bloodied towel in the house. But there was a laundered towel and female underwear on the clothesline.' She showed him the relevant photo in the police booklet. 'Ring any bells?'

He stared for a few seconds, then looked out to the shimmering water. 'I don't remember washing the towel. The underwear could've been in the washing machine but I don't remember hanging any of it out to dry.'

'Pity about the towel,' she said. 'It would have supported your account and explained why blood was on part of your clothing but not elsewhere. That's why Black asked you about a boiler suit.'

'Well, they can't have it both ways. I was either suited up or I wasn't. All or nothing, isn't it?'

'Not quite. I suspect they'll say you had the suit on for forensic reasons, then took it off to get blood on you consistent with your story of finding Lottie. We'll argue that, after the shock and your own injury, you destroyed evidence which would help you, not convict you. But it's a double-edged sword.'

He shook his head, not grasping the issue.

Sasha said, 'If the killer had Lottie's blood on his face and wiped it off, the towel with the killer's DNA was most likely with the boiler suit, probably burned or buried. Washing it and pegging it on the line required staying at the murder scene longer than necessary. But if it was a bloodied towel, it would be done to implicate you, on the basis you'd be the only person alive who would risk being seen.'

'I see. Logical.'

'What about that neighbour, Doris Knowles? Do you remember seeing her at the house?'

'She was constantly over here or Lottie was with her. Bloody busy-body.'

'So your first memories are the doctor and presumably going to the hospital?'

'Yes, I particularly remember the doctor. He was pissed off, kept going on about how he was on call. Then Black came to the hospital, looked at my clothes and shoes. Later a uniformed cop bagged them up and took them away. They took a few photos there as well, with blood on me.'

'And after – your dealings with the police?'

Tyler waved his statement. 'The day before Lottie's funeral, they asked me to come in and make this. I went in with Delia.'

'What was Black's demeanour when he asked you the questions?'

'I thought he was respectful, considerate even.'

Sasha took his statement and read aloud the bit about Lottie's matrimonial property settlement and how it was worth several million dollars. 'This bit tells me they've been digging around for a motive.'

'Well, they've got one now. On the day before the funeral, her brother, an executor of the will, told me she'd changed it when her divorce from Plummer was finalised. There's a million for her brother and four for me, including property, bank accounts and shares.'

'Was that will in existence before you got married?'

'I don't know when she changed it and I certainly didn't know the details. I floated the idea of a pre-nup but she was reluctant.'

'Do you know why?'

'At first, she didn't want to talk about it. I assumed the whole Plummer thing was just too painful so I never pushed. On the day we got married she said we were going to buy a holiday home. I said that one property mortgage would be enough debt for me and she laughed. I'd assumed we were more or less on an equal footing with assets. I let it sit for a while, then raised the idea of a post-nup agreement.'

'What good would that do?'

'Remove any suggestion I'd married her to get wealthy. About eighteen months ago I had her lawyer email me a document that basically said what we owned individually at the date of our marriage would remain our individual property.'

'The lawyer sent this?'

'Not to me but to Lottie, presumably because she was his client. She asked me if I knew what it was about. His cover note mentioned I'd been in touch.'

'That might be pretty important regarding your intentions. Have you got the document and note?'

'I signed it and gave it back to Lottie. Don't know what she did with it after that.'

'And the note?'

He looked uncertain. 'I suspect that went out in the trash.' He found the lawyer's business card in his wallet and handed it to Sasha. She didn't recognise the name and slipped it into her jeans hip pocket.

'You didn't think to tell Black any of this?'

'I just answered his questions. Delia said cooperate but don't elaborate. I don't think Lottie signed it so I thought it wasn't relevant to the will.'

As they set off back to the house, a roar from behind startled Sasha. Ben pulled her towards him while a lad on a skateboard passed them on the downhill slope. 'Idiot,' Ben yelled and received the middle finger response.

'In your statement, you mentioned your deputy had gone home sick that afternoon. Why did that mean you were later leaving than normal?'

'It fell to me to make staff decisions. Ultan wasn't the only one away sick. Our night editor was new on staff and she had enough to deal with.'

Ben kicked at a stone, watched it skip along the road. 'I can't think of anyone else who'd want to cause Lottie harm. Such brutality. So if it wasn't Plummer, I've no idea.'

'Do you know what she was working on?'

'No.' He gave half a smile. 'She was pretty secretive but, to be fair, we were competitors. I have a hunch it was political, a big story. I said as much to Ultan just before the funeral. I suspect the leaks inquiry Ellis announced might be part of it.'

'You think Lottie was worried about being caught up in that?'

'Possible, I guess.'

Sasha said, 'The inquiry would lead to pressure to reveal sources.'

'I don't think that's what would've been worrying her. It would be the consequences of not revealing sources, unsanctioned actions, an increase in mishaps, who knows?'

'That night, when you left work – about ten, wasn't it? Do you remember who was around?'

'Jane wouldn't have been. From memory, Ultan went home crook about lunchtime. We'd met in the morning and he was unwell then. I don't recall anyone else, except the production people and the night editor, and they'd have no reason to note the time I left, would they?'

Sasha thought that a fair point.

They walked in silence for a while. Sasha slowed. 'I need to ask you this question.'

Ben faced her, a look of apprehension.

'Were you faithful to Lottie, Ben?' She stared at him, unblinking.

He couldn't control the involuntary movement around his eyes. 'Fair question under the circumstances,' he said. 'There was one other woman, in Sydney. But Lottie and I weren't living together at the time. When Plummer introduced us, I ended it with the other woman. Quickly.'

This was when having had a long relationship with your client paid off. Sasha believed him. 'No others?'

'No others. I didn't kill her, Sash.'

The old familiarity was back. Sasha's thoughts went to that protective action of pulling her towards him seconds ago. They walked again, close enough to hold hands. She said, 'I'm thinking we might apply for a change of venue for the trial. You've had wall-to-wall media coverage and we can't be sure, despite your best efforts, you'll get an unbiased jury.'

He looked uneasy. 'I want this nightmare over but I don't want people thinking I'm running from a jury who knows me. And I'm not sure staying out of the media is working. People are not seeing the impact this has had on me.'

'For example?'

'It's the cruellest double whammy. I manage to keep up appearances when I'm with people but, on my own...'

Sasha could tell he didn't want to finish the explanation, to admit what it was like, the fickle finger of suspicion and the accompanying loneliness.

They arrived back at the house. 'I have to trust your judgment on this, Sash – the media thing. And if you want to go for a change of venue, okay.' He flopped into a chair at the table. 'I just want things back to how they were.'

The blood had drained from his face and the boyish confidence and partial grin with which he began the day had now been revealed as bravado.

She touched his arm. 'I'm really sorry about before. Lawyers can get a bit blasé, forget what it's like for clients. At least with you having reported from courtrooms, it won't be a foreign environment for you.'

He looked dejected. 'I guess.'

'I need to go,' she said, standing. 'What's next for you?'

'I won't be staying around here. I'm sick of the looks. I'll put the place on the market. It holds no attraction now she's gone.'

When he stood, Sasha said, 'Don't make any hasty decisions about money and property. Let things settle for a bit, eh?'

He nodded.

Without thinking, she offered a hug. He held her tight and she quickly regretted the comforting gesture and let her arms fall. She said, 'I should go.'

He pulled away, eyes moist. 'I was grateful for your call but I still looked for you at the funeral. Was it difficult staying away?'

'It was.'

She wondered what else she could say. The court case with Paul Diplock sounded like a weak excuse. Sure, their relationship was over but she knew she hadn't done the right thing by avoiding more personal contact.

'I understand,' he said.

'I'll be in touch after we've seen the disclosure file.'

He looked puzzled.

'What the police will use to try and convict you.'

24

IN HER OFFICE, SASHA read messages left by Kate. One from Edwin Yuile. She'd seen him only three weeks ago. He could go to the bottom of the list. Stan Newbold, the psychiatrist who saw Ben when he was remanded, was first call. She expected he would help her narrow the scope of the defence. She would call Ivor Grange after that. Staying in his good books was important too.

'More signs of neurosis than psychosis,' Newbold said, when she asked him for an overview.

'In terms of a Section 23,' Sasha asked, 'you're ruling out a possible insanity defence?'

'Correct. Insanity is out of the question.'

No great surprise. 'What have we got, Stan?'

'He can be a bit emotionally reactive, prone to kneejerk responses.'

'Caused by?'

'A high level of internal stress and agitation, especially if he's bottled things up.'

The image of the depleted Ben she left in Akaroa came to mind. 'Bottled up. Are you saying he could explode, cause the carnage he's accused of?'

'I saw no evidence to suggest that's what he'd do and besides, he came through the polygraph test well.'

No evidence. A psychiatrist had concluded this after a couple of visits. Sasha had seen no evidence of it over more than a decade. Although not infallible, the lie detector result was interesting but still inadmissible in any New Zealand court.

He continued. 'He was interested rather than apprehensive about what might be revealed. Fair to say he attempted to develop rapport with me, asked sensible questions, used a friendly tone. Overall, he was confident. And likeable.'

'Is there a "but" coming?'

'Not on the polygraph. But he was outwardly different across the two times I saw him. It suggests a changeable rather than stable mood. Unsurprising considering what he's going through.'

'In summary then, not insane, passed the lie detector, traits indicating neurosis. Could the bottling up issue be used against us?'

'I'd say nothing in his test scores, or my examination of him, would lead me to think he had blown his top.'

Sasha put the question Fisk would inevitably ask, should he have the opportunity. 'But you wouldn't categorically say he was incapable of killing his wife in the way that's been described?'

'No one could say that about anybody, Sasha. I can say he's likely to be independent minded, intelligent enough to manipulate and influence people, but then he wouldn't be good at his job otherwise.'

'Put aside the issue of gradually increasing tension. What about rage? Could Ben's emotional volatility have led him to act in the way the prosecution will claim?'

'Pretty unlikely. Most of his emotional reactions are internal. He may occasionally let his guard down so others see how he feels, but not enough to bring on the rage suggested by this killing. I think if he was capable, the scope of injuries inflicted might be in a bid to deflect attention to others, rather than a result of uncontrollable rage.'

'More calculating then?'

'Absolutely.'

'Well, we won't go there, will we?'

Stan chuckled and Sasha thanked him for his time and invited him to send his invoice to Delia. Without having his backing for an insanity defence, the rest of his opinions were unlikely to be admissible evidence.

She thought about identifying another possible suspect for the jury. Away from TV and movie courtrooms, it was a risky strategy and prone to backfiring. If they took responsibility for identifying the killer, the jury might shortcut to a consideration of her suspect versus Ben, abandoning reasonable doubt.

Anyway, why would Plummer wait until the third anniversary of being skinned by his wife? Surely an enraged killer wouldn't wait three years. To present him as cold and calculating as well as brutal, meant they'd have to show he had serious vindictiveness as part of his make-up, and show he'd come to New Zealand. Although she didn't yet have the full direction of the defence, she was more in control than when she started.

Sasha had no sooner finished with Stan than Kate put a call through. 'Ivor Grange, Sasha. I called earlier. Is it convenient to talk now?'

She sighed inwardly. 'Of course.'

'I just want to give you a heads up.'

Heads up. The vernacular had reached even the most formal parts of the public service.

He continued, 'This Taylor murder case you've got yourself.'

'You mean Tyler? Ben Tyler?'

The sound of paper rustling before Grange said, 'Yes. That one.'

'How do you know about that?'

Grange made a half cough, half chuckle sound. 'Contrary to popular belief, it's not just the pollies who leak like sieves.'

'Evidently. What's your interest, Ivor?'

'We did ask you about Mr Tyler, if you recall.'

Her stomach sent her a message of guilt. She should've said something by now.

He said, 'We think it best if you don't get too involved.'

'I'm sorry, I have no idea what "too involved" means.'

'It means, Sasha, we'd like you to give this brief to another lawyer, not invest any more in this case.'

'Excuse me, Ivor, I don't mean to be rude, but what's this actually got to do with you?' Her response sounded more intemperate than she intended.

'Hang on, Sasha. All we're saying…'

She cut across him. 'That's the third time you've said "we", but as far as I can tell I'm only talking to you. Let's be clear. You're authorised to make this call by the attorney general. Is that what you're saying?'

'Yes. And we don't think it's a good idea for you to defend an ex-lover charged with murdering his wife to score several million dollars. Not when the man prosecuting is someone you're still investigating, Sasha. These things get noticed in certain quarters.'

'Has anyone in certain quarters countenanced the possibility Tyler might be innocent of killing his wife, or, that Mr Fisk's appropriate action would be to stand aside until the investigation is completed?'

She heard a sniff of contempt before Grange said, 'I'm sure we both know prisons are full of innocents. Butter wouldn't melt in their mouth, Sasha.' He chuckled at his stale metaphor.

The royal 'we' again. She paused before asking, 'Are you warning me off? Is that what this is?'

'Not at all. You can, if you must, defend who you like. As I say, things get noticed, become, as it were, your judgments.'

Kate appeared in the doorway, her face serious.

Sasha wanted to tell the pompous prat to fuck off. That would get noticed. She wound her tone back. 'Appreciate the heads up, Ivor. I can see how certain quarters might be concerned but I'm afraid I'll have to go now.'

As Sasha replaced the receiver, she asked, 'What's wrong?'

'I just took a call from the hospital, Sasha. Mac's been admitted.'

25

SASHA WAS DIRECTED TO the resus beds. She looked away from the unfocused stare of one woman who had bathed herself in alcohol. She reeked from three metres away.

Poor Mac. When she reached him he looked as if he'd been inserted into the middle of a medical wiring diagram. Electrical sensors across his chest linked to a screen proving he was still alive. She whispered, 'Don't die on me, Mac, not now. Not when we haven't said goodbye.' She bit her bottom lip.

A woman's voice from behind her, soft and sympathetic, said hello. Her eyes were tired. She wore a hospital lanyard and stethoscope around her neck. She told Sasha she was a registrar and that she'd ask someone to bring her a cup of tea.

'Has he had a heart attack?'

'Doesn't seem so.' The doctor pointed at the waves on the screen. 'Each of the sensors gives us a readout. The combined readings and a blood test help us to determine whether there's anything serious to worry about.'

'I thought, with resuscitation...' Sasha paused, fingering the damp corner of an eye.

'It's just the name of the beds in this part of ED.' She smiled a reassuring smile. 'He was able to describe symptoms suggesting he'd had an angina episode. He initially thought he had indigestion but we're a wee bit concerned that, because he was resting at the time, his angina is unstable. We've scheduled him for stents, which will help.'

'Is he in pain?'

The smile returned. 'We've got that under control. Do you know if he's ever had any chest or arm pain before?'

'Not that I'm aware of.' It occurred to her, Mac tended to talk more of discomfort than pain, as if the latter was permitted only to those in serious strife. 'It's possible if he ever had serious chest pain I wouldn't know.'

'I know the type,' she said. 'His is the stiff-upper-lip generation. Please excuse me, I should move on.'

Sasha moved to Mac's left side. His face was grey next to the white sheets. He looked a hundred years old rather than eighty. She whispered his name and caressed his sun-spotted hand.

He opened his eyes and blinked a couple of times.

'I'm not going to ask you how you are. You'd tick me off me for rhetorical nonsense.'

He offered a wan smile.

Sasha said, 'I hope you're getting a kick out of the illicit narcotics. This is the one and only time the Law Society will leave you alone. Also, you've got a legally binding contract with the universe that you won't die, Mac. I'm here to enforce it.'

She felt the light squeeze of his hand on hers. 'No enforcer I'd rely on more.'

It was one thing to have the registrar's reassurance. It was something else to feel life in Mac's hand and hear his raspy voice. She would get to leave this place with relief instead of regret.

Shutting out the frenetic sounds of urgency and crying beyond Mac's shrouded bed, she mouthed the words, 'I love you', and kissed his damp forehead.

26

SCHEDULED FOR STENTS MEANT Mac would be in safe hands a little longer. It'd been a long day but Sasha still needed to see Clay. She'd kicked herself for not inviting him to stay with her and, try as she might, couldn't account for her reticence. Instead, he was staying at a motel in Papanui Road, expenses payable by Montague Media. He had independence. She resolved to be more direct about having Mac stay with her. He'd object so she would itemise the assistance she needed from him.

Sasha arrived at a bar on Oxford Terrace thirty-two minutes early, keen to figure out functions on her new BlackBerry. She knew how to call and text, but little else.

The bronze door handles to their meeting place were shaped like hands, fingers spread. Inside, the wall-mounted TV ahead of her was streaming live cricket from Australia. She didn't share Clay's interest in the Ashes series although in the past she'd pretended to because he got so excited about it. She decided she'd take the side in the booth that faced the screen, but he wasn't beyond sliding in on her side and nudging her along.

Clay had thwarted her plan. She picked him out through the reflection in the bar mirror beyond an assortment of coloured bottles. Engrossed in the cricket, elbows on the table, he rested his chin on linked hands. She sneaked up behind him and slipped her hands around his head and covered his eyes. 'Can't be trusted to focus on the bloody job, eh.'

He almost yelled, 'Christ, where've those hands been?' He pulled her fingers down and said, 'On second thoughts, say nothing.'

Sasha sat opposite him. Eyes still on the TV he said, 'They make hand cream to smell like disinfectant now?'

She gave him silence before he turned his eyes to her. 'It was disinfectant.'

'Oh.' Back at the screen.

She drummed her fingers on the tabletop. 'Jesus, Clay. Is this game life or death for you?'

'It's the Ashes.'

'I need a drink.'

He looked at her for a moment – a peculiar, almost querulous look. She said, 'Your round. If I get your attention after, I might reciprocate.'

'Fair enough.' He slid out of the booth. 'Chardy, is it?'

'Please. Oaked.'

As he moved to the bar, Sasha pulled over the larger of two files he'd brought with him. It was what she expected – statements, job sheets, photos – but after Mac, she realised she wasn't in the mood to take any of it in. She looked up. Clay was standing next to a woman at the bar, his back to Sasha. The woman was smiling, enthralled by what he was saying. She threw her head back and guffawed over the din of the bar. When she finished, she found his arm, made her hand linger. The barman presented the drinks and Clay handed over his plastic, without taking his eyes off the woman. She leaned forward and kissed him – on the bloody lips, no backing off on his part.

Sasha felt slackness in her jaw. Was she imagining this as mutual? He could at least bring her wine before he snogged the cow. She glanced back at the files, pretending interest. He'd wasted no time in finding female company. She could go and force the issue but she was struck by tiredness, the cumulative effect of the day's events.

The woman's hair, dark brown and blonde competing for space, was like a banana fast on the way to over-ripeness. Her skin was pale and she was dressed as a third world country's national flag. Her mauve top clashed with her short green skirt and she was wearing what look like orange trainers. For Sasha, it was an act of will not to shake her head. She knew she was no model, but who'd go out to a bar looking like that?

Sasha's shoulders slumped and the ache in her back returned. She felt battered and weary, a tiredness of being blown by every breeze.

For the first time in a while, Natalie's ghost popped into her head. It was the usual injunction – do the right thing, look after your father's good name. It was a voice of futility that answered: I've tried to keep things professional and look where that's got me. He's with someone else.

She was grateful when her BlackBerry winked at her with its red eye. It was enough to bring her out of another conversation with her dead mother, which was never enlightening or fulfilling. How much Natalie got out of it, Sasha had no idea.

It was a text from Clay. Help!

Sasha looked towards the bar and the woman was gabbling, drawing no breath. Between expressive hands and face, she touched his arm again, this time, her finger drawing sensuous lines. A stranger wouldn't behave like that, even if she was after him.

She started to text, 'Found a hot date?', deleted that and texted, 'Spin her around so you can watch the cricket.' She deleted that also, gathered up the binders and her bag over her shoulder, weaved around others to stand between them.

'…and she said, "Well, you've never done that with me. What is it she gives you that…"'

Clay looked at Sasha. 'Sorry, you must be dying of thirst.'

Sasha looked at the woman. 'I do enjoy my chardy chilled, how about you?'

The woman applied the handbrake and forced a plastic smile.

Sasha reached between them for her drink, then offered her right hand. 'Sasha Stace.'

'Bridget Felan,' she said. 'We're, you know…'

'Friends?'

'Good friends, so to speak.' The forced smile reappeared.

Clay said, 'You remember, Sean. Bridget's his sister.'

Sasha said, 'Unforgettable.'

'Anyway,' Bridget said, as if Sasha's appearance was a short intermission in her recital, 'Mel says, "What is it she gives you that I don't?" And he says, "What, apart from washing, ironing, cooking, cleaning and dog hair?"'

Bridget leaned back and bellowed again and when the decibels reduced Sasha said, 'Would you both please excuse me? I'm just going to check out the cricket score.'

27

BACK AT THE OFFICE, Sasha neither wanted nor needed Kate to stay and sent her off early.

It was quiet that day in the office when Kate dragged her down to the Hagley netball courts. Sasha once played on the wing, as a teenager, and had foolishly revealed this fact in conversation. She had a couple of centimetres on Kate and because Kate was playing goal attack on the weekend, she'd pleaded for Sasha to help her as 'live opposition'. Never did anyone look so pleased to be blocked.

As Kate left, Sasha wished her luck.

'Come down, help us in the warm-ups. You'd be great,' Kate said, genuine enthusiasm.

It wasn't the first time she'd asked. Sasha was at least twenty-five years older than most of them and didn't fancy being team mother, even if she could block and intercept.

Sasha pulled the Bombay Sapphire from the bottom drawer of her credenza, extracted diet tonic and ice from the fridge and settled into a double G & T. The last lemon looked like a grey fur ball.

Kate had left her another message from Yuile. The brightly coloured sticker glared at her from the edge of her screen. She took a bolstering swig of gin and punched the numbers. Yuile chastised her for not returning several earlier calls, as if she'd been recalcitrant with homework.

Ignoring or buying into this behaviour might draw more of it. Challenging it might result in Yuile having less confidence in her, ultimately damaging the opportunity to pursue Fisk. Challenging won. 'I hope I haven't done anything to suggest I'm your lawyer, Edwin, and I don't get paid to hold hands and offer solace. You might try Victim Support for that.'

It was a bit more acerbic than he deserved. In this mood, she was prone to engage tongue before brain but managed a half-hearted apology. She explained Fisk had been served with the papers. In an effort to bring the call to a close, she asked, 'Was there anything other than the case progress you were calling about?'

'As a matter of fact, yes.' A little cough. 'I suspect my phone is tapped.'

She tried Mac's sardonic 'Really' response, but didn't carry it off as well and simply sounded curious. The effects of her day were taking their toll. 'On what do you base this suspicion?' She was tempted to add that the society for protecting animals from cruelty didn't have access to such equipment. This time discretion won.

'Well, intermittent clicking noises, even when I'm just hearing the dial tone, and when I'm talking.'

She'd represented clients charged with drug offences who had to answer to their legally bugged but incriminating phone conversations. Yuile was an unlikely candidate for covert surveillance by the Government Communications Security Bureau or the Security Intelligence Service.

'Do you know anyone who might have reason to listen to your calls?'

'What about Quentin Fisk?'

'Well, we've discussed his interest in your credibility, but he knows what you're going to say. I don't see him having the time, interest and expertise to set up a personal bugging service.'

'He could be on good terms with a conspirator who would do it for him. Trying to dig for dirt.' Yuile sounded almost hopeful.

She took another sip. 'Well, best you keep the garden in order – make sure there's nothing untidy to turn up.'

'I don't think you're taking this with all due seriousness.'

He was right. She wondered who would. 'Is there any pattern to this clicking? For example, does it happen when you're talking to specific people?'.

'Not that I've discerned.'

'Have you called your phone company, registered a fault?'

'Well, no, because I don't think it's their problem.'

'Then I can't help you any further, Edwin. I suggest you try that and if you get no resolution, start to diary the dates, times, calls out and calls in when it happens. That might give you a bit more to go on.'

28

ON THIS LONGEST THURSDAY of her life, she now had shoeless feet up on her desk, gin in hand.

'Nice for some,' Clay said.

She pointed at the blue bottle on the corner of the desk. 'There's a glass on the left. Tonic's in the fridge below.'

'You seem irritated, not your normal composed self,' he said, as he poured the drink.

She gave him an appraising look, found neither guilt nor contrition.

He said, 'Well, what could I do? I didn't know she was in this country, much less in that bar. Rudeness doesn't come to me as naturally as it does to others.'

'That's directed at me, is it?'

'It wasn't so much what you said as the way you said it.'

'Well, I'm sorry to have made you and the other half of your comedy act uncomfortable.'

'She called you a stuck-up bitch.'

Sasha took a hefty swallow. 'As an insult, that's pathetic. She should stick to stand-up.'

Seconds of silence ticked by. 'Okay,' he said, 'what's up? This isn't like you.'

'I've had a shit day. I got nothing useful from Doc Newbold, except Ben passed the lie detector but that's inadmissible. He's potentially neurotic but not psychotic and he's considered manipulative. Then you are captured by a *Vogue* model.' She pushed the heel of a hand into an eye. 'I don't want to be a moaning Minnie.'

She swung her legs to the floor, not wanting to mention Mac, and grabbed the gin bottle.

Clay motioned for her to join him on the two-seater.

'That Bridget,' she said, sitting. 'Rare to see a woman who's colour blind. I'm confident in saying you didn't dress her this morning.'

He chuckled as he shook his head.

Sasha added, 'She was pretty forward for the sister of a good mate.'

His hand consulted his chin. 'Well, it transcended acquaintance level.'

'Bloody hell!'

'Not that surprising when you think about it,' he said. 'I first met her at a low point – after I'd done time for those unpaid fines and lost my ticket to practice. She was good company.'

'Was?'

'What do you mean?' he asked.

'The kissing and touching didn't look like she was consigned to history.'

He drank his gin. 'No. But she is. Bridge's lovely but she can be hard work. Quite different to her brother. Have to say, he sort of warned me off her. Wasn't surprised when we parted.' He tilted his head and gave her a curious look. 'Did Bridge meet the green-eyed monster back at the bar?' he asked.

He put his palm on her leg. The warmth was more than comforting.

'I've no idea who else she met,' Sasha said, confidence forced. She felt the heat rising in her neck and heading north. She hated that and looked away.

He said, 'Need to use your bathroom.'

Once he was out of sight, Sasha grabbed the notepad from the nearby table and fanned herself. What an idiot. How was she supposed to play it cool when she reddened like that? The booze wasn't helping either. Did he really not know that, for him, she'd drop her knickers faster than a girl on Manchester Street? She bet his timely exit was a move to reduce her embarrassment. Or his.

At the window, the lowering sun provided a warm light. A young blonde woman was walking on the grass with a little girl dressed in a pink and white gingham dress, lace around the bottom. The wee one clutched a soft toy, a teddy bear. She seldom saw such a sight without thinking, 'What if?' Even after thirty-three years. She told Delia she couldn't have managed. The boy and his family were long gone without a trace by the time her pregnancy was confirmed. She'd said that Natalie was right to take charge, to arrange an adoption. Delia didn't look sympathetic but Sasha didn't blame her for that. Once Delia learned she was adopted the effect of that news would never have left her. It would always be with her, as it was with Sasha.

'Cute,' Clay said.

Distracted by history, she hadn't heard him return.

She said, 'You missed out on all that, didn't you?'

'Wouldn't have been much good at it.'

She faced him. 'You don't know that.'

He'd said what she'd told herself for decades. He shrugged. 'No point living in the past.'

'No. How are things now, with Kylie?'

'We meet for coffee, that sort of thing. A slow start, but you can't expect anything else. We don't speak or text unless I contact her first, but it's a start.'

When Sasha looked out the window again, mother and daughter were almost out of sight. 'Take anything you can get, I reckon.'

'You ever think about it?' he asked, voice gentle. 'Having kids, I mean?'

'I met Ben when I was about thirty-five. Could've had kids with him but we were both driven around our careers.' She dropped her voice. 'That became the default position.'

Time to move off the subject, return to the couch and tell him the worst part of her day. 'Mac's in hospital – they rushed him in. I saw him in ED before I saw you. At first they thought he'd had a heart attack but he hadn't. They're going to put stents in his arteries.'

'Oh, no.' He touched her arm. 'I'm sorry, Sash. That would've rocked you.'

She took a healthy slug of gin to fight emerging tears. Why was it, when people intended comfort, they brought you closer to tears than if they'd said nothing?

Clay continued, 'His body might not be in great order, Sash, but he's still sharp.' He lifted his drink and toasted Mac's recovery.

They listened to the cars on the street below. Sasha's mind wandered to Grange. 'Can you keep a secret?'

Straight-faced, he said, 'I'm the biggest gossip in Australasia.'

'Well, I shouldn't even be thinking about saying this to you, very hush-hush. It's just I'm hoping Mac will be around for it.'

'Spit it out, then.'

'I've been invited to apply for the High Court.'

His eyes open wide. 'A judge?'

'I'd have hoped it wouldn't be such a shock.'

'It's terrific news, Sash. When would this happen?'

'There's a selection process. A formality, I'm told, after the AG's informal approach.'

'Really pleased for you, well deserved too.' His smile was warm and she squeezed his hand.

He frowned. 'But you sound flat. Is that about Mac? You know he'd be thrilled and if he were sitting here, you'd be getting a polite telling off for being morose about him.'

'You're right, but it's not just Mac.' She told him about Grange's recent call. 'It just feels like I've been warned off the case. Who I represent or how I represent them has got bugger all to do with the AG's office or the bloody government.'

'You said yourself, Tyler's got offside with the government.'

'He's an editor, for Christ's sake. It's his job to challenge, to hold public officials to account. Are journos and editors exempt from the right to a fair trial and defence?'

29

'LET'S COME AT IT a different way,' said Clay, annoyingly calm. 'I understand this city is pro-Labour, with an obvious exception or two, and therefore pro-government. Where's he going to get a jury of his peers to believe him with this?' He pointed to the files, the whole purpose of their meeting.

'The good news is he's just agreed to my suggestion we apply for a change of venue.' Impatient, Sasha added, 'Give me an overview of what we're facing.'

He stared at her for a second, doubtless concluding she was moody.

'Circumstantial case. No unreliable witnesses claiming to see him preparing, executing or covering his tracks.' He paused and tilted his head. 'Well, not quite. There's Knowles, the neighbour.'

'When was this supposed to have happened?'

'On the stroke of midnight according to her.'

'Can't be right,' she said. 'When Ben got there Lottie was already dead and the pathologist says death was between eight and nine.'

Clay just raised his eyebrows but Sasha pushed on. 'Other circumstances?' She leaned back and sipped.

Clay said, 'Looks like Lottie was planning to divorce him and he found out. The prosecution is using that to build a case around greed. Four million dollars' worth of motive.'

She brought Clay up to speed on what Ben said about seeking a post-nup agreement. 'Despite all that, Ben then murders her for money? It's bullshit.' She pulled out the business card for Lottie's lawyer. 'I don't know this guy so you may as well give him a call and verify what Ben's told me.'

Clay placed the card in his wallet.

'What about the weapon?' she asked. 'Where is it?'

He guided Sasha through the alleged chain of evidence, starting with the presence of a crowbar in Tyler's office, unable to be found after Lottie's death.

'Tyler's deputy, Ultan O'Rourke, is central to this evidence,' Clay said. 'And he'll also testify to the competition between Ben and Lottie. Delia's been helpful. She's uncovered some stuff on O'Rourke's background.'

Sasha told Clay the line they'd take with O'Rourke.

Clay said, 'Ben's relied on him to keep the paper going. He also sees him as a mate.'

'Too bad. Going soft on O'Rourke is a risk. We can't compromise the defence. I'll talk it through with Ben.' She pointed at the files. 'Anything in that lot worth following up?'

'Looks like the police asked for leads about Lottie on Crimewatch. A copy of the show has been supplied. They've done re-enactments of her going to Auckland airport and arriving in Christchurch the day she was killed. They used a red-haired model but supplied actual photos of Lottie on screen.' Clay frowned. 'There's a list of calls, those initially taken, about twenty odd, and those followed up. Three or four of those resulted in job sheets, the rest seem to be dismissed as cranks or no-hopers.'

'Sounds to me, Black liked Ben for this from the get go. Might be the case that anyone not pointing the finger at Ben will be a crank or no hoper.'

'Onto it,' he said.

'Ben's told me Lottie and her ex, guy by the name of Plummer, had an acrimonious split. Have the police looked into that?'

'There's a job sheet about calls they've made to Australia and to New Zealand Immigration, to Plummer as well. He hasn't returned calls. Immigration confirmed Plummer didn't travel in the three days leading up to and after the murder.'

Sasha asked, 'Why only three days?'

'Not sure days are relevant anyway. I'm not an expert on the New Zealand coastline, but if he had help getting into the country, the immigration authorities wouldn't necessarily know.'

Sasha poured more tonic mixer. 'We don't need to give the jury a murderer. But we do need to offer them a plausible angle the police haven't investigated. O'Rourke went home sick around lunchtime the day Lottie was murdered. See if you can connect him to Plummer.'

She mentioned the third anniversary of Plummer's and Lottie's divorce and her concern someone would wait that long for revenge.

Clay said, 'The prosecution will argue the brutality of the attack is part of Tyler's deflection – an attempt to point to Plummer's culmination of annual hatred.'

Newbold's similar comments came to mind. 'What they can bloody prove is more important. Plummer's on the Montague board in Australia. He's bound to know Tyler's the editor of *The People*. And if they haven't adequately investigated Plummer, and knowing Black, they won't have, we've got an opening.'

'Sorry,' Clay said, with a shrug. 'Your instinct about that third anniversary stuff is right. As far as motives go, our client's is stronger. If she was planning divorce, a jury will see that. He doesn't just get half on divorce. She dies, he gets the bloody lot.'

'Clay, I've seen how upset Ben is. He's devastated by Lottie's death.'

Clay sighed. 'Equally, he might be devastated he's been arrested. Or, he may now be devastated he killed her and denial is his easiest coping strategy.'

They sat in contemplative silence before Clay asked whether he could be honest.

'Of course,' she said, 'you know I need that.'

His face was a picture of anxiety. 'You said before your belief in Tyler is firm and real.' He leaned forward, his voice soft. 'But we have to face facts, Sash. The prosecution is going to argue he's set the whole thing up to look like the murderer has busted in and bashed her. He's tried to give himself an alibi but it doesn't fit with an earlier time of death and midnight's well out of the ball park.'

'You're saying he killed her between eight and nine, drove back to Little River cell phone towers to stage a texting phone call alibi, came back, then waited till midnight to fake a break-in? Come on, Clay, they're not going to fly with that, surely?'

'He could dig deep holes to dispose of weapons or whatever he liked in that time. My real point here is your past relationship with him is getting in the way of even considering that.'

'How so?' she asked, her tone defensive.

'You were with the bloke for so long and at the end of it all, it's just too hard to think that you've lived with a cold-blooded killer, that for so long he deceived you about who he really was.'

'Jesus Christ. You're not hearing me. He loved her, Clay.'

'Let me ask you this. Until you caught him in the sack with her, he was with you. Did you think he loved you?'

'We were going through a difficult time.' She gave a dismissive wave. 'Not the same.'

'Didn't you tell me earlier that Newbold said he's manipulative?'

'So what? Half the managers in the world attract that label. It's how successful managers get things done. What you're saying is, you think he's guilty.'

He stared back, an eternity. 'Yeah,' he said. 'I think he's guilty. He killed her.'

Combined with the effects of the long and difficult day, and the gin, this was like an assault. Sasha reeled, then realised her mouth was open.

Clay said, 'But I'm also a trained lawyer. I know I don't have to believe a client to be able to do the best for him. I won't be running on two cylinders here. I'll do everything I can to help you create reasonable doubt and more.'

'More?'

'Well, you know me.' He grinned. 'There's stuff I don't boast about.'

30

SASHA MET BEN AT the Russley golf driving range. She had chosen the activity to lighten the mood before going through the police case against him. Above all, she didn't want another emotional crisis like they'd had at Akaroa.

They were in a relaxed mood when they arrived at the house high above Sumner that Ben had inherited from his late stepfather. Delia was already there. Sasha looked at her watch but she was on time.

Ben put Thai takeaways into bowls, placed them in the microwave and punched in the beeping command. It'd been a warm day and, with the tide in, people were enjoying Scarborough Beach below. Half-moon waves endlessly lapped the sand. Delia picked up binoculars on the sideboard. 'Not guilty of murder, guilty of perving,' she said.

'I'll take it,' he said.

Delia offered the binoculars and Sasha adjusted the focus. People were eating fish and chips from paper parcels, ripped open at the top. Dogs not patiently waiting for donations were chasing balls into the surf. She handed the glasses back to Delia and faced Ben. 'You dodged my question about media coverage of the treaty debate. Is that because your paper is pro settlement payments?'

'You know yourself,' he said, 'that redress and reparation are cornerstone principles of the justice system.'

'I agree. I'm just not sure the case has been made out for redress based on ethnic background. A little Austrian with a funny moustache once had a similar selection system.'

Delia said, 'That's a bit out there as a comparison, Sasha.'

The microwave beeped – the food ready for a stir.

'Because the outcome is different?' Sasha asked. 'My main question isn't about the process of redress, it's about effectiveness.'

Ben brought a chilled Chablis to the table, condensation beaded on the bottle. It reminded Sasha of his past efforts to serve wine at what he called the correct temperature. Sasha raised her hand. 'I'm driving.'

Delia said, 'I'm driving too, but I won't say no.'

'Never been one to force it on anyone,' Ben said. 'But two glasses of wine with food is well below your tolerance, Sasha.' He turned and winked at Delia.

They'd obviously hit it off so far. Facing Sasha, he said, with his familiar boyish grin, 'Remember that time you got hold of those breathalysers and we got shit-faced as we worked our way to the illegal limit for driving?'

'I also remember how I felt the next day. I wasn't driving then.'

Anticipating the final electronic ping, he returned to the kitchen and called out, 'When the government takes your land, and keeps it for-bloody-ever, they can't claim no case for redress because the whanau or family are dead.'

'No. That's not my point. We're more than a decade on from large payouts with no impact on things like Maori health, employment or rates of imprisonment.'

Delia, doubtful, said, 'Is that really correct? What about Sealord? That's made a huge difference.'

Sasha said, 'But we've seen one tribe buy a rugby league club, for Christ's sake, and have to flog off the so-called depleted asset a year later.'

'Reparation with conditions.' Delia's tone was challenging. 'That's what you want?'

'All I want is more open dialogue. My questions should be the media's questions. Ben and his colleagues avoid them because they're afraid of racism accusations.'

Ben, indignant, said, 'That idiot Wright and his ONZ party are full of red necks. Not our job to give them a platform.' He brought the bowls to the table.

'But you do give them a platform, Ben,' said Sasha. 'What you don't do is back up either side of the debate with decent analysis. You may as well all be the *Daily Mirror*. Their contribution to the debate would be to have a topless wahine on page three.' Hearing her own exasperation, she said, 'You'd better pour me a glass of wine.'

As he complied, he said, 'I assume we're going to talk about my case, paling as it does against the bigger issues of the day.'

The food on plates, filled the air with garlic, ginger, citrus and coriander. Sasha's mouth zinged with the chilli and the food further weakened her resolve on the wine front.

Food consumed, and before drink stole her cognitive processing, Sasha nudged them to the real agenda. She acknowledged Delia's work while she and Ben had been at the golf course and suggested she summarise Fisk's case.

Ben smiled at her, encouraging.

'Fisk,' Delia said, 'will present Ben as a man troubled by increasing competition in his employer's business – point out his wife was at least partly responsible.' She stood and went to the window. 'He'll say the defendant felt increasingly envious at the difference in their financial circumstances. Then when he learned of his wife's plan to divorce him, he planned a pre-emptive strike. One weekend when Lottie returned to their idyllic vacation accommodation, funded from the spoils of her matrimonial property settlement, the defendant decided to kill her. He arranged to arrive at the house later than normal, an attempt to show a different killer had plenty of opportunity to murder his wife while she was alone. After the killing, he used Lottie's phone to text himself a message, leaving his own phone off until he arrived back at Little River. He then rang Lottie's phone and left a message he was delayed by a flat tyre, that he'd be late by half an hour.'

Delia turned and faced them. 'Fisk will probably argue your injury was self-inflicted, Ben. That you needed to fake an injury to explain why you didn't call the police until just before midnight. That, unbeknown to you, your neighbour saw a person in a white boiler suit skulking away from the property. The neighbour went to investigate what she thought might've been a burglary, which Fisk will say you also faked. He'll also say you used the time to dispose of the weapon. In summary, he'll argue you carried out a cold-blooded killing motivated by greed and the brutality was a calculated attempt to deceive and mislead investigators into thinking an unknown maniac carried out this heinous crime. Is that about the strength of it?'

Sasha looked at Ben. He had his head in his hands. Delia's matter-of-fact summary chilled her. In a strange way, she looked almost comforted by her smooth telling of a tale that, if presented in this way, would be utterly plausible and equally condemning. Then she said, 'But we'll get you off, Ben.'

The immaturity of her comment jarred Sasha – it was a statement an inexperienced lawyer might make – but she let it pass.

'A circumstantial case,' Sasha said, 'which makes any evidence of motive about envy and greed important. Clay will contact the lawyer who sent Lottie the post-nup agreement. Had Lottie even hinted she was thinking of leaving the relationship?'

'Not at all – nothing like that.'

'There are holes in Fisk's case but we need to be realistic, Ben. The case Delia just outlined – if witnesses hold up – it's damning.'

He bowed his head. 'I know. I know how these things work. I can't even begin to think about the possibility of a conviction. It's bad enough that my wife has been murdered without me spending the next twenty years in prison for a crime I didn't commit.'

Sasha felt the need to raise his spirits. 'The good news, if it can be called that, is we're not running a dodgy alibi. They can say what they like about the phone calls but your presence in the house deals to the forensic evidence identifying you as the killer. A big dampener on what Fisk likes to call "his silent but deadly witness".'

'The flip side,' he said, 'is there's no forensic evidence suggesting anyone else was in the house. The jury need to believe I got Lottie's blood on me when I found her dead.'

'True, but that's a double-edged sword. Whoever killed Lottie knew the importance of not introducing any forensic evidence. It's a prosecution witness who saw someone in a boiler suit and discovered you in the house without one. If I'm right, she's never said anything about seeing blood on you.'

Delia said, 'But they'll just argue that was part of Ben's deception, that he got rid of it.'

'But Fisk needs to prove the white suit wearer was Ben and at the moment he can't.'

Sasha looked at Ben. 'That's why the doctor who treated you is also critical.'

Delia looked confused.

'If the examining doc doesn't play ball about Ben's injury,'Sasha said, 'Clay's turned up information on him we'll be able to use.'

'What kind of info?' she asked.

'Misdiagnoses leading to bad treatment and death. He'd been stood down for years.'

'Well,' Ben said. A small smile, 'bugger me.'

Delia said, 'I think we should squeeze O'Rourke.'

Ben drew back and his smile disappeared quickly. She wanted to raise this issue with him in a more tactful way, lead into it gently. After a pause, Sasha said, 'Go on.'

'I've been thinking,' Delia said. 'He mysteriously takes ill the afternoon Lottie is killed. And you told me, Ben, he's never had a sick day the whole time he's been with you. And he tells you before the funeral that his white car painting outfit has been stolen. I mean, why would he bring that up then? It makes no sense unless he's trying to cover off the fact that you knew he had one.

Ben crossed his arms. 'He's a mate. He's…'

Delia interrupted. 'A mate who leads the cops to your office to recover a crowbar that's no longer there? Come on, Ben.'

'He liked Lottie,' Ben protested. 'He wouldn't kill her and besides, what's his motive?'

'Hang on,' Sasha said. 'How well did he know Lottie?'

'I don't bloody know. I could tell … hang on, are you suggesting there was hanky-panky going on?'

'I'm not suggesting anything. Not yet.'

Delia said, 'You told me he'd been to the Akaroa property, though.'

Ben looked dubious. 'Once.'

'That you know of,' Delia said, glancing at Sasha.

Sasha asked, 'Do you remember how that came about, the visit?'

Ben rubbed his forehead. 'I think he suggested he bring his partner over for the weekend.'

Delia said, 'He'd already met Lottie by then, hadn't he?'

'I think so.'

'We need to get this straight,' Sasha said. 'What was the time span between when you know for sure O'Rourke met Lottie and when he suggested that he and his partner visit?'

'Look, I don't know for sure when he first met her, okay? I know they came over about six weeks before the murder.'

'And stayed with you?'

'Of course. But I don't see where you're going with this.'

Sasha was about to explain when Delia jumped in. 'It means he knew the layout of the house, knew that he could hide in that little nook to attack someone if necessary.'

Sasha said, 'We need to explore this further. They're definitely relevant circumstances. Not impossible he was working on behalf of someone else. I can't help feeling Lottie knew her attacker.'

Ben and Delia looked at each other. She nodded her confirmation.

Sasha said, 'Delia, I need you to go through the file and look for any inconsistencies, but also anything that might be missing. Examine all Lottie's phone records. She had to be connected to her killer and given she was only a visitor to Akaroa, my hunch is a local isn't responsible. Clay will be doing the same thing but I'm getting him to focus on her work.'

'Not a problem,' she said.

'One last thing. Ben, I know you're in touch with friends at *The People*. Whatever we do, whichever direction we take, those things must be kept confidential to the defence strategy team. If not, Fisk will get to hear and you know he's not trustworthy.'

'Okay, but I'm still keeping in contact with Ultan.'

'Has he asked you anything about the trial?'

'No. We've just talked about the paper, staffing and story issues.'

Delia asked, 'Don't you think that's a bit strange?'

Ben said, 'Not really. He knows I'm concerned about the paper.'

'We're looking for a link between him and Plummer,' Delia said.

'What sort of a link?'

Sasha explained and when she'd finished, Delia excused herself. Her heels echoed on the wooden stairs. When she had driven away, Ben asked, 'What do you think of her?'

'You seem to connect okay. I saw your little wink earlier.'

'Avoiding the question?'

She had no intention of sharing the full story. 'I don't know her well. This is the first brief we've shared. She was keen to work with me, which suggests she'll take direction okay. That's as far as I can take it for the moment. What about you? Am I right that the two of you are hitting it off?'

'I agree she's keen but also professional. I feel I'm in good hands – all round. You know, seeing you in action here, it takes me back.'

Sasha was about to launch a defensive strike against nostalgia when he added, 'You're still hot, Sash. I hope you realise that.'

She was speechless. His tone, his familiarity, his attentive posture – they were all more than memories. She was guarded, but part of her needed what he'd just said, needed the flattery, even if it was from an ex-lover, now client. Seconds passed. The tongue-tied senior counsel. It was pathetic.

'What?' he asked. 'You think I'm coming onto you?'

His question triggered her release. As she stood, he followed. 'I think you like to play games, Ben.'

When she hitched her bag over her shoulder, he was the distance of a forearm away. He leaned towards her. An accomplished professional would have moved her head back, like a boxer dodging a blow. A clear message given. Or at least presented a cheek to a client – a friend. Instead she froze and his lips make contact with hers. They were warm, gentle and comforting. As she accepted them, the electricity they sent through her torso reached the back of her knees and turned them to jelly.

Part Two
THE TRIAL

31

DRINK IN HAND, FISK had had enough of the evening news and the SAS lance-corporal recently awarded the Victoria Cross for bravery in Afghanistan. He flicked from television to video and his mother's voice filled the room.

From behind him he heard, 'Motherfucker, motherfucker.'

Fisk snatched the video remote from the armrest of his leather chair and stabbed the pause button. It stopped in a place where Mother appeared harsh, even cruel. She squinted at him through one eye, a distrustful look under a cabled brow. It added to his annoyance with Graham, who always misbehaved when he replayed this video, as he did before most important trials.

'Naughty boy, Graham. You go to sleep, now. I don't want another peep out of you.' It was the same line repeatedly used on him in his childhood. He unfolded a blanket sitting on the top of Graham's cage and when the bird's home was shrouded, the cacophony stopped. How nice it would be to repeat this avian anaesthetic with the moaners at work. He once banged the top of the cage when reprimanding Graham and the bird wouldn't talk to him for a week. That had been a powerful lesson in parenting and he hadn't repeated the mistake.

He poured himself another gin and returned to his chair, lowered the volume on the player and pressed play. He knew Graham would still hear it but he was comfortable making the minor concession. For all her good qualities, Mother was never everybody's cup of tea.

He wondered why she looked so austere when she was dying. It wasn't just the tubes feeding her oxygen or even the rimless round glasses. It was her hair, dyed as black as a wet grave and pulled back so tight it wouldn't be out of place in a violin bow.

'... worthy end by unworthy means,' she'd said. 'You know that's populist nonsense, don't you? It was a creed your late father subscribed to, all part of his turn the other cheek philosophy and look where that got him.'

Her voice wasn't shrill as it always was when he hadn't met her expectations. On the contrary, although the message was tough, the tone was soft, almost hypnotic.

'He lost his resilience, lost his courage. I don't want that for you, son.' Fisk glanced at the photo of Queenie as he heard his mother say, 'The goal is all important. How you achieve it, less so. But you do need to achieve it.

'Close to that is the next myth: be the best you can be. Well, being the best you can be won't cut it, Quentin. It's the motto of those who think participating is more important than winning. Again, arrant nonsense. You can't control who your competition is but you can give yourself an edge. It's not necessarily cheating and anyway, the word cheat is used by the limp-wristed namby-pambies, as if it's a disease. How do you think the less able students get through law school? Through hard work? How do incompetent people become politicians? Hard work?' Her facial expression was pure derision.

Fisk fast-forwarded through several more examples illustrating his mother's point.

'Let bygones be bygones. A cliché for the spineless who subscribe to the forgive and forget creed. I say the fastest way to ensure people will take advantage of you is to let bygones be bygones. Where would Maori be today without redress for the wrongs of the past? You have to take your own redress. My personal justice register is full of redress and you'll do well in life to put this in place. I always found a visit to the justice ledger uplifting – seeing the red ticks, taking motivation from their absence. Don't ever let anyone try and get one over you without a consequence to them.'

The doorbell.

Exasperated, he sighed at another interruption and flicked the player and TV off.

At the door, his PA held up a bottle of red wine. 'Is tonight still okay?' she asked, trepidation in her voice.

He glanced at his Rolex. 'You're a little early, but otherwise, yes. Why wouldn't it be?'

'Well, you barked at everyone today, QF, including me.'

He glanced down. 'I'm sorry. That's normal for me about a week out from a big trial. I don't mean anything by it.' Fisk waved Averill in. Her silver-studded red leather jacket stopped at her hips, allowing her arse to rock along the hall like a prize-winning mare at a country show.

'I thought it was to do with the Yuile complaint. You know I'll say whatever's needed, don't you? The Law Society hearing's tomorrow, isn't?'

'I'm not worried about that at all.' A little smirk. 'It won't be going ahead.'

She shrugged, a couldn't-care-less gesture. It was what he'd seen teenagers give to parents who work at the office. He was about to tell her he didn't like that when she said, 'What smells so good?'

'My bolognaise.' He took the bottle she handed him. Pepperjack Shiraz. 'Barossa Valley. That'll go nicely, thank you.' Fisk moved to the heavy-bottomed pot on the stovetop and inspected the red-brown mixture. 'Would you stir this for me while I find the spaghetti?'

Averill smiled and Fisk knew why. He'd always been a bit scant on thank yous. Home was different. A part of him would like to be friendlier, a little less reserved in the office, but he'd accepted Mother's advice: staff can't be friends. Friendliness to employees, hints of warmth were, as she said, 'apt to be misguided by the giver and misused by the receiver'.

Averill twirled the wooden spoon. Fisk moved in behind her, placed his hands on her hips and pushed his pelvis into the soft seat of her blue jeans.

'That's nice,' Averill whispered.

'Me or the sauce?'

'What do you think?'

'Just nice?'

'Nice, or not nice. I like to keep things simple.' She guided Fisk's left hand underneath her Cashmere sweater. He felt the warmth of soft breast tissue unsupported by a bra and ran an erect nipple between two fingers. Her moan was soft, almost inaudible.

Averill said, 'You fancy dessert before dinner?'

32

FLUSHED AFTER HIS EXERTIONS, Fisk cooked the pasta, then reheated the bolognaise.

When they sat at the table, Averill said, 'Our third time here.' Her smile suggested it wouldn't be the last.

'Even defence lawyers can count to three,' Fisk said, with irritation. 'Well, a few, perhaps.'

'I was just wondering why, you know, we always do it that way.'

'You saying you don't like it like that?'

'No–oo.' She elongated the word.

He knew she wanted him to ask a different question, something about her likes and needs. He wasn't going there. 'How's the meat sauce?' he asked, feigning enthusiasm.

Her head was down. 'Lovely.' She paused, then said, 'The pistol thing. At my head. It's off-putting, you know.'

'When I'm behind, you shouldn't be able to see it. Besides, it may as well be a replica. I've no ammunition but it gives me a charge – Viagra without the chemicals. Eat your dinner.'

He didn't want to prolong this. 'Tell me, how's that legal exec from Sydney working out? You haven't reported in for a while.'

Averill looked concerned. 'You know I hate snooping on people, QF.'

'Don't consider it snooping. With my authorisation, you're gathering data to help me assess her performance. Only you don't need to tell her. Confidential, okay?'

'There isn't much to tell. Anyway, you selected her. Maybe you got her to turn around and touch her toes ten times.'

'Not funny, Averill. Stay on it, and keep me briefed about Zoe as well.'

'I thought she was in the camp already.'

'You can't be too careful. Her lack of info recently is one of the reasons I'm asking you. I've got a huge trial coming up. I want no surprises. You're officer in charge of no surprises, okay?'

Averill slid spaghetti off the prongs of her fork and into her mouth. 'How's the trial prep going?' she asked.

'They're going after that Doris Knowles woman. I knew that would come back and bite us,' Fisk said. 'Bloody Hart. Ignorant fat cop. He has his wife sew extra cloth onto the bottom of his shirts because his gut pulls the shirt from his pants. How the hell he passes his physicals I've no idea.'

Concern on her face, Averill asked, 'What's he done wrong?'

'He's only gone and written about her drinking in his job sheet. As a result, there's been a private detective sniffing around at her place on rubbish collection days.' He sat more upright in his chair, palms flat on the table. 'Still,' he said cracking a smile, 'I'll have a few surprises of my own to deliver.'

Averill reached over and touched his hand. 'You're still taking me to Wellington, aren't you, QF? When you get the AG's job.'

Another selfish woman, Fisk thought. 'My adorable Averill? How could I leave you behind?' He placed his pudgy fingers on top of her hand. 'Far too valuable to do that.'

33

IN THE AIR NEW Zealand Koru lounge, waiting to board a flight to Wellington, Sasha was a reluctant passenger. It was less than a week before Ben Tyler's trial, but Attorney General Ellis had thrown her a curve ball and she needed to respond. The good news was, despite scrutiny of her judgments, she'd proceeded through the vetting process. The bad news was, owing to the death of a High Court judge, her swearing in had been fast-tracked to this Friday. Her mission was to persuade Ellis to defer the ceremony for two weeks, ample time to have completed Tyler's trial. She'd heard Ellis liked to have most, if not all, important business done face to face, so she was hopeful a personal visit would swing it.

She sat with Paul Diplock as a constant stream of people moved to and from the breakfast bar. Paul was heading to the Supreme Court, also in the nation's capital. He told her it would be his first visit in the three and a half years since its establishment. She suspected her talk of the judge's death prompted him to inquire after Mac's health.

'I love him to bits,' she replied, 'but he's incorrigible and stubborn.'

'His best attribute at the bar, in most legal negotiations. The bugger wouldn't take no for an answer. What's he done to get you going?'

She paused for two boarding announcements to finish through the PA system. 'I shouldn't complain. He won't let me attend doctor's appointments with him. Says he hasn't yet turned full circle back to toddlerhood. I've told him I only want to know from the professionals what I can do to help. Can you guess what he said?'

Diplock grinned. 'Go on.'

'He said to use the internet or ring his doctor. He knows the doctor will be too busy to talk to me and, even if he did, I wouldn't learn anything I didn't already know. But I've had one win.'

Paul raised his eyebrows.

'I go to the cardiac care meetings with him. He resisted, of course, but I told him I wasn't going for him, I was going for myself. He scoffed, but I reminded him of my gene pool.'

'Ouch. His best mate.'

'Indeed. The Armagh Street Bridge. The only time in my life when he's had no answer.'

They watched the comings and goings of other commuters – serious faces, distracted looks. Paul told her more about his appeal and she told him more about her mission. He said, 'Well I hope he's in a better mood than he was yesterday.' He saw her frown. 'You haven't heard?'

'Heard what?'

'The AG's inquiry into public service leaks. Evidently they've caught two people, one from the Ministry of Foreign Affairs and Trade, the other from his own office. He'll be getting stick from the opposition over that, I bet. Here,' he said, passing her the newspaper.

But it was Yuile's photo on page three of *The People* that jumped out at Sasha. The small piece in a single column reported that he'd been missing for ten days. A police spokesman said that the fifty-eight-year-old, known to be reliable, was the type of man who meticulously planned his holidays in advance. Given that none of his bank cards had been used in the last week, there were now growing concerns for his safety.

Sasha was sure he wouldn't abandon his goats either. Diplock asked what she looked worried about. She folded the paper to highlight the article and handed it to him.

He asked, 'You know this guy?'

She told him the story, including Yuile's claim about his phone being tapped. 'Fisk's discipline hearing was scheduled for tomorrow.'

'Cold feet, you think?'

'Definitely not. Anyway, vanishing's a bit drastic to avoid going through with a complaint.'

Paul motioned with his head to a more private space, recently vacated. He dropped his voice. 'Don't be surprised if Quentin Fisk is behind this man's disappearance.'

'I know he holds grudges, Paul. But he doesn't strike me as a person with the necessary pull.'

'Between you, me and the gatepost, Sasha, the man's dangerously effective at getting what he wants.' He looked over his shoulder and back. 'They say that if there were a PhD in corruption, Quentin Fisk would be at the head of the queue. He has a way of commanding loyalty and silence so nothing ever sticks. If you get these Law Society proceedings over the line, you'll be doing us all a great service. That bloody Queen's honour you're looking forward to might come earlier than you expect. And you're absolutely right about grudges. Cross that man at your peril.'

'Thanks, Paul. Just the confidence boost I was looking for.'

34

THE AIRCRAFT CLIMBED TO a cruising altitude. Sasha, in a window seat, stared blankly at the Canterbury coastline. She was questioning her own insight. Should she have foreseen trouble after Yuile's last call only days ago? He'd left a new update on his enquiries with Telecom. He'd been told he was paranoid, there'd never been any interference with his phone. However, the clicking on the line had continued. Should she have been more proactive? Had she taken Fisk seriously enough? If Paul was right, and he wasn't prone to exaggeration, Fisk could've engineered Yuile's sudden disappearance.

The answers to these questions were plainly obvious. She'd never taken proper notice of the man's complaints about his phone. With Yuile's disappearance, the Law Society had no case. She'd let them down. Fisk's response to the complaint would go unchallenged. He'd sworn an affidavit that Yuile had summoned him to his property, insistent that Fisk see for himself the nature of a fencing dispute he had with his neighbour. Fisk had exhibited a copy of an invoice to Yuile, his costs for advice in the matter. He'd deposed that, while visiting Yuile, his client became hostile to advice that didn't support his case. Fisk had said that Yuile went on to raise the subject of the proposed land development, that he had sought representation but that he, Fisk, had explained the conflict of interest. His secretary, Averill Brandt, had also sworn an affidavit. No surprises that it corroborated everything Fisk attested to.

After receiving these papers, Yuile had emailed to say Fisk and his secretary had told the most appalling lies. He'd asked Sasha to ring him as soon as possible, to discuss how they would respond. She hadn't returned the call. It seemed he went missing the same day, or soon after.

It wasn't even worth trying to put Yuile's email before the judicial committee. Fisk would rightly object that he needed to have Yuile cross-examined. He'd argue that Yuile's allegations were malicious owing to what he believed was unhelpful advice.

Outside the Wellington terminal Sasha was greeted by several cab drivers and a southerly that was cruel to the cheek. Heading to the city, she again rehearsed what she'd say in the ten minutes the AG was willing to spend with her. She knew he was pressed. The leak of confidential information from within his own office was not the only thing on Martin Ellis's mind. The Criminal Justice Law Reform Bill was being debated in committee stages and he was expected to lead that.

When he appeared in the appointed anteroom at 9.32 a.m., he looked frustrated. 'Damn that opposition,' he said. 'Want judges to have carte blanche at sentencing time. Are they not listening to the public clamour for reform?'

'I'm sure there's a middle ground to explore,' Sasha said, pacifying.

He nodded, although it looked more like a gesture to hurry along than one of agreement.

'Thank you for seeing me, Martin. With this particular bill in the committee stages I can guess how busy you are, so I'll come right to the point.'

'Thank you.' He looked at his watch as if ready to say, 'Your time starts now.'

'I'm currently in the last stages of preparing the defence in a murder trial.'

'Yes.'

'The case has unusual attributes, which I won't detail unless you'd like more information. It's important for the defendant, who has no criminal convictions, and important for justice. Given it will be my last trial, it's also important for me.'

'Yes.'

'I know that in the normal course…'

'How long will it take?'

'I believe five to seven days.'

He nodded.

'I realise in the norm…'

'No.'

'I'm sorry?' Sasha said, taken aback.

'I have the horrible suspicion you're here to seek a delay of your swearing in.' He grimaced. 'The answer is no. Your swearing in is scheduled for this week. You will immediately preside over a rape trial the late Justice Sweetman was to hear, beginning that afternoon.'

'But this is a murder trial. I thought…'

'Ms Stace. You can either accept your appointment now, or relinquish all possibility of it being offered again. I strongly advise you to accept.'

Defend Ben Tyler or cast him aside for her career. His trial would have to be aborted and another lawyer brought up to speed. How had things come to this? Was this just about the death of another judge? Or was this the logical consequence of not heeding that 'heads up' from Grange, the unsubtle advice to ditch Tyler. The AG looked and sounded implacable. In the shock of his stony response, all she could say in the moment was, 'Thank you.'

'Excellent,' Ellis said, breaking into a smile. 'And now I need to return to that wretched bill.'

She turned and walked. She'd taken barely three minutes.

Away from the anteroom, Grange was standing in a dimly lit corridor with a group of officials. He tapped a folder in emphasis as he spoke. As Sasha strode towards him he looked up, muttered to his colleagues and turned away. Sasha gathered pace. His walk was brisk, avoidant.

'Ivor,' she called loudly. 'You're not running away, are you?'

He turned, a supercilious look on his face.

'This is down to you, isn't it?' she said. 'You don't want me doing the Tyler trial.'

'Sorry? What's down to me?'

'Butter wouldn't melt, eh Ivor. My sudden and urgent call to the bench, a call the AG has made clear I can't refuse.'

'The timing of your appointment has nothing to do with me, Sasha.'

'You knew, then?'

'Well, I had heard something, of course.' Palms up, he said, 'Look, if you don't do Tyler's trial, another lawyer will.'

She felt her jaw tighten. 'Oh, I'm doing it, Ivor. I will not be commanded. I will not be controlled. I'm bloody well doing it.'

35

AT 3.03 A.M., SASHA sat bolt upright and swung her legs out of the bed. Dressing gown on, she tiptoed down to her study, past the room Mac was sleeping in. No danger in waking him. His snoring was megaphonic. The wines they'd had with dinner were fuelling his nasal blasts. She was dry in the mouth as a result of drinking more than she normally would.

Delia had joined them for dinner and seemed to be building a rapport with Mac. His early aloofness had gone and been replaced by acceptance that Sasha and Delia were seeing more of each other, that Sasha was enjoying their relationship.

It was how Sasha thought it would be – like an older sister, a relationship that appealed, was realistic. She would never replace Delia's adopted parents.

When Mac had made a joke about Sasha's stubbornness, Delia had said that helped her understand more about herself. He'd pointed out Sasha was never good with ultimatums. When faced with a choice of what she wanted, or being coerced into an alternative, she always acted in a bloody-minded way – to her own cost. 'What Natalie didn't realise,' he'd said with glee, 'was she was building this one's resolve to be a lawyer like her father.'

Sasha could've added, but didn't, 'giving Natalie another reason to disapprove of me'.

Mac had completed Sasha's profile for Delia with stories of when her stubbornness turned to a cause involving a client and how that frequently paid off. His eyes had gleamed when he cited cases where Sasha hadn't accepted the obvious resolution.

At the end of it all, Sasha could say nothing about her visit to Ellis. If she'd thought giving up crime and introducing Delia were difficult subjects to discuss with Mac, she had no idea how to broach the cost of her latest stubbornness.

Sasha returned to a police job sheet she'd read on the plane back from Wellington. Discovery had come in dribs and drabs from Fisk's office. She'd been assured she had the last of it now. She could protest, but the very best outcome would be an adjournment and a censure for Fisk. It was tempting but wouldn't help Ben.

This last job sheet was about an Auckland-based police enquiry, carried out at Lottie's magazine premises. Staff had threatened to get lawyers in to deal with harassment. They insisted they didn't have a disk sought by police the first time they called, and still didn't have it. They professed to know nothing about Lottie having any disk. When Sasha first read that, it didn't make a lot of sense. She'd been distracted by the AG's intransigent stance on the swearing in date. Now, with a cup of tea, she could see the potential in exploring this enquiry but needed to put Clay to work. She made a note.

Existence of a disk? Relevant to Lottie's work? What and why police interest?

Back in bed, she heard the low percussive sound of rain on the roof. It was a comforting noise. That said, it was hard to forget that the government was out of love with her, an old lover accused of murder wanted to be in love with her again, the man she'd like to be in love with her wasn't, and the man she'd loved forever may not be with her for much longer.

Her mind went to Clay. She hoped he'd received her apology for not meeting his return flight from Sydney while she was having dinner with Mac and Delia. She missed Sydney. She missed her band – Tilly on bass, Angie on anything – and the gigs at the Landsdowne. She missed the barman's banter. He'd deserved a gold medal for tenacity in asking her for a date. His constant requests and her polite excuses became a harmless game between them. Clay and Sasha were once Sydney childhood neighbours. A man's man, was Clay. He didn't only push boundaries, he broke them. He never blamed anyone other than himself for his misfortune, and she liked that in him.

She could've selfishly made a case for Clay to stay until the trial, arguing his assistance with the defence was essential, but he'd started to make comments about going home. She wished she'd been as forthright with him as she had with Ben.

Following the kiss that turned her to mush, she came close to sleeping with Ben. Part of her wanted the comfort, the reassurance that, at fifty, she wasn't stranded in a sexual Sahara. And in weaker moments she told herself that she'd loved him for more years than not, that she had compassion. Fortunately, her head prevailed. She'd left him in no doubt. Their relationship would never be more than strictly professional.

But with Clay, she didn't have the courage to tell him how she felt. How could she be forthright about what she didn't want, yet so weak about what she desired? Once again, she'd failed to invite him to stay. If he'd asked, she'd have jumped at the idea, told him how sensible he was. No such luck.

36

JUSTICE NICOLA INKWELL'S OFFICE was part of the rabbit warren making up the High Court tower block in Durham Street. The corridors felt narrow and, as if in response, the behaviour in them was more constrained these days. In the old building, once an art gallery, now home to the Environment Court, there used to be lots of corridor banter.

Inkwell, formerly head proscutor in Auckland, was appointed to the bench when Sasha was in Sydney. She could be tough on counsel, although in the few cases Sasha appeared before her, they'd got along.

At the pre-trial motions, Fisk had strenuously opposed Sasha's motion for a change of trial venue. It was a difficult result to achieve. Inkwell ruled that Sasha failed to show they couldn't get a fair and unbiased jury. The good news about Inkwell presiding was that she was no fan of Fisk's antics in court. The bad news was she was still working prosecutions out of her system and kept the Court of Appeal busy.

Sasha's opponent stood beside her with his junior, Zoe Underwood – a pigmy between two younger Amazons. When Zoe spoke to him, he refused eye contact.

At 2.05 p.m. the lawyers were ushered into Nicola Inkwell's office. Perhaps as a sign that she was new to the bench, the judge emerged from behind her desk and pointed to aged leather chairs. Many other judges remained silent, steadfast in concentration on more inanimate objects, their signal counsel was interrupting. Other than toothpaste advertisement teeth, Inkwell was unremarkable until she spoke, in a modulated voice with precise diction. It was easy to imagine her having attended a London finishing school for young ladies. There was a silver fern pinned to the lapel of her charcoal grey jacket but it was her red shoes Sasha was drawn to and admired.

Inkwell looked at Fisk. 'Quentin, you prevailed on the venue motion.'

He looked smug.

Inkwell added, 'But that shouldn't be taken as a message you can do what you like in this trial. A man's life is at stake here. I won't have my courtroom turned into a circus or anything resembling a political grandstand.'

Fisk's look suggested the judge was off her trolley. 'Your Honour, please. Where is this attack coming from?'

'Attack? Who said anything about an attack?' She pushed back in her chair. It creaked in response. Her predecessor had been a big man in every sense of the word: in his day the chair had groaned. The judge continued, 'This is nothing more than a friendly caution based on our short history together. I'm sure you haven't forgotten my warning about courtroom misbehaviour, my intention to talk to the SG and the Law Society?'

Fisk looked into his lap. 'No, Your Honour.' He turned his head to face Zoe and whispered.

'Something I should know about, Quentin?' the judge asked.

'I've asked my junior to make a note of your reminder, Your Honour.'

Inkwell said, 'Sasha, any last-minute procedural issues?'

'As it happens, Judge, yes.'

Fisk glared. 'This is ridiculously late in the day, Judge, and hardly in accord with pre-trial directions Your Honour set months ago.'

'Pre-trial directions are predicated on full and complete disclosure, Your Honour,' said Sasha.

'What are you talking about?' he asked, affronted. 'You've had disclosure.' He looked to his junior for reassurance. She nodded.

Inkwell said, 'I take it that it's the fullness and completeness you have an issue with, Sasha?'

'Yes, Judge.'

'Do you have any evidence the prosecution has failed in this regard?'

'What I have, Judge, is disclosure of police job sheets trickling in as recently as two days ago.'

'I know nothing about this,' Fisk said, his arms spread. He looked at Zoe, who was impassive.

Inkwell said, 'How can that be, Quentin? Your office is responsible for overseeing disclosure after committal for trial.'

With nowhere to hide, Fisk reddened. 'I'll have to make enquiries, Judge.' He looked again to his junior, who wasn't rescuing him.

Inkwell glared at Fisk, then asked, 'Sasha, do you need an adjournment?'

'Not unless my friend intends to produce a witness based on the enquiries to which this job sheet is relevant.'

'I'm not calling any such witness because the enquiry has no relevance whatsoever.'

'I hope that's not why you withheld disclosure until now, Quentin,' Inkwell said. 'I'm unhappy about this. I want an explanatory report on my desk by the end of the day, copied to Ms Stace. Let me ask you now, do you have any witnesses to call in this trial not listed on the indictment?'

'Not from the need to present the prosecution's case as it is, Your Honour.'

'Obfuscation, already,' Sasha said. 'Fills me with reassurance.'

Fisk stared at the judge. 'I'm not limited at trial to the evidence in depositions, Your Honour.'

'Of course,' Inkwell said, 'but I'll adjourn the trial if I believe the defendant has been prejudiced by a surprise witness who hasn't made a deposition. I may even discharge the jury. You need to be careful you provide adequate notice of intention to call any additional witness, including a written brief at the earliest opportunity. Understood?'

'Of course, Your Honour,' Fisk said. 'I wouldn't have it any other way. I was more referring to the possibility that if defence counsel suggested a rebuttable defence, I needed to reserve my position.'

'Very well,' Inkwell said. 'Anything else, Sasha?'

'Thank you, Your Honour. Two small final points. We could do this before Mr Fisk opens tomorrow but may as well attend to it now. I will be asking for an order excluding from court all witnesses in the case until they're called.'

The judge looked at Fisk, who said, 'I ask that the usual exemption be granted for the officer in charge of the case, Detective Sergeant Rod Black.'

Sasha agreed and stipulated that Clay Tempero, whom she described as her case manager, also received the exemption.

Fisk frowned but the judge issued the orders.

'The other matter?' she asked.

'Concerns the booklet the prosecution has prepared for the jury.'

She was referring to the procedure outlining the indictment, the list of witnesses and a brief explanation of their status to help the jury.

Fisk stared at Sasha.

'I accept the contents aren't contentious,' she said, 'but I'd ask Your Honour to hand these to the jury through the court attendant. It's a small matter, but I submit having them come from the bench rather than the prosecution contributes to a greater sense of neutrality.'

Fisk sighed before he shook his head.

'A bit picky, Sasha,' Inkwell said, 'but I'll do it.'

37

ON THE COURTHOUSE STEPS Sasha walked past Fisk and Zoe Underwood without speaking.

Fisk paused and waited for her to pass. 'What the fuck happened in there? I expressly told you not to provide that Auckland enquiry job sheet.'

'I didn't hear you tell the judge that, QF.'

'This trial will be difficult enough without that bitch Stace getting Inkwell to put everything we do under the microscope. What am I supposed to say in this report?'

'I suggest,' Zoe said, 'that you blame an administrative hiccup, a miscommunication about who had responsibility to do what.'

Fisk turned to look at Sasha walking into the distance. 'Hoity-toity bitch,' he said. 'We'll take her down a peg.'

'She's not that bad. I don't think it's personal.'

'Oh, make no mistake, Zoe. It's personal all right. You don't know the half of it. Listen, I've got a little job for you. I need you to tell Black about the witness order. Make sure he gets a full police comms van parked a short distance away from the courthouse. I want all police and expert witnesses knowing everything that goes on in court during this trial, the moment it happens.'

'How will you do that?'

'Best you don't know the details. Just rest assured that if Stace pulls any other stunt, I will kill it stone dead. Understood?'

'That's effectively a breach of the order excluding witnesses.'

Fisk smiled. 'Inkwell ordered all witnesses to be excluded from court. And they will be.'

38

'**I'VE DONE WHAT I** can, Quentin. She's determined. You should've seen the look in her eye.'

Outside Graham's favourite bird seed supplier on Ferry Road, Fisk spoke in an untraceable mobile. He'd kept a furtive eye out for anyone he might need to avoid. A young man with a younger female teen, potentially jail bait, leaned against the brick wall of an old stores and supplies building. Leaning would slow the downward journey of the man's jeans. She was already threatening decency.

Fisk said, 'I never thought she'd take this bloody case ahead of a place on the bench. What is it with that woman, Ivor? Who in their right mind would make that choice?'

'Ellis was clear with her. It was now or never. Will you manage?'

'I'll have to.'

'We can't have that DVD appear at any cost,' said Grange. 'The best you could hope for would be the opposition benches. You realise that, don't you.'

Fisk said nothing about the Auckland job sheet being disclosed. He and Grange had agreed it would be buried. If it were reported to Ellis it would harm his ambition.

Fisk said, 'This bloke who's missing – Wheeler, is it?'

'What about him?' Grange asked.

'He's security services, right?'

'GCSB. He made the bloody thing.'

'It's not admissible, Ivor, not without him. Authenticity can't be proved and from what you've told me, there's no link between the DVD and the woman's killing.'

'For God's sake. We think that, but we can't be certain. If anyone can find the damn thing, Stace can. And if she finds it before we do, she'll have it produced and Inkwell will have to see it to determine its admissibility. All of a sudden, it's in the public domain. We can't have that.'

The young man against the wall tipped his head back. He dropped a substance from a thin aluminum tube into his nose. The girl, with enough metal in her face to set off any detector, did the same. The man saw Fisk looking his way, showed him his middle finger.

'Well, I can only control what happens at my end. You need to silence Wheeler. Squirrel him away like that idiot Yuile.'

'Don't you worry about Wheeler. You get Tyler convicted ASAP. We want no extant legal proceedings where that disk can be produced.'

'Christ, you think I don't know that? The whole team is focused on it.'

Fisk outlined his measures then paused. 'Ivor?' He made his tone suspicious, like his mother. 'Trust between us, yes?'

'Of course.'

'So, you can tell me. Strictest confidence. Nice guys don't win in this world.' Another pause. 'You had Charlotte Kaye silenced, yes? Had your man pin it on Tyler?'

Click. Ivor Grange ended the call.

39

'**THE WIFE AND I** were in Akaroa the Friday it happened. We're regular visitors. She was trying to get her new toys to work, a digital still and digital video camera – anniversary presents.' Vern Washbrook gave a look of disgust. 'Hopeless. Wouldn't let me show her. Thank God we don't have to pay for film to be developed, that's all I'll say.'

'On the phone,' Clay said, 'you mentioned calling *Crimewatch* about seeing Lottie.'

'I did, didn't I?' Vern launched the white ball into a neatly arranged triangle of reds at the far end of the table. Clay had to be signed in to the 'members' only' central city billiards hall. The man on the front desk looked displeased to see them, his demeanour no doubt a consequence of hurried adjustments of the ill-knitted and ill-fitted rug on top of his head.

'Well, they told me it was irrelevant,' Vern said. 'I didn't think anything more of it.' He stood back from the table and waved Clay to play, a mischievous grin on his face.

'Christ, Vern. Not a single shot on here.'

Clay planned to send the white back to the far end of the table. He'd snuggle it behind the coloured trio, prevent his opponent taking an easy shot. He failed. 'Did they say why your sighting of Lottie was irrelevant?'

Vern scratched the top of his head, taking care not to disturb too many strands. 'Because it happened – the crash, that is – it happened a fortnight before she was killed.'

'You talk to anyone in authority?'

Vern chalked his cue, leaned over the polished ledge and positioned the stick under the cleft of his chin. His stare down the length of his cue was merciless – enough to scare the red ball into the side pocket. 'The governor, bloke called Black.'

Bang. Another red ball down.

'Did he ask you anything, anything at all?'

'He asked what I saw. I told him. I said the whole thing. The woman, the one the *Crimewatch* show was about, I thought she was going to arse end our car.'

Vern examined the spread of balls on the green baize, his hunched frame stalking them around the table like a lion seeking the weakest prey. The shadows of men beyond Vern repositioned with slow movements, chalked their cue tips and marked the score of games. Most heads were down, engrossed in battles.

Vern said, 'I spent most of my time managing guests in the police cells each night so didn't dish out many speeding tickets. No expert, right? But I reckon she had to be doing a hundred and forty. Had to be.'

He narrowed his choice to either the brown ball, or the more valuable pink. He settled on the brown. It positioned him better for another red. He finessed the brown into the pocket and it plopped like a fishing sinker into soft sand.

'We were doing fifty-five – on account of the wife, like. A bit nervy with high speeds, know what I mean?' Vern looked apologetic for driving under the speed limit on an open country road.

Clay nodded. 'Some women are uncomfortable with high speeds.'

Vern's eyes widened. 'Not that Lottie woman.' He chalked his cue and slotted a red, brown again, red, blue, red and black before Clay said, 'Is anyone else allowed to play?'

Vern made a wry smile. 'She's ahead of us, see. This Lottie woman. Then she comes to this side road – Seabridge, I think. A T intersection. Well, her brakes light up and stay on. The back of her car rose up like a bloody snake in a basket – that's how fast she was going.' Vern, now in the flight of the tale, gripped the end of the cue in two hands as if he were driving a stake in the ground. 'Her brake lights go off and she's away. After stopping, this other bloke, he's off again. The woman can't help but ram him from behind. I says to the wife, "Unbelievable." I says, "That other driver's no better than that crazy bitch who just passed us" – 'scuse my French.'

'No one injured?'

'Nah.'

Vern realised it was still his shot. He potted another red but missed by millimetres doing the same to the green. He grunted dissatisfaction.

'Looks like you'll get to play after all. Don't blow your chance.'

Clay looked over the table and sighed. 'You miserable old coot. Not a bloody thing on – again.'

Vern's shoulders shook in a silent chortle.

Clay lined up a red for the far end of the table. It was ambitious but if the connection was right it was a straight shot, white on red. He sunk both balls, giving away points and the right to play on.

'You're a bit out of practice.' Vern said and updated the score slider. His marker was now more than the full length of the straight from Clay's. Back at the snooker table he said, 'This Lottie woman asked the bloke, younger than me he was, she asks him whether he got his driver's licence out of a cereal packet. He looks a bit sheepish, embarrassed like, and says he's sorry. Course, she doesn't admit to speeding. Instead, she's looking up and down the road, a bit uptight, mentions being a million miles from the airport.'

'Had you said anything at this stage?'

'Not much. Said we'd seen what happened.' He effortlessly sank another five balls. With little play left, Vern had an unassailable lead and Clay conceded defeat.

Vern continued, 'When she overtook us, I saw a tow truck in the mirror. A bit of good luck for this Lottie, 'cause her car's not driveable. His is, though the arse was well smacked.'

'What was Lottie driving?'

Vern smiled, almost in embarrassment, as he put his hand out.

Clay handed him two fives, the agreed stake. 'You hustled me nicely there, Vern.'

'Not allowed in here, mate. Reputable establishment, this. We pay a sub.'

Clay said, 'I need a coffee. You?'

At a mezzanine floor overlooking the tables, they sat in a low light. The sound of balls colliding below penetrated their quiet conversation. Vern said Lottie was driving a rented Corolla, the hood buckled and wedged upward.

'Broken light fittings and other carnage in front. And plenty of steam coming from under her hood. The tow bar on his car had done a great job.'

'No better defensive weapon,' Clay said. 'The tow trucker get involved?'

'A broad in overalls – looked like a bloke. Little tat on her neck. Bats for the other side, if you know what I mean.' He raised grey eyebrows, a knowing look. 'They run shows on the telly now, y'know. Reckon they can do anything. Started coming into the force after I retired. They reckon we're all redundant, mate.' He looked disconsolate.

'Well,' Clay said, unconvinced, 'only if we let them. That said, I'm never surprised by what women can do. She get the job, this tow trucker?'

Vern eyed him quizzically. 'Yeah, made out like she didn't mind a yes or no but it was obvious she wanted it. She hooked up the busted Corolla, but Lottie, she's more concerned about missing her flight. Then the bloke she rear-ended, he offers to take her – to the airport. He reckons she can still make it.'

'Had she mentioned her flight time?'

'Nope. And she didn't know him. Then she said her partner was too far away to come and get her. That's when he introduced himself.'

Vern extracted a notebook, no bigger than a cigarette packet, from his red and black checked shirt. 'Hamish Wheeler, that's his name. Oh, I forgot this bit. This Wheeler bloke, he has his own notebook. I recognised it. There was a crown on the black plastic cover.' Vern looked up. 'That's us or security services, maybe justice.'

'You tell Black this?'

'Told you, not interested.'

'Being an ex-cop – you mention it to Wheeler?'

'Nope. I saw his business card, the one he gave Lottie. It wasn't a police logo. He hands it to her, and she asks him what he does at Statistics New Zealand.' Vern looked incredulous. 'He says he's an IT manager.'

'You think not?'

'Not with that notebook.'

'Not ex-cop, turned IT, purloined the notepad as a parting gift?'

Vern's face contorted. 'Never a cop's arse,' he said, contempt high. 'Had airs and graces, like he's from a pommy university. Mouth full of plum. We'd sooner take them lesbianese and the like on, providing they don't try and convert the rest of us. But not his type.'

'Presumably Lottie introduced herself?'

'She gives him her card and he says he's read her work. He gave her a look.'

'What kind of look? Sad? Angry?'

Vern squinted while he thought. 'If I had to guess, I'd say he looked as though he knew her a bit, not only her work. Know what I mean?'

'Well, if you're right about his background before Statistics, you think he might've researched her. Is that what you mean?'

'Could've.'

'Are you thinking the accident wasn't an accident?'

'Buggered if I know, mate. When Black said it wasn't likely to be connected, I didn't give it another thought until you called.'

'What about the tow trucker? Anything to identify her?'

'She had "Rescue Services Limited" across the front of her green overalls and "RSL" across the front of her cap, in red. She gave her card to Lottie. It only had the tow company's name and phone number on it. Mighta had an address for pick-ups.'

'Don't s'pose you got any of that detail.'

'Nope. Said her name was Shazza. Spoke a bit like yourself, Aussie accent. The wife got pictures of the cars and that. How we were certain it was the woman, the other one, not…'

Clay interrupts, keen. 'You have those?'

Vern extracted a camera from a well-used leather satchel. 'New toy. She'd have photographed the grass growing so she wasn't going to miss out on an accident scene.' He handed Clay the camera.

'Have you printed these by any chance?'

'Nope. Not after Black said we were wasting his time.'

'He said that?'

'Not in so many words – more in the tone. He was a bit pissed, maybe more disappointed than pissed. I know how it is.'

Clay buttoned his way through the digital camera file. 'These aren't too bad. I'm keen to get a few printed – at my expense, of course. Will you come with me?'

Vern drained what was left of his coffee. 'Sure – if you think it'll help.'

On their way to Fotoshop, Clay asked, 'How come you were on that road that day?'

Outside, a southerly wind punished exposed skin and pushed on-comers toward them. Clay hunched, tightened the collar around his leather jacket and Vern zipped up a heavy-duty puffer and pulled a black beanie over his head. With his shave needing work, he looked like a retired bank robber. He said, 'We'd had our fiftieth anniversary there. Go to Akaroa every second month, rain or shine. The wife loves it more than I do, to be honest, but, you know how it is.'

'Whatever makes her happy?'

'You got it.'

'You'd almost be a local?'

'She reckons we are. We were in Akaroa the night that Lottie was killed. Some bastard went through a stop sign nearly took us out.'

'Wasn't Hamish Wheeler?'

Vern chuckled. 'Reckon he'd seen enough of Akaroa roads. Odd bloke. Missus had the video cam on that night too. Just crap, mind. Nothing useful.'

Clay rubbed his chin. 'You being a local, you wouldn't by any chance know a Doris Knowles?'

Vern shoots him a look. 'Why'd you ask?'

'Important prosecution witness in the case against Ben Tyler.'

'Doris Cole is? You're having me on.'

Clay was about to correct him when Vern made it obvious Cole was Knowles's nickname. 'The village knows all about Doris Cole.'

40

'NOT GUILTY,' BEN TYLER said, resolute.

In the High Court dock, courtroom one, he was wearing a dark suit, white shirt and blue tie. Fisk sat at the front table, his back to Sasha. Before court started the court clerk told Sasha that Fisk rolled his eyes at the jury when defence counsel made a telling point.

Both juniors, also in sombre black over white, sit to the left of their leaders. Ben's support crew gathered in the media box to Sasha's right, along with their competitors. The latter would say the right things but secretly hope the high-profile defendant was found guilty. That verdict would be a much bigger and better story for them.

Sasha's team had talked in her office, about how the first day of a murder trial can be harrowing. She caught herself constantly jiggling her right foot. There was not much like it for atmosphere. Clay light-heartedly compared the ambience with the opening session of the Boxing Day cricket test in Australia, without the coin toss. No expert, Sasha could see similarities – high stakes, tactics, errors and even the possibility of no result after several days.

It wasn't only lawyers and the media who understood this. It was the reason people bunched together, shunning the usual conventions of social space. As if to make a point of unity, the police involved in the case stood shoulder to shoulder, lining the walls at the back of the court.

The clerk of the court called the names of people summoned for jury service. Ben, Delia and Sasha had pored over the jury list, identifying who to include or exclude if chance permitted. They wanted an intelligent and disciplined juror – one who would weigh evidence focusing only on reasonable doubt, who wouldn't criticise the defence for failing to prove another person did the crime.

They also wanted younger, educated types, people who had not yet made their way in the world and acquired wealth. No older, more cynical types like Clay, whose starting premise was to presume guilt if the police brought a defendant into court. Conversely, an antagonistic juror could be hard-bitten in relationships, someone who'd accept that a man would kill a woman for money alone. That meant they would challenge a woman who might be financially independent, likely to overidentify with Lottie's circumstances. As Clay said, laughing, 'You, for example, Sash.'

Two people successfully sought excusal from service, including a juror Sasha was hoping to secure. After she and Fisk had used all six challenges available to them, she was positive about the final seven men and five women selected. The average age would be close to forty-five, though three would be twenty years older. Ten were Caucasian, one Maori and one man of Chinese descent.

The popular belief that only the elderly and indolent served on juries hadn't proved to be true. Nine people were in the workforce, including a management trainee, an advertising executive, a music tutor, a nurse aid and phramacy trainee. Sasha considered the last five her ideal jurors. They were the youngest and, she hoped, the most intelligent; the most likely to deliver what she would ask of them.

After instructing the jury about its own conduct, Inkwell focused on their need to choose the right person as foreperson. Seeing her at work, Sasha couldn't help but think about the derailment of her judicial appointment. She was now fractionally more sanguine. Initially she had been caught up in rebellious and resentful thoughts, but it eventually came to her that she'd assumed she would sit on the Christchurch bench. That might not have happened, or it might've been some time coming. Mac had reminded had her there was an older convention requiring new judges to sit, for an appropriate time, on a bench away from the bar at which they practised. That wouldn't have worked for her or Mac in ensuring he had the right care.

When the sworn twelve retired to choose their foreperson, Sasha took the chance to get Lottie's brother into court before he was required to be excluded. She wanted people to see Tyler and Grayson Kaye together, shaking hands, giving each other a hug. A bit of tit for tat for the angelic police line-up at the back of the court.

When it happened, they were hovering near the dock. Fisk saw the charade and charged towards them, demanding to know what they were doing with his witness. His shouting quelled the chatter from all corners. Sasha smiled inwardly.

Ben Tyler, annoyed, was loud. 'He might be your witness, but he's my brother-in-law.'

Fisk, facing the gallery, sneered, 'Not any more, he's not.'

It couldn't be better. Sasha pretended to look more horrified than she was and said, 'You're still going to call him?'

Realising he'd been played, Fisk returned to his table and Clay winked at Sasha.

She said, 'Our side can still be civil, Quentin.'

'Civility is for losers,' he said, his back to them.

Team Tyler's little victory was short-lived. The chosen foreperson led the other eleven back into court. She was a middle-aged business woman from a wealthy part of the city. Just the sort of juror Sasha would have excluded had she had another challenge in the bank.

41

IT FELT LIGHT YEARS since Sasha had written on the bottom of the Andrews file, 'Final criminal trial'. The old feeling of invigoration, of gladiatorial contest, had returned. It helped that you believed in your client, but belief also weighed like an anchor around the neck. In the lead-up to this trial, Sasha had felt that weight.

The jury filed into two rows of six, one behind the other. The young man who taught music made eye contact. Sasha gave him the smile.

Before she called on Fisk to open his case, Inkwell instructed the jury to ignore all prior publicity. She inclined towards them, as if sharing a confidence. 'You may well find people will want to discuss how the trial is going, perhaps even quiz you on your view. Please resist such overtures as they may end in your dismissal from the jury and the costly aborting of this trial.' She turned to Fisk and nodded, his cue to begin.

He rose and gave the customary response, 'As Your Honour pleases.' He fastened his suit coat and offered the jury a plastic smile. Hesitant in his early phrases, he seemed unable to leave his notes. Perhaps yesterday's embarrassment was still with him. Sasha wondered whether in his own mind, he'd staked his career on the outcome of the trial. In ignoring Ellis and Grange, she knew she had.

Fisk referred to Lottie as a multimillionaire, milking the motive for all it was worth, a high spot in his address. 'You will hear evidence leading you to conclude that Lottie Kaye's and Ben Tyler's personal relationship was deeply rooted in professional conflict. The prosecution says once the defendant discovered his wife's plans to leave him, she was on borrowed time.' He paused to let the motive sink in.

A hushed murmur reverberated around the courtroom. Some jurors looked towards the gallery. Others appraised Ben in the dock, including those Sasha had hand-picked. Fisk would rely almost exclusively on Doris Knowles for this evidence. It would be sensible to take a pre-emptory strike, putting his slant on this witness's drinking and disarming her cross-examination, but he said nothing about it. Nor did he mention her claim to have seen a figure in a white boiler suit after midnight. Perhaps he was concerned about her reliability. Sasha made a mental note to have him squirm.

Studious in her note taking, Justice Inkwell had acquired the look of a person who'd whiffed something obnoxious. Sasha guessed her discomfort was because Fisk was still on motive, laying out Ben's intentions like black tar. It was far from the simple recitation of the facts required at this stage of the trial. Sasha folded her arms and stared at the ceiling. She'd wanted Inkwell to interrupt, put Fisk off his stride. When she'd given up hope, Inkwell said, without looking at him, 'Mr Fisk, is it not a little early for the rhetoric of a closing address?'

Her question helped bring him to a close, although after half an hour it was difficult to see that anything had been left unsaid. It struck Sasha how accurate Delia had been assessing Fisk's approach. A positive sign to balance her crass optimism about an acquittal.

Sasha, on her feet, bid the jury good morning, then said, 'Ben Tyler is not guilty of this brutal murder. We will expose this case for what it is, for what Ben is actually guilty of.' She paused, catching the eye of most of them. 'We all know my client is guilty of holding people to account – people who would prefer to have their actions hidden from the glaring light of public scrutiny. He's guilty of being a fine editor, of setting this city's news agenda, of overseeing the exposure of corruption and incompetence. Who in this courtroom has not been saddened that these failings have extended to the people in whom we give our trust? The police and the prosecution service itself have not escaped the scrutiny of *The People* and, I submit, have been found wanting.

'The prosecutor has shared his elaborate theories but I suggest you'll find the evidence flimsy. It won't withstand any rigorous test. We're here because Ben Tyler's lack of fear and reluctance to overlook gross incompetence have blinded the prosecution from the outset. They've fixed on a theory of domestic murder motivated by greed, then determinedly worked to prove that, to the exclusion of all else. I don't say this is a wilful conspiracy to convict an innocent man. I say it is more of the same – more incompetence, perhaps with an element of subconscious vengeance, perhaps driven by political ambition.' She looked pointedly at Fisk.

Inkwell said, 'Ms Stace, you may be venturing onto the same ground Mr Fisk occupied a few moments ago.'

Sasha bowed at the gentle rebuke. 'Quite so, Your Honour. I have been inspired by the rhetoric of my learned friend.'

Everyone in the court enjoyed the exchange – everyone except the two counsel sitting at the front bench.

'Ladies and gentlemen,' Sasha said, 'speculation is no substitute for fact. A crime novel written by the prosecution, narrated by its protagonists in the witness box, is not evidence beyond reasonable doubt.' She looked for the eyes of her friendly five, those she hoped would keep the others on track. 'Reasonable doubt is not a trick conjured by defence counsel to ensure the guilty go free on a technicality. Reasonable doubt is the cornerstone of our criminal justice system. It's what you would want for your family and friends – if they were ever in the terrible position in which Ben Tyler now finds himself.'

42

'**SHE TOLD ME A** few days before she was murdered that she'd had a story go south, that two weeks of journalist time had been wasted. She was frustrated she couldn't talk to Ben about it because they were fierce competitors, more than she wanted them to be. She said he insisted on business secrecy between them.'

Doris Knowles was thirty minutes into her evidence, gaining confidence as she went, occasionally touching her coiffed hair. A picture of probity, she wore a cream shirt under a rose-coloured woollen suit.

Fisk's big gun, she would be primed, both as Lottie's confidante and as a critical eye witness. Insisting it was Ben who required secrecy in the relationship put her at odds with his version of events.

Fisk asked, 'Did she confide in you about other factors in the relationship?'

'Evidently there'd been recent problems in the bedroom department.'

Sasha let this go, only because her objections as to relevancy and gratuitous nature were considered in pre-trial motions. They were overruled. Fisk cocked his head and played the naive inquirer. 'The bedroom department?'

She glanced at Tyler before adding, 'Erection problems, something like that. Don't ask me any more about it. I'm not an expert.'

A definite titter rode through the court and four jurors covered their mouths. Sasha was concerned they liked a witness she'd have to attack.

'Did the deceased ever indicate that erection problems were the subject of discussion between her and the defendant?'

'Yes. Ben became defensive about an innocent comment she made to him about a female staff member straying with her golf pro.'

Sasha rose, arms spread. 'Your Honour! Will there be no limit to this second-hand account? Now we have characterisation of conversations by this witness.'

'Mr Fisk,' Inkwell said, 'I think that's a fair point. I've ruled on the boundaries and constraints on hearsay. Unless the evidence is about what the defendant did, I think we've gone far enough.'

Fisk returned to his witness. 'What, if anything, did the deceased tell you about what the defendant did at this point?'

On her feet again. 'I don't understand that question, Your Honour. I'm not sure how the witness can.'

The judge asked, 'At what point, Mr Fisk?'

Fisk looked flustered as he thumbed through a pile of papers, seeking inspiration.

Frustration in her tone, the judge said, 'Can we move on, Mr Fisk?'

Zoe leaned over and whispered.

Fisk said, 'Evidence will be given that certain medications were found in the house, Mrs Knowles. Did the deceased make any mention of those to you?'

Fisk was referring to Viagra – it was in the file. Because Doris Knowles didn't find it, Fisk couldn't put those words in her mouth. She looked confused before she spluttered, 'They were for Mr Tyler's depression.'

More murmuring in court. There was nothing in her pre-trial deposition about this. Inkwell stared at Fisk.

'Are you certain about the medications being for the defendant's depression, Mrs Knowles?'

Knowles's cheeks turned the colour of her suit but she picked the cue from Fisk. 'No, I'm not certain about that.'

'Good,' he said, as if his witness hadn't erred. 'Let's turn to what happened on the fateful night. You made a formal statement to the police. When was that?'

'The day after Lottie was murdered.'

'But you spoke to them on the night?'

'I spoke to a Detective Hart, yes.'

Fisk picked up a document. 'He recorded you as saying your first inkling something was wrong followed the midnight time pips on the radio, then the sound of smashing glass.'

'I said that. I was mistaken.'

'In what respect?'

'About the time. It was much closer to 9 p.m. than it was to midnight.'

Sasha shot upright as if she'd sat on a pin. 'Your Honour, this is appalling.'

'No. It's not appalling, Ms Stace. It's a variation from her deposition. You're entitled to question her on that and the reasons for it. When your time comes.'

Fisk continued, 'How have you come to this realisation about the time you heard glass smashing, Mrs Knowles?'

'Because Detective Hart said police were well on their way to the house at midnight.'

The jury looked impassive. A couple nodded their heads, acceptance the witness was fixing an honest mistake.

'I thought about it and realised I was wrong. It was the shock, you see. It was near the beginning of the movie, not the end.'

'What do you mean the beginning of the movie?'

'I heard the smashing sound during the movie – *Bewitched*. It was on Sky TV at 8.30 that night. Nicole Kidman was in it. She was good but the story was garbage.'

Laughter in the courtroom. Most of the jury joined in.

'You ignored the smashing sound, then?'

'Well, no. I got up and went down the drive about nine and saw a man in a white boiler suit disappearing around the corner of Lottie's house. I assumed it was a glazier, come to finish a job.'

'At nine o'clock at night?' Fisk asked with the incredulity Sasha would use if she was asking.

'Lottie has – had – quite a bit of money. I'm sure she'd get any tradesman at any hour if the money was right. And besides, black for a burglar, not white. That's what I thought.'

'Well, you went over to her house. When was that?'

'Before the movie finished. I lost interest in it after a while. I thought a good neighbour would check out a disturbance properly, see everything was okay. The smashing sound – it played on my mind. Lottie was a lovely person, like a younger sister to me.'

'So you checked out the sound, saw the person in the white boiler suit about 9 p.m. and returned to your house?'

'Yes.'

'The movie was scheduled to finish just before 10.30 p.m. What time did you actually enter Lottie's house?

'Some time between 10 p.m. and 10.15 p.m.'

Did you see the defendant arrive at the house?'

'No – not until after.'

Fisk had her identify Ben. It was an overdramatic move. The whereabouts of the defendant in court was always obvious. Blind Freddie could've pointed Ben out.

'Did you see the man in the boiler suit again?'

Sasha objected that the witness saw only the back of a person whose gender could not be identified. Inkwell agreed.

'Was there anything about this person's walk or other mannerisms that looked unusual?'

'Not that I can think of.'

'Did you get any sense of how tall the person was?'

'He seemed tall, tallish.'

'You've met the defendant?'

'I have.'

Sasha knew where this was going and objected before the question was put. 'Your Honour, this evidence, in the absence of identification of other physical attributes, is worthless. The population is full of men Ben Tyler's height.'

Fisk still standing, said, 'Not that many in Akaroa.'

The exchange caused more muted comment in the gallery. Inkwell quelled it and asked Fisk to move on.

'When you went into the house, what did you see?'

'Broken glass. Glass everywhere inside the front entrance. The downstairs lights were off but my eye was drawn to the stair lights. I stood at the foot of the stairs and called out to Lottie.'

She stopped as her face crumpled.

Fisk acquired a Victim Support worker's tone. 'Please, go on.'

Jaw quivering, Knowles said, 'She didn't answer. I went up and near the top, I saw blood on the carpet.' She lifted a trembling hand to her mouth. 'It turned into a trail leading to the bathroom. I saw her bare foot through the gap in the door.'

Fisk paused, allowing suspense to build in the quiet court. 'Did you push the door open?'

She nodded. 'It wouldn't open.' She dabbed a tissue under her eyes. 'I only knew it was Lottie because of her red hair. It was terrible, so shocking.'

'Now you saw the defendant after that. When was that?'

'When I came downstairs. I turned on the lights because I was shaken. He was lying in the hall leading to the back door.'

'You said earlier, you stood at the foot of the stairs and called out to Lottie. Did you not see the accused then?'

'No. As I said, the place was in darkness and my eye was drawn to the light up the stairs.'

Fisk showed Knowles the floor map of the house. When she oriented herself, he asked her to show where Ben was when she saw him. When she pointed, he asked, 'Did he appear to be badly injured.'

'No. He looked like he was waking from a sleep, as though he'd been drunk or exhausted.'

'Did you talk to him?'

'No. I…'

'What is it Mrs Knowles?'

'I was frightened. I ran off, got home, locked and bolted the doors and called the police.'

'Just answer defence counsel's questions please, Mrs Knowles.'

Sasha rose and adopted her preferred pose in cross-examination: one arm across her torso supporting the elbow of the other, chin resting in her palm. 'Rubbish movie, you say, Ms Knowles?'

'Yes.'

'Better or worse than the story you've told today?'

Fisk threw his pen down. Both counsel looked at the judge, who showed no sign of intervening.

Calm, Knowles said, 'I don't think the two can be compared.'

'No?' Sasha asked, feigning surprise. 'Has there not been a little magic trick played in the changing of your evidence?'

Indignant tone, 'I don't know what you mean.'

They discussed the relevant dates of her statements, her attendance at Lottie's funeral. 'Did you see Ben arrested on the day of the funeral?'

'I did, yes.'

'Ben made a formal statement to the police the day before he was arrested. What do you say to his statement he arrived about 10.30 that night?'

'I didn't see him.'

'Pretty close to the time you say you arrived in the house? What time was that?'

'I believe between 10.15 and 10.30.'

'After the midnight radio pips. That's what you said, wasn't it?'

'I was mistaken.'

'Not drunk, but mistaken about the time you went snooping?'

Fisk jumped up. 'Your Honour!'

Inkwell glared at Sasha.

'By the time of the funeral,' Sasha said, 'your statement about the midnight smashing of glass hadn't been changed. We've established that, have we not?'

Knowles's wary look was encouraging. Sasha had seen it many times. 'The day after he was arrested, you received a visit from Detective Hart. Yes?'

Knowles nodded and Sasha asked for a verbal response. She obliged.

'What happened? Did he twitch his nose at you, Ms Knowles?'

Inkwell looked at the court clock above the jury box and cashed in on the humour. 'The witching hour, Ms Stace. Let's have lunch.'

When the judge left, Clay approached from the back of the court.

'You booked for Auckland?' she asked.

He looked solemn. 'I'll meet *Uncover*'s acting editor later this afternoon. Doesn't believe she's got anything useful to say, though. Got to dash I'm afraid, cab waiting.'

Sasha knew how he felt about flying and offered a sympathetic smile. 'I'd let you go by boat if there was one, but we don't have the time.'

He gave her a fortifying hug.

43

FISK AND ZOE WALKED past Sasha without speaking but Zoe offered a small smile, no more than the acknowledgment of an opponent.

Out of earshot, Fisk said, 'We don't fraternise with the opposition, okay?'

Zoe was tight-lipped.

Fisk said, 'Look, we're lunching with Black. I need to know where he's at on a couple of matters.'

Zoe said, 'They made Knowles change the time, didn't they?'

'They told her the truth,' Fisk said. 'Madness to allow her to believe she didn't discover the body until after Black and Hart were on their way.'

'I'm not talking about that convenient excuse,' Zoe said. 'They could've done that any time. Why did they wait until they had Tyler's statement?'

'Don't concern yourself about that. Hart cocked up. Suited me, though. I found an opportunity to create conflict between what Knowles would say and what Tyler had said. Refined her evidence to our advantage.'

About to leave the courthouse, Fisk slowed, looked for jurors, then hung back. A couple of them caught up. 'Now we fraternise. Smile nicely,' he said, 'and say, "Enjoy your lunch."'

Zoe's jaw dropped. 'I'm not doing that. We're not supposed to communicate at all.'

Fisk gave his dog-like smile. 'Has no one around here got a sense of humour any more?'

Back at the office, he clicked fingers at his PA. 'Lunch, Averill. Guests are here. Chop, chop.'

Zoe rolled her eyes and Averill said, 'Already in there, QF.'

He made no response. Black and Hart followed and when they were all in his office, Fisk instructed his junior to remove the aluminum wrapping from the warm food platters.

Hart looked at the food and muttered, 'Been a long time since breakfast.'

Zoe revealed platters of crumbed fish with a sweet chilli dipping sauce, sausage rolls tidily sliced into bite-sized chunks, sandwiches with a variety of breads and fillings. It was accompanied by a platter of peeled and sliced orange, grapes and chocolate-dipped strawberries.

'Enough here for an army,' Black said. 'What do you hide this under in your bill, or has the state allowed an increase in prosecutor pay rates?' He winked at Fisk, who gave a royal wave across the food. 'Help yourselves.'

Fisk munched on a sausage roll, then said, 'Detective Hart, I assume you're up with the play. Is my mike and transmitter coming through?'

'A bit crackly when you're fiddling with papers,' mumbled Hart through a mouthful of sandwich, 'but otherwise it's pretty good.'

'You can hear the witnesses?'

Hart mumbled a yes, his mouth full.

Fisk moved to his window, his back to the detectives. 'I assume Cadveron will come up to brief – he'll be resolute on the time of death, no later than 9 p.m.?'

'He's experienced, QF,' Black said.

'And Spiers will support him with the blood?'

'Ditto.'

'Just as bloody well,' Fisk said, 'given that village idiot you've provided as a key witness. Are you hearing what bloody Stace is doing with her? And you, Detective Hart, you've not helped in the slightest here. I thought I'd asked you to amend the job sheet of her interview, water down the drinking issue. Christ, man, what were you thinking, recording that?'

Hart, had raced through the savoury platter. Mouth full again, he started to answer, and pastry flew from his mouth. He chewed more and swallowed. 'Well, that's how it was and I don't go around doctoring job sheets. She said she'd helped herself to a drink for medicinal purposes.'

Black intervened. 'We shouldn't fixate on this. The jury will see the correct context when you bring it out in re-examination. I was a bit surprised you didn't address it head on in the opening. We both saw her in tears that night. More than once.'

Fisk sat at his desk, cupped his hands behind his head. 'You better be well prepared for the grilling you're going to get on that fucking change of statement. Why'd you leave it so long?'

Hart said, 'We didn't notice.' He shrugged. 'That's it.'

'Christ,' Fisk said. 'That'll go down like a shit sandwich.' He got up and popped two strawberries into his mouth. A few crunching jaw movements, then he looked at Zoe. 'Give us a few moments, will you, Zoe.'

She picked up a plate of fruit, unhappy, but left in silence.

Fisk asked, 'How are we doing with defence witness, Alan Markham, that lawyer Stace has about the post-nup evidence?'

Black said, 'He's clean. Not a person of interest.'

'Is that right? I take it you've had a proper look?'

'Of course.' Black sounded annoyed.

'Well, let me tell you this. He's a mate of that judge who was stood down, the one who viewed porn in his office while a jury was considering its verdict. Got caught in an IT sweep by the Justice Department.'

'So what?' Black said. 'Proves nothing.'

'Markham's a supplier of ... how do I put this? Popular art for perverts, if you get my drift.'

'You know this for fact?' Black asked, disbelieving. 'How?'

Fisk's mirth was dismissive. 'I'm connected. How the hell do you think I know? I'll get you what you need for a warrant, but don't piss about. I want him arrested before we close our case.'

44

'**ROAST BEEF AND TOMATO** sandwiches today,' Ben said. He dropped his voice. 'We're doing okay, yes?'

Sasha smiled and patted his arm as he resumed his position, flanked by the prison escorts. The jury would see it. They always watch the defendant, trying to get a bead on their emotional state. They'd see a woman lawyer offering comfort to the man accused of the brutal killing of another woman and they'd ask themselves why.

Sasha was standing when the court attendant announced the judge's arrival with the usual command for silence and to be upstanding. On time at 2.15 p.m., she bowed to counsel and they reciprocated. Inkwell didn't make a meal of it like some of her colleagues. It was more an exchange of little head movements, almost curt.

Doris Knowles stood in the witness box waiting. Sasha rubbed the spot above her left eye she'd noticed after the morning shower. In her imagination it was now the size of a gob-stopper, the oversized sweet Mac used to buy her as a kid, probably to shut her up. It received her fingertip with all the comfort of a blunt needle.

'I'm a little confused,' she said to the witness. 'Mr Fisk was calling you Mrs Knowles this morning. You haven't been married, have you?'

'No.'

'Let's look at what you had in common with the deceased, shall we?' Your financial circumstances, Ms Knowles. Have you...'

Fisk objected but Inkwell knew where Sasha was going and allowed it.

'Have you been successful with property or investments?'

'No.'

'Are you a professional writer or editor?'

'No.'

'In fact, you're retired after working as a cook, yes?'

She looked haughty, gave a sniff of contempt before her answer. 'A chef, actually.'

'And you saw the deceased, Lottie Kaye, about once a fortnight, is that right?'

'Every time she came from Auckland.'

Sasha pressed the point. 'About once a fortnight, yes?'

She nodded.

'For the microphone, please.'

She leaned forward. 'Yes, once a fortnight.'

'And did you keep her informed of the comings and goings in Akaroa between her visits?'

'She was interested. As a journalist, she was naturally curious about people.'

'Do you need me to repeat the question?'

'I kept her up to date. She was interested.'

And you told her all she needed to know?'

'I like to think I was helpful, yes.'

'In fact, more than she needed to know. Isn't that the case?'

The skin over Knowles's face had tightened, her jaw stiff. 'It is not the case. I resent the implication I'm the village gossip.'

'That's your word, Ms Knowles, not mine. You'd have looked forward to her visits, yes?'

Fisk was irritated. He again introduced his pen to the table, then looked at the ceiling. He wanted the jury to know this was a tiresome waste of time, to be annoyed with Sasha. But Sasha was not letting Vern Washbrook's comments to Clay pass without getting mileage.

Knowles said, 'We enjoyed each other's company.'

'Have I got this right? Having nothing in common whatsoever with the deceased, you would have us believe you were her confidante.'

'I was first of all a friendly neighbour.'

'A friendly neighbour to whom the deceased poured out the most intimate and private details of her relationship with Ben. Is that right?'

'She did that, yes.'

'I understand, Ms Knowles, you're widely known by the nickname of Doris Cole.'

'Not to my knowledge, I'm not.'

'Are you aware of the TV character, Norris Cole, in the English soap opera, *Coronation Street*?'

'I've seen the show.'

Sasha saw that Knowles knew what was coming. She paused to increase her discomfort. 'Would it be fair to say that the Norris Cole is an interfering busybody, an incorrigible gossip?' Sasha glanced at the jury. A couple of the women and one man clearly agreed.

Doris looked towards the bench but the judge wasn't offering any solace.

'I suppose so.'

'Ms Knowles, is that not the reason why you are known as Doris Cole?'

Fisk objected that the witness has already disavowed any knowledge of her alleged nickname.

Inkwell raised her dark eyebrows at Sasha.

'Happy to move on, Your Honour. 'Ms Knowles, when did you last speak to Ben Tyler?'

She glanced at him. 'I can't remember. It was his wife I had a relationship with.'

'Did you not speak to him the weekend before Lottie was killed?'

She looked at Fisk but he had no idea what was coming. Sasha said, 'I don't think Mr Fisk can help you with this one. It was the previous weekend, wasn't it?'

'It might've been.'

'He told you Lottie was under stress with work, didn't he?'

'I think so, yes.'

'He asked whether you could give her a bit of time to settle in and relax with him before you delivered the weekly update on village comings and goings.'

'I don't recall that.'

'Given you and he didn't speak much, you would recall, wouldn't you?'

In her silence, Knowles's lips were tight.

'You were embarrassed by his approach, weren't you?'

'I thought he'd deliberately exaggerated.' She glanced at Ben. 'He was rude to me.'

'And you said, did you not, "She's lonely. If you were a half decent husband, she wouldn't go looking for other company."'

'Well, that was true.'

Sasha, pointed to Delia on her left. 'In the lunch break, did you notice my junior in the bar with you?'

Knowles looked at Fisk but he had his head down. The witness flushed and Sasha wondered whether the jury had seen that.

She answered, 'I'd have said it was more of a restaurant than a bar.'

Sasha gave her the smile. 'I bow to your expertise, Ms Knowles. You were having lunch on your own?'

'No.'

'Oh,' she said, as if surprised that Delia hadn't given her a full account. 'Who did you have lunch with?'

'Well, your co-counsel,' she said with a little smirk, much to the amusement of the court.

Sasha played along. 'How much wine did my co-counsel have, Ms Knowles?'

The smirk disappeared. 'I've no idea.'

'And you, how much did you have?'

Fisk stood in front of Sasha. 'Your Honour. What the witness eats or drinks today is irrelevant to what she says she saw on the night of the murder.'

The judge said, I think I can see where this is going, Mr Fisk. I'll allow some latitude.' I also think we can speed up, Ms Stace, can we not?' She turned to Doris Knowles. 'You can answer counsel's question.'

'I enjoy one or two glasses of wine with a meal.'

Sasha asked, 'Well, today, was it one or was it two?'

Knowles flashed a look at Delia. 'Two.'

'And you do this for enjoyment or for, medicinal purposes – to get you through the day?'

'I don't drink because I'm addicted, if that's what you're insinuating!'

Sasha asked Delia for some notes. They were nothing more than the case chronology but neither Knowles nor the jury knew that. She flicked through several pages and tilted her head. 'I suggest two would be the minimum at lunch, most days. More before and after the evening meal, not so?'

Knowles could say it wasn't so but she hesitated and Sasha filled the gap. 'Do I need to ask you about your glass recycling, Ms Knowles?'

Fisk half stood. 'Might we have one question at a time?'

But all eyes were on his witness. Sasha had rolled the dice and as they rolled, she was helping the jury believe that this star witness was hiding or minimising something important - again. They'll see more hesitation, assume she feared she'd been watched and the truth will out.

She still hadn't answered.

'Is it fair to say you don't quite remember the general pattern?'

Knowles, not considering what the bald court transcript would look like later, accepted the suggestion. She nodded.

'For the microphone, please.'

'I don't remember.' She added, indignantly, 'I don't count the bottles every week. I don't know anyone who does.'

'On the night Lottie was killed how much alcohol had you drunk before you went to her house?'

'Nothing.' She almost spat her answer into the microphone.

'None at all?'

'That's right.'

'You live on your own. Is that right?'

'Yes.'

'You had no one over to watch the movie that night?'

'No.'

'No little comforting wine or sherry that night?'

'No.'

'Can you think of any reason why Detective Hart would say you smelt strongly of alcohol?'

'That's not fair. I was upset, but coherent.'

'I'm not asking whether you were coherent, but whether you were reeking of booze.'

Fisk snapped, 'She also said she didn't think that was fair.'

Inkwell glared at him. He hadn't got to his feet this time. 'This is not television, Mr Fisk.' Then, to Sasha, she added, 'That said, Ms Stace, his objection to your response is reasonable.'

Sasha wasn't concerned. She had what she needed to present

Knowles to the jury as someone who had crossed swords with Ben and was a drinker. These factors, taken with her changed account at the police behest, would allow Sasha to suggest that, on critical matters of timing, Knowles was unreliable.

'Ms Knowles,' Sasha said, 'what would be a fair description of your consumption of alcohol that night?'

Doris Knowles slung her bag over her shoulder and was out of the witness box and heading towards Sasha before anyone reacted. 'You and your fucking high horse,' she yelled.

Loudly, Sasha asked, 'How much brandy?'

The judge's call for Knowles to return was lost as the witness shouted again. She was close enough for Sasha to see the down above her top lip. 'I don't need this bullshit. I'm not playing your dirty little games.'

Delia stood as if to protect her leader but it was too late. Doris Knowles stormed from the court, slamming the door behind her.

Sasha's heart rate had doubled in seconds.

Inkwell said, 'A short adjournment. Counsel to my chambers, please.'

45

THE JUDGE INVITED COUNSEL to sit in the club chairs facing her desk. Since the last visit, Inkwell had upgraded the artwork on the walls – three oil paintings of Paris on one wall, three of Rome on another. All in simple, up-scale frames.

'Sasha, I've had this message from the jury,' Inkwell said, looking down. 'It suggests neither of us is in their good books at the moment.' She unfolded a piece of lined paper and read: 'Is it acceptable in this court that witnesses can be bullied about their private life?'

Sasha flushed and before she could control it, her hand moved to her mouth.

The judge said, 'Anyone want to suggest what we do next? Anyone want to ask me to have Doris Knowles arrested and returned?'

Sasha looked at Fisk. His look was not just of the cat that'd swallowed the cream, but all the dessert and the budgie that had taunted it all its life. 'I intended to ask Ms Knowles in re-examination about how she came to be smelling of alcohol and why. I understood she'd had a little brandy to settle her nerves after the horrific scene she encountered.' He looked at Sasha. 'I've been deprived of making that clarification. Counsel could stipulate into the record the defence accepts that as the case.'

Sasha looked at Inkwell. 'It looks from his brief as if Detective Hart is going to give that evidence. I'll undertake not to object on the grounds of hearsay.'

Fisk said, 'I'm sure the jury will be struck by your generosity.'

Inkwell ignored the sarcasm. 'That's reasonable. What about this note, Sasha? There's an implied criticism that I've given you too much latitude – permitted the bullying of a witness. I need to respond, wouldn't you say?'

It sounded as though she was more concerned for herself. Fair enough. Sasha couldn't know how many of the jury supported the sentiments in the note but she believed it was directed more at her than the judge. Nicola Inkwell was, at worst, an accomplice. Any sanction sustained would be Sasha's to bear in the form of an alienated jury.

Fisk muttered, 'This'll be good.'

The judge stared at him for a second. 'Quentin, let's not forget that your witness stormed from the court, screaming at counsel as she left. This showed the same lack of self-control she exhibited when she stole brandy or whatever it was from the deceased. Don't think you've suddenly acquired the moral high ground here.'

Fisk looked contrite.

'Perhaps, Judge,' Sasha said, 'you might comment on the need for the robust testing of a witness's credibility. Some witnesses come through well, others don't.'

Inkwell replied, 'I think that's mostly fair but I won't imply that Ms Knowles lost credibility. I'll tell them that the credibility of any witness is a matter for them to decide but it is very common and normal to have credibility questioned through cross-examination.'

In court, the Inkwell said what she had planned, adding, 'Having taken an oath to tell the truth, witnesses were in a privileged position. In the end,' she said with a reassuring smile, 'you are the sole judges of fact. For the prosecution to prove its case beyond reasonable doubt, it's essential the evidence before you is properly tested. Justice is not well served without that.'

Sasha felt more at ease. Inkwell had done a good job but she suspected the majority of the jury were still unhappy with her. The mouths of three women in the back row, one of them hand-picked by her, were tight, and each of them squinted at Inkwell as if trying to identify a distant object well offshore. In a way, they were. Concepts of reasonable doubt had confounded many a jury. There was no head-shaking, though. The optimist in her hoped the expressions were more of concentration than disillusionment.

With Inkwell's nod to proceed, Fisk called Professor Patrick Cadveron to the stand. Cadaverman, as he was widely known, was the most experienced of two forensic pathologists in the city. Sasha realised it was the first time she'd seen him since her return to Christchurch.

In the last ten years he'd acquired a small but noticeable limp, balded neatly and now, as many with a shiny pate did, compensated with a goatee. His pastry-like complexion, not dissimilar to those of his refrigerated charges, was in stark contrast to his dark suit. Fisk led him through his qualifications – a fellow of this and a life member of that – then his practical experience in forensic pathology. As if to bolster his credible presence, he confirmed he had given evidence for the defence.

He told the jury how he'd examined the deceased at the scene, taken her temperature and that of the room and concluded Lottie Kaye would have died no later than 9 p.m.

Fisk said, 'I ask you to look at this electronic receipt for a meal of hamburger and chips.' He showed a copy to Sasha who objected that this was the first time she'd seen the document.

Inkwell asked the jury to leave while legal issues were discussed. She looked at the press box. 'For the moment, I'm going to suppress from publication any discussion or legal argument about this receipt. Is that clear?' The assembled media nodded and the judge checked for the presence of other media in court.

'Ms Stace, this document was in fact before the court long before this trial started. It came as a supplementary exhibit after the defendant was committed for trial.'

Smugness oozed from Fisk. 'Quite so, Your Honour.'

Sasha said, 'But withheld from me, Your Honour. It's presented now as it's intended to be – an ambush.'

'I resent that, Your Honour. Bear with me, please.' Fisk leaned over to Zoe and Sasha confirmed with Delia that she also knew nothing about the receipt.

Fisk came up with another document, which he showed Sasha before passing it up to the judge via the court attendant. It was a copy of a foolscap page receipt signed by Kate for two supplementary exhibits. The first was additional evidence of a witness the prosecution had dredged up from a woman who claimed Ben told her he knew of Lottie's plans to divorce him. The second was the receipt, accompanied by an additional brief of evidence from Hart who said it was found in Lottie's jeans pocket. The receipt was timed 7.38 p.m. Sasha knew from the autopsy report how Fisk and Cadveron would use it.

When the judge looked up, Fisk said, 'I ask the court to admit the evidence.'

'Before that happens,' Sasha said, 'I ask the prosecutor to produce the original receipt.'

'For goodness sake,' Fisk said, 'that's uncalled for.'

'Your Honour, I said before this trial started I was concerned about discovery and here we are. The court has something I don't have.'

Fisk barked, 'Look to your PA.'

Inkwell rubbed her forehead. 'You'd better produce the original, Mr Fisk.'

He looked at Zoe, who trawled through her documentation without success. 'I'm sorry, Your Honour, we can't locate it,' Fisk said. 'However, I can assure the court I delivered it to defence counsel's office in the format it's now in. I will swear an affidavit if necessary. Ms Quigg signed for it because her boss was visiting Mr McClintock at the time.'

All plausible. The judge would allow this in and Sasha, in Inkwell's shoes, would do the same. But it was devastating.

Inkwell confirmed Sasha's fear. 'It's probative evidence supporting the time of death. We'll adjourn for the day and Mr Fisk can swear that affidavit in front of Ms Stace's co-counsel and I will see that affidavit before we start tomorrow.'

46

THE RIDE FROM BRITOMART train station in central Auckland to Otahuhu had six stops. Clay endured the twenty-minute journey as he endured all forms of mass transit – loathing a necessary evil. Sitting on grubby seats and squinting through dirty windows was preferable to negotiating clogged motorways and unfamiliar central city traffic. Sasha told him his experience living in Sydney would serve him well. In truth, living and working in the same building meant he didn't do much driving at home.

The premises of *Uncover* were as inconspicuous as they were inauspicious. The signage was low key and the narrow, cemetery grey, two-storey building was hidden down a tapered lane in central Otahuhu.

Pine air freshener assaulted Clay when he emerged from the elevator on the second floor. He meandered to a silver metal sign, shaped like an old-fashioned name plate on someone's office desk. A bell sat on top of a stylish black counter. Around him, framed covers from past editions of the magazine adorned pale walls. His eye was drawn to one on which the headline read, 'We got him' and underneath, in the sidebar summary, 'Abuser Imprisoned'. The by-line was Lottie Kaye's. Clay photographed the frame, adjusting the lens for the glare on the glass. He tapped the bell and, while waiting, learned of the magazine's success in hunting down a young man who had eluded police for several months. The fugitive had frequently changed his identity while he continued to indecently assault teenage girls. *Uncover*'s investigations proved pivotal to a successful prosecution. Clay decided to email the photo to Sasha.

A large, pear-shaped woman emerged. 'Kia ora. I'm Ngaire Mahuta. People call me Hut, eh?' Her smile revealed a set of square teeth between plump lips. 'On account of my slim-line shape.'

'Clayton Tempero.' He offered his hand. 'Everyone calls me Clay.'

Hut's grip was stronger than he expected and the dairy white smile returned. 'I thought you sounded like an Aussie on the phone.'

'Just don't get me onto rugby.'

'Fair enough,' she said.

In an airless little room away from the front desk, they indulged in small talk that ended with Hut's hope that the magazine's board would soon confirm her appointment as editor.

'You said you were a private investigator – something about Lottie's case. What's your interest?'

'I'm helping in the defence of her husband.'

Hut tilted her head. 'There's a defence?'

'He says, and his lawyer believes him, someone else killed her. I'm exploring that angle, looking at what the cops might've missed.'

'What's to miss?'

'Not sure yet. Good to know if there was anything. You said on the phone there'd been some issues in her life.'

'She was a bit down,' Hut said, with a hint of sadness. 'She'd chanced on this guy, it was all mysterious.'

'An affair?'

'I didn't get that impression, eh.' Hut wrapped a strand of dark hair around her forefinger. A crimson painted nail emerged. 'I asked her how she met him and she wouldn't even say. The only thing she told me about him was he worked in the public service. I think she said he was blaming her for being watched.'

'He meant spied on?'

'I guess. He wanted to know if she'd told anyone about their meeting.'

'Well, she told you.'

'Yeah, but I never said anything. Not till now. What was to say? That she met a guy down south who's a public servant. Hardly the scoop of the year, is it?'

'How did she react to his concerns?'

'She told him he was being paranoid. That's what she said.'

'To his face, do you think?'

'Don't know about that. Might've been email, phone – who'd know. Whatever was going on between them seemed to cause her mood swings. I know that much. One minute she was up, the next down. Not her usual way and nothing else behind that except him, I reckon.'

'If he was a bit paranoid,' Clay asked, 'could he have been the source of a story?'

'More than likely. Paranoia's fairly typical. People want to tell us stuff but they don't entirely trust us to protect their identity.'

'Perhaps phone calls or emails might not be the preferred way.'

'Sometimes a source is happy to meet in our lawyer's office. We and the source would turn up at different times for the same meeting.'

'Cloak and dagger.'

'That's nothing. They might have emailed each other using just the one email account.'

Clay frowned. 'How does that work?'

'The source gives us the login and password to their account. We go in and save messages in their draft mail folder. The source replies in the same way, deleting the first message. You can keep a conversation going for ages without meeting or speaking and it'll be beyond interception because the mail never goes anywhere.'

Clay laughed. 'I'll have to bear that in mind for personal use. If this bloke was a source of something big, wouldn't you expect her mood to be more up than down?'

Hut winced, wobbled her hand. 'We'd lucked out on something big in Rotorua – a cop on the inside, talking serious shit. The trail went cold. Contrary to popular belief, we're not made of money. We don't have endless resources. It was partly why she was a part-time editor and part-time journalist.'

A moody journo with a paranoid source. Where was this taking him?

'What about socially?' he asked. 'Did you two ever do anything together, maybe see her with anyone?'

Hut played with her hair again. 'She knew I had a contact at Ticketek. She asked me to get a couple of tickets for the U2 gig. I was a bit surprised. I'd never heard her talk about them. It was at the stadium gates, the bag check. I thought it was strange that she rifled through her bag as soon as she got it back from the security guy. It was as if she thought he might've nicked something.'

'Did you say anything?'

'Didn't see the point.'

Hut told him about finding their seats, how the rain stopped at the end of the warm-up act.

Clay asked, 'Did she speak to anyone other than you, or did anyone attempt to talk to her?'

'One guy up from Christchurch, but he was with a woman. He sat between the woman and Lottie – small talk, I think.'

Clay listened patiently while Hut recounted the set the band played. 'Lottie applauded but I knew she wasn't into it. At the break, before the encore songs, she wanted to go, beat the rush, and said she'd phone me in the morning. I remember she shuffled in front of me to get to the end of the row and then she stopped, turned around and came back, saying she would wait.'

'What happened?'

'No idea. But she was looking at her phone when she came back. I think she got a text.'

Clay rubbed his chin. 'Sounds like she was going to leave but was told not to.'

'It was like she didn't want to be there, eh? She wasn't enjoying it, which sort of made me pissed. I was lucky to get those tickets.' Hut looked up at the ceiling. 'When we all filed out we were tightly bunched. People were pretty happy. I reckon she was the only one who wasn't. About thirty metres from where we sat I saw her grab at her shoulder bag, pull it around in front of her, in a hurry. It was like someone had tried to reach into it and she'd stopped them.'

'Big crowds. I imagine ripe for pickpockets.'

'Yeah. Anyway, she half pulls out a plastic cover with a plain disk inside it. I'd swear she didn't have it going into the stadium.'

'What did you say?'

'Nothing. She looked like she was hiding it from me so I thought it best not to mention it. Later I thought about when she went to leave, that first time. Whoever put her off leaving might've been the one who put the disk in her bag.'

'How was she after that?'

'Next day, she thanked me for taking her out of herself. That was the way she put it. She was her usual self, in fact better than usual. I didn't see the point in bringing up the disk. Then, basically, I forgot about it until you called. To be honest, I still can't see how any of that's relevant.'

Clay said, 'The police are required to disclose who they've talked to and what their sources say.'

Hut nodded. 'We know.'

'A job sheet, late release to us, referred to police coming here to look for a disk. It was a bit confusing. It implied that police tried to find this disk but failed.'

'I remember that, now. But I've no idea how they would they even know about the disk.'

'Did the cops take her computer?'

'They took all our bloody computers. Smart arse dicks in suits, eh. Demanded to know where the disks were. I only had our normal back-ups at home. I wasn't going to tell them about those. They didn't give a stuff about the fact we had a magazine to put out.'

Clay produced a photo. 'The person who put the disk in her bag. Could it have been this guy?'

Hut looked. 'I didn't get a look at him. Don't recognise him.'

Clay produced the photo of Shazza, the tow trucker. 'What about this woman? Ever seen her with Lottie?'

Hut stared, doubt in her face. 'Don't think so.' She pushed the photos back with a sympathetic smile. 'Sorry, I've been no help.'

Clay left the photos on the table between them. 'I wouldn't say that. The disk is interesting. Given the way she acquired it, I don't see it holding entertainment files.'

Hut agreed.

'That concert. When was that in relation to your next publication deadline?'

'I can find out. Hang on.'

Clay pondered the idea of Wheeler contriving to meet Lottie through the vehicle accident. Perhaps that meeting was the catalyst to their secret communications thereafter. Sometime between that first meeting and the concert, one or both of them have been distressed. Why? After the concert, Lottie had seven days to live.

Hut returned. 'Eleven days from the concert to publication deadline. If that disk involved a big story, it might not have made the deadline, of course.'

'But if a breaking story was on that disk and the relevant party knew, they'd do something – fast.'

'But we never had any injunction papers.'

'They'd need to know what to injunct you on. That requires declaring what they know and putting it into court records. Thing is, your editor was killed a week after the concert and four days before the deadline.'

'But any of us could have… Oh, sweet Jesus. That's why they took all our computers. Not only Lottie's.' New urgency in her voice. 'She has a computer at home.'

Clay looked resigned. 'I think we can reliably close off that avenue.'

'You talked to Jonno?'

'Jonno?'

'Her cranky neighbour. They sort of looked out for each other. He might know something.'

47

DAY TWO WAS MUDDLED by Cadveron's overnight illness. Fisk called the first cop attending the scene, a young man who attended to Ben and saw his injury before he was taken to hospital. After getting the uniformed cop to discuss his first aid training, Sasha asked, 'Would it be fair to say Mr Tyler looked somewhat disoriented?'

Fisk looked up at his witness.

The cop moved his head from side to side, indicating maybe, maybe not. 'If he was, it wasn't obvious to me.'

Not what she hoped for. A change of tack. 'You would've been struck by the amount of blood on his clothing, not so?'

'Yes, that was noticeable.'

'Fair to say, at first, it might've looked like he'd been stabbed?'

'That's fair.'

That was enough for her closing address – a young cop was unlikely to note evidence of a head injury when he was looking at something he thought was a lot more serious.

When Cadveron was recalled, the judge confirmed she'd read Fisk's affidavit about the receipt. Overnight, Sasha asked Kate about it. The PA distinctly remembered only the brief of evidence about the new witness. She said there was nothing about extra evidence from Hart or the receipt. Fisk had lied. Sasha was tempted to put Kate's statement into evidence but knew the judge was always going to allow the receipt in.

Fisk recapped for the jury, then asked, 'Does that receipt indicate an expense for $10.05 was for a meal paid for at 7.38 p.m.?'

'It does.'

'And when you examined the stomach contents of the deceased, what did you find?'

'Partial digestion of a hamburger and chips.'

'How long does it take for food to be digested?'

'About two hours. Although digestion of the recent intake of food may be suspended if a person suffers trauma, even emotional trauma.'

'Drawing on all your experience, Professor, would knowledge of the time the deceased consumed that meal help you in concluding a time of death?'

'Yes, absolutely. Very little of the meal the deceased consumed, had been digested. I believe, taking account of the receipt and the undigested food in her stomach, time of death was much closer to 8 p.m. than 9 p.m.'

Fisk took Cadveron through the brutality – injuries to the head and face, arms, hands and fingers. Sasha wasn't challenging any of that evidence. The receipt evidence was huge for the prosecution. She had to force herself to concentrate. It was difficult.

The prosecution's telco expert put the text to Ben's phone at 9.12 p.m. If Sasha could've pushed Cadveron more to 9 p.m., based on uncertainty over the time of Lottie's last meal, she'd have had wriggle room. Now, the text from her phone had to be sent after she was dead.

It was 4.32 p.m. when Fisk asked Cadveron to remain in the box for her questions. Inkwell asked if Sasha needed any time. Her tone conveyed hope she'd been able to put today's late start to good use. She shared her observation that several of the jury were, understandably, looking pale.

The judge turned to the jury box. 'Despite our later start, I think we'll take the adjournment a little earlier. Please remember to keep an open mind and not to discuss the case with anyone.'

Delia offered to take Sasha for a drink. She was keen to discuss the setback but Sasha needed to talk to Ben. He'd know the significance of the hit they sustained. Sasha excused Delia's attendance, and suggested she visited *The People* and find out if there was any scuttlebutt about what O'Rourke would say tomorrow.

She received a text from Clay expressing hope the day ended well. He also said, 'Gd mtng with L's deputy. Will contct Davo in Sydney 4 relev phn info.'

Davo was a hard case cricketing mate of Clay's who worked for a Sydney telco. If there was a gold medal for endurance mastication,

Davo would win it. He raised concurrent chewing and talking to an art form. Sasha had no idea what line of enquiry lay ahead. She hoped it would be something to raise her spirits.

In his unlocked cell Ben was pale, the rims of his eyes were the pink of dawn and, despite the cool ambient temperature, sweat beaded on his forehead. He undid the top button of his shirt and wrenched the tie loose. 'You'd have warned me, right?'

Seeing him distraught, her own anxiety ratcheted up. 'We can't be surprised he'd pull a stunt like this, Ben. And when he signed that affidavit, I know he lied. The word of an experienced prosecutor against an inexperienced PA. He'll have picked his timing to perfection.'

He yelled, 'He's set you up. Ambushed you, like you said.'

The indictment in his tone was clear. She should have been above this, an impregnable force repelling all deceptive conduct. She wanted to yell back, tell him to stop being a cry baby.

She turned her frustration dial back. 'Listen, Ben. The telco says the text from Lottie's phone was sent at 9.12 p.m. You didn't get it till ten. By then, Lottie was dead. There's no point in trying to defeat this. We won't be calling him or Cadveron liars.'

'What the fuck am I supposed to do? Just suck it up? Jesus Christ, Sash. You're better than that.'

It was an act of will not to respond in kind. On reflection, Delia should've been here to share this. To see how difficult and challenging the stages of a high stakes trial can be. 'Our strategy' – she had no idea where her calmness was coming from – 'is more or less that – to roll with the punch. It was the killer who texted your phone and they did that because they'd seen the receipt and knew how to play it. It implicates you in an attempt to create a false alibi. We'll get there.'

He looked more thoughtful.

Sasha asked, 'Do you know you had a reporter at the scene that night? A woman, my sort of build, long brunette hair. Wears a cap?'

He frowned. 'Don't know of any your height. Our crime reporter is fat.'

'I recognised all the others, or it was obvious where they were from.'

'You think she might be able to help?'

'I thought if she was one of yours she might've seen or heard something useful.'

He filled his cheeks with air, then blew it out. 'I'm sure she'd have said by now. I couldn't tell you everyone who was on the staff back then. Ultan will tell you for sure who was there on that night.'

Sasha wouldn't be going near O'Rourke, but Ben didn't need to know that.

48

AT THE BACK DOOR, the mouth-watering aroma of a boeuf bourguignon greeted Sasha like an old friend. The lights were on, the curtains drawn and the table was set, for two.

Sasha hung her ankle-length coat over a hook she had once screwed into the back of the door.. She considered herself to have limited practical skills so was still pleased at its longevity. Over the top of a game show leading into TV One's six o'clock news she called out, 'That smells divine.'

The genial game show host shouted above applause. Mac peeked around the side of her recliner with a smile as warm as the comforting temperature he'd set for the gas-fired burner. He killed the TV volume.

Pushing down the leg rest, he made to get up, but Sasha motioned him to stay put and poured them both a cabernet merlot. Peeled potatoes and cut beans were in their respective pots. She enjoyed arriving home to a cooked meal, one she hadn't prepared. How long had it been since that had happpened? She joined Mac by the fire and handed him his wine.

'Took the hint,' he said. 'Thought I'd make myself useful.'

He'd been more vibrant in the last six months. The stents in his arteries had done their job. 'And you thought my insisting you stay was for your benefit.'

'Sly.' He grinned. 'You get that from your father.'

Sasha stopped herself from saying Natalie was much more in her face, more direct. That what Natalie intended was beyond question, even in pointed silence. For all her faults, unseen by Mac, he loved her. There was no point abrading her personality now. 'Cheers.' She touched her glass to his. 'I wouldn't know about that, but you may well be right.'

'See,' he said, smiling, 'the living proof.'

Sasha chuckled. She wondered if this is what a long-term marriage was like.

Seated on the couch opposite, she asked, 'Did you get out, today?'

'The other hint I took. I caught up with your mate, Diplock. He thought he should come here but I said I wasn't an invalid.'

'How did that go?'

'He tells me he made a half-hearted attempt at talking you out of the bench.'

Half-hearted was a fair description. She related her version of the conversation, and finished with, 'Doesn't matter now.'

The reason it didn't matter now appeared on the TV screen, the lead item in the news. They watched footage of Fisk asking Doris Knowles to identify Tyler in the dock. It was ridiculously out of context. Then Sasha's cross-examination about gossiping and drinking. To her relief, there was nothing shown of the storming out, which could only be because the camera operator had left the courtroom. The lack of footage didn't stop the reporter from describing what she called high drama. Then there was film of Cadveron detailing all the injuries.

Mac said, 'I know from experience that won't accurately reflect the day.'

'It was awful.' She told him about the note from the jury and its aftermath.

'Sounds like Nicola Inkwell managed it well,' Mac said, his usual bolstering way.

'Fisk pulled a dirty trick with the evidence today.'

She explained it in detail, pausing only to light up the gas under the potatoes. Mac was reassuring. He called her amended strategy of rolling with the punches defence counsel's t'ai chi.

Later, at the dinner table, a delicious meal devoured, she asked, 'Okay about tomorrow?'

'I'll show you what I've done.' He fetched a document from the table by the recliner. 'This is separate to the will,' he said.

Mac had neatly handwritten into a printed template. The form was headed, in bold type, 'My Advance Directive'.

Words grabbed her – 'contact the following people', her own name, 'preferred place to die', 'organ donation' and 'seriously ill'. Her stomach turned when she read 'and unable to speak for myself'. The second page listed several options of care for Mac to consider in the event he could not speak for himself. The one he'd ticked said, 'I would like to receive only those treatments which look after my comfort and dignity. I do not wish to receive any treatment aimed at prolonging my life. I understand this means cardiopulmonary resuscitation will not be attempted.'

'Oh, Mac, is this really necessary?'

No hesitation. 'We should all do it.' The steely look in his eye suggested he was well prepared for an argument.

Sasha didn't want to argue. 'And what? You sign this up with your doctor tomorrow?'

'After she's assured herself I know my own mind and am fully cognisant of the options.'

'If you must do this, will you at least allow the option that says your health professionals will make the decision in consultation with me?' No sooner had she said those words when she realised why he'd chosen the other option. She looked at his stony face. 'You think I'll pressure them to resuscitate you, give you treatments.'

'I don't think that. I know that.' His face broke into a grin, but this only underpinned his resolution. 'I remember what you said at the hospital.'

With false cheer, Sasha said, 'I don't know why I'm worrying. Since you've had those stents, there's another decade left in you yet.'

'May well be. Nevertheless, we won't have people worrying about what to do with me when it's time. In my view, this form relieves considerable burden all round.'

His old authority was back. They discussed how the form would be used and who needed to know where it was. It would be less straightforward than he thought unless he had it on him at all times. Her thoughts went to that bloody bridge in Armagh Street. If he collapsed there or anywhere else, and the paramedics arrived, she knew damn well they'd attempt to keep him alive – even with the form. They were all about keeping people alive, not letting them die.

She'd get past this and be happy for him – not because he faced death with rare calmness, but because he accepted that the life he'd lived was as good as it got. Melancholy seldom called at Mac's door. Sasha was careful not to project her own feelings about his son John, a corporate lawyer in London who had no time for an ill and aging father.

'I wish I had your strength,' she said and sensed the onset of stinging behind her nose. She hurried to kiss his cheek and left the table, pretending an interest in making tea.

'Course you have,' he said, almost gruff. 'You just don't know it.'

49

CLAY WAS ABOUT TO turn away from the cream Mt Eden bungalow next door to Lottie's house when he heard two bolts slide on the other side of the wooden door. It creaked as it came ajar. A Maori man, lined face the colour of caramel fudge and hair in a Willie Nelson ponytail, appeared in the gap. 'What?'

Clay passed his card through. The man stood back an arm's length to read it then eyed Clay, full of suspicion.

'Got no fuckin' need for a honky lawyer, sonny,' he said, dropping the card between them. 'What the hell does "legal investigations" mean?'

'I'm here about the woman who lived next door. I'm tidying up her estate matters, property and such.'

'I know what estate is. She's been dead for ages. Had bugger all to do with her.'

He started to close the door when Clay said, 'Cops treat you okay?'

'Whadaya mean?'

'I'm picking you might stand out in this neighbourhood, people might make assumptions about you that aren't right. Cops are no different. They can be a bit disrespectful, assume you're ignorant about everything.'

The man released the chain, opened the door. He wore grey striped PJs underneath a red towelling dressing gown, and dilapidated brown slippers.

'Get that a bit,' he said. 'Used to it. I spoke to 'em. Two lots.' A toothless smile. 'The second lot were fucked off. The first lot, no suits and ties – they'd taken her computer and the next lot, they knew nothin' about it. I told 'em, eh. I says to 'em, you buggers won't catch any crims if the left hand don't know what the right's doin'.'

'Did she seem to have any unfamiliar visitors in the days before she was killed?'

'Listen, mister, I'll tell you what I told them fuckin' cops. I ain't no curtain peeper. Right?'

'Sorry.' Clay paused, then produced two twenty-dollar notes. 'Your time is as valuable as anyone else's. I appreciate it.'

'You for real?' The man grasped the money and put one note between a beady brown eye and the naked light bulb.

'Of course.'

'What's the estate got to do with strange visitors?'

'There might be property of hers that others are after,' Clay said, 'something they're not entitled to.'

The man looked at the money. 'Maybe something else,' he said. 'Come in if you want.' He stepped aside. Down a dingy hall, Clay was assailed by the sound of an argument and the smell of cat piss and boiled cabbage. The argument, two women fighting over a man, came from an old console television with a portable aerial. In a darkened room, the TV gave off a blue hue. In a galley kitchen at the end of the hall, several chipped and soiled plates were stacked on a grubby bench. The carpet was as worn and threadbare as its owner, who pointed to a chair. With care, Clay lowered himself, trying not to displace the wad of cardboard under one wooden leg.

'Getcha tea or coffee? Only bags and instant,' the man said.

'Put one out not long ago.'

The man raised a grey chevron brow.

'What do they call you?' Clay asked.

'What's it matter?'

'Only being polite.'

'Jonno. John Hart. Ex-coach of the All Blacks.'

'You've grown your hair a bit since then,' Clay said.

Jonno gave a belly laugh until he started coughing, the explosions turning to a paroxysm. Composed again, he said, 'Need a fuckin' ciggy. You?'

'Every day since I stopped.'

'Mug's game.' His one-handed craft with the tobacco was efficient. He lit up and his eyes rolled back, nicotine striking its mark. Smoke mitigated the cooking smells – oil, and fat that permeated nearby walls and surfaces.

'You saw something else then?' Clay prompted.

Jonno forced smoke out of the side of his mouth. 'This bloke come round after dark. On a pushbike. Not usual for round here. Says he's been next door and can't raise the woman. Did I know where she was, when she'd be back? I told 'im I wasn't her dad. He looked as if he was gonna cry.' Jonno took another vicious draw – a third of the cigarette glowed. 'This bloke says his name's Hamish. Would I give her a message? Almost on his knees he was. Desperate. "What message?" I ask. He says, "Tell her I need the disk back." I says to 'im, "Disk, whadya mean disk?" He says, "She'll know and she's to communicate the usual way." He was almost cryin' at the end.'

'Did he give any clue about what was upsetting him or what was on the disk?'

Another draw, the rollie almost incinerated. 'Nah. Coulda bin a Frisbee for all I knew. But he kept lookin' round, expectin' to see somebody. Like he thought he was being watched or followed.'

'You pass the message on to Lottie?'

Jonno poked a black-nailed finger into his mouth and picked out a tobacco strand, examined it as a jeweller would an unfamiliar stone. 'Never got the chance. Reckon it was only a coupla days before the cops came round sayin' she was dead.'

Jonno looked vacant. Clay suspected there was more, waited him out.

'She was a nice lady. Smiled at me most days, gave me a wave. Brought me cheese scones one day. Fuckin' good they were, too.' He lifted his head. 'I know where this Hamish bloke lives.'

Surprised, 'He told you where he lived?'

'Nah. He came round before I went out to get milk and baccy from the 24/7 down the road. When he left, I wrote down his message. Done that, got the Harley out and headed for the shop. Saw the bloke, didn't I?'

'At the shop?'

Jonno wiped a finger under his nose. 'Nah. Saw him there but followed him for a bit, ten minutes or so. Wrote his address on the same bit of paper I wrote his message on. Had that in my pocket, didn't I?'

Clay pulled out Wheeler's photo. 'This the bloke?'

Jonno extended his arm in front of him as far as it would go. 'Memory's not the only thing that's fucked, eh.' He cocked his head. 'Reckon that's him, though.'

50

AFTER TAKING MAC BREAKFAST in bed, Sasha reread the contents of a probation officer's report. Her client was up for sentence at 9.15 a.m. When she got to the courthouse, dozens of people were walking in all directions. Delia was several metres ahead of her, talking to another woman. Neither of them looked comfortable and Sasha slowed. Each gesticulated at the other but words were unclear over the noise of a busy courthouse. Sasha stepped to the side of the main thoroughfare and watched.

The other woman was Frances Rule, a lawyer who practised in the family court. Not yet forty, she was about four or five years older than Delia. Rule once briefed Sasha on a hotly contested matrimonial property case, husband and wife lawyers fighting over chattels. Sasha guessed Delia and Rule were arguing legal issues. She sped up and Delia was first to notice her arrive. She pulled away from the other woman.

'Morning, you two,' said Sasha. 'Everything okay?'

Rule said, 'Nice to see you, Sasha.' She held out her hand and they shook. Frances looked at her watch. 'Look, sorry. I've got to dash. Let's catch up properly soon. It's been a while.'

She left without looking at or speaking to Delia. When she'd gone, Sasha asked, 'What was that about?'

Delia said, 'Nothing a court won't fix.'

Sasha tilted her head, remained silent.

Delia said, 'We're opponents in a civil case. She was giving me a hard time because I haven't complied with an order for discovery. I told her I have the documents but my client's on holiday till next week and can't swear the affidavit till then. We'll be ten days late. You'd think the world was about to end. She thinks she can charm everyone with that Virginian accent of hers. But she can't hide from me what an unreasonable bitch she really is.'

'You both looked pretty pissed.'

'Some people just wind you up.'

51

IN COURT 2, ALFONSE Cretin stood in the dock, on two counts of attempted arson. He'd been acquitted by a jury of the attempted murder of his wife Esmeralda but still faced sentence on the alternative and lesser charges of arson. Two attempts, two failures. The couple had been married for over twenty years. Sasha was certain his acquittal on the attempted murders was less to do with her advocacy and more to do with sympathy for the unfortunate prisoner's name. That and the bungling nature of the fire setting, which involved wet kindling, followed by Alfonse's wait for the fire trucks to arrive.

Esmeralda had delivered vituperative vitriol to her husband from the witness box and Sasha was sure the jury were consumed by sympathy for the poor man.

Now, having got whatever frustration she had out of her system, she'd informed the probation officer that she wanted to reconcile with Alfonse. Also in his favour were his previously unblemished record, commonly referred to by the cynical cops as 'hitherto having avoided detection', his conscientious employment ethic and voluntary work in the migrant community. Sasha proffered several character references that confirmed Alfonse's attributes, their heart-warming authenticity obvious in their insecure command of written English.

Zoe Underwood was scheduled for the prosecution, but Fisk turned up instead. Sasha wondered whether Fisk's attendence was to send her a message of some kind. How ironic. Fisk made brief submissions, acknowledged the jury's verdict, but submitted that Parliament nevertheless still regarded attempted arson as a significant crime, as evidenced by the maximum of up to ten years' imprisonment. He submitted that Sasha's submissions for a community-based sentence were as muddled as her client.

In the end the judge sentenced Alfonse to twelve months' periodic detention and community supervision for afters. A sensible outcome. After the judge and the court staff left the court, Sasha gathered her thoughts about the trial. Fisk approached and stood over her. 'A little win for you, Stace. You'll be pleased.' His dog smile appeared. 'But don't expect you'll get more of those any time soon. I don't know what planet you were on when you turned down the bench to defend your murdering ex, but I'll tell you this much – I'm nowhere near done with him.'

52

BACK IN HIS OFFICE, Fisk extracted his justice ledger from a locked drawer and turned to the back page. As he did before and during every trial, he studied a smaller copy of Queenie's photo. It transported him back to that long-ago birthday party.

'How many, Mother?' he asked.

'How many what?'

He could almost taste the vanilla ice cream in the cardboard tubs. Mother had buried them under ice in the blue cooler box with the white lid. He saw the little wooden spoons pressed into the cardboard tops. He pointed.

'One each,' she said.

He pouted. 'I want two.'

She turned her back to him and poured lemonade into plastic cups. 'If you have two, someone won't be able to have one.'

'Peter.'

Mother turned around, serious face. 'Challenge him to a race in the pool. If you win, I'll think about it.'

Standing at the far edge of the pool, Queenie wasn't playing with her friends. She'd been keeping watch for the postman, had been all morning. Quentin smiled, thinking about what he would do to win that race.

Queenie shouted, 'Quentin, Quentin! He's here. The postie's here!'

As she ran down the drive, someone shoved Quentin from behind and he tumbled into the cold water, with only milliseconds to hold his breath. The water raged around his submerged head, settling by the time his feet touched the bottom. Looking up, he saw shimmering figures. When he breached, kids pointed and laughed. Even Mother enjoyed the joke at his expense. She called everyone to order.

As he dried off, Mother asked where Queenie was.

'The postman finally arrived. She's probably opening parcels.'

Mother was annoyed. 'Go and find her, Quentin. We're not doing gifts yet and we won't start without her.'

Quentin looked in the direction of the letterbox but saw only the tabby cat that Mother hated for shitting in the freshly weeded flower beds. He ran inside the French doors beyond the pool and shouted his sister's name, several times. The radio – someone complaining about something. On the other side of the living room, venetian blinds rattled in front of an open window. But no sight or sound of Queenie. He ran upstairs to her bedroom, called as he went, doing his best to mimic his mother's cross tone. Her door was open but she wasn't there. He looked into his own room, no belief she'd be there either. The bathroom – the only place left. He'd opened the door before he'd realised he hadn't knocked. Empty. Only the smell of cleaning fluids.

'I can't find her, Mother,' he said, glancing at the children sitting patiently around the table, two places left. 'I've looked everywhere. Honest.'

Mother glared at him, hands on hips. It wasn't his fault he couldn't find her, but Mother blamed him – he knew she did. That always happened. She and Queenie were ruining his birthday and that wasn't fair. Mother looked away, towards the house, and her face changed. The anger had gone. She started to run.

From inside the house she screamed Queenie's name. He started to cry, not really knowing why. It wasn't his fault.

Mother came back outside. A different face now but her voice was high. 'I'm sorry, children, but you all have to go. We can't find little Queenie. We'll do the party soon, all right?'

The other kids look confused. One girl started to cry when another said, 'Queenie's lost.' Everyone was slow to move and Mother clapped her hands and shooed them like Grandma shooed her hens away from the wire door. 'You may take a piece of cake with you,' she said, smiling. He'd seen that face before. The unhappy smile, Father called it.

Soon a police car with its flashing light came up the drive. It was exciting but Mother didn't look happy. She had both hands over her mouth. She sent him to sit by the pool. The policeman came and asked him questions about the pool. When the policeman bent and put his hand in the water and pretended he wanted a swim, Quentin wanted to push him in. He asked about Queenie. Quentin told him he didn't make her go away. The policeman also had the unhappy smile.

When Father came home, Mother cried. He asked the same questions as the policeman. Quentin didn't know what to say. He wanted to say the right things. He wanted to make everyone happy but he didn't know the words. He wanted Queenie to come back. That would make them happy, make them smile properly.

Now, Fisk touched his sister's cheeks in the photo, brushed away imaginary tears and then locked away the ledger.

According to his mother, his lawyer father, Randolf, had few desirable qualities. When she was sober she described him as a 'cheek turner', 'a man with a blind eye when it came to serving justice'. But when she was drunk, Randolf was no more than a lily-livered coward, a shiver looking for a spine to crawl up.

But in truth, they'd all changed after Queenie was murdered, Randolf most of all. His father was in the office, the same room along the corridor from his own, now occupied by Tom Carson. There would be no 'like father, like son' as far as he, Quentin Fisk, was concerned. The days seemed like years before Queenie was found in a shallow grave in the dunes of Waimairi Beach.

The biggest red tick of all was only days away – Tyler imprisoned for life and Stace in a dark hole of ignominy, no longer the darling of the Standards Committee.

53

'PROFESSOR CADVERON,' SASHA SAID, 'before we get to the matter of the receipt, you said yesterday you thought the injuries were consistent with a crowbar?'

'I did.'

'Pretty common tool for the DIY handyperson.'

'I suppose so.'

She reached down and heaved up a carton. Inside were four of the blackest and most menacing iron bars she'd managed to round up in the last week. One she purchased, the other three were on loan. 'Have a look at these, please, will you, Professor.'

Cadveron inspected each one as if he'd discovered a foreign object inside a body's cavity.

'Is it fair to say, that apart from minor differences in the grip and the pinch end, they're remarkably similar?'

Cadveron agreed.

'In your expert opinion, Professor, could any of those four crowbars have killed Lottie Kaye?'

'Yes. Each of these could've caused the injuries that led to her death.'

'This sort of implement would be commonplace, not so?'

'That's possible.'

'Thank you.'

The crowbars were returned to her table.

She said, 'I understood you to say yesterday that, you initially believed death might have occurred up to 9 p.m. Then, once you became aware of the time of purchase of the meal, you were influenced to pull that back nearer 8 p.m. Is that correct?'

'Yes. It's within my remit to consider all evidence that might suggest an accurate time of death.'

'Quite so. And to be fair to you, you would take supporting evidence at face value, coming, as it did, from Detective Hart.'

'That's fair.'

'No concerns as to the authenticity of the receipt?'

'No.'

'Had that receipt not been made available, we might have been having a conversation about time of death occurring around 9 p.m.'

'Yes, but based on temperatures, I always thought that was at the outer edge of time.'

'Again, to be fair, you wouldn't suggest, in the absence of supporting evidence, that this timeframe would preclude 9.05 or 9.09 p.m., would you?'

She glanced at the jury. Three were leaning forward. 'I know of no experienced pathologist who would suggest the time of death to the minute unless there was clear evidence to do so.'

Sasha thanked him as if he'd made a significant concession. 'Professor, let's assume the receipt in question relates to the contents you found in the deceased's stomach and not to the killer's burger and fries meal.' She shot a look at the jury. First point made. 'Do you remember seeing, in the house that night in Akaroa, an oven and a microwave?'

He looked like he knew where she was going. 'I don't, Ms Stace, but if you say those items were there, I'll accept that.'

Side on to Sasha, Fisk glared at Zoe. The jury would see that too. Sasha beckoned the attendant and asked him to obtain an exhibit. 'Professor, the document shown to you now is an inventory of items noted by Detective Hart as present in the house that night.'

'Yes, I see that.'

'You see one item listed in the refrigerator was uncooked fish, along with carrots and broccoli.'

Fisk objected that the questions had not the slightest relevance to a brutal murder. The judge said she'd allow a little more latitude.

Cadveron acknowledged the references.

'And I think you're aware that Lottie Kaye was killed the day she arrived in Akaroa.'

'Yes. But if you're suggesting that was the deceased's dinner, it appears she changed her mind.'

'I'm suggesting, Professor, that the food in the refrigerator was for the defendant. That Lottie waited for him to arrive, intending to reheat her meal so they could eat together.'

Fisk jumped to his feet. 'Speculative. Also the defendant had plenty of time to buy that food.'

Sasha responded, 'Where's that receipt, Mr Fisk?'

Smirking at the jury, Fisk said, 'It's where he put the crowbar and the boiler suit.'

Nicola Inkwell, shouting over the eruption in court, said, 'Enough, you two. This is a courtroom, not a public bar. Sit down, both of you.'

When order was restored, Inkwell faced Cadveron. 'Ms Stace is addressing two things. The first is whether this receipt can be reliably tied to the meal the deceased consumed. Was it, for example, given to her by the establishment responsible, or was it placed by someone to be found later? In that regard, Mr Fisk, I'm assuming Detective Sergeant Black will be able to produce the relevant bank statement. It's not a matter for the pathologist.'

Fisk said, gratitude in his tone, 'Indeed, Your Honour.'

'The second issue is, even if the receipt is found to be the deceased's, you cannot say with any certainty whether the meal was consumed at or around 8 p.m., or saved and eaten somewhere around 9 p.m.'

Cadveron repeated he thought 9.00 p.m. was at the outer range for time of death.

'Do you have any further questions of this witness, Ms Stace?'

The attendant handed Sasha a note from Ben. 'No, Your Honour, but I may be able to save the police time. I'm instructed that the sum of $10.05 was indeed debited to the deceased's bank account on the day in question. This would deal with the first issue Your Honour has summarised.'

Inkwell glared at Sasha. 'It would have been helpful to have had that earlier, Ms Stace.'

Fisk had no re-examination. He called Henry Spiers, the government's forensic scientist in the city. Like Cadveron, he had a long list of credentials.

After half an hour of tedious science, Sasha persuaded Inkwell to intervene and get on with it. Sasha knew Fisk would be miffed as he faced the witness and she smiled inwardly.

'Mr Spiers, you were asked to examine the defendant's clothing, said to be worn on the night the deceased died?'

'Yes.'

'What did you find?'

'I found blood on the defendant's shirt, including both front panels, the sleeves and the inside or underside of the cuffs on the sleeves.'

'Whose blood?'

'The blood belonged to the deceased.'

'Did you find any blood on the defendant's trousers or shoes?'

'Nothing on the trousers, but smudges on the shoes'.

Fisk hammed it for the jury, pretending surprise. 'Only smudges of blood on the shoes?'

'Correct.'

'Mr Spiers, the defendant told detectives he was attacked inside his house before he discovered his wife's body. Did any of the blood you examined on his clothing belong to him?'

'No – all blood matched the deceased's.'

'I understood you to say, blood fell from the head and face of the deceased, but also from the weapon used to kill her.'

'That's correct.'

'Can you account for blood on the defendant's upper body clothing but not the lower?'

Sasha was about to stand but saw the judge's arm rise as if she was about to start a race. 'Mr Fisk, the defence is that the defendant was not present when his wife was killed, but was present after the event.' She turned to Spiers. 'You said the blood on the defendant's clothing was consistent with smears or smudges rather than splatters.'

'Yes, Your Honour.'

'But there were no smears on the lower half of the defendant's clothing and no splatters.'

'That's correct.'

'Is it your expert opinion,' Inkwell continued, 'that the defendant was not present at the killing, or he was present and wore protective clothing against inevitable splatters of blood?'

'Those are two options, but they're not necessarily mutually exclusive,' Spiers said, authoritative. 'We're not talking here about new blood and then substantially aged blood. It's conceivable the killer may've protected his clothing from splatters then, having discarded the protective clothing, returned and received the smudging.'

Sasha felt tightening in her shoulders and jaw. That was the trouble with judicial intervention at times like this. It would've been bad enough for Fisk to have led this evidence but the fact the judge did so will give it credibility in the jury's eyes. Inkwell handed back to Fisk and gave Sasha a sheepish look.

Fisk, almost rubbing his hands with glee, said, 'If the killer were to do as you suggest, protect his clothing then discard the protection, what, in your expert view, would that say about his intentions?'

Sasha objected. 'Your Honour, Mr Spiers is an expert in forensic science. The prosecutor has led no evidence as to his expertise in psychology.'

'I agree.' Inkwell sounded almost relieved. 'Both of you are free to argue theory in your closing addresses.'

After getting Spiers to look at Ben's shoes and drawing the same protection/no protection answer as before, Fisk changed direction.

'Now Detective Hart asked you to examine additional samples of blood and hair. He'll give evidence about where these were found, but is it correct these samples did not belong to the deceased?'

Spiers confirmed they belonged to Ben. Sasha looked at Delia. Something wasn't right here, particularly the bit about Hart saying where the samples were found. This was new. She whispered to Delia, 'In the hall by the nook, right?'

Delia whispered back, 'I presume so.'

Sasha asked her to go over his brief and job sheet.

Fisk thanked his witness and sat. It was a few minutes before the scheduled afternoon adjournment. The judge said, 'I'm thinking we're all in need of a refreshing drink. Is now a convenient time, Ms Stace?'

'I'll finish before 3.15, Your Honour.'

She looked pleased and invited Sasha to continue. It was nice to be back in her good books.

'Mr Spiers, is Detective Hart's inventory still in front of you?'

'It is, yes.'

'Does it refer to a bathroom towel?'

'Yes.'

From a supermarket shopping bag, Sasha withdrew the towel Ben had given her. 'Your Honour, I will put this to the detective as the towel in question. However, with your leave, I'd like to show the court a reconstruction of how it was possible for blood to appear on the defendant's upper, but not lower body.'

'How do you propose to do that?' the judge asked.

'The court clerk, who is the same build as the deceased, has agreed to let the defendant demonstrate on her.'

Fisk jumped up and objected to what he called theatrics that demeaned the court. 'If counsel wants to do that, Your Honour, I submit the defendant needs to give the relevant evidence under oath.'

'Fair point, Ms Stace.' Inkwell sounded resigned.

'I'm not asking for an evidential point to be made. I'm asking the witness to consider the possibility that the evidence he found is consistent with a theory other than the prosecution theory.'

The judge faced the witness. 'You understand what's going on here, Mr Spiers?'

'I think so, Your Honour.'

She asked, 'Could a situation exist where a towel might be used to protect the lower clothing but not the upper?'

'Yes, of course.'

Sasha wished she could see Fisk's face.

Spiers continued, 'I could demonstrate with the clerk.'

Fisk got to his feet again. 'That would have no probative value whatsoever, Your Honour.'

Inkwell said, 'I'm inclined to agree, Ms Stace.'

Still standing, holding the towel, Sasha decided that if the jury hadn't seen Fisk as an obstructer of justice, she'd help them a little. 'Given the prosecutor won't agree to a demonstration, I have one remaining question.'

Fisk threw his head back in exasperation and the judge came to his rescue. 'No, Ms Stace. I won't have that. His objection is proper and it's my decision.'

She gave the outwardly respectful response, 'As Your Honour pleases.' Then she asked Spiers, 'Is it possible the options you discussed earlier could be added to?'

Spiers looked at Fisk then back at Sasha. 'Possibly.' He sounded unsure.

'Might one such scenario involve a towel coming between the deceased's blood-soaked body and the defendant's lower clothing, yet permit her blood coming into contact with his shirt as you've described.'

'Speculation, but possible.'

'Evidence will be given that a towel was found on the washing line on the property. Were you given such an item to examine?'

'No.'

'Depending on how that towel was washed, would it have been possible to find traces of blood in the fabric?'

A long pause. 'It's possible.'

'Thank you.' Sasha sat.

Inkwell looked pointedly at the clock. 'Now we'll adjourn.'

It was close to 3.30 p.m. Sasha was back in the judicial fridge.

54

AFTER THE AFTERNOON TEA adjournment, Fisk was back to his old tricks. He had Barry Hart explain that he'd made a mistake in his brief of evidence supplied to the court. His error, he said, uncomfortable, was to exclude from his statement that he'd found Ben's hair and blood on an outlet pipe at the back of the house. Instead, he'd given the measured distance from the back door. The prosecutor had noticed the omission before court started that morning. The judge, showing her frustration, offered Sasha an early adjournment.

'I wonder, Your Honour, if I might briefly confer with my co-counsel and Mr Tyler without having everyone leave the court?'

As Delia and Sasha headed towards Ben, the two prison escorts withdrew a short distance, giving the defence privacy to whisper.

Sasha said, 'With this change, Fisk will argue your injury didn't happen inside the house.'

'Meaning no assailant,' Delia added.

'He can now say there's forensic evidence of self-inflicted injury rather than rely on theory.'

Delia's whisper was almost too loud. 'Christ, Sasha. You're not going to suggest it was planted evidence.'

Ben, emphatic, said, 'No. The previous fortnight I did crash my head into that bloody pipe after I bent to pick up the key from under a pot plant.'

Sasha said, 'You've never said that.'

'I'd forgotten.'

Sasha bit on her bottom lip, suppressing irritation. 'Okay. Anything else?'

Ben shook his head.

Back at her table she said, 'Your Honour, I'd like to reserve the right to recall Mr Spiers but for now we can proceed.'

Facing Hart, Sasha was close to screeching. 'This isn't simply an omission from your brief of evidence, is it, Detective?'

'I'm not sure what you mean.'

'Look at your job sheet. You refer to finding the defendant's hair and blood within three metres of the back door, don't you?'

'That's correct. The outlet pipe was three metres from the back door.'

'Not three metres inside the house.'

'I've never said that. That's the defendant's story.'

'And not attached to an outlet pipe. You never said that either?'

'As I said, Mr Fisk felt I should be more specific.'

'Kind of him. You've misled the defence right up to this point, haven't you?'

He moved his bulk in the witness box and bent towards the microphone. 'I haven't been deliberate about that. I apologise for not being specific.'

'Generous of you. But not the only mistake about evidence you've made, is it? There's the matter of the receipt you claim to have found in the deceased's jeans pocket.'

Hart, concerned, glanced at Fisk. 'That mistake was a matter of timing rather than the location of evidence. I should have ensured my original brief was more specific.'

'Mr Fisk didn't ask you to leave it out?'

'No, he did not.'

'Mr Fisk didn't ask you to alter the location of the blood and hair evidence, to be less specific until today?'

Sasha noticed Zoe look at Fisk, a shimmer of doubt on her face. All she could do with Hart was to sow seeds of doubt with the jury, signalling something was wrong here, that the prosecution was playing games and making up the rules as it went. Before she let Hart go, she revisited the delay in correcting Knowles's statement, milking the cumulative effect of all these mistakes. Hart looked tortured by the end of it and glared at Fisk as he left the box.

55

THE RED DOTS ON the radio clock winked at Clay in broken sleep every two hours. Rising from a hollowed mattress at 8 a.m., he felt as though his head had been in a vice. Also the night's debauchery was in his mouth, throat, stomach and bowel. Who? That crazy journalist, Hut, that was who.

Loose fragments of Wednesday night started to cohere. A place called the Viaduct, its familiarity to Darling Harbour comforting. A meal and drinks at Wildfire, an Irish bar, or was it two, more drinking, then gambling at Sky City. A visit to a brothel, sans Hut, in a road at the far end of Queen Street. A road with a long Maori name beginning with K. He remembered his companion – tall, thin faced, emaciated almost, giving him his card. A connection to Hut, possibly. An ex-journo or something.

He cringed as the first water passed his rasping throat. A delayed shudder then immediate trouble. He shuffled to the toilet seat, dropped his boxers and held his head in his hands. Scottish comedian Billy Connolly came to mind, something about the uncontrolled spray of a fire hose. That bloke last night. What did he do with his card?

A shower, the rose set to wash his pubic hair more than his head, did little to make him human again. His knees ached as he bent to catch a water flow delivered with all the force of a man suffering from advanced prostate problems. He'd look for the guest happiness survey in the room. He filled them in to kill time, minutes he knew were utterly wasted.

Dehydrated, he thought of downing more water but the way he was, the odds were short on regurgitation. As he was towelling off, there was a knock on his door. It was an 'I know you're in there, you bastard' knock – confident and insistent.

Towel around his middle, he was greeted with, 'Shit, mate, you don't look too good.'

He blinked at the man, mid to late forties, shades, pale green shirt under a crumpled suit the colour of old bark. He might pass for security staff, perhaps a protector of an upmarket car yard, but this was last night's drinking companion. When Clay said, 'What's your name again?' he heard the change in his own voice. He'd gone from baritone to bass overnight.

'Gave you my card, last night. You got short-term memory problems, mate?' The man's smile revealed teeth that would fund a lucky orthodontist for a luxurious week in the South of France, with a panoramic view of the Mediterranean.

'That's a distant fourth to cranium, bowel and liver problems. What the hell are you doing here, Phil? It is Phil, isn't it? Phil from Immigration, or was it Statistics? Or was it Internal Affairs, whatever the fuck they are?'

'Breakfast meeting, mate. And yeah, done time in all three.'

'The done time bit doesn't surprise me. What breakfast meeting?'

'Ultan O'Rourke. Get dressed,' Phil said. 'I'll remind you on the way.'

At the wheel, Rivers said, 'You were banging on about this Irish bloke, all night.'

'What Irish bloke?'

'O'Rourke. Except I don't think that'll be his real name.'

Rivers was taking Clay to what he recommended as the benchmark in hangover terminations.

'Kill or cure in K Road,' Rivers he said. 'Either way, gone by lunchtime.'

Clay realised he wasn't alone with pronunciation difficulties.

At the café, the men reunited with Hut, who was initially the centre of their attention for her prodigious alcohol consumption. Clay's ability to become legless on a variety of beverages had endeared him to the two Aucklanders. He couldn't think why. In the cannabis-infused interior of Rivers' dented Mondeo, Clay suggested the man's CV might, to a discerning recruiter, convey he was an occupational bed hopper.

Rivers, spurred by the use of the term, said, 'Speaking of beds, you failed to get your leg over last night. Slept in the massage parlour foyer while I paid to service a young lady. Not a good look on your part.'

'Merely resting my eyes. I recall it wasn't a long rest.'

Hut moved them along and said she'd used her sources to acquire a photo of Ultan O'Rourke. She put it on the table between them.

'Any idea what his real name is?' Clay asked.

Rivers looked unsure. 'When he was at uni, he was going by Ultan O'Malley. O'Rourkes and O'Malleys are common enough, but Ultan, a bit less so.'

'How do you know this?' Clay asked.

'When my folks moved to the UK, I went with them. Met Ultan at Oxford.'

Concerned, Clay asked, 'What did I say about him last night?'

Hut gave her toothpaste smile. 'Nothing complimentary.'

'Well, I feel a bit of a dick. I don't know the guy. I do need more on him, though.'

Rivers said, 'We both did political science at Oxford. He likes a drop. He's great company when he turns on the Irish, but he's full of bullshit.'

The chilli beans were much better than Clay thought possible at this time of the day. They went well with the fried egg and pork and fennel sausage. Human again, now more aware of his surroundings.

A fat cook, of Greek extraction, partially wrapped in a stained apron, was unreceptive to negative feedback about his barista skills.

'Isn't that part of the Irish charm?' Clay asked.

'Yes, but I'm talking serious bullshit, mate. He was obsessed with secrecy and security shit. I couldn't give a fuck who knows what about me, but he's off the other end of the scale.'

'People don't come in here for da coffee,' the cook shouted. 'You gotta get your priority right.'

Frowning at the intrusion, Clay raised his voice, 'I wish I knew where this fits in the picture.'

The customer yelled, 'But you're charging for horse piss, calling it coffee. I've got consumer rights.'

'You reckon,' the cook shouted back. 'I burnt those with da fuckin' coffee. Fuck off, 'fore I call the cops. Your bullshit is messin' up my floor.' He gave a belly laugh.

Hut said, 'You mentioned you were looking for a connection between him and Orson Plummer?'

'Really? What the hell did you buggers pour down my throat last night? And look at you both, not a thing wrong with either of you. Where's the bloody justice in this world?'

They picked up their long blacks. They weren't eating. Perhaps they were not as well as he'd assumed. Clay poured tea, his usual preference for the day's first hot drink.

Hut said, 'When you said Plummer's name, I was curious, eh. Lottie mentioned him. Said she'd got rid of a controlling bastard. We ran background on him. I don't know why, bloody nosiness I guess.'

'Anything that might help me?' Clay sounded hopeful.

Hut explained Plummer sold the plans for technology he was working on when he was in the States. 'That was long before Lottie met him in Australia. He made a killing out of it. All hush-hush, so much so, he hired his own security firm to keep it that way.' She looked at Rivers.

He said, 'O'Malley and Co., an outfit based in Charlottesville Virginia, created a tight security ring around and inside Plummer's lab. Being a local firm, they'd done contract security and been advisers to the CIA.'

'What the hell was he making?' Clay asked. 'Nuclear weaponry?'

'Not quite,' Rivers replied. 'Plummer had shared in plans for a machine that could fly a single person – safe take-off, navigation, flying and safe landing. He saw military implications and took to developing an armed and armored prototype.'

'Bit like that show on the telly in the sixties,' Clay said, smiling, 'without the firepower. What was it called?'

Hut said, '*The Jetsons* – the space age family.'

'*The Jetsons*. Enjoyed that almost as much as *The Flintstones*,' Clay said.

Rivers continued, 'He's called the military version the Jetson.'

'I imagine,' Clay said, 'the security surrounded military...'

Rivers interrupted. 'He sold out to the Chinese military. The strict secrecy was down to the extremely unpatriotic action involved. Plummer didn't want that out at any cost. Many Americans consider they owe the Chinese so much money they're now effectively owned by China. If he'd sold to the American government, the money would've stayed in their economy. They might've had military advantage for

Navy Seals flying under the radar – literally.'

Clay asked, 'You guys think O'Rourke had something to do with this?'

'Before his time,' said Rivers. 'But it was Ultan's father's firm.'

'What's with the name change?'

'News of the deal was leaked. Then old man O'Malley went missing. Plummer's security was so watertight it was rumoured O'Malley senior had leaked the news himself – perhaps a pang of conscience, perhaps it was greed.'

'Greed?' asked Clay.

'Market analysts assessed the deal as worth a billion dollars. It was cheap for the Chinese – they had exclusive production and distribution rights. O'Malley may have felt his contribution had been undervalued.'

'Lottie would've had no idea,' Hut said. 'She knew Plummer was rich but not that rich.'

'So Ultan O'Malley became Ultan O'Rourke and moved to Sydney. Would he have met up with Plummer?'

Hut looked dubious. 'Given the lack of a happy ending, seems unlikely. We dredged the archive files but can't see any connection between the two. You're the first person to think there might be.'

'Just a theory. Not one I'm strongly attracted to.' He set out the idea of O'Rourke helping Plummer to enter New Zealand illegally.

'If he was a vindictive bastard,' said Hut, 'Plummer was more likely to go after O'Rourke than his ex-wife. He'd visit the sins of the father on the son.' She sat back in her chair. 'No. I reckon what Lottie took him for was no more than a bag of crisps, from his point of view.'

'Shit,' Clay said. 'This isn't the secret I was hoping to uncover.' He turned to Rivers. 'You said before, O'Rourke was obsessed with secrecy and security. I wouldn't have thought that made him the best qualified to be a journalist.'

Hut said, 'Makes him well qualified in terms of protecting a source.'

'That reminds me...' Clay pulled Wheeler's photo from his jacket. 'Hut tells me Lottie may have had a news source that concerned her.' He passed the photo to Rivers. 'Have you seen him before?'

Rivers had a long look, shook his head. 'No. Pretty sure I haven't seen him before.'

'Believed to have work for Statistics,' Clay prompted.

'Plenty of people there I haven't met, but enough I'm on good terms with. I can make enquiries. Email me the photo. I'll see what I can do.'

Hut said, 'You were saying last night Wheeler wanted that disk back from Lottie.'

'Well, Jonno Hart was definite about that. Though I had a feeling he had something else to tell. Seemed like he and Lottie got on, though.'

Hut said, 'Took a while to build trust, eh. You leave your card?'

'Initially, he dropped it outside the door. Told me he had no need for a honky lawyer. I've been called shonky before, but not honky.'

56

FISK ASKED, 'WHAT DID the accused tell you about the extent of professional competition between himself and Lottie?'

Ultan O'Rourke stood tall in a buttoned tweed jacket over a black roll-neck sweater. He lifted his head. 'He told me they both knew they were fishin' competitively in the same small story pond. He thought it added to their stress levels.'

'And how, according to the accused, did this competition and stress affect the couple?'

'You'll understand,' O'Rourke said, 'I only formed such views from the things Ben said, and to be fair, he didn't say a lot.'

'But?' Fisk asked as a prompt.

'He did say it got pretty fierce at times.'

Fisk whispered something to his junior, who handed him a folder. 'You did tell Detective Sergeant Black you met Lottie Kaye in their Akaroa house?'

'I did. Once, not long after she bought the place – a couple of years ago.'

'What views did you form?'

'I thought they were a lovin' pair.' He sipped water placed on the ledge of the witness box.

Fisk asked, 'Did he say anything else about their discussions?'

'He said the only work-related conversations they had were about bitchin' staff, who was complainin' about management and who wasn't, who was offerin' sexual favours for significant by-lines and so on.'

Fisk said, 'Go on.'

'Ben said they didn't talk about their respective business finances, stories, potential stories or business management issues. They were frightened to watch the TV news together for fear one would find a deeper line of enquiry that needed to be kept from the other.'

'Who initiated this level of secrecy between them?'

'I believe Ben said Lottie did.'

Fisk smirked at the jury.

'Did the accused identify other difficulties in his relationship with the deceased?'

O'Rourke sipped more water. 'He said the commute to and from Auckland didn't help. He'd hoped it would be a case of keepin' their relationship vital but she'd said it didn't quite work like that. Physical exhaustion, mental tiredness – they played their part.'

'Evidence has been given of Viagra found in the Akaroa house. Did the defendant ever indicate he was suffering from erectile dysfunction?'

'I wouldn't imagine that to be a popular topic of conversation between men.'

Laughter reverberated around the rimu panels of the courtroom.

'Do you know if…'

Inkwell said, 'Mr Fisk, your use of the word "if" suggests you're asking a witness to speculate. Perhaps it's time to move on?'

'Indeed, Your Honour.'

'Do you recall a time at *The People* office when you were unable to access staff files? Tell us about that and when that happened.'

'The week before Lottie was killed, we'd failed to meet a deadline for staff salary reviews. The union was pressin' us. I needed access to the files, which were kept in a locked cabinet in my office. The key was missin' and I asked Ben if he had one. He didn't. I searched extensively for the key and asked a number of people – without success.'

'Did you get access to the files?'

'Eventually. I'd rung two locksmiths but had no luck. I can't remember why, but we were havin' some buildin' alterations done on our floor. I asked Ben about breakin' into the cabinet, using a crowbar – force the lock, as it were. He said, given the urgency, there was no better alternative.'

'You used a builder's tool?'

'Shouldn't have, but things were gettin' a bit urgent. We needed to show we were serious – takin' action.'

'The accused watched you break in successfully?'

'He did.'

What did you subsequently do with the crowbar?'

'Put it back in the bundle of tools.'

'You do that in front of Mr Tyler?'

'I believe so. It was hardly a grand gesture. We're talking a matter of a couple of metres.'

'Presumably the builder took the tools away.'

'No. We still have them. He was arrested for forgin' his qualifications. He hasn't come back yet.'

'At some point you were visited by the police?'

'The same time I noticed the crowbar was missin'.'

'You say missing. Are you sure someone didn't shift the tools?'

'Absolutely. We checked.'

The murmur from the public gallery was loud and Fisk shot a glance at the jury. Sasha hoped they remembered the four crowbars in court yesterday, common as hammers and nails.

When it was quiet again, Fisk asked, 'Did you tell the police it was missing?'

'Not immediately. I had to think about the timin', etcetera. By the time they came, it was common knowledge Lottie had been beaten with a heavy blunt instrument. I thought I'd better tell them.'

'Thank you, Mr O'Rourke.' A little lilt of joy in Fisk's voice. 'Please answer defence counsel's questions now, will you.'

Sasha looked at the clock above the jury box. Inkwell took the hint. 'I think that's a convenient time for refreshments.'

Hoping for news from Clay, Sasha heard urgency in his voice message to call him back.

'Well, it's another piece slotting into the big puzzle,' she said. 'We're taking big hits here and as we suspected, I'm going to have to go after O'Rourke when we resume. What the hell's happened to your voice?'

'Various parts of my anatomy are casualties of chemical warfare. Let's say I'm considering joining the temperance movement.'

She scrawled a note for Delia. The site this Hut woman gave would be a good start for research.

'And here I am, trying desperately to save a man's future, and you're swanning around Auckland having fun.' She turned away from Delia and dropped her voice, 'Are you missing me?' A frustrating crackling sound. She looked at the screen. The call time was still running. 'Clay, are you there?'

No response.

A second identity for O'Rourke would interest the jury but it wouldn't get them far. She dashed to the loo, thinking about apparent coincidences underpinning this case – the so-called accident Vern Washbrook saw, then a tow trucker on hand, all not being well with Lottie in the fortnight before her death. Secret communications channels, paranoia about spying. What sort of a story was big enough to have the SIS or the GCSB involved? Could O'Rourke, with his background, be a fit for that?

These and other flights of fancy danced across her cortex as Inkwell charged up the few steps to her seat, keen to see the trial moved to a conclusion. Sasha didn't blame her. She and Fisk had squabbled like siblings in a supermarket while a long-suffering mother did her best to keep the peace.

57

SASHA NEEDED TO GET under the self-assuredness that O'Rourke had oozed from the witness box. He'd enjoyed the opportunity to perform, charming the jury with his Irish brogue. She asked Delia to hand her the product of her internet search, three sheets of paper she'd run off on her portable printer.

'Mr O'Rourke,' Sasha said with a puzzled look. She pretended to read the sheets for long enough to let him and the jury become curious, but not so long to provoke a rebuke from the judge. She put the papers down and folded her arms. 'How long have you been known by that name?'

Fisk whispered something inaudible to Zoe.

O'Rourke blinked, looked at Fisk. 'I don't follow your question.'

She cocked her head and delivered Mac's 'Really?', nailing it this time. 'I suspect the questions might get more difficult, Mr O'Rourke.' This drew hearty laughter from the gallery, but not from the jury. They sensed something was up. 'Now you've had a little time to think, perhaps the truth will be forthcoming.'

Fisk jumped up, objected to the appropriateness of the statement, said suggestions to the contrary were baseless.

Inkwell said, 'Let's just get on with it.'

O'Rourke said, 'For a long time. Is this a roundabout way of askin' how old I am?'

An ego here, but sparring wasn't always a good thing in the witness box. 'I don't need to use a roundabout way, Mr O'Rourke. When did you stop calling yourself O'Malley?'

He looked at Fisk.

'The prosecutor doesn't know, Mr O'Rourke. At the moment, you and the defence team are the only ones who do.'

O'Rourke stared. 'Well now, you'd be the one tellin' the story, Ms Stace.'

Irritated, Inkwell said, 'Answer the question.'

'About seven years ago. It was when I left Virginia, after completing my MBA.'

'Your passport is in the name of O'Malley or O'Rourke?'

'O'Malley.'

It occurred to Sasha that his degree from Oxford and his MBA would also be in that name. He'd have had to explain the discrepancy in his CV material.

'You haven't legally changed your name by deed poll. Is that because you didn't want the change on a public register?'

'In a manner of speakin', yes.'

'Your personal documents say one thing but you tell everyone something different. Yes?'

'You could put it like that, I suppose.'

'You've engaged in deceptive conduct for seven years, have you not?'

'Not to achieve any dishonest outcome, I assure you. Somethin' happened with my family in Virginia that led to me changin' my name and leavin' the US.'

Sasha didn't want the whole story out. It might give O'Rourke the opportunity to build trust with the jury.

'That family situation involved a Mr Orson Plummer, did it not?'

'Yes.'

Fisk objected on the grounds of relevance.

Sasha said that the prosecutor knew it was relevant because investigators checked on Plummer's movements as part of their enquiries. The judge waved for her to continue.

'It's correct, isn't it, that Plummer and the deceased were once married in Sydney, where, as a journalist, you wrote about them.'

He looked wary. 'I think so.'

Sasha asked the attendant to approach and take a document. 'I suggest you know so, Mr O'Rourke. Look at this article you wrote in October 2003 for the *Sydney Morning Herald*.'

O'Rourke took the document from the attendant, then looked up.

'In that article you described a public and acrimonious divorce between Lottie and Plummer, did you not?'

'I remember now, yes.'

'You estimated, based on a commercial transaction years earlier involving your father, that Plummer got off lightly in the divorce?'

'I believe he did.'

'And recently, Plummer has become a member of the board of Montague Media?'

'He has, yes.'

Sasha had established she knew about his background. Using the rest of Clay's information, she got two concessions from O'Rourke. He was concerned Plummer might come after him and that his father felt he had been short-changed in the deal, that Plummer had been greedy. His use of that word was a bonus.

O'Rourke denied, however, knowing anything about the police enquiries into Plummer.

Until now, she'd been reasonably sure of her ground, as any good advocate would be. O'Rourke confirmed the good oil Clay came up with, presumably because he thought Sasha knew more than she did.

'Did you not tell police before Ben was arrested, you thought Plummer might have been responsible for killing Lottie?'

After a pause, he said, 'I can't remember'.

Sasha poured incredulity into her response. 'You can't remember?'

He shook his head.

She suspected he was worried about the existence of a police job sheet that showed he had said that, hence the lack of an outright denial. That was good enough.

'You had a reporter attend the scene on the night of the murder, didn't you?'

'Yes. As a matter of fact, she's sittin' right here.' He nodded towards the media box. The woman smiled. But this wasn't who Sasha had seen on the news clip.

'Just the one reporter to cover this case for *The People*?'

'We're not made of money, Ms Stace,' O'Rourke said with fake indignation.

She tried not to show her confusion and paused to signal a change of tack. 'At one time you owned, did you not, a white boiler suit?'

'I had a pair of overalls I used for paintin'.'

'White?'

'By the time they were stolen, they had many colours on them, Ms Stace.'

'And you told Ben they went missing in the days before the deceased was killed?'

'I'm not sure of the timin'.'

'And the day you told him about them going missing was the day of Lottie's funeral. Yes?'

'I can't remember.'

'He knew you owned them?'

'Yes. I thought he'd be interested.'

'On the day of his wife's funeral?'

'It was simply a harmless distraction.'

'So you're not implying today that you lent them to Ben, are you?'

'Of course not.'

'Or that he stole them?'

'Certainly not.'

In your pre-trial deposition, did you not estimate your painting outfit went missing a week before Lottie was killed?'

'I may have.'

Sasha asked Delia to hand her O'Rourke's deposition. 'Would you like me to read it to you?'

O'Rourke rolled his left shoulder. 'No. Now you mention it, I remember it was about the time I had a visit from Montague's counsel. She came to obtain my signature on an affidavit for legal proceedin's that needed to be filed that day.'

Sasha looked at Delia who whispered, 'An employment case.'

Sasha covered her mouth. 'You could've told me.' She looked back at O'Rourke. 'My co-counsel, here?'

'Indeed. She was very helpful, Ms Stace.'

When the laughter at her expense died, Sasha said, 'You told the prosecutor that when the police came calling at *The People* you mentioned the missing crowbar.'

'I did.'

'You used that crowbar a week before Lottie Kaye was killed. Is that your evidence?'

'That's as I remember it.'

'You had no reason to check on its whereabouts every day.'

'Of course not.'

'You couldn't swear exactly when it went missing could you?'

'No.'

'It could well have been in your office on the day of the murder and sometime after?'

'I don't know.'

'But you had no qualms about pointing the finger of suspicion at your boss?'

'I don't think that's fair. I wasn't doin' that.'

'No? More diverting focus away from you perhaps?'

'I didn't need to do that either, Ms Stace.'

Throughout her questioning of O'Rourke, Fisk sat back with his arms crossed. She could imagine the smug expression on his face.

'You told the jury that you visited Lottie in the Akaroa house about a couple of years ago. Is that right?'

'I did.'

'Just the two of you there at that time?'

'I think that's pretty unlikely, but I don't recall. I've had no reason to recall that.'

'Let's look at more recent times. You and your partner visited Lottie and Ben in Akaroa six weeks before she was murdered?'

'A social occasion, yes.'

'Am I right in saying you instigated that?'

'I don't recall that, just that we had a nice time.'

'If you had to, could you describe the layout of the house?'

'At a pinch.'

She had O'Rourke look at the police photos. 'It has a little nook about three metres from the back door, to the left as you enter. Is that right?'

'Yes, I believe so.'

She now had what she needed – enough to show he was familiar with the layout to help make murderous plans. There was a fine line between asking too few and too many questions.

'On the afternoon of the day Lottie was killed, you weren't at work, were you?'

'I was ill.'

'There in the morning, gone in the afternoon.'

'That's the nature of gastroenteritis, I'm afraid.' His confidence was back.

'You saw a doctor about this?'

'I didn't intend to, but by 5 p.m. I was no better after restin' so I took myself off to the doctor. Within a short time, I was admitted to hospital.' He gave Sasha a sly smile. 'I was kept in overnight.'

Oh, Jesus! What had she done? Fisk faced his junior but his broad smile was for the jury.

Sasha thanked O'Rourke and sat down, trying hard to conceal how she now felt.

Fisk delivered the coup de grace. 'Do you have any record of that overnight stay?'

O'Rourke pulled a document from his tweed jacket, his discharge sheet, and produced it as an exhibit. It didn't matter that it failed to prove he'd stayed in the hospital for the whole time. She'd walked straight into Fisk's trap.

58

'YOU TOOK YOUR TIME, mate,' Clay said.

'Mate. I'm not your fuckin' PA, you know. This is unpaid and dirty work.' Davo emphasised every third word with a meeting of his upper and lower jaws. 'And I had to call in favors from Kiwi mates. You owe me big time, fella. Real big.'

'A man's life might hang on this, but I'm grateful.'

'So, how many sheep have you've shagged so far? I hear them ewes are more fuckin' frightened of you than a farmer's dog. Mind you, Kiwi ewes – not the same as ours for courage.'

In his mind, Clay saw his Sydney cricket mate Al Davidson grinning at the other end of the line: a short man, a torso like a seed potato on steroids, wiry limbs that seem to go everywhere. He sported a haircut that made him look like the survivor of a severe electric shock.

'Anyway,' Davo continued, 'you need to get near a fax in the next five minutes. Or has that technology not yet arrived in the Shaky Isles?'

'They have email here, mate.'

'Fuck. You come down in the last shower? That's where the spooks live. They don't monitor faxes any more.'

An hour later, Clay had the dates, times and numbers of the calls made to and from Orson Plummer's Sydney home, and his mobile, in October last year. The same for Ultan O'Rourke and Ben Tyler. Everything entered into a spreadsheet and sorted by frequency. Using the telephone directory, he cross-referenced the New Zealand codes after +64; the Australian ones he knew. Calls and texts between Tyler's and O'Rourke's mobiles all occurred within normal business hours. Nothing unusual and certainly no contacts between Tyler and Plummer. But the worst news, no link whatsoever between Plummer and O'Rourke. Frustrated, Clay drank a Diet Coke, belched almost immediately. He had his big favour ticket well clipped and got bugger all to show for it.

He rang Sean Felan's office. The girl at the front desk sounded as though she had a heavy-duty clip pinching her nostrils. She thought her boss was down at the King Street court. 'What's your name, again?' she asked. 'Spell it out for me, please.'

Clay complied, asked if she was new. Both of Felan's staff had known who he was for the last twenty years.

'As a matter of fact, I'm a temp. It's a good agency.'

'Will you get him to call me, please?'

'On what number?'

'My mobile,' Clay snapped.

'Does Mr Fegan have that?'

'Your boss's name is Felan, Sean Felan, and yes, he's had my mobile number ever since mobile phones became available.'

In an hour, Clay read the *Herald*, front to back, focused on the quarter-page story of the trial in Christchurch. It looked like Tyler was getting a hiding at the hands of the prosecutor, but little coverage was given to Sasha's line of questioning. Then he remembered the newspaper was from an opposing stable to Tyler's. He tossed it aside and was struck by a craving for decent coffee.

At the kitchenette, a two-ring hob, an old pop-up toaster and a kettle, cutlery the Salvation Army would refuse. He fingered through the little wooden box with tea and coffee sachets. Instant only. Then he noticed the television was bolted to the wall. What chance would a coffee plunger have? The whole interior wasn't worth more than a hundred bucks.

He decided to go in search of something drinkable. His mobile vibrated on the bedside table. Felan. The coffee run would wait.

'My secretary impressed upon me the urgency in your tone.'

'Ah. Mr Fegan, is it?'

'What?'

'Your temp. She's been as accurate in expressing my tone as she was in remembering the name of her boss.'

'Hard to get good help, mate. You'd know if you had a real job. We've been invaded by Kiwi women who can't speak proper – tattoos, rings and studs on or in every visible orifice, and Christ knows where else.'

'You come across Ultan O'Rourke when you were hobnobbing with the literati of the media world?'

'The literati are in another world altogether. Many of the media, those describing themselves as reporters, are in fact, illiterate. They know how to ask impertinent questions but that's about it. Mr Ultan O'Rourke found this out not long after he arrived on these shores.'

'You acted for him?'

'No. McAdam QC. Met him?'

'Not that I can recall.'

'Trust me. You would recall. Rupert McAdam not only looks like a British bulldog, he's got the loving slobber to go with it. The fortunate few who are warned come equipped with surgical masks. I'm sure the silk believes most of his colleagues divide their time between law and medicine. Anyway, the old bulldog managed to get O'Rourke out of a large hole. In a story intended for the *Sydney Morning Herald* O'Rourke accused a New Zealand Cabinet minister in the previous government of favouring a crony in a tender. If memory serves, new security equipment for their paid eavesdroppers, that sort of shit. To add insult to injury, O'Rourke questioned the minister's sexual proclivities, and I'm not talking about batting for the other side. Reckoned said minister gave new meaning to the term "under age".'

'How come they don't know anything about that over here?'

'You're in New Zealand. You need to ask that question?' Felan's tone suggested Clay was the class dunce.

'Seriously, mate, a story like that is incendiary, to say the least. Everyone'd be talking about it.'

'O'Rourke and the *SMH* got injuncted before it ran,' Felan said, disappointment in his tone. 'It's been confined to the Montague vault, despite rumors of copious corroboration on both counts. What's your interest in O'Rourke?'

Clay updated him on O'Rourke's story and suggested the Irishman might have friends in the current New Zealand government.

'Not an unreasonable conclusion,' Felan said. 'The truth is, O'Rourke is in the government's debt. Montague over here didn't have the stomach for the legal fight. Well, that's the official reason they gave for hanging O'Rourke out to dry. Certain New Zealand opposition politicians who were privy to O'Rourke's story are now government ministers. Not only did they fund the bulldog to defend him, but they gave him the home straight to run in when it came to a new tender for that security technology I mentioned. They bought themselves a new crony. Had to, having compromised the other outfit.'

'Hang on. I'm confused. O'Rourke ran a damning story on a New Zealand minister in the National government. And now the government supports him?'

'The current New Zealand government supports him because they fed him the story when they were in opposition. However, it cost O'Rourke his job and credibility. Because the story also burned a security company, they ensured he was rewarded when the time came. The new outfit's called Soter Security.'

'And this is O'Rourke's company?'

'Well, the names of his mother and brother are on all the papers. However, not long after his mother came out to Sydney the poor old duck was stricken with dementia. Thought every man was her long-lost husband. She's in that outfit resurrected by Sasha Stace a few years back.'

'Garden View.'

'That's the one. O'Rourke's brother is back in the States running one of those trendy rehab clinics the Yanks are so fond of. Between the two of them they know as much about security as you and I.'

59

IT HAD BEEN A tough first week but with the next witness sworn in, Sasha was looking forward to scoring important points.

Fisk said, 'Please describe your relationship with the deceased, Lottie Kaye.'

Michelle Vercoe, tall, in her mid-thirties had the looks of a model. The brown hair that touched her shoulders was fortified by enough chemicals to warrant a health and safety inspector's improvement notice. She had enviable cheekbones and wore fire engine red lipstick.

Her voice, though, was nasal. 'I first met her about two years ago when Ben brought her to a charity function sponsored by *The People*.' She brushed the left lapel of a cream designer suit jacket that permitted a discreet show of cleavage. 'We got on well and maintained phone contact when she lived in Auckland.'

Fisk asked, 'Was there a point last year when she confided in you about her relationship with her husband?'

'Yes. About a year ago, I'd said to her in a couple of calls that she seemed flat. It was her tone. I told her I thought she sounded depressed.'

Fisk's expression feigned concern. 'What did she say?'

'Lottie said she knew Ben didn't love her, she was sure he was seeing someone else. She said, in a way, she still loved him but he wouldn't divorce her.'

'Did she tell you what she planned to do?'

'She told me she'd make it easy for him. She didn't want a repeat of the awful divorce experience she'd had with her first husband. She felt a failure.'

'Make it easy?'

'Yes. She would initiate a divorce but needed to tell him face to face – in Akaroa.'

'Did she seem apprehensive about that conversation?'

'Very much so. She said she'd seen him go berserk when he didn't get what he wanted and she was sure it was only her finances keeping him in the relationship.'

Judging by the gasps and talk coming from the back of the court, many people thought this was the death knell to the defence. They'd heard Fisk promise there was a four million dollar motive and now he'd delivered. The attendant called for silence. Sasha and Delia glanced at each other, both poker-faced. The loud chatter continued. It prompted a bellow from the attendant, a second call for silence.

Fisk enjoying the commotion, turned and smirked. 'You can take it from here.'

Sasha started to ask her first question before she was upright. 'In the last six months of Lottie Kaye's life, how frequently would you have spoken to her by phone?'

'Three times a week. I was concerned for her.'

'You're a photographer at *The People*, are you not?'

Michelle Vercoe looked pleased with herself. 'Senior photographer. I won a Qantas Media Award for the paper last year.'

'Congratulations. You rang the deceased from your work or personal phone?'

'Personal.'

'Never work?'

'No. That wouldn't be appropriate.'

'Quite so. From your home phone or your personal mobile?'

'With three-dollar calls, I'm sure it was the land line.'

'You have only the one mobile phone?'

'Yes. A monthly plan.' She offered perfect teeth for the camera, smile.

'In the last six months before she died, how often would she have called you?'

'Once or twice. It tended to be the other way.'

'You calling her?'

'Yes.'

Sasha asked the attendant to hand the witness a sheet of paper. 'I won't read your numbers out loud in open court, but please confirm the numbers on that paper are your home and mobile numbers.'

The witness took an age to do so. Sasha knew Vercoe would be wondering where this was going. Fisk's agitation suggested he too, had concerns.

'Those are your phone numbers?'

The early smiling had ceased. Now it was a look of wariness, knowledge of a trap but not where it was laid. Vercoe said, tentative, 'That's correct.'

'No others?'

'No. No others.'

'Lottie Kaye called you once or twice in the last six months. How often did you call her?'

Fisk did the exasperated pen and table thing and stood. 'Your Honour, will there be no end to counsel's irrelevant fishing excursions?'

He was giving his witness more time to think. The judge told Michelle Vercoe she could answer.

'I didn't count.'

'You say you were concerned for her?'

'Of course. She was affected by Ben's attitude towards her.'

'You were concerned, but you didn't call her at all in the last six months of her life and she didn't call you. Correct?'

Fisk objected to the two questions.

Sasha said, 'Let's just focus on your calls to her then, shall we?'

'I don't think that's right.'

Sasha asked for the attendant again. He handed the witness another document, a printout of Vercoe's phone records for the two numbers. Calls made and received for the numbers she agreed were hers.

Sasha said, 'We've written Lottie Kaye's phone numbers at the top of each of those pages. Will you accept from me, that you neither made nor received any call from her?'

Vercoe blushed and kept her head down, pretending to check off all the numbers. Sasha hoped the jury would see it.

Sasha said, 'It would be understandable for you to get a bit tired of caring for your boss's wife, wouldn't it?'

'I got incredibly busy, distracted I suppose. I thought it was a lot more.'

'More than zero?'

'Yes.'

'This distraction you had. Are you saying you were distracted by your boss, Ben Tyler.'

'No. With work,' she said, annoyed.

'You found Ben attractive, didn't you?'

Vercoe glanced to the well of the court where Ben sat flanked by two prison officers. 'He's an attractive man, in a rugged sort of way.'

'You went after him didn't you?'

'I don't know what you mean.'

'My apologies. I'll be clearer. You pursued him for a sexual relationship, did you not?'

Her jaw dropped. 'No. Of course not. I was sympathetic to his wife.'

'Ever write to him in what might now be called the old-fashioned way, pen on paper?'

'Not that I can recall. Email is so easy now, no one does that.'

Fisk whispered to Zoe, 'How have you missed this?'

'Please, look at this document.' Sasha waited. 'That's your handwriting, yes?'

'It looks like mine, yes.'

'Did you send it to Ben?'

'I suppose so.'

Sasha read, '"Dear Ben, why are you ignoring me? It's not fair. Please, cancel on Lottie. Let's get away one Friday night. She'll never know".' Sasha paused. 'There's another line. Do I have to read it?'

Vercoe sneered. 'Please yourself. I never meant it.'

Sasha read each word slowly. 'The other line said, "I dream of you inside me. Make my dream come true." And you signed that, "Love Chelle". Correct?'

'He asked me to write that. He said it would be a turn on.'

Sasha smiled. 'Of course he did.' She asked that copies be handed to the jury.

'So turned on that he never took up your invitation on a Friday or any other night, Ms Vercoe?'

'No.'

'What did he do with the note, did he say?'

'I don't remember.'

'He showed it to Lottie, didn't he?'

She scowled. 'I don't know – ask her.'

There was a collective intake of gasps around the court. It was a good place to finish. Sasha sat down and looked at the jury, giving them the tiniest of headshakes along with an appropriate look of disgust. She expected Fisk to get her to say that Ben initiated a relationship but he wanted her out of the court as soon as possible. He had no re-examination.

Sasha with her back to Michelle Vercoe, whispered to Delia, 'Game, set and match.' Vercoe stopped her courtroom exit at Sasha's table. 'Think you're clever, eh?' she said.

Sasha spun around to find Vercoe withdrawing papers from her handbag, tears of rage washing over a contorted face. She slapped two photos on the table in front of Sasha. One captured a woman, face on to the lens. Delia. Another photo, side profile, showed Delia and Ben kissing. It was dated and timed the afternoon of the murder. They were high-quality digital shots. There was no mistake.

Sasha gawped at the photo, searched for signs of reluctance in either of them, hoping this was a case of the camera lying – an unfortunate but misleading moment. Her hope was in vain. They were tight in their embrace, feeding on each other – no mistake about mutual intent and desire. Sasha turned them face down on the table. Delia reached out but Sasha nailed them to the table with a closed fist.

'Has he not tried it on with you?' Michelle Vercoe screeched over the courtroom din. 'My guess is, it won't be long. You'd still be within his age range – at the outer edge.'

Ben's words in her mind – You're still hot, Sash. I hope you realise that.

The attendant moved towards them, calling for silence. Amid the cacophony around her, Sasha was the only one complying. She couldn't speak. Vercoe turned and strode away. Fisk now stood in front of Sasha and ripped the photos from under her hand. 'We'll have those, thank you.'

60

IN THE CAB TO her office, a distance easily covered by a walk, Sasha said nothing. Her eye caught the tariff card fixed to the passenger side of the dashboard. The fine for vomiting in the cab was set at $350. She took a deep breath, tried not to swallow.

When Michelle Vercoe dropped her bomb the judge offered an early adjournment. Sasha left Delia without telling her what had happened. She was in no hurry to ease her junior's shock. Delia might know intuitively, although Sasha had no doubt that Fisk would share the news with glee. All she told her was to seek a longer adjournment if necessary. Nothing about what she was doing or where she was going. Similarly with Ben. Just a command for him to follow her. Now, he sat in the front seat of the cab, pretending nothing was wrong, answering the driver's inane prattle – political news and what was wrong with Maori being dependent on Pakeha.

'Never works,' the driver said, glancing at Ben. Rat-like, the driver twitched his nose, as if a hair was tickling him. 'Look at what the Aussies did for the Abos all those years ago. Built them lovely new houses. What did they do? They dug up the floorboards and ripped out the window sashes for firewood, didn't they? To say nothing of them shitting in the corners of their rooms. Nah, mate. Give people something for nothing, never works.'

At her office, Sasha gave the driver a twenty-dollar note and told him to keep the change. It was twice the fare but Sasha didn't care.

Striding inside, Sasha barked at Kate. 'No calls, tea or coffee. We're not staying.'

Wide eyed, Kate gave a single nod.

Sasha slammed the door behind Ben and stared at him.

His face was a picture of innocence and angst.

'Well,' she shouted, 'what the fuck was that about?'

'What? The cab driver?'

She realised he hadn't seen the photo. It didn't leave Fisk's hands before Inkwell adjourned. Sasha explained, finished with, 'So don't even think of feeding me bullshit about an innocent explanation. Not when you had your fucking tongue down her fucking throat. And if that's not bad enough, it was taken the afternoon Lottie was murdered.'

He stepped towards her.

She recoiled.

'I can explain. She...'

With all the derision Sasha could muster, she said, 'Oh, you can explain – that fucking cliché. You know what that says, don't you? Another full load of shit coming down the pipe at me as if I haven't had enough already. After all I said to you, to Delia, to your general manager. I was clear. Couldn't have been clearer. You can't deny that. I said if you lied to me, I'd be gone. You accepted the condition. There was no argument. And what have you done? You've fucking lied to me and deceived me again. Sydney revisited. After all I said about not wanting this case, what do you do? You play me like you were playing me at your place, telling me I've still got it. Telling me, I'm still hot.

'And me?' Sasha pointed at herself. 'What did I do? I let you kiss me. Christ, I feel sick. You knew I needed to hear those things and you manipulated me, played me big time. You've lied right up to the trial. To think I believed you when you told me Viagra was to help you overcome work stress so you could perform. All the while it was to help you fuck two women. Christ, what was I thinking? That leopards change their spots? Well, it's over. It's fucking well over. I'm off the case.'

Ben inhaled deeply. As he let out his treacherous breath, he asked, in a soft voice, whether he could say something.

Sasha remained silent.

'I'm innocent, Sasha. I'm innocent. I did not kill my wife.'

He stared at her and she stared back.

'For what it's worth,' he said, voice still soft, 'Delia came to me. We got on well when we did that employment case. Later she rang me out of the blue. God knows, I made it clear I was with Lottie. She asked me questions about her, about us, sympathised about her commute, about the difficulties of a relationship with partners geographically separated. Over drinks, she flirted with me. She's attractive. I was flattered. Very flattered. I admit it, I was weak. I succumbed.'

He pitched this with an apologetic tone but she felt immune, inured to his plea.

Undeterred, he continued. 'Look, I'm a weak bastard, but I did not kill Lottie.'

'Well, you tell me,' Sasha said, 'what would you do now, in my place? If you'd told a client, if there was any lie, any deceit, you'd be gone?'

He looked out the window, the first time he'd broken eye contact, then back at her. 'I hope I'd always see the big picture. I hope I'd remember that people lie for all sorts of reasons, not least of which is the fear of embarrassment, to avoid an imminent threat. I'd hope, when I uncovered a lie, I'd stand back and take a fresh look at the ultimatum I'd given. Maybe ask myself whether a client, desperate for the best possible lawyer on a horrible charge, could've done anything but agree to any condition I asked for. All I'll say is, if you walk away, you've done no more than you said you would. But I'm innocent.' He dropped his voice to a whisper. 'Walking away from me ought not to be the same thing as walking away from my defence.'

61

THEY WALKED BACK TO court separately. Sasha, with leaden feet, gave Ben a head start. Kate, bless her, attempted to comfort her. She heard all of what Sasha said, but little of Ben. Sasha told her what he'd said when she'd challenged him.

Kate said, 'Forgive us our trespasses as we forgive those who trespass against us.'

Sasha expressed surprise Kate knew the Lord's Prayer.

'We were made to say it every day, in school assembly,' Kate said, her tone flat. 'Now I'd say forgive, but don't forget.'

Metres from the courthouse, Sasha saw Fisk and Black sharing a joke. They looked like two men who knew the curtain was about to fall on their triumphant production. She tried to ring Mac but couldn't get an answer. If ever she needed his advice, no time was more important than now.

And yet, despite how he'd felt about her taking this case, she intuitively knew what he'd say. Walking away wasn't the answer. Criminal law hadn't changed. Nothing had changed except her attitude to deceit. Mac would say police sometimes perjured themselves in misguided efforts to lessen their burden of proof. That it was too much to expect defendants to be better, to always tell the whole truth, with no minimising culpability.

Forgive but don't forget. In a way, those four simple words from her PA helped reboot her thinking. That, and Mac's example. He'd never walked away from a problem in his life.

Something else came to her as she walked back to court. She had dropped the necessity for professional detachment and replaced it with irrational naivety. Yes, people with their backs to the wall would lie. Taking responsibility for behaviour was an anathema in the world of criminal justice but it didn't mean those prone to lying should be deprived of a defence. Even Ben could see that. *Walking away from me ought not to be the same thing as walking away from my defence.* She'd believed her own maturity would give her insight, when all along, she'd been judging and condemning those who'd offended her personal code.

Back in the courtroom she was thinking options. Withdraw or continue. Withdraw was justified for all the reasons she'd said but with judicial ambition destroyed, and no outcome for her. What a waste. Continue with what now seemed a hopeless case, made so by the deceit of her client and co-counsel. What a choice.

Yet if he was innocent. The thought pushed her down the neural pathway of trial tactics from here, defusing that bomb. Fisk and Black would want the photo in as evidence. They'd argue it showed Ben's emotional state, his interest in another woman on the same afternoon his wife was killed.

She could argue it was irrelevant to the issues in the trial – that the kiss represented no more than an unprofessional crossing of boundaries. Fisk would counter-argue it was evidence of Tyler's duplicity. Maybe she'd be on more stable ground objecting to the photo's authenticity. That couldn't be proved except to recall its author, a woman now so obviously scorned and humiliated as to be unreliable, given her ability to manipulate images.

Fisk saw her return, strutted to her table. She told him what she intended and, with his canine smile, he said he welcomed the debate.

The familiar shoulder pain returned, accompanied by a thumping headache. She reached into her briefcase for the pills she needed, thinking something stronger than paracetamol was needed. A client capable of telling the truth would be a good start. For that matter, a junior counsel who had a better understanding of professionalism and a willingness to be more open. She was pill popping when an official with a worried look hurried towards her. 'We've been trying to call you, Sasha. Your phone's either been busy or off.'

She requested Sasha urgently call the charge nurse in the hospital's emergency department. As soon as she left the courtroom she punched in the numbers. When she heard the news, Sasha staggered, her knees weak, then collapsed in a waiting room chair.

62

MAC LOOKED PEACEFUL, HIS pale and lined face above a pristine white sheet, his eyes closed, never to open again. In the quiet of a private room, Sasha thought back to a time when they played hide and seek at her Glandovey Road house. He'd reveal his hiding place the moment he sensed that she was frustrated, couldn't find him. She'd have been five years old.

Delia touched her hand. She was waiting for her when Sasha got back to court, crying and full of apologies. In despair that her duplicity had been discovered, she practically begged to go to the hospital with Sasha, worried she would be permanently excised from her mentor's life. Appalled at Delia's behaviour, Sasha couldn't do that. And the sad fact of her life was, that apart from the good friend she had in Paul Diplock, engaged in a civil case next door to her trial, there were few she could immediately call on to offer moral support.

Delia's eyes were wet again. Sasha wasn't there yet. Too much adrenalin. All those thoughts about Mac dying, thoughts that would sometimes lead her to tears and now that it'd happened, she was dry-eyed.

'Give me a minute please, Delia?'

Sasha's mind was a potent mix of memories and sadness. Glandovey Road, her visits to Mac's office when he was bewigged and gowned, imitating the father she never knew, discussing trial tactics. Mac, more than any other, was responsible for nurturing her interest in the law.

Hospital staff told her that Mac had managed to ring for an ambulance and somehow left the door ajar for the paramedic to get inside the house – that he died on the way to the A&E. Where did she find comfort in that? He'd died with paramedics and not alone? Her thoughts went to his advance directive, his end of life care plan. He hadn't wanted to be resuscitated. They'd have tried. Could Mac have been stubborn enough to give up on life despite their best efforts? Would he have tried to ring her like the hospital did? She willed that last thought away.

Nicola Inkwell had been good about the situation. It wasn't customary for a judge to telephone counsel during a case but she'd called to offer condolences. She'd assured the jury that an ongoing adjournment was inevitable but unrelated to the trial and asked Sasha to keep Fisk informed of developments.

When she rang Fisk, he sounded as though he'd been drinking. 'Well, that's up to you,' he'd said, running his last three words into one. 'Seems there's no cost you're not prepared to endure to see this trial through.'

Sasha was at the point of ending the call, but asked, 'What's that supposed to mean, Quentin?'

There was a long pause. 'I've said enough about your lack of ambition. Tell me, Sasha. Given Tyler can't access his new-found riches, are you now on legal aid?'

'I don't believe for a minute you're concerned about me being paid.'

'You should have concerns about your investigator incurring unnecessary travel costs, an Auckland junket chasing wild geese. I'll be making submissions about that at the appropriate time.'

'What he's doing has nothing to do with you. You manage your grudge case and I'll manage the defence.' She ended the call with considerable regret that she'd made it.

How dare he suggest that she'd be doing something inappropriate. Outside the hospital, she braced against a scything, malevolent winter wind.

63

AT HOME, EXHAUSTED AT 10.30 p.m., Sasha could barely remember it was still Friday. She phoned Mac's son in London. He said it would be another three days before he could make it to New Zealand. He showed no sign of urgency to depart. At one point, Sasha wondered whether he would come at all. She sent a message to Inkwell to say she'd be ready to reappear Monday. She thought, if she could defend a client charged with attempted rape the day after she was raped, she could finish this trial. Mac wouldn't want her to do it any differently. As he'd said many times, 'You don't get to be good at this job without overcoming a few setbacks.' And if she wasn't walking away, she certainly didn't want to start over again.

Paul Diplock came as soon as he could. He had lovely things to say about Mac and recalled their recent conversation. He offered to speak at the funeral, something Sasha wasn't ready to think about – tomorrow's job. She'd left the sad news in a message for Clay. Ben offered to stay the night, just to have someone else in the house. She sent him and Delia on their way. They had the decency to come at different times but, with their secret out, it made little practical difference. There was a look about Delia, as if she was more concerned about her relationship with Sasha's ex than her professionalism.

Take a cup of tea to bed. She hauled herself out of the recliner, a comfort she'd always given up for Mac. He'd sometimes push himself back in the chair after they'd shared good food and wine and then fall asleep. She filled the kettle and thought about his snoring, once comforting, replaced now with a cold silence. How easily she'd give up that chair to have him back now, even to say goodbye, to tell him how much she loved him. There would be hundreds of millions of people in her situation every year, denied that desire, that ability to say goodbye. Instead, she'd kissed the cold head of a man who'd only ever been warm to her.

She dropped a lemon teabag into boiling water. Fisk entered her consciousness, an unwelcome intrusion. He'd never come and see her, or attend Mac's funeral. Or perhaps he might attend the funeral to be seen, avoid having his absence noted and adversely commented upon. That would be a knock to his ambition.

The more she told herself not to think about Fisk, the greater his intrusion on her privacy. It was like the times she woke in the night's wee hours, telling herself to go to sleep. Utterly futile.

I've said enough about your lack of ambition.

As SG, Marshall Hall wouldn't gossip about upcoming judicial appointments. Law Society? Yes, they'd be knowledgeable. Tell Quentin Fisk? No. He was persona non grata with the society at the moment. Yet he knew she'd elected to defend Ben ahead of being sworn in as a judge. This had to be Grange or Ellis.

Her heart pounded. Not good. All tiredness gone, she reached for her phone. What sort of person could be back in work mode the same day her dearly loved stepfather died?

Another call to Clay went to voice mail. 'Clay, please be careful pursuing that police job sheet about a disk. Fisk knows you're in Auckland and he'll know why. I might be out on a limb here, but I think that the disk and the AG's concerns about leaked information are connected.' She paused. 'I'm missing you. Call me when you can.'

Was the invitation to express an interest in the bench a play from the start? No. The timing was wrong and what would be gained? Grange's pressure to drop the case, her swearing in scheduled to conflict with Ben's trial – these might've been in response to pleas from Fisk.

Sasha couldn't shift the screwdriver winding and unwinding at the edge of her mind, that Fisk was behind Yuile going missing. Somehow, a close connection to the AG made the possibility of what happened to Yuile a bit more likely. Someone had the pull to muster the resources.

Her eyelids gave her a message to turn off her barnstorming brain. The radio should do it. She'd usually fall asleep listening to a calming compere or soothing music. National Radio was a good friend, never offended when she fell asleep during its late night programme.

The midnight news was all but over when she heard police had arrested a Christchurch lawyer on charges of possessing a large volume of child pornography. More work in the pipeline of disciplinary hearings.

As she went to switch off her cell phone, it trilled in her hand, too loud for the time of night. Delia.

'Sasha, sorry. I had to tell you ASAP.'

She knew why Delia was calling. You just knew. 'It's Alan Markham, isn't it? Our witness about the post-nup.'

'Yes, but how did you know? It was Markham himself who told me. His name hasn't been released.'

She paused before replying. 'I don't think the timing is a coincidence. Let's say that I've come to know Quentin Fisk and his abilities quite well.'

64

'**WASN'T SURE I'D GET** you,' the voice said. 'Me, I'm late up, late to bed, like ruru.'

'Who the hell's that?' Clay asked.

'Ruru's an owl.'

'Well, at this hour, I've got the patience of an eagle, Jonno.'

Flat tone, almost uninterested, he said, 'I hear patience has its rewards.'

'You've got something else?'

'What I don't have is a lot of my baccy left.'

Clay scratched his head. 'Royal Port, isn't it?'

'Observant. I like that. A good brand, Royal Port. Well rounded. Makes a good connection with a man's internal drive, his hard-wired needs.'

'Doesn't sound to me as though it's a fix that can wait.'

'My store's closed for renovations.'

'I'm not far from a 24/7.'

In the interior of the cab preserved by garlic breath, it took twenty minutes from Great South Road to Horopito Road via the convenience store. Clay paid the bearded, turban-wearing driver in cash and walked towards the naked bulb that enthralled a swarm of insects over Jonno's front door. About to knock, he heard the bolts slide and the door creak ajar. In the reflection of the porch light, Jonno eyed the cab suspiciously as it pulled away, then jerked his head towards the hall.

Clay walked through the same invisible but malodorous curtain of cabbage and cat. Two of the offenders screeched at each other in a room off the long hallway. In the kitchen, he took the distinctive orange plastic package from his leather jacket.

'Something to trade?' Clay said, dropping the tobacco on the table. It partially covered five interlinked heat stains, reminiscent of the Olympic rings without the colours.

Jonno shuffled to the grubby lime green cupboards above the enamel bench, reached above his head, winced in discomfort, and pulled down a Queen Anne chocolate box. It was a deep receptacle, once home to three layers of assorted confectionery in little paper cups resembling corrugated iron. Now, under the lid, disordered piles of black and white photographs. Scattered throughout, small, square, coloured pics.

Jonno said, 'You wouldn't guess I had family, would you?'

Clay picked up one photo. Three boys, bright smiles, white teeth, black hair encroaching on eyes. Each of them holding a large fish.

'Good-looking boys. Happy boys. Yours?'

Jonno's jaw tightened. 'Taken not long before they died. My biggest regret was missing them growing up.'

'What happened?' Clay asked.

'Their mother killed 'em.'

'Oh, Jesus, Jonno. I'm sorry.'

He nodded, not looking for sympathy. 'Dig in the box.'

Clay fished inside. It took him back to lucky dips at the school fair. He withdrew a hard, thin package wrapped in plain brown paper, the ends folded into envelope flaps and Scotch taped.

'Open it,' Jonno said. 'It's how she gave it to me. What that bloke wanted, I reckon, the one I told you about.'

Clay used a short fingernail to lift the edge of each piece of tape, unfolded the paper as if it were an explosive devise. He stared at the plain plastic casing, the unmarked silver disk inside. A piece of A4 paper, folded twice, sat loosely on top. A typewritten note.

To whom it may concern:

You're reading this because my good friend and neighbour Jonno Hart has trusted you to do the right thing, in the country's interests and in my interests. I can't control what happens to this disk but I respectfully ask, when the time is right, you provide its contents to my team at Uncover before anyone else in the media.

The man who recorded what's on this disk and passed it to me goes by the name of Hamish Wheeler. I don't know if that's his real name but Wheeler works under cover for the Government Communications Security Bureau posing as an IT executive for various government departments. His job has almost exclusively focused on determining the source of leaks of confidential information within the public service. Whether he serendipitously recorded this, as he says, testing new surveillance equipment, or whether he has turned against his employer, the contents of the disk speak for themselves.

'Why you, Jonno?'

Jonno drew on the nicotine, a subterranean pull on the newly lit cigarette, then lifted his head, adding smoke to the stained ceiling. 'Coupla reasons. I don't have anything to play that thing on, so I've no idea what's on it. Not interested in knowing. Also Lottie knew me well enough to know nobody would think someone like her would have anything to do with the likes of me. The cops that tried, I gave a hard time.'

'You crafty old bastard.'

Jonno produced a weak smile.

'Why now?' Clay asked.

'If anything bad happened to her, I was to give this to someone I trusted. The only cop I trust is my brother – he's out of the country. Then there was you and your lawyer arse card. I didn't think the cops would be dumb enough to pull that. And I'm not feeling brave any more. While back, losing my boys, I wouldn't have cared what happened to me but I've moved on, sorta. That bloke who wanted this,' Jonno said pointing at the disk, 'he's dead.'

'Wheeler's dead?'

'Tonight's news. They pulled his body from the Waikato River. Hamilton cops reckon he went over the Huka Falls. They say no suspicious circumstances. So, two people I know have had their hands on this and they're both dead. All right with you, I'm playin' pass the parcel, mate.'

'I'll show you the content, here and now.' Clay indicated the computer in the bag over his shoulder. 'You deserve that, at least.'

'I'd rather not know.'

In the cab back to the motel, Clay didn't notice the car that stayed with them all the way. Ear plugs in, he was captivated by the disk in his computer. Job done, he dropped the lid and whispered to himself, 'This blows Fisk apart.'

It was minutes after 1 a.m. Friday, when he got back to his motel. He cleared Sasha's message about Mac, left over an hour ago, and a second call urging him to be careful. He punched the speed dial for her mobile and it went straight to her voice mail service. He left thoughts about Mac and a promise to call later in the morning, but made no reference to the video. Tomorrow, if she was up to it, it might lighten her day a little.

An hour later he was disturbed by voices somewhere outside his room. His was at the end of a line of motels organised in a U shape, the front desk and office in the centre of the two wings. The voices, male, were getting closer. 'This is unacceptable, totally unacceptable.' Clay recognised the Indian owner.

Another man said, 'Too bad. National security matter.'

'What do you mean national security? Since when do security men cover their heads and…'

'Shut up, curry muncher, and open his fuckin' door – now.'

Clay, in boxers and T, bounced out of bed and ejected the disk from his computer at the dining table. He heard a door knock.

A man's voice, 'Don't knock, just unlock the fuckin' thing.'

A key in the door. Then a second key. A man said, 'For fuck's sake, get out of the way.'

A jarring noise, the result of a forceful kick.

Clay launched the disk, Frisbee-like, to the top of the old wooden wardrobe between his bed and the kitchenette.

A second kick, and the whole room shuddered as the door burst open. The Indian proprietor ran in first. 'I'm very sorry, sir, very, very sorry. There was nothing I could do.'

Two men were silhouetted by the outside light in the car park. One stepped forward and felled the Indian with a baseball bat to the head. The crack of aluminum on skull was sickening.

Clay flicked a light on. Both balaclava-wearing assailants were clothed in black, a post box slit for their eyes. The motel owner groaned as he held his head and blood oozed between his dark fingers. Alive, for the moment.

The batter asked, 'Where is it?'

Clay glanced at the other man, a dwarf in comparison. He carried what looked like jumper leads that would give life to a dead car battery – two spring-loaded clamps converging into a red insulated cable. The leads passed through a black box with button controls and converted into a mains plug cable the other side.

Clay said, 'What the fuck are you on about?'

The batter said, 'Clever boy, eh? This'll be good', and swung the bat. Hit in the midriff, Clay doubled over and collapsed on the floor with an involuntary groan.

The dwarf with the black box said, in a squeaky voice, 'Let me have him, mate. Let me spark life into those balls of his.'

Clay was still holding his stomach when he felt the batter tug at the elastic band of his boxers, pulling them halfway down his bum. The man used the bat to part his buttocks. Clay winced.

'What's it to be, sunshine? Tickled testes for late night supper? Or hand over the disk and you go back to bed and sleep like a baby.' He sneered, then called to his mate, 'Over there.'

Dwarf went to Clay's computer and pressed the DVD button to eject the contents. 'Nothing here, mate.'

Batter said, 'Duct his hands, feet and wire the cunt up.'

Tape ripped off the roll. For a second, Clay's mind was back in Sydney. He'd tortured a man for information and now he was to be tortured.

Hands and ankles bound, Clay said, 'Tell me why you think I've got a disk.'

'A good brand, Royal Port,' batter said. 'Well rounded. Makes a good connection with a man's hard-wired internal drive, et-fucking-cetera. Tempero, you're not dealing with wet-behind-the-ears schoolboy bullies.'

That was persuasive enough. He wasn't brave, wasn't macho. Nothing more than a small practice solicitor who'd done time for unpaid fines, albeit quite a few. 'Up there, on top of the wardrobe,' Clay said.

The batter looked around, gave orders to the dwarf and looked back at Clay. A smirk. 'Not up for the Victoria Cross, this year, Tempero.'

Dwarf dragged a chrome-legged chair to the wardrobe. Too short to see over the ledge, he felt around, blind, pulled a face in the stretch. Voice straining, he said, 'Got it. 'Now, let me charge him, mate. Set the bastard's balls alight.'

Batter replied, 'Client says not to hang around any longer than we need to.' He extracted pliers from the back pocket of his jeans and cut the motel phone cable. 'Grab his computer, and get his fuckin' mobile while you're at it.'

65

SATURDAY MORNING AT DOMESTIC arrivals, they locked eyes. She'd put make up and lippy on but was sure Clay would think she'd aged a decade. It was how she felt. He looked sad, much more than she'd expected. In the depths of her own grief, she'd overlooked that Clay and Mac, despite their obvious age difference, were good friends.

He dropped his overnight bag with a thud and wrapped his arms around Sasha. In the long and comforting embrace, their silence said everything. When they stood back, she dabbed her eyes with tissues. His looked damp.

He didn't need to ask, but she said it anyway. 'I'm fine, honestly. When he had those stents put in, I got a warning. I've always known the day would come, but not so sudden, so soon.'

He said, 'Bloody shock for all of us, Sash.'

She reached for his hand and squeezed it gently. He gave his own smile, no glint of gold this time, tight-lipped. They walked to her car, buffeted by the cool north-easterly and she outlined the funeral arrangements. She knew she had to tell him about Ben and Delia, but had no stomach for that now. But the subject would be like an untended itch, something she'd have to deal to soon, relieve the discomfort.

Once the car was released by the mechanical arm, she said, 'You know the saying, "I've got good news and bad news"?'

'I don't think I want any more bad news,' he said. 'Tyler's trial?'

'Sort of. But he can wait, if that's okay?'

'Sounds intriguing.'

'The good news is personal. Deeply personal. And when I first learned of it, quite a shock.'

'Really?' He drew out the word with a suspicious tone.

'Well, a confession first, though it's not something I've deliberately withheld from you.'

'Yes?' Same wariness.

In the pause, she exhaled. 'When I was seventeen, I had a baby. I was still at school. Natalie thought it best I adopted it out.'

He took a few seconds to absorb this. 'Hell. You kept that a closely guarded secret, Sash. And for a long time.'

'Yes and no. There was sadness and shame for a long time. Then I got on with my life.' She mentioned reminders of her past, like the cute tot in the green square below them just a few months before.

They were at a red light in Memorial Avenue when he said, 'Why have you decided to tell me now?'

'Does Delia Lang remind you of anyone?' she asked, casually.

'Well, to be honest she reminds me of... No!'

The car behind sounded its horn and Sasha hurriedly turned from his shocked look and planted her foot on the gas.

'How long have you been looking for her?' he asked.

Sasha explained the circumstances.

When she'd finished, he said, 'Christ, what a turn-up.' A little pause. 'Are you sure this isn't a sick trick, to get you to take the Tyler case?'

She glanced at him. The apprehension she heard was also on his face.

'The timing does seem a bit improbable,' he said.

'I went through all this with Mac. She asked me to be her mentor a while ago, well before Ben's case. She knew back then. I took her request at face value and recommended someone else. But she's increasingly been in my sight and I've thought nothing of it. She told me she was looking for opportunities to tell me.'

For a short time, they drove in silence. Then Clay asked, 'How are you feeling about it all?'

'Pretty good. I'll never be more than her biological mother, of course, but at thirty-three, she doesn't need a mother.'

Sadness in his tone, he said, 'We all need our mothers until they leave us.'

Clay's mother was driven to suicide by his father, an event that kept father and son estranged for decades. She glanced again. 'I'm sure that's true, but you know how I feel about Natalie.'

'I wonder what the old bird would say about this turn of events.'

'I don't care to think about that. I suspect she'd be negative, guilt driven. At least Delia met Mac before he died. He wasn't supportive about her as my junior counsel.'

'Well, Mac and I would be in the same camp. If you remember, I didn't think you should be Tyler's counsel.'

At busy Fendalton Road, Clay said, 'Look, I don't want to appear cynical or anything, and I acknowledge she's been really helpful, but I think it best we say nothing about my trip to Auckland.'

'I wasn't intending to. She's on a strictly need to know basis from here.'

'Oh?' He sounded surprised.

'This is where the bad news comes in.'

'Jesus, what's happened, now?'

'You remember the photographer, Michelle Vercoe?'

'The one who claimed to be a friend of Lottie while lusting after her husband?'

'That's the one. She didn't take too kindly to being exposed as a liar, nor for that matter being scorned. Walking out of court she dumped two photos on my table, both of Delia, one capturing her and Ben feeding their tongues to each other.'

'No way! When? I mean, did he seduce her leading up to the trial?'

'Worse than that. Said photo was taken on the afternoon before Lottie died.'

'Oh, Christ, Sash. He's a bloody serial offender with shagging women. Fisk's right. Lottie will have found out about him, probably even confronted him and mentioned divorce. After all, she could never really be free of suspicion could she? I mean...'

'Indeed,' she said, closing off his recollection of Ben two-timing her. She knew this news would play to his belief that Ben was guilty. She showed him a two-millimetre gap between thumb and finger. 'As you might expect, I was this close to walking out on him, as I'd promised.'

'Why the hell didn't you – leave him to Delia?'

'Ben turned into a liar and a fuckwit, Clay. It's beyond dispute and even he doesn't contest that.' She filled him in on her reasoning and finished with her continued belief in his innocence.

Clay clicked his tongue in disgust. 'He doesn't deserve your help, or the evidence you sent me to get.'

66

A LOW, WEAK SUN made Sasha's living room feel warmer than it really was. She and Clay sat facing each other on her cream three-seater sofa. It had been a moment of madness purchase, no thought given to its appearance after several years of hand sweat and sundry smudges. They'd eaten Greek salad, focaccia bread, roasted lamb fillets and washed it down with good pinot noir from Central Otago.

As they drank the last of the wine, she told him about Fisk's trial antics and her suspicions about an unhealthy relationship between Fisk and Ellis. 'I've never seen him work as hard for a conviction before, and that's saying a lot.'

'He's bloody ambitious, I reckon.'

'Exactly right. He sees everyone else through that lens. His determination to prevail in a show trial like ours means he's taking extra risks. Your unscheduled visitors, I'm sure, were a direct result of telling Ellis where you'd gone and why.'

'I'm just pissed off I didn't see them following me. Anyway, you look calm, the calmest I've seen you since I came over last summer.'

Dare she tell him that's because he was back? Her loss of Mac was undiminished, her disappointment in Delia no less sharp. Yet somehow she did feel calmer.

'How long are you booked in at that Papanui Road motel?' she asked.

'Until the end of the trial, which hopefully, given what we've got, won't be far away. Is the expense a problem?'

'No. That's not the problem.'

A silent moment between them, unblinking eye contact. Then the sly appearance of the gold glint, a broader smile. Clay said, 'I think the problem is I haven't thanked you sufficiently for the taxis and refreshments.'

'What, the motel doesn't do that for you? Outrageous.'

Thankfully, he made the first move. He leaned towards her. That was all it took. In less than two minutes she slid her hand below the crisp, white sheet on her bed and felt the warmth of Clay's left quadricep. 'I enjoy having a man in the palm of my hand.'

'Well, bits of a man. You're still prone to exaggeration. I feel that.'

'I now feel some embellishment myself.'

'No argument on facts, Your Honour.'

'Let's not be too precipitate. The voters will need to do their thing before I'm running that race again.' She rolled on top of him. 'In the meantime,' she said, 'I accept I'll need a few lower grade races to stay in condition.'

'Lower grade? We'll see about that.'

67

FEELING SLIGHTLY FLUSHED, SASHA hit the right pointing arrow in the middle of her screen. Grange and Ellis were in view, facing an unseen camera, seated together on a park bench.

Grange: 'It's incredibly fucking risky.'

Ellis: 'The Tories took a risk on that "Kiwi – Not Iwi" slogan. That was in everyone's face and the bastards nearly got home on it. We'll be more subtle. We're the party least likely to be suspected. Tories on the take – a more credible story. We, on the other hand, are the government of the people, for the people.'

Grange: (laughs). 'Even so. How…'

Ellis: 'The beauty is, apologies to Maori still happen, the recompense for land and lost opportunities is still paid. It's all a matter of timing. Under strict secrecy, we sell the land under Maori claim to the Chinese government first. Those wankers at the Overseas Investment Commission are kept well clear. The Chinese then lease it all back to us at a peppercorn rent. We use the sale proceeds from the Chinese as treaty settlement funds – less our personal commissions, of course. The result is budget surpluses continue throughout our term on the Treasury benches while we supplement our retirement plans.'

Grange: 'But we still give the land to iwi?'

Ellis: 'Of course, for their unfettered use and development as everyone expects. The leases are good for thirty years. The Chinese are in this for the long haul. We're their market garden, a source of water, milk, produce – whatever they want for which clean air and water is essential and which they've got a snowball's chance in hell of producing.'

Grange: 'Viable leases in which Maori, or whoever they sub-lease to, develop the land in readiness for the Chinese to take over?'

Ellis: 'Exactly. Hence the peppercorn rents.'

Grange: 'Do the Chinese know what's going on, that there's a shit bomb with a thirty-year fuse?'

Ellis: 'No. The Chinese think that iwi are in on the deal and Maori are guaranteed the full, exclusive and undisturbed possession of their lands. That only we, the government, can buy and sell that land. I've also explained to the Chinese that Maori are happy to have a thirty-year deal to maximise their use of the land, taking whatever profit they can. After that, we take ownership then hand it over to the Chinese.'

Grange: 'Surely, the Chinese won't swallow that?'

Ellis: 'Why not? They're a country of peasants run by richer peasants who want to get richer. The average paddy farmer doesn't know there's anything beyond his region, much less the country. Like much of America, when you think about it.'

Grange: 'The Chinese government won't keep this quiet. I'd have thought it's a huge coup for them. A big celebration.'

Ellis: 'Beauty of the deal. Cancelled the moment it's in the public domain and they lose a significant part of their settlement funds, which they pay progressively over ten years. And of course we deny it, vehemently. If it has legs, we'll discover documents blaming the Tories for trying to set us up. Secrecy's in the make-up of every chink, Ivor. Also, they say they have other international interests to protect, whatever that fucking means. I suspect they don't want the Japs and others knowing this shit – all part of their plans for global domination. They want the jump on their neighbours.'

Grange: 'Still, a huge risk.'

Ellis. 'I can manage the worst – if it happens, which it won't. Don't look so worried, mate. In thirty years the bloody treaty will be irrelevant. We'll have widespread interbreeding and our Asian population will outweigh Maori significantly. We'll make sure of it with appropriate immigration policies. We'll be truly multicultural. Bloody biculturalism has had its day. The world doesn't need that. And the best thing? When this shit bomb, as you call it, goes off, we'll be seeing out our years sunning ourselves in the South of France. No one will give a fuck about us.'

Sasha pushed the stop button. 'That motel man. Will he pull through?'

'Looks like it,' Clay said. 'As soon as they were gone I rang the cops and ambos from his office. They thought it was bad concussion.'

'After all that, how did you get this to me?'

'As soon as I finished watching it in the cab, I copied it to my hard drive. The second I was back in my room, I emailed it to you and, in case you were mysteriously burgled last night, to Kate as well. Then I deleted the file and deleted the sent mail record, and deleted the deleted file from the trash. It would've taken them a bit of time to make those discoveries. Fortunately, they didn't have it. Even then, they'd need forensic analysis.' He pointed to the blank screen. 'But with Wheeler dead, there might be authentication problems with this. I've arranged for Jonno to give us an affidavit attesting Lottie handed it to him for safekeeping. He'll exhibit her handwritten note.'

'Great.' She smiled. 'I suspect that might be enough for Inkwell to subpoena Ellis and Grange.'

'Love to be a fly on their wall if she did that.' His cheerful expression disappeared. 'The real issue will be whether those two discovered Lottie knew, that she had acquired the disk from Wheeler. Otherwise they're not linked to the murder.'

'To create reasonable doubt, it's almost immaterial. The government announced an inquiry last year into leaks of sensitive information by public servants. Wheeler was specifically but secretly employed to hunt down leakers and get evidence. He gets evidence of something altogether different, something that could bring down the government. He put the evidence in Lottie's hands for the purpose of exposing the corruption. Ben knew Lottie was working on something huge, something worrying her, according to Hut. Now we turn to O'Rourke.'

She told him what happened in court.

'But we can't prove a connection between O'Rourke and Ellis or Grange, can we?' asked Clay.

'Not forensically, but this is another line of enquiry the police should've investigated. Far from O'Rourke assisting Plummer, he'd prefer to have him out of his life and we can show why, a compelling motive. Ben's been set up to make it look as if he committed that incredible violence simply to point at someone else. Yet we know with O'Rourke, he's had the opportunity and means, knowledge of Ben's and Lottie's movements and an opportunity to clear his debt to the government.

Sasha mentioned the mysteriously disappearing crowbar and white painting overalls. 'Perhaps he was worried someone might've remembered he had that painting outfit, so he told Ben it'd been stolen. He set himself up with a hospital alibi but we can argue a discharge note did not account for every minute of his presence at the hospital. We legitimately question if there'd been a full and proper investigation, who knows what the police would've turned up. Let's not forget the risk Ellis and Grange were taking. They needed to have intelligence on the ground about story angles, breaking stories and finding leakers. What if O'Rourke wasn't breaking stories about the government but helping to cover them up?'

'Fuck!' Clay exclaims. 'What a cover.'

'Ben told me about Montague's sharing news policy. If he ran it right, O'Rourke could've had the inside running on anything breaking anywhere, at least in the Montague Media stable. Lottie had to be silenced and Ben was collateral damage. We don't need to prove O'Rourke or anyone else killed Lottie. Nor do we need to prove Ellis or Grange organised it with someone who did. We don't have to prove anything but we've got enough for reasonable doubt. We play this right we can kill this trial stone dead.'

'How?' Clay asked.

'Leave that to me.'

68

THEY WERE BACK IN Justice Inkwell's office at 9.30 a.m., Monday. The judge said nice things about Mac and told Sasha the whole High Court would close for the funeral. She said, 'Now I understand there's been something of a dramatic turn in this case.'

Sasha said, 'Yes, Judge. With your leave I'd invite my investigator to show you a DVD recorded by an employee of the GCSB.' She looked at Fisk and saw the colour drain from his face. 'Given the content, and in fairness to the prosecution, I thought it best we view this in the privacy of your room.'

Inkwell looked dubious. 'And I have your assurance this is relevant, Sasha?'

'Oh yes, Judge. This, I'm afraid, goes to the heart of whether the man in the dock should've been arrested, much less put on trial.'

Inkwell looked at Fisk. 'Quentin?'

Fisk looked ill, his face now grey and pinched. 'The man who produced this is dead,' he said, stiff jawed. 'I strenuously oppose its viewing and admissibility.'

Sasha leaned back in her chair, glee in her voice. 'So you know about this undiscovered disk, Quentin. One left for the defence to turn up.' Sasha glanced at Inkwell who looked shocked.

He said, 'Wheeler, no doubt burdened by his deceit, committed suicide. I know that.'

Inkwell asked, 'Who's Wheeler?'

To Fisk, Sasha said, 'Will you tell or will I?'

'This is your circus, not mine.' Childishly, he turned his face away from Sasha and the judge and pretended to be captivated by a painting. Sasha explained the position, emphasising that Wheeler passed the disk to the deceased and Clay would attest to the chain of evidence thereafter.

The court clerk fetched Clay, who was introduced. He played the recording, rigged to his screen and portable speakers so everyone could hear.

At its end, Inkwell said, 'Mr Tempero, I need to ask you some questions on oath.'

Clay took an affirmation to tell the truth, then produced the affidavit Jonno Hart had sworn in front of an Auckland solicitor the day before.

Sasha said, 'Judge, although the man who recorded this is dead, I submit we have a viable chain of authenticity that is damaging to the prosecution's case, perhaps to the government itself.'

Inkwell looked at Fisk. 'What do you say about this?'

'It's a smokescreen, Judge. I repeat my objection about admissibility.'

Sasha shot a look at Delia. She was beaming like a small child with a longed for toy. But she had to be wondering why this was the first she'd heard of this evidence.

Fisk continued, 'It's not relevant to whether the defendant murdered his wife and it's certainly not exculpatory of the defendant. In fact, I submit it's a major red herring.'

'I agree,' the judge said, 'that in itself, it is not exculpatory.'

Inkwell paused and Sasha's heart sank.

'But it is admissible given the deceased had, at one time, possession of this disk and Mr Hart has deposed that others came looking for it well before Mr Tempero. That possession raises an important question about the police inquiry, in particular whether it has been wide enough to justify settling on a circumstantial case against the defendant, alone. No matter what happens here, I will ask the police commissioner to investigate the matter.'

Fisk said, 'In that case, I'll need to take instructions from the solicitor general, Judge.'

'How long do you need?'

'Subject to his availability, probably an hour.'

69

THE END WAS RAPID. A churlish Quentin Fisk approached Sasha in the corridor leading to Inkwell's office, unable to look her in the eye. 'Tyler's as guilty as sin,' he said. 'I know it, you know it, we all know it. That photo shows the real Tyler – and your co-counsel, his next floozy in waiting. Black's team and I are at one on this. But you and that incompetent bench bitch have allowed an appalling travesty of justice here. Your old boyfriend gets to crawl back under a rock, continue his grubby philandering and benefit from his greed. But what can I do?'

Her jaw tightened but she kept calm, tried to look unruffled. 'I'm happy to proceed, happy to have the jury see the tape.'

Still reluctant to look at her, Fisk said, 'I'm instructed to ask you to seek a discharge under Section 347 and not to oppose it. If Inkwell won't go with that, we jointly request her to direct the jury to acquit.'

'They don't want the DVD in court, do they?'

He sneered. 'What do you think?'

'What do they say about it, Quentin?' It was hard to suppress the little bliss in the question.

He almost spat the answer. 'If they said anything, you're the last one I'd tell.'

He turned and walked four paces, somehow looking shorter than he was when he started the trial. Sasha was glowing inside when he suddenly turned, the whites of his eyes prominent. 'Don't think this is over for you, Stace.'

70

SASHA DIDN'T NEED THE photo John McClintock emailed her – the similarity in complexion, the straight black hair. Not the same eyes as his father, but the same hedge-like eyebrows.

In memory of Mac, she'd hoped to make a connection with his son, establish a relationship of mutual value, but John gave off all the wrong signals for that. He'd been reluctant to come earlier, something about a civil trial he was involved in at the Old Bailey. Sasha switched the listening button off when she heard the whining tone, an indicator his father's death was more of a serious inconvenience than a substantial loss.

His presence now mattered only to himself. It was difficult to know why he'd bothered, but she would be cordial, for Mac's sake.

'John?' she said, when he was a step from the bottom escalator at Christchurch airport.

'Ms Stace.'

Mac's last squeeze of her hand had more life than this cold fish greeting. There was alcohol on his breath but, given the situation, she wouldn't hold that against him.

Stiff and aloof, he said, 'I'm sorry to meet you in these circumstances.'

She wanted to say, 'It would've been good to see you at your father's bedside' but she settled for, 'Me too.'

She wasn't with him long. His hotel room was a short ride from the airport. In the car, he told Sasha he was here to attend the funeral, not to speak at it, but would talk to one or two of his father's friends – people with whom Mac had shared an investment property. 'I'll be discussing estate matters with the appropriate solicitor and then I'll travel to Queenstown to ski.'

Sasha was unable to hide her surprise. 'It's a hell of a long way to come and not speak at the service.'

'Perhaps.' His tone was more dismissive than provisional. He added, 'I didn't know my father well.'

'But Mac had several trips to the Privy Council. I know he stayed with you.'

He sniffed. 'Well. One does one's duty. I tended to have evening appointments when he was there.'

Her urge to slap him was almost overwhelming. She disliked the feeling, but John McClintock's attitude was like rubbing lemon juice into an open wound.

At the hotel, she thought about offering him a ride to the service tomorrow. 'Do you know how to get to the chapel?'

'It was in your email.' A pause. 'I appreciate you driving me here. I need to rest now.'

He showed no interest in the arrangements for his father's funeral. It was as though he expected everything to have magically fallen into place by 11 a.m. tomorrow. It was bloody difficult to see this man as Mac's progeny.

As he left the car, he said, 'Oh, one should say thank you, Ms Stace – for attending on my father, the arrangements and such like.' He gave a curt, military nod.

Unable to reply, she thought about his suitcase in the boot. He read her mind. 'Don't get out, I'll get my bag.'

He disappeared into the hotel entrance without waving or looking back. That much, Sasha was satisfied with.

71

'BUBBLES FOR YOUR VICTORY?'

Mac's words were in her head when Sasha spotted Delia waiting by the Coffee House steps, a look of concern on her pale face. She offered a hug and Sasha accepted, taking comfort from the embrace.

Part of forgiving Delia involved accepting the inevitable link between defensiveness and deceit. Delia and Ben had feared a puissant mix of embarrassment and threats. Ironically, it was Ben with his candid admissions who helped her to see that. He'd lied out of fear she would refuse to represent him if he was truthful. Delia had been a willing party to the scam, but her credibility was on the line with her firm. And she'd been supportive over Mac's death. Sasha forgave her immaturity but would not forget. She never did forget, something said of Quentin Fisk. *Don't think this is over for you, Stace.* She didn't like that he was someone with whom she shared a likeness, almost a disability.

A waitress who'd attended to Mac many times showed them to a table and others smiled their recognition. Sasha was torn about sharing the sad news. Right or wrong, she decided now was not the time. Once their coats had been collected and hung up, and a warming shiraz delivered to each woman, Delia asked, 'This still okay for you?'

'After meeting Mac's son, essential. I think about Mac in this place. Always will. We'd been coming since the place opened. Before that, when I was little, he'd take me in an old Austin to Ice Cream Charlie's for a glass dish after visits to the gardens and feeding the ducks. Sometimes it was the museum. Later we came here, in good times and bad. We argued and agreed, he cajoled and he listened. There were times when I think his faith in me transcended reason.'

'And I bet he got plenty in return,' Delia said, warmly.

'I don't know about that. I know I'm struggling with the fact I wasn't with him at the end.'

Delia touched Sasha's arm. 'I don't have much experience of these things outside the death of my own parents. What would you say if our roles were reversed, if I was the one struggling with what you're going through?'

Sasha looked into mid-air, resignation in her tone. 'I know. I'd say, you don't blame yourself. I think we both know, though, that there's the rational and then there's the emotional.'

Delia looked away. When she faced Sasha again, she said, 'I can only imagine how disappointed you must be in me. I am so, so sorry.'

'You know, I can understand it from Ben...' Sasha let the rest of the sentence go unsaid.

'I was at Lottie's funeral,' Delia said. 'We both looked for you. When you didn't come, he was convinced that if he was arrested, it would be impossible to get you on board. And he said it would be hard enough for you to agree to represent him without also knowing we were a couple. He was desperate to get the best lawyer possible to combat Fisk. I went along with him but I should've been more up front.'

Odd that Ben had never said he thought he might be arrested, but Sasha let that go.

'You realise, Delia, that each time he has a relationship with a woman, he finds someone younger?'

'My eyes are wide open. To be perfectly honest, with what's happened, if I had to make a choice, I'd want my relationship with you to flourish.'

'I'm not asking you to make a choice, just to be well informed.' Sasha drank more of the shiraz, the warmth and velvet feeling in her mouth, soothing.

After a pause Delia asked, 'Do you really think O'Rourke was the link between Lottie and the attorney general in a murder plot?'

'It's exercised my mind for a while, but I doubt it. The evidence is too thin to put either of them in the dock. The best thing about that appalling DVD was it opened a line of enquiry no one had traversed. I'm sure we'd have got an acquittal from the jury if they'd been allowed to see it. Ironic, isn't it? The prosecution's big motive for Ben being the killer was greed, yet it was greed that undid the prosecution.'

'You do believe Ben's innocent, don't you?' There was anxiety in her question.

Sasha gave her the smile. 'I couldn't have gone back to court after that awful discovery with the photo if I'd thought there was the slightest chance he was guilty. Clay had accused me of letting my head rule my heart, of having an overwhelming desire to want Ben to be innocent. In a weird kind of way, my gut feel is that Ben knows something he hasn't told either of us. What the hell it is, I've no idea. It's possible he has knowledge that protects someone else. What's he doing now?'

'He's having a drink with Ultan. Trying to repair the damage caused by your cross-examination. Ultan sees Ben as complicit with our tactics.'

'Bit naïve on Ultan's part I'd have thought. We had little choice.'

'I asked Ultan to think about it more. I asked him whether he had any leads or probable suspects.'

Sasha looked into the gathering gloom in the courtyard. 'I'm sorry, Delia. I was a little distracted. What exactly did you say to Ultan?'

She looked slightly perplexed. 'I asked him, "Do you have any leads or probable suspects?" You know, a bit of a challenge because he was pissed off with Ben, didn't seem to recognise that Ben was in such a deep hole that he needed anything and everything to climb out.'

She started to talk about Mac, but Sasha wasn't concentrating. A man who looked like the hen-pecked arsonist, Alfonse Cretin, walked into the café. And then it hit her. In the same way Cretin waited for the fire trucks, the real killer couldn't resist returning to the scene, to learn of progress.

'What?' Delia said, a concerned expression on her face. 'Sasha, what is it? You think O'Rourke's the murderer after all?'

Sasha drained the dregs of her wine. 'I'm sorry, Delia, but I need to attend to something urgently, but it will be nice to see you at the funeral tomorrow.'

She touched her daughter's hand briefly and hurried back to her car.

72

IT WAS NOT EVEN 5 p.m. and nearly dark outside. Drizzle appeared in the beams of the car lights below. Sasha drew the crimson velvet curtains she'd once bought as a bit of a joke. Pulled back, they added colour to the otherwise conservatively presented room. Drawn, they looked hideous. But tonight, visited by vague feelings of vulnerability, she had no interest in aesthetics.

She wanted to let this case go, like she'd wanted to let all the others go. Instead, she listed on a whiteboard all the names of possible killers, Ben's at the top. Then she rubbed it out. Liar, adulterer, but not murderer. She could never accept that.

Despite what she'd told Delia, she wrote O'Rourke's and Plummer's names on the board. She added 'at behest of Ellis/Grange'. She stood back, wondering who to add. Wheeler? No. Shazza, the tow truckie? No. The teenager Lottie helped send to prison? Revenge was a powerful motive. What became of him? Michelle Vercoe, a woman scorned, unable to kill the man she desired but with no compunction about removing the obstacle in her way.

The familiar shoulder ache had returned, the physical price she paid for not moving on. Despite an increased awareness of her morbid need for certainty, she couldn't help herself. It was like a sickness, she had to know all the answers. Always that voice, ruinous to relaxation, 'Do the right thing'. And when she gave in to it, always the same question, win or lose. What was a just outcome?

She knew the just outcome in Andrews before the jury did their job. But here, in Tyler's case, the just outcome had eluded everyone.

There were copies of the Vercoe photos on her desk. She turned them face down and connected the video player to the monitor. She rewound to the beginning of Fisk's impromptu press conference outside the hospital in Akaroa. No one was wearing any lanyard identification, though that was unsurprising. The angles and the light were different to how she remembered. She started to doubt herself. Then she saw the reporter she thought was from *The People*, the one Ben had no recollection of and totally unlike the woman O'Rourke identified in the court media box. In the low light, the hair below her cap was dark. But the face wasn't in full shot, barely a half shot profile. Was this unknown person involved? She played and replayed the muffled audio. Frances Rule? Michelle Vercoe?

Clay had given her Vern's wife's pictures of the alleged accident scene two weeks before the murder. Vern had also said they were in Akaroa the night of the murder but there was nothing useful on the video. She had to see it. She looked at her watch. Clay was due soon but there was time to call him and make sure he had both the Akaroa footage and his video analysis tools with him.

As she waited she returned to the whiteboard: means, motive, opportunity. The futility of it pained her.

When Clay arrived, the footage was revealed as a jerky amalgam of shoes, grass, asphalt, trees, fences, letterboxes, a late evening sky.

Clay said, 'It's complete crap.'

'Until that car,' Sasha said.

'What's all this about?' he asked. 'I seem to remember we won.'

'Unfinished business.'

Clay fast-forwarded. 'There's always mystery with you, isn't there?'

She stroked his arm. 'Would you have it any other way?'

Clay connected his equipment to allow a better look at the video. They both stared at the screen, looking at rubbish which, in a strange way, was less ridiculous on fast forward. After a few seconds Sasha said, 'This looks like where it gets interesting.'

The car's movement was slow and the steadied camera produced footage of houses, gates and footpaths. The camera recorded the time at 20.05.

Sasha asked whether Clay recognised the area.

'Looks like the place where I did my spying on Doris Knowles.'

'Quite right – these houses in shot are back from the beach at Akaroa, between the two ends of town.'

The angle of the lens changed to a more front-on position. A side street rose away from where Vern was driving. A blue car appeared suddenly, ran the stop sign to traffic coming down the hill.

Sasha almost shouted, 'Stop.'

Clay chuckled as he obeyed the command. 'He told me this happened to him. I'd forgotten. We joked that Wheeler had returned.'

'See that?' she asked. 'Zoom in there.' She pointed to the licence plate of the car. 'An H inserted into the middle of the silver grille above the plate.'

While Clay zoomed, he said, 'At Fotoshop, when we were getting copies of his wife's pictures, Vern said something about nearly being cleaned out by a driver. This Honda must've been the one.'

'Not much time to digest the burger and fries,' Sasha said.

'Eh?'

'Timing's almost a glove fit with what Cadveron said at trial.'

Four out of six numbers on the plate were discernible. 'You have Vern's number?' Sasha asked.

Clay punched the keys and hit the speaker phone.

Clay and Vern bantered about snooker hidings and con artist arrests then Clay introduced Sasha to Vern. To the numbers on the Honda plate, Vern told her he had a mate who could help but it might take an hour or two.

In the time before he rang back, Sasha told Clay about her meetings with John McClintock and Delia.

Seventy-three minutes later, the phone rang at Kate's desk, piercing the quiet of the office. Sasha pushed the number nine, then speaker, to take the call in her office.

'Sasha Stace.'

'Vern Washbrook, Sasha.'

'Thank you for calling back. Any luck?'

'A bit, but I'm afraid with the two unknown numbers in the plate, I've ended up with three names, addresses for each. Actually there were more but we've eliminated others. You got a pencil?'

She looked at Clay, saw tension on his face. 'Go ahead, Vern.'

'I reckon the car involved was a Honda Civic. At least that's what I told my mate. I'd hate to put you wrong.'

'Anything at this stage is better than nothing, Vern.'

'Good-oh! George Stockley, Herman Bolt and Frances Rule.'

'Frances Rule? You sure?'

'Yep. Frances Rule.'

He gave the three addresses and Sasha thanked him for his time. 'Clay tells me you pay a subscription at City Snooker.'

'That's right, respectable place. He thinks otherwise.'

'No. He just needed an excuse for his humbling loss. Your sub for the next year,' Sasha said. 'It's taken care of, Vern.'

'You don't have to do that.'

'Good as done,' she said.

After the call, Clay said, 'I can check the police job sheets but I don't think any of those names have come up in the inquiry.'

'You don't need to check. I know Frances Rule, she's a lawyer. She briefed me years ago and I saw her in the courthouse during the trial. Kate will have recorded the others' names.'

Sasha thought about adding Rule's name to her list. She called up the file on Kate's database. 'As I thought. You're right. Vern's names are new. Let's split the task? I'll talk to the lawyer. She expressed interest in a catch-up.' Sasha gave her tight-lipped smile. 'Now I have the perfect excuse.'

Sasha explained what she needed. 'Can you do the other two?'

'No chance of a quiet night before the funeral?'

She stared back and said nothing.

'Of course,' he said. 'How long have we got?'

'Tonight.'

'Not urgent then.'

73

FRANCES RULE WAS A suburban solicitor working on her own: estate, conveyancing and family law. Her internet profile said she'd been born and educated in Virginia and had completed post-grad management studies at Darden after graduating with a law degree. Hadn't O'Rourke gone to Darden?

Heart thumping, Sasha rang Rule's office number, but at 6.46 p.m. she was calling an hour past office closing. She listened to Rule's office hours several times, an attempt to recognise the solicitor's tone and cadence. Rule was a tall brunette, hair past her shoulders. It was imperative to determine if Rule's was the muffled voice that had asked Fisk about probable leads and suspects. The voice message put her no closer to the truth.

Many suburban lawyers had offices attached to their residence, particularly sole practitioners such as Frances Rule. She lived in Clyde Road, west of the city. Sasha tried the mobile number again. Same result.

The worst of the commuter traffic was over as Sasha headed west. In complete darkness, the rain and red car brake lights combined to produce blood-filled puddles. An erratic wind occasionally tugged at her wipers. Oncoming headlights were determined to blind her. The joys of winter night driving didn't make it easy to spot house numbers either.

Her BlackBerry winked at her from the passenger seat. Clay's text. 'Herman 90. Lvs alone. No one driven car in 3 years. Luck 4 U?'

She texted Clay back, 'Not yet.'

The shoulder pain had intensified. Damn. She hadn't replaced the last of her painkillers. She dug fingers into the spot, an attempt to fight a knot of tension that her mind, rather than her posture had caused.

Rule's house was close to the Fendalton village, an L-shaped arrangement of shops bordering a car park that included a bakery, café and Indian restaurant. Sasha sat opposite, hoping the lights she saw behind curtains meant Frances was in rather than a standard precaution against burglars. She called the mobile number again, knowing that the lawyer had set her voice mail message to kick in after seven tones. Sasha was at six and resigned to failure when Rule answered with her name.

Her heart lurched. 'Frances, Sasha Stace here.' Her mouth was dry. 'Probably not the best time to take up on your invitation to catch up, but I was...'

'I was just about to get changed to go out, Sasha.'

'Of course. I tried ringing you earlier and when I couldn't reach you I decided to drive over. A silly impulse, I know. I'm in my car opposite your house.'

'Oh. That's a bit awkward.'

'To be honest, there is something else.'

'Really? Sounds important.' Her tone indicated more curiosity than apprehension but there was a noticeable pause. Sasha could almost hear the cogs in Frances Rule's brain turning over. 'You'd better come in,' she said. 'I've got the fire going but you'll have to excuse my sweatpants and fluffy slippers. As I said, I was just about to change to go out.'

Under a striped awning at the front door, Sasha hunched against the cold. Frances led her inside and Sasha promised not to detain her long. The warmth inside the house was immediately comforting. They passed a living room on the left, corn-coloured curtains almost floor to ceiling, big paintings on the walls. An open door led to a dining room. To her right, a large kitchen with more bench space than Sasha had in hers. They headed left to where a wood burner cracked like a distant gun, dry willow blazing in the firebox. Frances pointed her to a blue upholstered sofa. On an adjacent table, a wine glass, near empty with a red lipstick mark at the edge. 'May as well have a civilised little red seeing as you've come out here on a horrid night.' She went to the sideboard in the corner of the room.

Frances was tall even in her flat-soled slippers. She poured wine, then held up her glass. 'Anyway, I heard the news. Congratulations,' she said. 'A triumph for justice in front of ex-prosecutor Inkwell?'

Sasha searched her face for signs of concern. There were none. 'Thank you. Although, it's a little unusual to get that far through a case and see it pulled from the jury.'

'Yes. The media made it sound a bit mysterious. Was it?'

Sasha took her briefly through her belief that the police had formed a working theory about Ben too quickly, which suited a prosecutor with a grudge against him.

'So you think there's a killer on the loose?'

'I think that's the only reasonable conclusion.'

'I saw Delia in court with you. How did she go?'

Sasha was momentarily taken aback. She didn't know Frances had come to the actual trial. Other trial lawyers often stopped by in big cases, particularly those who had a sense of occasion. But Frances wasn't a trial lawyer. Was she there because of Delia, an opponent with whom she had crossed verbal swords? Or was she there because she had more than an unusual interest in the case?'

Not answering, Sasha said, 'Obviously the two of you know one another.'

'You could say that. How does someone like her become your second chair?'

Someone like her. That was a phrase suggesting antipathy was mutual. 'Ben Tyler was a client of her law firm and she came to me needing senior counsel.'

Frances appraised her, as if considering an important purchase. 'Well, you probably didn't come to talk about Delia.'

'No. But there *is* something of a loose end I'd like to tie up about the trial.'

Frances tilted her head slightly. 'Goodness. I can't think how I can possibly help tie up your loose ends, Sasha.'

There was no lack of confidence in her demeanour, no concern that she might be implicated in a murder.

Sasha said, 'Had the trial not taken an unexpected turn, our defence would've relied on video evidence of a car leaving an area close to the scene of the murder at a time almost immediately after. The driver was in a major hurry, ran a stop sign. That driver was a woman.' She looked for the little tell-tale movements in and around Frances Rule's eyes. There were none. 'You've obviously followed the murder so you'll know it was in Akaroa in October last year.'

Frances nodded, looked mildly curious.

'The nub of the matter, Frances, is that the car in question was a Honda Civic with a registration number indicating you're the owner.'

It was overstatement. In fact, there were several overstatements. But it was too late in the day for niceties.

'Me?' She was clearly startled before she looked into the fire. 'I don't get that.' She turned back to face Sasha. 'I haven't been to Akaroa or that area for what – over two years, I'd say.'

Sasha let her answer sit in the silence, waiting for Frances to process the issue.

'You don't think... Is this the loose end? I'm supposed to be the... Oh, Sasha. Really?'

Rule was incredulous and indignant in equal measure.

'It's more that I'd like to rule you out of any ongoing inquiry, Frances.'

'What ongoing inquiry? Don't tell me the police are now interested in pursuing someone else.'

The temperature of the skin on Sasha's neck increased. She said, 'I'm sorry for the embarrassment. Could I at least check the plate, make sure there's no mistake?'

'Didn't you just say it matches my car?'

'I said the number indicated you're the owner. The truth is, a couple of digits aren't clearly identifiable.'

'I see,' she said, in the tone of a disappointed headmistress. 'Well, I don't know how it will help.' She rose. 'It's in the garage. Follow me.'

Through the kitchen, into a long hall, one small bedroom on each side, they turned right at the end. It was cooler at this end of the house, rather like their discussion. Sasha imagined the talk in the coming week. How a senior member of the bar accused a respected suburban solicitor of murder. About how she was taking her role as a leader of Law Society misconduct proceedings way beyond any sensible boundary.

Inside the internal access double garage, Sasha stood in front of a red Civic and a two-tone blue sixties Austin, which she recognised immediately. She pointed to the old car. 'This looks special.' The tyres looked as if they'd been recently blackened and the paintwork was clean and undented. The abundant chrome gleamed under the fluorescent tubes on the ceiling. Sasha added, 'In lovely condition, too.'

'It was my dad's,' Frances said. 'He bought it off a lawyer, local, I think. Wish I could remember his name.' She ran a hand over the hood. 'Old leather inside,' she said, smiling.

'Brian McClintock. Was that the lawyer?'

Frances looked surprised. 'Yes. How did you know?'

'It used to belong to Mac, my stepfather. I knew he'd sold it. I looked for it on the streets for years, without success.'

The change in the other woman's expression was unmistakable, indignation gone. She said, 'Sit in it if you like.'

Sasha couldn't resist. When she opened the door and slid into the passenger seat the intoxicating smell of old leather and oxidised wine was still there, along with wood polish on the dash. When Frances saw her with knees up under her chin, she said that the seat adjustment couldn't be fixed. Sasha remembered that.

Out of the car again, Sasha noted the reason for ambiguity with the registration plate on the Honda Civic. A number that looked like a seven was in fact a one, and what looked like a three was in fact an eight. The angle of the shot and the blurred image both contributed to the uncertainty. Sasha explained the situation and thanked Frances.

As they walked back to the warmth of the living room, Frances said, 'I keep a social diary, Sasha. Let's tie this up properly.'

In the kitchen, she removed a small hard-covered book from a drawer under the sideboard. 'What date exactly?'

'18 October.'

She frowned as she flicked a couple of pages. 'Hanmer,' she said, giving a little nod of satisfaction. 'Mike took me to Hanmer. See for yourself.'

'You say, took you to Hanmer?'

'Yes, he drove. From memory he'd bought a new Lexus. Well, not exactly new, but red.' She smiled. 'Keen to give it a run on the open road. Aren't they all the same? He'd have the receipt for the overnight motel. Actually, now that I think, I might even have photos in the office.'

'And your Civic? In the garage here, was it? While you were away?'

'Well, presumab....' She stopped and looked down at the bench, then at the diary. 'Wait a minute. That weekend, I lent my car to...' She looked at Sasha. 'I lent it to Delia.'

'Delia Lang? Are you sure? Why?'

'It was stupid. I did it out of guilt. And because she'd said there'd been a delay in getting hers back from the mechanic. She needed a car to take her brother somewhere. The hospital, I think.'

There was much to unpick here. 'I don't follow the part about guilt.'

Frances stroked her neck with a finger. 'Before Mike and I were together, he was with Delia. It was all a bit untidy.'

'That day in the courthouse, when the trial was on. I interrupted the two of you. You seemed to be having an argument.'

'It was about Mike. I thought she was over all that.'

'And not about a case, her failure to meet a discovery deadline?'

Frances looked confused. 'No. I don't have any case where she represents the opposition.'

'Are you sure?'

'Yes. Of course'

More deceit.

Sasha asked, 'Did you meet Delia's brother?'

'No. But I did ask why she couldn't use a cab. She said something about him freaking out with strangers. I didn't push the issue. As I say, she'd come to me still wanting us to be friends.'

'You didn't think that was unusual?'

'I did. But I've known her since we both did the work to be admitted to the bar. Normally, I'd have been well ahead of her chronologically, but I had to step backwards when I came to New Zealand. To be honest, when I think about it, she's always been a bit needy. It was a problem between them – her and Mike. He was like a father figure to her and I was a bit like an older sister. All changed now, of course.'

Sasha could see the irony. 'Because you and Mike are a couple?'

'That's it. But she's proven to be pretty volatile since. Again, I think that's down to the situation.'

'What have you noticed specifically?'

Frances scratched her head. 'Look, I feel a bit awkward. Talking about her like this – it doesn't feel right.'

'I'm sorry, Frances, but this could be very important. You'll understand now, that if Delia drove that car to Akaroa then…'

'But surely she had no connection to the victim.'

Clay's emailed photos at *Uncover* flashed through Sasha's mind. Also the headline, 'Abuser Imprisoned', the young offender eluding police and then Delia's brother's suicide. 'I'd like to think so.'

'When you came in,' Frances said, 'I asked you how she was because I'd hoped working with you would give her stability. I thought she'd been pretty fragile. Mike left her for me about September last year. When she wasn't screaming at us down the phone, she was crying about her brother.'

'She had only one brother. Did you know that?'

'That's my understanding.' She frowned. 'You said, had?'

'He committed suicide.'

Frances brought her hand to her mouth. 'She never said a word. When?'

'Her parents were killed in an accident about ten years ago. Sometime after that, I believe.' Sasha allowed time for Frances to consider this. Then she asked, 'Was your car in good condition when it was returned?'

'I'll say this for her. It was probably in better condition than when she borrowed it – well, except for the tyre lever. But then that might not have been her.'

'What do you mean?'

'I couldn't find it when I had puncture a couple of months ago.'

'You might have lost it?'

'Unlikely. But it's possible it might not have been part of the kit when I got the car.'

'You said she brought it back in better condition?'

'When I lent it to her, it was untidy – bit of a mess, to be frank. It was spotless when I got it back. The boot had never been cleaner. I called to thank her, and to tell her that her brother had left his cap behind. Somehow it had got into the well where tyre-changing kit was kept.'

74

'I'M SO SORRY IT'S turned out this way, QF.' Averill was at Fisk's back door, wine bottle in one hand, box of chocolates in the other.

'You and me both, Averill. You and me both. Thank you for coming. I feel tonight I need you more than ever. I'm only beginning to appreciate how you've been my rock, a guiding light in all you've said and done for me. And what have I done for you?' Fisk looked at his shoes.

Averill grabbed Fisk by the hand and led him into his kitchen. Placing the gifts on the marble-like bench, she turned and pulled him to her. She kissed him firmly, pushing her tongue into his mouth.

Drawing breath, he said, 'Let's have a drink and go out to dinner. I want to treat you.'

'Not before we've had each other, QF.'

In the lounge, she unzipped and removed her black boots. Leaning against the sofa, she unrolled her fishnets, grinning at him as she did so. Fisk swallowed a mouth full of saliva. Raw lust assaulted him again and caused his blood to flow south.

He went to his mother's mahogany table on its spindly legs, legs that looked nothing like Averill's. Hers were strong and that arse – how he would miss that arse.

Graham was quiet. It was as if the bird had a sense of foreboding. From the little table drawer Fisk pulled his Smith and Wesson .38 revolver.

'Do you have to hold that, Quentin?' Averill asked, in the tone of a whining child. 'You know I don't like it. We've talked about this before.'

'But you know why I do it. Don't make me beg, Averill.'

Disappointment painted her face and Fisk, placatory, said, 'Look, I promise you, this will be the last time.'

'You promise?'

'I promise to promise. That's what I said.' He smiled. It was his jury smile. 'You know I keep my promises.'

She gave her little smirk, then lowered her knickers and kicked them away as if all the troubles in their world together had disappeared. Struggling to keep the seal on his contempt, Fisk felt his spleen was about to burst. He'd been struck by the fact she was but one in a cast of the perfidious and incompetent. There was Ivor Grange, the snivel servant. Sure, he teed up the resources to deal with back-stabbing Yuile but he and Ellis had let him down when it mattered most. Zoe Underwood, to whom he'd extended every consideration, every opportunity in the trial of the decade, a difficult but potential protégé who had not only provided the Auckland job sheets to Stace against his directions, but couldn't carry her weight in the trial. Her inadequate briefing of Michelle Vercoe had allowed a key witness to crash and burn in the witness box. But closest to him of all, his own PA – Averill's integrity had dropped way below average. Betraying his most intimate secret to Underwood was unpardonable.

'I want you to watch a little recording,' he said.

'Not your mother, QF. I can't make love in front of your mother.'

'It won't be Mother. I've decided to retire Mother. Does that please you?'

'It does, QF. You're better than that – better than depending on her for guidance. Much better.'

Fisk positioned the sofa so when Averill knelt on its seat, she splayed her elbows across its high, soft top. In that position she would see the monitor. Her back to him now, she pushed her arse back in his direction.

'I know. It's taken a lifetime to realise but you're right.' He unzipped his fly and dropped his pants.

When he slapped each of her buttocks, she made a cooing sound as if she'd been handed a new puppy. It was pathetic. She bent a little more and waited for his thrust. When he was inside her he grabbed the DVD remote.

'Hold this for me while I work the remote,' he said. He placed the gun in her hand, the barrel facing her head.

She said, 'A porny for the horny. I like it.'

The grainy black and white picture rolled. Fisk's empty desk was centre screen, the doorway to his office, off to the right. Averill asked, without apprehension, 'What's this QF? Did you record our first shag?' She giggled.

Their first time, he'd taken her as she spread-eagled herself over his desk. He remembered her comment about his passion, how she loved passion but also loved romance. He didn't give a fuck about romance.

The overture kicked into life and Fisk manoeuvred Averill's stubby forefinger inside the trigger guard. Captivated by the monitor, she paid no attention to the gun.

She giggled again. 'Why are we watching your office?'

'I think you know why,' he said, giving no clue in his tone. 'But it will become apparent.' His heart rate increased with excitement.

'But there's no sound,' she said.

'None needed, listen to the overture.' He thrust his pelvis forward, timing the contact with the first round of the overture's cannons.

The camera above his desk picked up two figures entering his office. Averill was the first, Zoe Underwood, the second.

'Oh, my God,' Averill said.

'Indeed,' Fisk said. 'You're a star, Averill.'

The monitor showed Averill leading Zoe to Fisk's locked drawer. The overture was near its end. 'La Marseillaise' had played for the last time and the final cannons fired. On screen, Averill, spare key in hand, opened Fisk's desk drawer and removed the ledger.

'Oh, no. No,' Averill said.

Fisk thrusted, resisting the obvious, 'Yes, yes.' His right hand tightened on hers gripping the revolver.

On the last of the cannons firing, Fisk ejaculated and whispered the hymn title, 'O Lord, Save Thy People'. The picture showed Averill opening Fisk's justice ledger. On the last of the church bells, he increased the pressure on Averill's finger over the trigger.

Fisk's head rang with fury and he rolled off his dead secretary. In the kitchen, he'd covered Graham's cage. Graham was the only one who deserved to live. He couldn't bring himself to harm, much less end his chirpy little companion's life. What happened to the parrot would become someone else's decision. For the moment, he would live with that.

Confident he had remembered accurately, he checked the death notice column in *The People* last week.

Brian McClintock QC

After a short illness, in his 81st year. Dearly loved partner of the late Natalie, much loved father of John (London) and dearly loved stepfather and mentor of Sasha Stace.

Through his kitchen window he saw the lights were off at Ted's house. Give them another half-hour, just to be sure.

75

THE CLEANEST AND SHINIEST vehicles on the road were always reserved for the dead. Mac's black hearse, in front of the Merivale church he sometimes attended, put any other car in the vicinity to shame, including Sasha's.

Standing a few metres from the hearse was the full High Court bench, black suits huddled together. It was inconceivable any well-balanced judge would say a bad word about Mac, but not all those attending would meet that description. Three of them were here because they would feel the need to be seen.

The president of the Court of Appeal walked over, escorted by Paul Diplock. Sir Neil Havers, ruddy face, shorter than Sasha, offered his hand. Sasha had appeared before Havers only once. He had a great reputation and struck her as a more courteous judge than most.

'Paul's been telling me you were Mac's daughter.' His tone was in condolence as he added, 'I knew you were close but didn't realise how close.'

'Thank you, Your Honour…'

His hand came up – polite, not a stop sign. 'Please – today it's Neil. In fact, any time out of court, if that's all right with you.'

She smiled at the friendly gesture. 'Thank you. I was really Mac's stepdaughter. Mac and my mother lived together for many years.'

'At the bar, Mac had that lovely balance of incisiveness and humility,' Havers said. 'A huge loss to you and many others. He will be missed, considerably so.'

Her heart swelled. 'I hope you can share stories with me over refreshments, Neil. You too, Paul. Thank you for coming.'

They wandered off to break up the judicial cabal. Piped music called them to order. She was starting to feel a little weak at the knees. The moment had approached, all too fast.

Inside the church, many of Sasha's bar colleagues were already seated, including Frances Rule. Delia was not. She had sent a text message. She was ill. She'd expressed disappointment she couldn't attend and wished Sasha well. The Montague crowd were there, people from the court administration, the legal faculty. The pews were full, but for the first time in her life she hadn't counted the number. Had it taken Mac's death to rid her of this quirk?

The vicar preceded Sasha and John to the front of the church. Clay sat one side of her and John McClintock the other. John blinked at Sasha, then looked at Clay but said nothing. Sasha introduced the two men and told John that Clay was a good friend to his father.

The vicar, impressive in a white cassock and stole that contrasted sharply with her black bobbed hair, approached, her face an appropriate mix of sadness and welcome.

76

FISK LET GRAHAM OUT of the cage and inspected the droppings as he always did. No change. The parrot flew to the top of the sofa on which cold Averill had spent the night. The bird, looking inquisitive, cocked his head to fix a beady eye on the body below.

Determined that Graham's routine would be normal, Fisk put fresh food and water in the cage and turned on the radio.

He'd asked Carson's secretary to let the firm know he was indisposed and that he'd given Averill the day off. Others would come for her later, when they pieced together what had happened. It struck him he knew nothing of Averill's family. She had never volunteered information, no doubt correctly assessing he wouldn't have been interested.

Yet through his mother's video she had come to know the influence on his life, of the better, but seldom seen, side of his mother – the helpful and encouraging side.

When they came, they would also take away the recordings of calls between himself and Ivor Grange. Did he have prescience that things would be as they were, that even in defeat he would deliver justice? No. The recorded conversations were to avoid the role of solitary fall taker. Grange and Ellis had both let him down and they would both pay for incompetence and for losing him his most coveted opportunity. He tossed the mini cassette tapes onto the dining table and penned a note for them to sit on – 'Give Ivor my best! QF.' He stared at the tapes and conjured a newspaper image of his accomplices' forlorn faces in the dock, of himself marking a nice big red tick through the page.

Fisk picked up the framed photograph of his twin sister. 'I'm sorry, Queenie.' He lovingly placed the photo upright in a cardboard box, then checked the revolver. One bullet down, four to go, but these would be fired only if he encountered resistance or obstruction. He placed the gun near the full gin bottle in the box and extracted the Tchaikovsky CD from the player. The final item for the box was petrol-soaked strips of cotton bed sheet, which he had placed in an airtight container.

He checked his watch. The funeral would start in less than half an hour. He didn't need to be there for the beginning. In fact, the possibility of being seen before he was ready would be counter-productive.

In the garage, Fisk positioned the box in the passenger seat of the car. As the garage door rose, he noticed the postman depositing an envelope in the letterbox at the end of his drive. He closed his eyes and the old vision of Queenie racing to get birthday parcels returned. He didn't retrieve the letter.

Ted approached the fence and made a beckoning gesture. In no mood to talk, Fisk called out, 'Sorry, Ted. In a bit of a rush. Heading away for a while.' He pointed toward the vegetable garden. 'There's a few leeks here you might want to help yourself to while I'm away.'

Ted looked serious. 'Bit sudden, isn't it?'

'No, why?'

'You want us to look after Graham?'

Fuck. Why did he say he was going away? If it was planned properly, he wouldn't be leaving Graham's care to the last minute. That was careless. 'Taking him with me. A little change of scenery will do him good. Appreciate the offer, though.'

Ted hadn't finished. 'The missus reckoned she heard a gunshot last night. Then your car going out about 3 a.m.'

Keep this up, Ted, and there's a bullet with your name on it. One for Mrs Ted as well.

'I'm sorry, mate. I had a few too many last night. Tell you what – buy her a box of chocolates from me, flowers as well, if you must. I'll fix you up when I get back. How's that?'

Ted waved his okay and retreated.

77

THE VICAR WAS SOMEONE Mac had got to know at the Cardiac Companions meetings. She had attended with her ill sister. Mac had confided in her and she'd agreed to commend him to their God. Sasha had met her twice before Mac's death and could see why he'd warmed to her. She had ready access to a strong voice, a bawdy joke, a hearty laugh and a fine single malt. She didn't fit the church stereotype of the quiet hand-wringer, telling the patient and the curious that the world was a better place for an eternal God who chose who suffered and who thrived, who lived and when they died. Her robust approach wouldn't be to everyone's taste, but if Sasha were ever to be a church goer, it would be this vicar's church that she'd attend.

She tended to keep her views about religion to herself. It wasn't that she eschewed it with contempt. Sasha admired people with faith. The stronger their faith, the greater their serenity approaching death. Today, it was about respecting the views of the man she'd always loved, his faith.

78

TED AND HIS WIFE decided a leek and potato pie would be just the ticket for tonight's dinner. The leeks in his neighbour's garden were a good few centimetres in circumference. He forked up three and rubbed the dirt off them.

Produce gathered, he started back down Fisk's smooth asphalt drive, a drive he'd always envied. His own was cracked and rumpled concrete, the result of silver birch tree roots. In his peripheral vision, Ted saw movement. Was it inside Fisk's house? He stopped and stared into the kitchen window. Odd that the cream blind was up. Fisk normally covered the windows when he was away. He peered in to make sure everything was okay. It's what his neighbour would want him to do.

As he leaned into the glass, a hand to shade the glare, there was a thud right in front of him. He jumped back in fright, gasping. It was Graham. What the hell was the bird doing with the run of the house? Fisk had said he was taking him on holiday. Come to think of it, he'd never done that before. It would be odd, wouldn't it? A prominent and respected lawyer like Fisk carting a caged bird around with him everywhere he went. Ted moved to the far side of the house. Fisk had sliding doors out to a patio leading to a grassed area and the school beyond the front fence.

Ted stepped up onto the patio. The lace curtain had been partially drawn. Graham reappeared, gliding, then landing on the other side of the glass, less than a metre from Ted's feet. The bird turned and waddled across the cream carpet.

What had the parrot jumped onto? Ted squinted, peered hard into the corner of the room. A foot? An ankle?

Ted saw the whole body now. The leg extended out from a sofa, toes to the floor. It was the woman they'd seen call on Fisk. 'Holy shit.'

By the time Ted had jogged back to his house, he'd realised his wife hadn't imagined the gunshot in their quiet neighbourhood. They'd thought nothing of the woman arriving in a cab last night.

Ted had thought good luck to the lawyer – more discreet than trolling Manchester Street.

'Call the cops,' Ted shouted at his wife. 'The woman, last night. The one who went to Fisk's house. I think he's done her in.'

Five minutes later, standing at the edge of Fisk's drive, Ted said, 'That was quick.'

'Got diverted here from another job,' the uniformed driver said. 'This the place, then?'

Ted lifted his arm, crowbar in hand, and pointed down the drive. 'You'll need to go round the front.'

Suspicious, the cop asked, 'What's that for – the crowbar?'

'Thought you might need help to get in.'

'Got our own key,' the cop said. 'In the boot.'

By the time Ted joined the two cops on the patio, one had grabbed a door rammer from the boot. It took two blows before the back door gave way.

79

FROM THE LECTERN, SASHA looked out over a black and white sea of sympathy. Tearful faces, strained faces, anxious faces, all willing her to get through this. John McClintock looked down, as if in prayer. She had no idea what he was feeling. That saddened her.

Sasha's head hurt in sympathy with her left shoulder and her tongue was like old leather. She cleared the constriction in her throat.

'For those of you who don't know me, I'm Sasha Stace. It's a little difficult knowing where to start with Mac, to do justice to the life of a wonderful man, a man who was, to all intents and purposes, my father.' She spotted Havers and smiled. He reciprocated.

'A man who, in his office, would lovingly mimic the cross-examinations of the father I never knew, telling me that I had exactly the same mannerisms. A man who inspired and encouraged me, a man who supported and loved me as his own daughter.' Her voice faltered and she dug thumbnails into the pads of her index fingers. John looked up at her, expressionless. It was enough to help her go on.

'Brian McClintock QC was universally known as Mac. He was without airs and graces and had what is sometimes referred to as the common touch. No client's affairs were trivial or unimportant, no matter who they were. He enriched all those whose lives he touched. I know, without doubt, that my own will be diminished by his death. I feel...'

Her voice was straining now and she paused in the struggle for composure.

'I feel something has been amputated from me, if not in body, in soul. And in saying that, I hear Mac on my shoulder urging me to be less melodramatic, as he so frequently did.'

80

FOR THE FUNERAL, FISK wore a charcoal grey court suit and white shirt, no tie. He filled his Subaru with petrol, letting the end of the hose dribble into the airtight container holding the cotton strips. The material was still damp from earlier preparations but a bit more accelerant wouldn't go amiss. He made eye contact with a woman at an adjacent pump. She was curious about what he was doing. Too curious. Fisk watched her fasten her belt and drive away. She didn't pick up a mobile phone. Good. The man on the till tried to sell him confectionery. When Fisk declined, he smiled and said, 'Have a nice day.'

Fisk replied, 'I intend to.'

Driving away, bottle to lips, he took his first gulps of the gin. He kept a steady fifty kilometres an hour to the church, his second visit this day. He had no desire to shoot a cop. As a result of the recce in the early morning darkness, he knew where, hidden from view, he'd make his final preparations.

His thoughts went to Lottie Kaye. Wheeler had looked for an outlet to betray the attorney general but nobody had found out how he and Lottie established and maintained communication or who had leaked what he'd done back to Ellis. After that it was panic stations.

Fisk had argued to the solicitor general there was no evidence linking the politicians to Lottie's death. He'd urged the man who reported to the AG to accept the disk was a smokescreen. He'd said he could pressure Inkwell not to let it in – she'd lost enough appeals so she'd act cautiously. But no. The gutless pollies caved. To save their own skins, they'd let a murderer walk.

81

'HIS PA,' BLACK SAID to the uniforms, putting two joined fingers on the pulse line. 'I'd say by the amount of blood from the exit wound, she was killed here. But is Fisk the killer? Or has it been set-up to look like that?'

From the temperature of the woman's skin he knew she'd been dead for several hours.

A uniform handed him the note.

'Who the fuck's Ivor?' Black asked.

The constable shrugged. 'Found with mini cassette tapes on the kitchen table, boss.'

'Look for a player. And the gun,' Black said.

In the master bedroom, the amount, type and size of clothing suggested only Fisk lived at the house. The bathroom and other bedrooms confirmed it. As Black walked into the spare bedroom, he thought how little they knew about Fisk outside or away from court. No clues here at all, no boxes of crap that would tell the story of the man's life outside work.

Except for the bloody bird. Black's own neighbours kept two parrots, which ran their lives. They attended to them like little children. The parrot alone suggested it was unlikely Fisk was doing a runner. Unless...

He moved to the kitchen table as the uniforms systematically went through drawers in the house. Black noted an ink ring around a funeral notice in *The People*. The deceased was the old lawyer who had died during the trial. What were the odds Fisk would attend the funeral and leave a dead body in his house?

'Someone put that fuckin' bird in its cage, for Christ's sake. Bloody thing keeps dive-bombing me.'

'How do we do that, boss?' one asked.

'Don't tell me they left that out of the syllabus at Porirua. Get a bloody towel and cover it. Smother it, for all I care.'

Black strode through the house. Had the Tyler trial pushed Fisk over the edge? It had happened before. His maternal grandfather had prosecuted in a famous trial in the 1950s. He'd ended up committed as a special patient by the psychiatrist he'd ruthlessly cross-examined.

Black paused at the doorway of what was clearly Fisk's home office. Magazines on bird care and vegetable gardening sat on top of a hand-carved desk in the corner. A similarly styled but near-empty bookshelf stood nearby. 'Sad bastard,' Black muttered.

Manila folders tied with thin strips of green and pink ribbon lay across the desk and three were scattered on the floor. His laptop was off. That might be more revealing about the man's life.

He opened the top drawer of the desk – a stapler, paper clips, compliment slips from Fisk, Carson & Co., a couple of pens, a roll of Scotch tape. In the second drawer, he lifted a photo turned face down. Underneath it, a mini cassette player and charger. Yes! As he carried the player to the kitchen he read the message on the back of the photo. 'For the future AG. All my love AB.' The photo was of Fisk and the dead woman. Black guessed it was taken in the Botanic Gardens, a short walk from Fisk's office. She had her arm around him. He didn't look particularly happy about it.

He connected the player and power, starting with Side A.

Fisk: 'If you want this trial to go well, I need something from you, Ivor.'

'You're the man in court. Martin and I can't do anything about that.'

'Stace is pursuing me for the Law Society. I did your bidding on that shoddy piece of land in Selwyn and look where it got me.'

'You were well remunerated for that, QF.'

'Not the point. That idiot Yuile is a pit bull, slobbering over the prospect of biting human flesh. My flesh, Ivor, and we know what Stace is like. I've got my PA behind me but I need insurance. I need him squirrelled away.'

'Leave it with me.'

Black fast-forwarded through silence. Hearing the gabble of helium-like voices, he stopped the tape, rewound and was about to hit play when he heard the urgent call. 'Sir!' Black jogged to the internal access to the garage at the other end of the house.

Strips of burnt cotton had left a long, narrow stain on a clean concrete floor. Black picked up the material and sniffed. 'Petrol,' he said. He bent to sniff part of the stain. 'Ditto.'

'I'm thinking fuse, boss,' the uniform said, pointing to a pack of blue adhesive. 'A practice run, maybe?'

At the boot of their car, Black unlocked the firearm security cabinet and withdrew three Glock pistols and ammunition. 'Come on,' he said, 'we're going to a funeral.'

82

INSIDE THE PETROL-SOAKED interior of his car, Fisk focused on the mourners through binoculars. Stace would be a temporary nemesis only. At least she didn't have the satisfaction of running a disciplinary hearing against him. Paul Diplock was holding her hand. Fisk had nothing against Diplock but if he stayed close to her, he risked becoming collateral damage.

Mouth dry, he guzzled the gin as if it were water. There was Tyler, head high. The arrogant turd had had a narrow escape, thanks to the prick he was standing next to, the man who'd think he was so fucking clever getting that DVD to Stace.

Fisk turned up the volume of the overture and wiped away tears with the heels of his hands. He couldn't remember when he'd last cried – maybe Mother's funeral. A radiant Queenie looked out from the box and his thoughts turned to his father.

Fisk was at university, his twentieth birthday, when Randolf disappeared. His father had been under suspicion because no one could remember seeing him in the law library at the time Queenie went missing. Suspicion diminished, but with it went Randolf's resilience and character.

Someone found his father's decaying body inside a grey business suit hanging from a pine in the Balmoral Forest. Lying at the foot of the tree, a leather briefcase, the initials 'RF' marginally visible through the grime. No note. Not long after, his mother's vitriol intensified.

Every trial he'd ever run was for his sister, every loss a permanent scar, setbacks to securing justice for all the Queenies of this world.

Feeling slightly anaesthetised, Fisk had difficulty threading the petrol-soaked cloth through the adhesive loops he made last night. Alight, it would run from his driver's door to the passenger door behind him and then through the final loop, where the fuse would drop into the open petrol tank at the rear of the car. He slipped out of his driver's seat, the door facing away from the chapel, and crawled on hands and knees, fixing the Plasticine loops to the side of car.

Back in the car, he couldn't remember how long the fuse lasted before it hit the gas. But he knew last night's practice that told him that he had the right length of fuse. At worst, a second or two delay on impact. No more. Everything in place, he swallowed more gin.

Flashing red and blue lights in the rear-vision mirror. Surely they weren't coming for him. Not that fast. The overture, loud now, meant he heard no siren. Now. Go now.

Tyler and Clay Tempero were headed for the same vehicle. Stace and Diplock were behind them. Nice and tidy.

The goal is all important. How you achieve it, less so. But you do need to achieve it. He unbuckled his seat belt and planted his foot on the accelerator. The power of his turbo-charged firebomb propelled him back in his seat as he surged forward.

83

OUTSIDE THE CHAPEL, THE air was still, little warmth in the sun. In the shade, concrete puddles were frozen and the low cut grass remained white. Paul asked, his voice low, 'How come Mac's son didn't speak?'

When Sasha explained in a whisper, he looked as shocked as she was resigned.

'He was persuaded to be a pallbearer.'

John McClintock headed the sextet in black. They placed Mac's casket on the rollers inside the hearse and did it exactly as she would have – unhurriedly and with care.

Sasha startled at a squeal of rubber on asphalt, a sound followed by the throaty roar of an engine urged to go at warp speed. It was close, too close. The car chewed up the distance between it and the mourners, yet things were slowing down. People turned their heads in slow motion, reluctant observers to an intrusion on solemnity, almost uninterested. No one was concerned. Clay and Ben were in the car that would take the four of them back into the city for the wake. Sasha and Paul were ten quick strides away.

Then Sasha realised. She screamed, 'It's Fisk. No!'

He was close enough for her to see his death grip on the wheel, his face twisted in grim determination to kill.

In milliseconds she turned and shoved Paul, the effort powered by her right shoulder and arm, her good shoulder. She hit the asphalt a moment before Fisk ploughed into Ben's car, an explosion consuming the air around it, the force an invisible thrust over their prostrate bodies. Arms over her head, she heard glass disintegrating, the tearing and wrenching of metal in its death throes, the final groaning before submission. Pieces of metal hit the hard ground near her. The sound of sirens was close and her watch beeped on the hour, midday.

On top of Paul she lifted her head and asked, 'Are you okay?'

He croaked in the affirmative and Sasha could smell his aftershave, but also petrol. There was another explosion and the world turned orange.

84

ON HER BACK, SASHA woke in a strange place, the taste of oil in her mouth. A man in a white shirt and black trousers stood over her, a stethoscope around his neck. He was smiling, a sad little smile. When his lips moved she struggled to hear. Her ears felt like they did when an aircraft cabin depressurised in prep for landing. Sasha thought he said she was okay.

Instinctively she pinched her nostrils and blew. Her eyes were raw, a month's worth of grit in the sockets. Her hands and wrists were dirty, covered in something soot-like.

Was that Paul Diplock's voice she heard nearby? She propped herself up on her elbows. He was on her right, also lying down. They were both in an ambulance.

She held out a hand to him. 'You're okay?'

He nodded.

'Clay? And Ben? They were in the car.'

'Haven't heard,' he said.

She coughed. 'It was Fisk. He tried to kill us.'

Black stepped into the ambulance, his expression grave, and Sasha feared the worst.

'Hello, Sasha. How are you feeling?'

It would be the voice he used when he encountered victims.

'Tell me what's happened, Rod.'

He paused, seeming to judge whether she was up to it. 'We're taking a tally of the injured. We're in ambulance three. As far as we know, two dead – Fisk and,' he paused, 'Ben Tyler. I'm sorry.'

'Clay Tempero?' she asked, too quickly, and held her breath.

Another pause.

'Haven't seen him. We'll account for him soon enough, I expect.'

She let the air go.

Black said, 'Fisk rigged his vehicle, set it to blow after the impact. He'd planned it, practised the bomb fuse. And he shot his PA.'

'Do you know why?'

'Can't be certain. Tyler's trial pushed him over the edge. It's happened before. He was a bit flaky throughout. He's left plenty to follow up on. You don't know someone called Grange, do you?'

Sasha wanted to have a piece of Black for again being part of a hastily led investigation. But his mention of Grange doused the urge. 'Ivor Grange. He's the attorney general's parliamentary secretary. What did Fisk tell you about the reason the trial was halted?'

'Only that the AG got the solicitor general to make the call. Something about new evidence which Fisk said he couldn't discuss, except to say it was a crock of shit. Reckoned you were behind it.'

'Well,' Sasha said, her voice weaker now she was talking, 'what we put to the judge was legitimate. We got hold of a DVD. If you guys had it, it ought to have taken your enquiry in a completely new direction.'

Black's neck coloured. The both know their shared history wasn't pretty.

'Is that so?' He sounded sceptical.

'It is so.' Sasha rocked her head on the pillow. 'Doesn't matter now.'

A paramedic stepped up into the ambulance. ''Scuse me, folks. Now there's another ambo on the way, we've got to go.' He looked at Black. 'We'll have her overnight, sir. Maybe you can visit in the morning.'

Black stared at Sasha. He looked uneasy.

Almost whispering, she said, 'Tomorrow, Rod, okay? I'll give you something to follow up on, a chance to get real justice for Lottie.'

All the way to hospital, her thoughts were with Ben. She needed to trust that if Clay was dead, Black would have told her. He's probably been injured, crawled away and been treated somewhere. He was a survivor.

But Ben. Poor Ben. He was so grateful to her when he was free. 'I knew you'd do it, I just knew.' None of that arrogant, fist-pumping Andrews behaviour.

Now, eyes closed, she saw the boyish grin that day at court when they met all those years ago.

'And for the most part, warm and loving. Yes?'

Why couldn't she say yes? Only the living have regrets. First Mac, now Ben. He came to Mac's funeral, as much for her as to pay respects to Mac, despite the things she'd said to him.

She told herself she shouldn't have denied him that truth.

'Yes, Ben, warm and loving.' She wiped away tears.

85

THREE MONTHS LATER

THE CHOSEN TWELVE WERE about to file in to the jury box, for the fifteenth and final time in the three-day trial. The solicitor general, Marshall Hall, had sought her help – the final catalyst in excising her disillusionment with criminal law. Ironically, he called on Sasha because of Quentin Fisk's death. That and the inevitable retirement of Fisk's boss, Tom Carson, due to ill health. The prosecutor's office was now short staffed and she'd taken Zoe Underwood under her wing.

They had just finished prosecuting a man for raping a prostitute. The old pre-verdict feelings returned. Her body temperature rose, her heart quickened and her palms felt damp. She could smell the anticipation in a packed court. It wafted from the wall and ceiling panels and was underscored with a whiff of fear. All ears were tuned to avoid missing a single word of the drama.

The court official had the jury foreman confirm they'd reached a unanimous verdict. As usual, Sasha make no eye contact.

'Guilty.'

Now, she looked at them and hoped, as always, to appear dispassionate, something Fisk could never bring himself to do. She looked for signs of collective composure. Serenity was a bit much to ask for, but if someone had had their arm held up their back to agree, there was always a sign.

When everyone left, Diplock for the defendant, congratulated her. 'Good to have you back in here, Sasha.'

'My emotions are still evolving on that, Paul, but thanks.'

He was stern in his sincerity. 'Mac would approve. I've no doubt about that whatsoever.'

She gave him the smile. 'Neither do I.'

'You seem to be bearing up, coping well.'

'Have my moments. You'll know what it's like.'

He nodded. 'The emotional slaps around the head, I call them. But over time, they become fewer and less intense.'

'Clay's been good. He calls me from Sydney several times a week. He's engaging in subtle persuasion to join him.'

'Well, nothing to hold you here now, Sasha. Especially, if that's where your heart is.'

She didn't tell him she was torn, what it was that might hold her here. 'You just want to improve your bloody win rate, Diplock. I know you.'

He chuckled, a rare occurrence. Then he said, concern in his voice, 'You hear the news this morning?'

'I did. Rod Black was kind enough to phone me last night. As a matter of fact, I'm heading out to the prison now. She's asked to see me.'

86

SASHA SAT IN AN unwelcoming grey room that felt as though it was in the bowels of the prison. She'd never got used to it. The smell of isolation and fear was as pungent as it was pervasive. The plastic chair provided minimal comfort and she sat behind a table that was bolted to the floor, a precaution for an unsupervised visit.

A sturdy-looking warden in green knocked on the open door and showed Delia in. Sasha thanked her. Allowed to wear her own clothing on remand, Delia was in blue jeans, a grey shirt and a blue sweat top zipped up the front. Her face was thinner, taut. She'd aged.

As Delia sat, Sasha said, 'A warden with a smile. Might break the mould.'

In seconds of silence, Delia stared back. 'It was you, wasn't it?'

'What was me?'

'Who told Black?'

'Delia, you asked to see me and I'm here.' Sasha could hear the frustration in her tone. 'I'm here to see what help or support you might need on the outside. I've had many clients sitting where you sit. I know it's not easy. I'm prepared to help if I can.'

'Guilt, isn't it? Not wanting to abandon me three times.'

They stared at each other in silence. Sasha caught herself exhaling nosily.

Delia said, 'If you want to help me, start by telling me where I went wrong.'

'I don't understand what you mean by three times. I've never abandoned you. I couldn't keep a baby when I was seventeen, not without support.'

Delia looked incredulous. 'Lots of girls keep babies when they're that age.'

'Not back then they didn't. And not when their mothers were telling them to put their baby up for adoption where it would have two parents, desperate to have a baby to love, cherish and support. Like yours did.'

She scoffed in derision. 'You know nothing, Sasha. My loving parents told me I was adopted when I was seven. Then they split up when I was fourteen. Do you think I was a pawn in their custody battle?'

'I'm sorry. I believed you when you said they died in an acc...'

Delia leaned forward, her chin jutting in a way Sasha hadn't seen before. 'I told you that because I hate the truth. There was no custody battle. I had to beg them not to put me in care. Do you think that worked? No. It didn't work because neither of them wanted me in the end. Foster care was the easy way out. I'd have taken either of them, it didn't matter which, so long as one of them wanted me. You dumped me on people who didn't want me, effectively abandoned me twice.'

'I'm so sorry, Delia. I couldn't ... no one could've foreseen that. The screening adoptive parents go through is...'

'Never enough. And hopeless in my case. At eighteen I was determined to find out who my birth mother was. It took me years. When I qualified, and that's another story, I joined Child Youth and Family Services. I knew I'd find you then. That story about a boyfriend...'

Her voice started to break and her bottom lip trembled. Sasha reached for the tissues she kept in her bag.

Uncomfortable, Sasha ripped the packet open and put it between them. Delia's eyes went to the packet but she used the sleeves of her sweat top to wipe her cheeks. For the first time, Sasha saw bitten nails.

Her voice was higher now, child-like. 'There was no boyfriend. I started to fall for this guy in CYFS. He led me on, two-timed me. From that moment I was determined it wouldn't happen again. I would be the one who was in control, calling the shots. I studied how people in authority behaved, learned how to control my emotions.' She sniffed. 'I've had a string of men, dumped them all when they started to get intimate. I didn't need intimacy. What fucking use was intimacy? You know what I'm saying?'

Sasha couldn't keep saying how sorry she was. She lifted and lowered her head, slowly.

'I needed sex, not intimacy. Until I met Mike. Then something changed. He's a counsellor. But he told me to see someone different, that he couldn't be involved in counselling me because we were seeing each other. That's what I thought until that bitch Rule snatched him from me. I had started to come right before that.'

'Until you found out about Lottie Kaye's award.'

'After Peter's suicide, that was too much. I snapped. I went to see her, to have it out with her about the way she hounded him. She knew I was his sister. You know what she said?'

Sasha could only think of those brutal images in that bathroom, the force of the blows.

'She said, "Take a look at you, your family. With parents like yours, a sister like you, what support did he really have?"'

Sasha was as certain as she could be that this was untrue. Lottie was killed in her bathroom, naked, extremely vulnerable. With knowledge from Ben where the back door key was, Delia had chosen her moment. A tyre lever or crowbar – it didn't matter now. Sasha wasn't going to argue. Delia was justifying the vengeance coursing through her system that night.

Sasha's old feeling of rising bile returned. She suppressed it by shifting her thoughts away from that bathroom. 'How did you connect with Ben? Through Montague?'

'Partly.' Delia sniffed, this time wiping her nose, further up the sleeve. 'Research. I found out she'd worked and lived in Sydney. That was the easy bit. Found out about her and Plummer, their divorce. But I chanced on a picture taken at a media awards function, a picture of her and Ben together.'

'I see.'

'I got back in touch with him, purely social. With the right attention from me, he was a mine of information.'

'I don't get it. You got on so well. Why set him up to be arrested?'

'I knew you'd show that he had been set up. I didn't want him to go down but if he did, sooner him than me.'

'Which is why you pushed for the squeeze on O'Rourke when we discussed strategy over dinner at Ben's place?'

She leaned back in the chair. 'Useful getting that extra history about the Jetson and family tensions between O'Rourke and Plummer.' There was a hint of a smile. 'Too bad we didn't need it in the end.'

Sasha massaged her forehead with the heel of her hand. 'Delia, that's all over now. What do you want from me?'

She crossed her arms. 'You've got a shot at redemption, Sasha. I want you to defend me. Create reasonable doubt. You're great at that. You got Ben off, you'll get me off, too.'

'For Christ's sake – I can't defend you.'

'What? Because you're my blood. I've got news. It's not thicker than water. You can defend me. You're not my mother. I've had no real mother. You gave that up thirty-three years ago. At the first chance, you dobbed me in to Black, abandoned me again.'

Delia's bitterness rode on every word but Sasha refused to defend herself. It would only make matters worse.

'Look, you did what you thought was right at the time,' Delia said, calmer now. 'Just as you did when you gave me away. I'm not surprised you blabbed to Black.' She paused. 'But you can put that right. You can put it all right. Stand by me. Don't abandon me again.'

There was no look of desperation, no hint of anguish in her voice. She'd thought about this, thought about how to manipulate. With Ben, it was sex for information. With Sasha, it was emotional blackmail. But Sasha owned no guilt. She was sorry for what Delia had been through. Who wouldn't be? But a blackmail victim needed to avoid something, to choose the lesser of two evils.

'Delia, I'll be a prosecution witness. I'll be expected to testify against you.'

'There's no value in your evidence,' she said, derisive. 'You told them to look for my party wig. So what?'

'Come on, Delia. The cap had your DNA on it and that was in Frances Rule's car. She can establish she couldn't have been in Akaroa and Hanmer at the same time. Despite your clean-up, there are minute traces of Lottie's blood in the boot. And it was you who washed the towel, wasn't it? You wiped her blood off your face and realised your DNA would be on that towel.'

'The towel's a red herring. Any towel with my DNA would be with the boiler suit that's never been found.' She gave a malevolent little smile Sasha hadn't seen before. 'Who'd be stupid enough to wash a towel and hang it out to dry?' She stared back at Sasha. Long seconds of silence passed.

Sasha was about to ask if her defence involved denying she was in Akaroa on the night of the murder. Delia spoke again. 'I'm only asking you to do what you did for Ben. Create reasonable doubt. It's what you do well.'

Reasonable doubt. The expression tripped off the tongues of most barristers. But Delia saw this as a ploy to get guilty people off. Some in the community, familiar with the term, might think of it the same way. Andrews saw it like that. It sickened her then as it sickened her now.

She put up her mother's stop sign. 'Please, Delia. They'll have voice recognition software of you at Fisk's conference. Don't do this. You might have a defence of extreme provocation but to get that over the line, you'll have to admit being responsible. Don't insult anyone's intelligence about not being involved. Please.'

Delia pushed her chair back. 'Just as I expected.' She shook her head in condemnation. 'I'm not surprised. You've only ever looked after number one. Ben said as much. You didn't want kids with him. You didn't want kids – full stop and fucking exclamation marks. Face it and stop pretending you're here for me, Sasha. See the light.'

'It's the darkness in here that allows me to see perfectly well.'

She sneered and said, 'All the words, but none of them for me.'

Delia Lang, her long-lost flesh and blood, banged on the door and the warden let her out. She paused, turned and gave Sasha an evil little smile. 'You think I did all that in Akaroa on my own, don't you?'

Sasha let the question go. She reached for the tissues that Delia had refused. Time to give Clay a call.

A humble request

Last, but not least, a big thank you to you, my reader. If you have enjoyed this book, please tell others. Reviews are like the author's life force – not for ego, but because they are central to encouraging people to read my book and help me achieve my purpose of entertaining others. The more reviews of a book, the more the book stores promote that book to potential readers. That's how the system works. I would be hugely grateful if you could post a few words of comment about what you liked about this story on the site where you found this book.

Contact

Please contact me through my website, https://www.mcginncrime.com or https://www.facebook.com/MarkMcGinnAuthor